Semisweet

ISBN: 1-4538-0837-X
ISBN-13: 9781453808375

Semisweet

A Maggie and Odessa Mystery

Jill Brock

Also by Jill Brock

A Maggie and Odessa Mysteries

Pennywise
Drop Dead Delicious

This book is dedicated to my family and friends who love and support me, and NIA who always inspired me to write.

chapter 1

I STOOD IN the middle of a near empty restaurant with Horace Fouke. He held a knife to my throat and threatened to cut me open like a turkey on Thanksgiving Day. He wanted his soon-to-be ex-wife to let him back into their house and her heart. If she didn't, Thanksgiving would never be the same for me, and I liked Thanksgiving. I got myself into this position because I decided to play waitress and bring out the dessert order to Mrs. Fouke's table. Her dining partner was her divorce lawyer and a friend of mine—Aaron Boyer. I wanted to say hello. Aaron often brought his soon-to-be divorcees to my family's restaurant, The Blue Moon, in Queens, New York. I was the dessert chef, and he loved my key lime pie. Nothing helped better after the destruction of a marriage then a piece of my German chocolate cake.

Horace's sudden appearance at Aaron's table put a damper on the celebratory mood. Mrs. Fouke demanded controlling interest in Fouke's bug extermination business, the house, two cars, and the family cat. According to Mrs. Fouke, Horace's side of the deal was for him to disappear off the face of the earth. Horace's chances on improving his day lessened with the two anxious policemen who stood in front of us. Besides the knife at my throat and the possibility of dying in a hail of bullets, I had to deal with Horace's gin-laden breath. If anyone lit a match near us, we'd go up in a ball of flames.

"For Christ sake, you idiot, let her go," Mrs. Fouke said, her voice cutting through my panic like nails on a blackboard. Yeah, Horace, listen to the woman you hate with each gin-soaked breath you take. The woman hadn't helped the situation. Ever since Horace began this no-win scenario, Mrs. Fouke has called him every disparaging name she hadn't called him while they were together.

"Relax, fellow," one of the uniformed officers said, trying to calm everyone down. Yeah, Horace, listen to him, though it was hard to do this because he'd made a bib out of his napkin. His lunch was interrupted by the Foukes' afternoon family feud.

"Please let Odessa go," Aaron said.

Being the Odessa in question, his sincerity touched me, but I knew in the back of his mind, he wondered if Horace succeeded in ending my career as a dessert chef, who would make his favorite key lime pie. Aaron tipped the scale at nearly three hundred pounds. His priorities for his visits to the Blue Moon were scotch, the barbeque hash open-faced sandwich, key lime pie, and conversations with me, exactly in that order. I had no illusion of my place in Aaron's world.

"Everyone shut the hell up," Fouke said, sending out waves of his gin-laced breath. He tightened his grip on me. I didn't know if my weak knees came from fear or inhaling the alcohol fumes.

"You can't talk to me like that. We're getting a divorce," Mrs. Fouke said with a little too much glee. Her joyous satisfaction only infuriated her husband. He placed the steak knife closer to my throat. The cold steel pressed into my flesh, and I winced at the pain as an abbreviated version of my life passed before my eyes. I was too terrified too pay attention to the good parts.

"Married to that woman for over ten years and all she did was complain I wasn't good enough!" he screamed. He swayed and righted himself.

"Don't worry, he won't do anything; he never does," Mrs. Fouke said. She had a thick Long Island accent, which sounded like a watered down version of anyone from Brooklyn. Her tone was nasal and grating. Talking to this woman too long would drive anyone to murder.

So there we were—the cops, the lawyer, the battling Foukes, and the dessert chef. What didn't belong in the picture? Me. I wanted everyone to relax and take a deep breath, sit down with a cup of coffee and my chocolate chip cream cheese pound cake. I wanted Mr. Fouke to get the knife off my neck and stop breathing in my face, the cops to get their hands away from their guns and finish lunch, and Mrs. Fouke to find another time to tell her husband exactly what she thought of him.

"You're all show, Horace. You ran the company into the ground and slept with your trashy secretary," Mrs. Fouke said and cackled. This must have enraged Horace, because he pressed closer to me, his short, rapid breaths sounding like a freight train ready to crash. He would kill me because his wife had no grasp of the obvious. Was this woman insane? You don't poke a snake. You don't light a match at a gas station, and you don't insult a drunk with a knife. Aaron told her to be quiet. One of the policemen looked as if he might shoot her. Someone needed to shut the woman up.

"You women are all alike. You'll suck a man dry," Horace said.

Despite my precarious position, I took offense to this. I was nothing like his wife. Mrs. Fouke's searing dark eyes reminded me of a mongoose. She had pasty skin and straw-colored hair teased so high it looked like a hotel for pigeons. She wore too much makeup and a permanent scowl. I knew pit bulls with better dispositions. The possibility of her husband dying in a hail of bullets only made the woman giddy. I wondered if pushing him beyond the point of sanity was a daily pastime for her. I concluded we had nothing in common.

As for me, I believed most people could be a bit self-serving, but no one deserved to die in a shootout. The ending of a relationship should be private and not done in the middle of a hostage negotiation. The last time I checked, I hadn't driven anyone to kidnap or murder.

"What the hell is going on here?" A familiar voice bellowed in the near empty dining room. My sister, Candace, stood behind the two police officers with hands on hips and a face full of righteous indignation. She was tall, like me, but had more weight to her and was curvy in places most women envied. A beautiful woman with a dark caramel complexion, copper-colored eyes, and her hair styled in elaborate braids. All this beauty vanished in an instant when her temper emerged, as anger flushed her cheeks and her lips set in a tight line. Everyone stared in awe.

Candace had been next door at the travel agency owned by a family friend, Mrs. Deforest, when the incident occurred. She was helping Mrs. Deforest finalize her plans for her retirement party she wanted to have at the restaurant. When Candace returned to the Blue Moon, she found the place under siege and her sister held hostage. A petite female cop, who could pass for a sixteen-year-old, tried to keep my sister back with little success. In truth, I was extremely gratified to see her; finally, someone was going to make sense and bring this party to an end.

"Miss, you need to leave," the bib-wearing cop insisted. Candace's appraising glance turned scornful. The cop flinched.

"This is my restaurant, and that's my sister," she said, pointing at me as if I were the cause of the trouble. "I'm not your problem; this worthless jerk with the knife is, so stop talking to me and do something."

"Who you calling a worthless jerk?" Horace said, griping me tighter. "This is none of your damn business."

I groaned. Thank you so much, Candace. Here was yet another woman belittling him and telling him what to do. She should have told him he was an upstanding human being and violence wasn't the answer or offer him free dinner for a month, if he got the knife away from her only sister's neck. Christ, will no one have a clue?

"I'm a Christian woman." She put a hand on her chest and looked up to heaven, letting everyone know that the Lord was on her side. "So, I'm going to pray for your pathetic soul. Because when this is over, and there's anything left of your sorry self, the devil will need a broom to get up the pieces. You little..." She stopped. Her eyes widened in surprise. The anger drained from her face, replaced by what looked like a smirk. Had she lost her mind? Before I could ask,

I sensed a large presence behind me but couldn't turn because of the knife at my throat.

Without warning, someone yanked Horace away. He was there and then gone. I grabbed my neck and thanked God when I didn't feel blood. I turned and saw George Fontaine, the Blue Moon chef, clutching Horace by the hand. At six-three, two hundred and thirty pounds, George towered over Horace and everyone else in the room. He reminded people of a black Pillsbury doughboy, only with a lot more muscle and no cute smile. No one would ever poke George in his tummy and expect a giggle. You might expect a stern look and, at worst, a broken finger.

Horace's body trembled as he stared up at George's large, round face, and a puddle of liquid pooled by his feet. George snatched the knife, expertly flipped it, caught the blade, and flung it into the far wall. A graceful move any circus knife thrower or ex-Marine sergeant might appreciate.

"Where the hell did you come from?" the officer with the bib said. Finally noticing what he wore, he yanked it off.

"Downstairs in the basement, checking the meat in the walk-in fridge," George said, as he walked a timid Horace over to the police like a puppy on a leash. Candace pushed through the small crowd and went where the knife had gone into the drywall. She pulled it out and inspected the hole.

"I'll pay for the wall, Candace," an apologetic Aaron said. Her eyes raked the room. Her lips curled into a sneer as she headed for the kitchen.

"I'm gone five minutes, and the place goes to hell." She slammed through the kitchen's double doors. I watched her go, somewhat stunned. I'd just survived a hostage situation and she went searching for what–lunch?

"Thanks for asking, Candy, but I'm alright," I said, rubbing my neck and thinking about the possibilities. My life had passed before my eyes, and I was too scared to pay attention. I sighed. Aaron came over, put his massive arm around my shoulders, and gave me a squeeze. As comforting as the hug was, it didn't calm my nerves.

"Are you okay?" he asked.

"Give me a minute," I said and took a deep breath. It didn't help.

Horace began to weep as they cuffed him. One of the cops came over to speak to me, but I held up a finger for him to wait. I peeled out of Aaron's embrace and went to the bar. The bartender ran out with the customers when this mess began, so I had to help myself.

"Ma'am," the cop said. He probably wondered if I was in shock. At the moment, he impeded my efforts to steady my nerves. I kept my finger up, walked around the large oak bar, and found a bottle of Tequila. I first picked up the cheap stuff, put it down, and went for an expensive one that sold for sixty dollars a bottle. With the cop and Aaron watching intensely, I twisted off the cap and drank straight from the bottle.

"Lady, are you all right?" the concerned officer asked. I ignored his alarm, took another swallow, and shook my head. The liquor burned as it went down, begging my jumbled nerves to calm themselves. Aaron seemed unsure of what to do for me. Luckily, for him, Candace came storming back from the kitchen. She joined me behind the bar and snatched the bottle away, spilling some of the Tequila on my hand, which I promptly licked off. I had my hand in my mouth when she pulled me into a hug so tight I almost lost my breath.

"Odessa Marie Wilkes, you're alright," she said, in that commanding way of hers. Wilkes women didn't fall apart. They didn't have meltdowns, especially in public. There were strong and fearless and took on kidnappers who held knives to their throats. As the alcohol worked on my nerves, I wondered if I was adopted. After a moment or two, the Hallmark moment between us made Candace uncomfortable. She released me. My cell phone rang, saving us both continued embarrassment. I pulled it from the pocket of my apron. Candace took this as a cue to step away from me. The LED display read Maggie. I answered, ignoring my shaking hand.

"Hey." My voice quivered, and I cleared my throat.

"Hey yourself," she said. "Are you alright?" Maggie Swift was my best friend since high school and could read me like a book.

"I've had better days." A confession that didn't ring true, but I forced a smile. Candace stared at me for a moment, perhaps waiting for me to turn into a pile of mental goo. When it didn't happen, she turned and walked away, leaving me to my phone call.

"What's wrong? " Maggie said.

"A problem with a customer," I said.

"You know what they say about the customer always being right," she said.

I wasn't too sure about that being true as I watched them lead Horace away in cuffs and a yelling Mrs. Fouke close behind them with a few more things to say.

"Not this time," I said.

"Well, sorry you're having a bad day. Maybe I've got something to take your mind off of it." Her voice was light and cheery because she knew I needed light and cheery. "I need your help."

I glanced around the restaurant and the puddle left by Horace. One of the busboys began cleaning the mess up under the supervision of Candace. This could have gone so differently, I thought.

I said, "Great, whatever it is, I'll do it."

chapter 2

TWO DAYS AFTER Horace Fouke, I sat at a small table in the back of the Blue Moon watching Jenny Esposito stare at my boyfriend's butt as if it were the prize winning ham at a country fair. Lee stood up front by the bar chatting up Trevor, the bartender, oblivious of this attention. I was comforted by the fact that he believed only I held any interest in his posterior.

Beneath the table, Maggie gripped one of my hands so tight I started losing feeling in my fingers. She wanted me cooperative and silent. In truth, I hadn't planned to utter a single syllable to Jenny. I wanted only to grab her by her hair and toss her out on her narrow butt. Unfortunately, Maggie stymied my desires with her vise-like grip.

Maggie kept throwing me pitiful looks in the hope I could keep my jealousy in check and not embarrass myself. I wanted to ignore her, but her grip got tighter. My smile morphed into a grimace when Jenny asked about the guy with the red tie by the bar. I cut Maggie an exasperated look, which she paid no attention. I bought him that tie for Christmas, for heaven's sake.

I had to admit, any woman with a hint of estrogen would find Leland McKenzie attractive. His wire-framed glasses gave him a studious appearance, a little like Clark Kent. You half expected him to rip off his tie, toss his spectacles aside, and materialize into blue tights.

Perhaps reading my mind, he turned in my direction and gave me a playful smile. Of course, Jenny took this the wrong way.

"Well, I'll be," she cooed, as she twisted her seat for a better view. Her form-fitting floral dress protested as various regions of her anatomy wanted to escape. When Jenny's attention turned back to the table, she smiled at me. I didn't smile back.

"Can you stay focused for five minutes, Jenny?" an impatient Eloise Verde said, glaring at her best friend and maid of honor. Jenny appeared to comply with a halfhearted attempt, as her attention drifted toward anything shiny or with an XY chromosome passing in her line of sight. The fifth person at the table, Mrs. Thea Verde, groaned.

"Jenny," Mrs. Verde barked, in a pack-a-day gravel voice that made Jenny stiffen and my liver shrink. Her voice appeared out of character for a tiny woman in her sixties. Boney, angular features, thin lips, and dark deep-set blue eyes made her appear hawkish. She sat at our table like a queen, saying little, but her withering gaze spoke volumes about her discontent.

No one had any doubt Mrs. Verde held the checkbook to what Eloise wanted for her wedding. This included hiring my business, *O So Sweet Cakes*, to make her wedding cake. For whatever reason, Maggie convinced Mrs. Verde to hire me. Her jovial daughter needed a wedding cake in less than three weeks. Whether or not I would be Eloise's wedding cake-maker depended on her maid of honor shutting down her heat-seeking man radar and Maggie's grip.

"I am focused, but you can't let a good view go to waste," Jenny said, in an irksome baby doll voice. Mrs. Verde cleared her throat, and this seemed to refocus Jenny, at least for the moment. Maggie released her hold on me, and I stretched my fingers to get some blood back into them.

"I know him," I said, catching Maggie's irked expression. "He has a girlfriend." I ignored Maggie because Jenny wasn't sizing up her man for a Happy Meal.

"Can we focus on the wedding?" Maggie insisted as she went searching for my hand from beneath the table. I eluded her.

"It has to be perfect, like on one of those wedding shows on television—grand and super elegant. I want lots and lots of flowers and lights." Eloise prattled on about the television shows. I got the feeling she was happy the conversation centered around her again. Jenny's attention span failed her as her eyes drifted back to the bar. I tried to ignore this and focus on the problem at hand—a last-minute job jammed into an already crowded wedding schedule.

"I'm booked right now, but if we keep the cake simple, I think I can handle the job," I said in the hope of regaining Jenny's attention. In truth, short of jumping Lee in the middle of a crowded restaurant, I wanted to believe she had some sense of propriety. At least, I hoped.

"This is the only wedding I'll ever have, and I want to be a princess," Eloise said. Mrs. Verde shifted in her seat as if someone stuck a hot poker up her butt. Everyone noticed. She raked the table with a hard glare, sending a chill down my spine. Eloise lost her smile as her eyes darted away from her mother.

Eloise—a plain girl with a spoon-shaped face, soft features, and olive skin—had large, dark, expressive eyes, which betrayed her every emotion. She reveled in her role as bride-to-be. Somewhat unsure of herself, she acted almost punch drunk with the newfound attention.

"There is so little time," Eloise said. She struggled to keep her smile as her eyes kept drifting toward her mother.

"The wedding will be held at a place called Darbonne Winery. It's small and recently started doing special events," Maggie said.

"We have a cake, and now I need a dress," Eloise said and looked at Maggie.

"Eloise isn't having much luck, so I told her I'd help her find one," Maggie said. Though she tried to hide it, she didn't seem thrilled with the idea.

"Don't worry, honey. We'll get everything together," Jenny reassured, patting Eloise's hand.

When Jenny's attention floated back to the table, she spent much of her time countering derogatory barbs Mrs. Verde made toward Eloise. Jenny would swoop in with a compliment or flattering remark, to the consternation of Mrs. Verde. An odd competition developed to determine which woman could irritate or appease Eloise more.

"It will be wonderful," Eloise cooed. Like some child who believed in the tooth fairy or Christmas, she dared anyone to tell her otherwise.

I knew weddings were like a military deportment to a foreign country. The good ones took time, planning, and money. The bad ones lacked all three. Depending on how generous Mrs. Verde was, money wouldn't be a problem. Planning was the issue. Eloise didn't have a wedding planner and she had three weeks to achieve her dream of a magnificent wedding. I wanted to give Eloise a rap on that thick forehead of hers to knock her back to reality. Maggie must have read my thoughts because she tried to grab my hand again. She missed.

"We're done here," Mrs. Verde said without warning. Everyone at the table collectively stopped breathing.

"Mommy," Eloise whined. "There are still things—"

Mrs. Verde shot her daughter a withering glare as color drained from Eloise's face.

"Ellie, let's go get the car," Jenny said, taking the younger Verde's hand. "I'm sure your mother has to talk about dirty old money."

"What about the cake tasting?" a disappointed Eloise said.

"Why don't you come back with your fiancé so you can do the tasting together," Maggie suggested.

"Yes, Henry has to be here," Eloise said. She did a little hop in her seat and clapped. I guessed showing off her fiancé made her happy. The two women got up from the table. Jenny smoothed out her dress and ran her hand along her hips as if something shifted in transit. A few dining room patrons turned to stare at the show. Eloise gave a nervous laugh before smoothing down her oversized tee-shirt and saying goodbye.

They headed for the door but stopped when Jenny reached the bar. She made a detour straight to Lee. She leaned in close and spoke to him before following Eloise out of the restaurant. To Lee's credit, his eyes didn't follow. Instead, he turned in the opposite direction, saw me looking at him, and gave me a lecherous smile. I shook my head, and he covered his heart with his hands and feigned a wounded look.

"Sometimes I wonder if she's right in the head," Mrs. Verde said.

"You wonder?" I said with surprise. Jenny was the type of girl in high school you found beneath the bleachers sucking face with your boyfriend.

"Jenny said your priest offered to do the ceremony at your church in Brooklyn. Why didn't you take him up on the offer?" Maggie asked.

Mrs. Verde's lips curled into a sneer.

"I'm not having this circus anywhere near my church. People know me there," she said, pulling out a cigarette from her tiny handbag. She rooted around until she came up with a lighter.

"You can't smoke in here," I said.

Mrs. Verde's tepid attitude toward me turned frigid as she dropped the lighter back into her purse.

"I better go, or they'll come back and waste the rest of my day," Mrs. Verde said as she stood up from the table.

"I'll call you with any news, okay?" Maggie said, also standing.

Mrs. Verde turned her dark eyes on Maggie and pointed a wrinkled finger at her.

"You got less than three weeks, or I'll take the matter into my own hands," Mrs. Verde said as she turned to leave. As Maggie's eyes followed her out the restaurant, my eyes were on her.

"You want to explain that?" I asked.

Maggie sighed.

"You remember you promised to help me," she said as she plopped back down in her chair.

I sighed.

In the past, keeping Maggie's promises ran from babysitting her hyperactive son, Rocket, to helping her do a background check on a philandering husband. A private investigator in training, Maggie assisted a local P.I. in the hope of one day having an office of her own and a list of clients who appreciated her remarkable deductive skills.

Hence, when she asked me to do a wedding, I appreciated her help in my specialty cake making business. However, I remembered what she did for a living.

A perky, height challenged, blue-eyed redhead, a woman of good intentions, dipped in a healthy dose of sweetness, tenacity, and as duplicitous as a Girl Scout, Maggie was an excellent wife and mother. Often mistaken for a lack of shrewdness, her pixie demeanor put most people at ease and susceptible to her inquisitive nature. Secretly, deep down, she was a closet superhero, as evidenced by her innate curiosity and her penchant to help people. Therefore, when she called and begged me to take on the Verdes as clients, I suspected something.

I sighed.

"If I don't stop this wedding, Mrs. Verde is going to get rid of her future son-in-law."

"What do you mean, get rid of?"

"You know." Maggie's eyes widened.

"I know you dragged Lucrezia Borgia, her dewy daughter, and the slutty best friend here to convince me to make a last minute cake," I said with a straight face. "You almost broke my hand because the reality is Eloise's wedding isn't going to be the dream she thinks her wedding should be. Now you tell me the mother–of-the-bride wants her future son-in-law whacked."

"Odessa Wilkes, don't be so dramatic," Maggie said.

I blinked.

"You come in here and tell me Mrs. Verde…" I pointed to Mrs. Verde's empty seat. "…will kill her daughter's fiancé."

She started playing with her hair, a familiar stalling tactic.

"Maybe," she hedged.

Exasperated, I glared at her.

"It's like being pregnant, Maggie, either you are or you aren't." I folded my arms and waited.

"Yes, okay. Are you happy now?" she said with some annoyance. "Mrs. Verde will try to kill Eloise's fiancé if he tries to marry her."

I blinked.

chapter 3

IT'S NOT EVERY day your best friend tells you someone you just met planned to have someone you haven't met before killed. News of Mrs. Verde's intention toward her future son-in-law made me take a deep breath. I stared at Maggie as if she were crazy. The news sounded absurd coming from her. Imagine Minnie Mouse telling some Senate s-committee on terror that the Axis of Evil was Goofy. I would admit the elder Verde could scare dogs and small children, but a murderer?

"I'm serious, O," she said. Maggie's big blue doe eyes stared at me unwavering.

"Right," I said with not much conviction, but nodded anyway.

Maggie stepped close to me and whispered. "She said she knows people. Are you listening? She *knows* people!"

"So what?" I said. "This is New York City. You can't throw a rock without hitting someone who has broken the law." A patron stopped eating and stared at me. I smiled until he got interested in returning to his meal again.

"O, you said you would help me." She crossed her arms like a petulant child.

I did promise, and I needed to get my mind off Fouke. I started seeing the little man all over the place. Every short, desperate-looking, middle-aged, slightly balding guy was him. A decent night's sleep was elusive. He'd begun to invade my dreams. I dreamt he snuck into my house, stole all of my butter knives, and then hid beneath my bed.

"Come on, you won't let me do this on my own, will you?" She gave me one of her most engaging smiles.

"Fine," I said with little enthusiasm.

We'd been close since high school. To most, our friendship seemed odd. A part-time, stay-at-home mom, Maggie lived in a modest house in Hicksville, New York, with her insurance salesman husband, Roger; son, Rocket; and their dog. She dreamt of world peace and getting her private investigator license.

Over a year ago, my promising career in advertising fell apart when an embezzling scandal forced me to leave a job I loved. On the day of my termination, security guards escorted me out of the building with the remains of my dignity and the contents of my desk in a cardboard box. Waiting for me out on the street was my perfect boyfriend, who proceeded to dump me. On the subway ride home, a tunnel fire trapped me on the train for hours. The aftermath of my most disastrous day left me with little blue pills for an anxiety disorder, employment working alongside my overbearing sister at our family's restaurant, and the notion no man would ever love me again.

Through all my drama, Maggie stood by me, being my best friend. She encouraged me not to give up and throw myself under a bus. Eventually, I conquered my fears, learned how to work with my sister, and found someone to love me. Therefore, even when she sounded crazy, I tended to listen.

"Just tell me this isn't one of Frank's crazy cases," I said. Her vanishing smile confirmed my suspicions. "Speaking of Frank, where is he?"

I scanned the crowded dining room filling up with early evening patrons. No sight of an overweight, poorly dressed, retired New York City ex-cop anywhere. Frank McAvoy was Maggie's boss. To get a private investigators license in New York, you needed three years of experience or mentoring by a licensed investigator. As for Frank, she would get more guidance from SpongeBob. Frank's priorities included getting paid, eating, and gambling, and not exactly in that order.

"He's busy with an insurance fraud case Roger set him up on," she said.

"You didn't want to turn down the Verdes, did you?" This had to be true, because McAvoy Investigations barely made ends meet. The business stayed afloat because Maggie kept the books and their few clients satisfied. Part secretary, gofer, office wife, and research assistant, she ran the small one-man detective agency single-handedly. She'd gotten friends and family to throw work Frank's way, but sometimes it just covered office expenses and Maggie's meager salary. Turning down work wasn't an option. I wouldn't put it past Maggie to think she could handle the case and get the agency paid at the same time.

"Listen," she said. "Frank is busy with the thing for Roger. He's doing surveillance on someone faking an injury. He's gone a little ... Captain Ahab."

"What?"

"You know, the white whale, Captain Ahab."

"I know who Captain Ahab is." I rolled my eyes. I wanted to get to a point sometime in the near future.

"Frank is obsessed with the guy. He sits in his old, stinky car waiting for him to make a mistake."

"So Frank doesn't know about the Verdes?" I said.

"No."

"Are you going to tell him?" I asked.

"No." She stuck out her chin, defiantly.

I shook my head, annoyed with her stubbornness. I was about to tell her so when I saw something extraordinary, something not seen since the last moon landing. Lee and Candace talking, not just talking, but they looked congenial toward each other. What really set my radar booming was the sight of an unidentified man's arm around my sister's waist.

I ignored Maggie and stared.

"Are you listening?" she asked.

18

I was too intrigued with the idea of my sister and some amorous stranger. This from a woman who believed any public display of affection was bad for digestion. She even bristled seeing Lee greeting me with a peck on the cheek. The unwritten rule at the Blue Moon was no P.D.A.

"Who is that guy?" I asked.

Maggie turned around and followed my line of sight.

"Seems like she and Lee are getting along better," she said.

"Well, yeah," I said. At best, Lee and Candace tolerated each other. She expected me to date and marry someone tall, dark, and handsome. I clearly didn't get the dark part right. Then again, Lee McKenzie's Scottish ancestors might wonder why he cohabitated with an opinionated black woman. Some days you can't please anyone.

"No, the guy with his arm around Candace." I could ignore Lee's and Candace's sudden civility toward each other; rarer things have happened.

"He's handsome," Maggie said.

"He's alright if you liked guys who grope." I got up from the table and started to walk over to them when George came out of nowhere and blocked my way.

"No you don't," he commanded.

George loomed in front of me like a brick wall. When I tried to walk around he, took me by the arm and redirected me toward the kitchen.

"What the hell?" I yelped, and George guided me through the double doors.

"Odessa, what about the Verdes?" Maggie called out, to no avail.

The Verdes were the last people on my mind. My concern had to do with George's intent. He didn't look overjoyed, and I couldn't imagine why. When he finally stopped manhandling me, I found myself in front of my work space. I understood his anger immediately. The place was a mess.

In my defense, I had so many cake orders. I no longer had the luxury of working at home. I brought some of the work to the Blue

Moon. Normally, I wasn't this messy but somehow my baking equipment and supplies had a fight and George's kitchen lost.

"Clean it up," George barked.

I pulled away and smoothed out my rumpled clothes. I didn't have time to deal with the mess; I needed to find out about Candace's mystery man.

"I'll do it later, George, I swear." I crisscrossed my heart and gave him a disingenuous smile. He folded his arms and stood before me like an immovable fortress.

"Now," he said, his eyes narrowing and brow furrowing.

Maggie stepped into the kitchen, assessed the situation, turned around and left. Even she wasn't going to take on George.

"Come on," I pleaded.

"If you ever want to cook in this kitchen again, do it now," he said, nearly growling.

I couldn't argue. Even though I was part-owner of the restaurant, I carried no weight in the kitchen. It was George's domain, and I was just another peon.

"Fine," I said, my tone unapologetic. I began to clean.

By the time I finished, Maggie had left to pick up her son, Rocket, then headed home to start dinner and turn back into a housewife. Candace's mystery man was gone as well. She stonewalled me when I asked about him. When I tried to ask George, he turned a deaf ear. I was even desperate enough to try to elicit information from the young sous chef, Bebe Bernard.

A few years ago, a local family court judge talked my sister into taking on the 16-year-old former wannabe gangsta and sous chef in training as part of a work program for first-time youth offenders. She half expected him to kill her or at least steal from the register. He did neither. Bebe came under the tutelage of George, who discovered Bebe's natural talent for cooking exceeded everyone's expectations.

"You won't tell me?" I said.

"No," Bebe said flatly. Recently, he'd been working hard at improving his relationship with my sister. It was a wonder to me why he tried. Bebe could become the next president, but if you asked Candace, he'd still be the kid in the droopy jeans, oversized tee-shirt, backward baseball cap, and potential criminal.

It annoyed me that no one would divulge Candace's mystery man's name. This only intrigued me more. Dejected, I bagged my trash under the watchful eye of George and went to the dumpsters outside the kitchen. The late afternoon summer sun faded low in the sky, casting shadows and a sun glare. I squinted as I walked over to the large double dumpsters. I never saw Horace Fouke coming out between them. Dressed in dark clothes and a skullcap, he looked like a middle-aged ninja. I didn't know anyone dressed like that who amounted to any good.

I jumped at the sight of him. Instead of letting out a bloodcurdling scream, I yelped. Fear had stolen my breath. I sounded as ferocious as a toy poodle. I held up the garbage bag, ready to throw it at him, hoping he was more concerned about his ninja outfit than hurting me.

Don't," he said, pointing at me.

"Stay away for me," I yelled, finally finding my voice. He stepped toward me, and I screamed so loud, they heard me in the Bronx, Brooklyn, and parts of Staten Island. Horace's eyes widened as he took another step toward me but stopped when George rushed out from the back door, followed by Bebe. I pointed at Horace, like one of the pod people from a B-movie. Pointing and screaming, screaming and pointing, I had this move down pat.

"Hey you!" George shouted. The small man recoiled at the sight of him, probably remembering their last encounter. He turned and ran. Without saying a word, Bebe sprinted after him as both men disappeared around the corner. I continued to scream and point. George grabbed me by my shoulders and gave me a little shake. I guess he found the only off switch that would work on me. I stopped screaming.

"You all right?" he asked.

I nodded.

A crowd of gawking kitchen workers gathered at the door, and I felt foolish. Horace hadn't laid a hand on me. A moment later Lee burst through the doorway and pushed past the small group.

"Are you okay? I heard you in the dining room," Lee said as he pulled me into his arms.

I shook my head.

"What is his problem? Why doesn't he pick on his wife?" I said as I pulled away from him a little. I still had the garbage in my hand, and some of it oozed out. It made a stain on Lee's shirt, but he apparently didn't care and pulled me closer.

"You recognize him?" Lee asked.

"He's the guy with the knife and the ex-wife," George said as he took the bag of garbage from me and tossed it into the dumpster.

"Why isn't he in jail?" I asked. I took slow, deep breaths as my heart raced. I stepped back from him because I needed some air.

"I'm going to find out," Lee said and pulled out his cell phone.

Bebe reappeared, drenched in sweat and heaving hard. It took him a moment to catch his breath.

"The little bastard is fast. He had a block on me and then got into some van with a bug on top of the roof," Bebe said.

"A bug?" I said in disbelief.

"Yeah, a big ass bug on the top. I think a cockroach or maybe an ant." Bebe didn't seem certain.

"Horace Fouke, the Bug King, got out on bail twenty-four hours ago." Lee snapped his phone shut. He stared in the direction Horace ran, possibly hoping the man would be dumb enough to return. Horace threatened me, not once but twice, and Lee needed to deal with it the only way he understood, by putting the man so far under the jailhouse, he'd take his bathroom breaks in China.

Lee's anger didn't surprise me. He had an even-tempered disposition most of the time. His calm demeanor morphed into chest-beating, possessive superhero, determined to save me. It was stupid, but after awhile I stopped fighting it. No twentieth-century feminist logic was going to beat out the genetic anomaly in his man code. I'll admit the screaming pod people thing didn't help.

"I'm being attacked by the Bug King?" I said in disbelief.

"I'm going to talk to the detective in charge of the case and get that son-of-a-bitch Fouke back in jail," he said. He clutched his phone so tight; I thought it might snap in two.

"That would be nice," I said and yawned. I'd screamed myself into a state of weariness and needed to sit down. I pulled a resisting Lee back into the restaurant. I got a feeling he still wanted the chance of giving the Bug King a little more than a piece of his mind. I preferred dinner and world peace as George ushered everyone back to work.

"Show's over folks," he said.

I hoped he was right and Horace was scared off, because I didn't want another visitation from the Bug King.

chapter 4

AFTER MY UPSETTING encounter with the Bug King at the Blue Moon, Lee drove me home. In an attempt to take my mind off Horace Fouke, he ordered pizza and opened a bottle of wine. We sat on the couch and watched a movie on television. I didn't think about Fouke for a while. I wanted to believe he would stay as far away from me as possible after his run in with the Blue Moon kitchen staff, especially George.

As I relaxed in Lee's embrace, I felt safe enough to utilize my time perusing a more constructive endeavor, like convincing him to divulge the name of Candace's mystery man. Before George and the Bug King interrupted me, I had intended to find out. Alone at home, I had a better chance of getting the truth out of him than anyone else. In the courtroom, Lee excelled as a lawyer, a champion of justice, a defender for the little man, but in bed, he turned to putty.

After a long hot shower, I slipped on a recently purchased Victoria's Secret burgundy lace camisole. I'd been saving it for his upcoming birthday. When he came upstairs to go to bed, it took about forty minutes, a second bottle of wine, and a promise I would never tell Candace he cracked. Who would have thought Lee was Candace's weakest link?

"Christ, Dessa, I'm finally having conversations with the woman without her calling the NAACP on me," he said. He lay there, breathing heavy, shaking off the last remnants of my persuasion. I snuggled close to him and listened as he complained about his fragile relationship with my sister. He and Bebe should start a support group, for Christ's sake. I took pity on him and gave him a kiss that left him silent for awhile.

I pulled away and said, "Trust me, sweetie, you don't want to be too friendly with Candy."

"She's your sister. She should like me." His wounded expression only depressed me.

My bedroom had too many people, first Fouke and now my sister. Rolling onto my back, I stared up at the ceiling wondering how I could get my sister out of my bedroom and Lee's head. He and Bebe believed that Candace's friendship had benefits. I grew up with her; trust me, there weren't any. She required subjugation and allegiance. In Candace's world, you had to leave any opinions by the door.

"I love my sister, but she's a controlling pain in my butt. The only reason she hasn't begun to run your life is she expects at any moment I'll come to my senses and dump you."

"Dump me?" Lee sat up and stared down at me, startled, his brow furrowed in confusion. "I thought she was starting to like me."

"You know she's still friends with Davis. He is my ex-boyfriend and she talks to him as if he doesn't have a wife or a home of his own," I said. Lee's foolish belief that my sister's dislike for him had waned was wishful thinking on his part. The woman was only biding her time. I sighed in disgust and a little frustration. Maybe sensing this, Lee wrapped me in his arms.

"Let's forget about Candace," he whispered into my ear. I nodded and grinned. He planted kisses along my neck and worked his way down when he suddenly stopped.

"Just don't tell Candace I told you about Leon," he said.

I laughed. "You wimp."

***

The next morning, Lee made noises about staying home with me, but I insisted he go to work. He only agreed when I told him I had plans to meet with Maggie about a cake. When his resistance remained, I threatened to tell Candace about his late night slip of the lip. That got him out of the house. As he drove off to the office, I went out to Long Island to see Maggie at her office.

McAvoy Investigations resided in a strip mall thirty minutes form Maggie's house. Sandwiched between a martial arts studio and a pizzeria, the place smelled either like pepperoni or like sweaty kids depending on the direction of the wind. I found a frazzled Maggie going through some files. Dressed in jeans and a baby blue tee-shirt, with her long, red hair scrunched up in a haphazard ponytail, she seemed too young to be a mother and a wife. Truthfully, she hadn't changed much since I first met her in high school, except for the scowl on her face. When she saw me walk in, she brightened. I always liked her ability to change emotional direction on a dime. If I tried it, I'd snap something.

She cleared off a chair by her desk Frank must have gotten from the town dump, and I took a seat. Pictures of family and friends cluttered the desktop. Most were of her son, Rocket. In constant motion, in every photograph, the 8-year-old didn't get his nickname for being stationary. A miniaturized version of his mother, my godson didn't inherit her even disposition, only her red hair. Rocket at rest was a near impossibility. I loved him to death, but the child was why strong and effective birth control was essential.

"Where's Frank?" I asked. I surveyed the tiny office. I hadn't seen the big man in days.

"He's still on the stakeout, remember?" Maggie said. She cleared off more papers and took a seat across from me. "I can't believe Horace Fouke tried to attack you after I left."

"Try being the operative word," I said. I didn't want to talk about Fouke. I'd had enough excitement from the Bug King. "Why aren't you doing the stakeout thing with Frank?"

She frowned.

Frank had antiquated ideas about women being private investigators. He didn't mind if she worked in the office and answered the phone or did a little research, but that was it. Deep down I didn't think Frank believed Maggie would make a good P.I. He was clueless.

"I understand I'm a lowly secretary, coffee-maker, and office cleaner, but I have opinions about things." She yanked out the hair clip holding her hair together, ran her fingers through her tresses, and redid the ponytail, a habit she did in frustration. If she worked with Frank any longer, she'd go bald.

"Get real. Frank hasn't left the seventies yet. Hell, he's still carrying around the sixties. I bet if you checked his closet, the fifties would be there," I said.

Maggie laughed.

"I'll forget Horace Fouke, and you can forget Frank," I said, and that made her smile.

"Well, I'm doing the Verde case whether he wants me too or not," she said, sounding determined.

"What do you mean, wants you to or not? He still doesn't know?" I said.

Maggie said nothing. I shook my head.

"Maggie, I think you're missing something here," I said.

"What?"

"First, technically, it's Frank with the P.I. license, not you. You can't run around telling everyone you an investigator," I said.

"I didn't tell anyone that I was. Mrs. Verde came in, asked about hiring the agency, and I just agreed," she said and blinked her eyes at me. I wasn't buying her innocent demeanor. I sighed in exasperation.

"She hired you to stop a wedding that isn't going to happen anyway," I said.

"What do you mean?"

"A patch of grass in the middle of a vineyard and a cake does not a wedding make. The way things are going, there won't be a wedding to worry about," I said.

"Yes there will or Eloise and Henry will elope. Eloise threatened to do it unless her mother gives her an unforgettable wedding."

"And Mrs. Verde agreed to this? The woman looks like she hasn't agreed with anyone since the Eisenhower Administration," I said.

"She thinks the three weeks will give me time to find something out about Henry that could stop the wedding," Maggie explained.

"So the wedding is a delaying tactic?"

Maggie nodded.

"Eloise is going to figure it out when there aren't any preparations made for the wedding," I said, aware of her short-sightedness. "I've been around enough brides; trust me, they notice these things."

"The wedding is being planned," she insisted.

I gave her a doubtful look.

"By who?"

"Me."

It took me a moment to realize she was serious.

"What? Are you crazy?" I said. "You expect to do a wedding in three weeks, investigate the fiancé, and keep the whole thing from Frank?"

I laughed. Maggie didn't.

"If you help me," she said, her eyes filled with confidence and a hint of delusion. I was sure this was what Butch said to Sundance about going to Bolivia.

"Maggie, this isn't Rocket's birthday at Chuck E. Cheese. You can't throw a wedding together like a late-night snack," I said.

"Well, Eloise believes I'm her wedding planner." Maggie stuck out her chin.

"Honey, you are a lot of things, but you are not a wedding planner. You're organized and you run this office wonderfully, but wedding planners are a whole different beast. Four-star generals could take lessons from them."

"You've been to lots of weddings. You must have picked up something," she pleaded.

"I show up with the cake, Maggie, that's it," I said. "You're at least married."

"The only thing I remember about my wedding was Roger getting sick on my wedding dress, his mother calling an ambulance and the cops on me. The woman thought I poisoned him." Maggie cringed at the memory. I remembered the event. Roger's mother made Candace seem like a Girl Scout.

Candace! The idea danced across my mind like running on hot coals. I knew it was crazy of course, but when you had nothing, next to nothing seemed great.

"In a perfect world I could ask Candace. She's done tons of weddings for Blue Moon Catering. She knows about food, flowers, the whole thing," I said.

"You think she'd help me?" Maggie asked. This time I had to laugh.

"Hell no," I said. Candace didn't think much of Maggie.

"If you asked?"

"Double hell no." My sister loved me, but she didn't always like me. My choices made me dubious in her eyes. Disappointed I didn't continue my career in advertising; I made no effort to save my relationship with my ex-boyfriend, Davis; I lived with Lee and had Maggie as my best friend. My sister didn't trust me to make a sane decision.

"Mrs. Verde will pay for the wedding. She needs to buy time," Maggie said.

"How much is she willing to pay?"

Maggie's lips curled in a crooked smile.

"Her words were, 'Whatever it takes,'" Maggie said.

I thought about possible work for the restaurant and without a doubt, Candace would take the catering job in a heartbeat. Helping Maggie arrange the wedding was another thing.

"Let me work on her," I said. I tried to hide my uncertainty at the prospect my sister would help her. This didn't stop Maggie from smiling and jumping up and down in her happy dance, a spastic contortion of arms and legs. You'd get more rhythm from a psychotic chicken. I motioned for her to sit down.

"You don't believe Mrs. Verde is going to have Henry killed, do you?" I asked.

"The Verdes originally came from Brooklyn or the Bronx, where Mrs. Verde's family...." She averted her eyes. "Let's just say she had family connections with people in the meat-packing industry."

"She comes from a family of butchers?" I said, trying hard to read between the lines.

"You know," she said, hinting at something sinister.

"I don't want to know," I said, shaking my head.

"Listen, O, first let's worry about Eloise and Henry. I'll arrange the cake tasting for them. When she brings him around for the tasting, tell me what you think. Tell me if something is hinky," she said.

I raised an eyebrow.

Maggie was under the delusion that I had the ability to recognize devious and duplicitous men because my previous jerk of an ex-boyfriend. In truth, Davis honed my ability. She considered this one of my super powers. She believed everyone had at least one. The only certainty was if I met another man like Davis, I'd run the other way because he dumped me on the worst day of my life. Then Davis stalked me in the hope that I would forgive him for his transgressions against me. Not only was he crazy, but he was an idiot.

I sighed and gave my friend a long scrutinizing look. She'd taken on this case despite the fact she had no license. Her boss didn't have a clue what she was up to, and she planned to stop someone's wedding. I hadn't met Henry, but Eloise seemed pleasant enough. She wanted a dream wedding Maggie was determined to ruin. It was so unlike her, the queen of happy endings.

chapter 5

I'D LEARNED OVER time when approaching my sister for a favor, you had to come up along her blindside—money. This overrode most of her usual dislikes, including Maggie. The Verde's wedding would be costly, and if the Blue Moon did the catering, it was a winning situation for the restaurant—and my sister, of course. My only hesitation had to do with asking my sister for a favor. Helping Maggie plan Eloise's wedding was no small feat. Depending how I asked, Candace might interpret the request as a favor I'd owe her. If that happened, there wouldn't be enough time and subjugation in the world for me to pay her back. I wondered, as Candace stood by the front of the restaurant greeting customers, how I would accomplish this without owing her my firstborn.

I approached her under the guise of telling her the restaurant had a full dessert case. This would make her cordial. At least I hoped so. Her biggest problem had always been I never made enough desserts to please her. There wasn't enough time in the day or enough flour and sugar in the world to make her happy. Ten feet before I even got near her she spotted me and frowned. News of my recent inquiries regarding Leon Pendarvist had gotten back to her. She didn't appreciate my sticking my nose in her personal business.

I received a brief reprieve when a customer leaving the restaurant complimented Candace on his wonderful meal and she gave him a million dollar smile. Amazed at her ability to turn on the charm when a customer stood within a hundred feet of her, I watched in admiration. Lacking this ability, I tended to stay far away from the customers. When the patron left, she returned her attention on me, and her frown came back.

"Hey, Candy," I said. I gave her my warmest smile.

"What?" Her terse voice snapped, and my smile wavered.

"Wanted to let you know the dessert case is full, and there are extra cakes in the refrigerator in the kitchen," I said.

This garnished an upraised eyebrow and a vigilant gaze from her.

"Do you plan to disappear for a couple of days?"

"No," I said, somewhat indignant at the implication that I only filled up the dessert case when I wanted a few days off from the restaurant. A day maybe, but never a couple of days. I had some sense of responsibility.

"Good, you will have time to do Mrs. Deforest's retirement cake for her party. She's closing the shop in a few weeks," she said.

I knew the travel agency next door planned to close, but this was the first time I'd heard of me making a cake for the party. Mrs. Deforest had been a friend of my mother when she first opened the Blue Moon. Candace inherited the friendship when she took over the restaurant.

"Sure, no problem," I said. "What's going to happen with the agency?" I asked. Candace always hinted at expanding the restaurant. Now she had an opportunity to do it. Since I was partial owner of the Blue Moon, I didn't have any objections. Not that Candace would even ask my opinion.

"Also, Aunt Renne wants you to make cupcakes for the church choirs."

"What?" The request hit like a body blow because the First Baptist choir had over 150 members. Also, I hated doing cupcakes for large groups.

"Do you want me to tell Aunt Renne you won't?" she asked snidely, knowing I would never deny my elderly aunt anything.

"When?" I said, between clenched teeth.

"Next Sunday." Candace didn't care if it were the height of the wedding season. Already booked for several engagements this month, over a hundred cupcakes would put a sizeable dent in my schedule. I gritted my teeth and agreed. Remembering Maggie, I'd lost enthusiasm for subtly and stealth. I took my chance on the truth.

"I have a wedding in less than three weeks. The customer needs a caterer," I said. Candace laughed.

"I think McDonalds is available because we're booked."

"So am I, yet you still told Aunt Renne I'd do over a hundred cupcakes and let's not forget Mrs. Deforest," I said.

"That's family, and she's a friend," she shot back.

"Which means I won't get paid. At least the catering is money," I said. "Thousands for the budget for the food."

Candace's eyes lit up.

"Liquor included, of course." I knew she was working the math in her head.

I nodded.

"Three weeks, yes or no?"

"Yes." She smiled at me.

"There's a catch." I grinned back.

"What?" Her smile faded, and her eyes narrowed.

"Maggie is planning the wedding," I said. "If you want the job you have to help her."

"No way." Candace shook her head.

"Then no catering job and no money." I folded my arm and matched her raised eyebrow.

"I thought she worked with that fat detective, what's his face." Candace never remembered Frank's name.

"She is, but she's making a little money on the side," I lied. "So, I can tell Maggie you'll help her?"

Candace huffed and nodded.

"Thank you, Candy." I grinned at her and headed for the kitchen. I turned to leave but stopped when she spoke.

"George said you made a mess in his kitchen," she said as she wrote in the reservation book. This surprised me. When did George go running to Candace for anything?

"He shoved me in a corner, and I need a little more space. George will deal with it," I said.

"No he won't, you will." She finally looked up at me and stared at me like our mother used to when I didn't take out the trash.

"With Lee in the house, there isn't much space. Come on, Candy, you don't want me to turned down jobs, do you?" I said, hoping to plead to her monetary demons.

"Either manage your space with George or kick Lee out." Her tone had no humor, and I thought she meant it. I rolled my eyes, turned, and headed for the kitchen. I counted to ten beneath my breath.

I pushed through the kitchen double doors to find George going over the evening menu with one of the kitchen staff. He hated interruptions, but I didn't care.

"You complained to Candace," I said with hands on my hips. He turned to me, pointing in the direction of my workstation. Many of my cooking pans and ingredients had spilled over to another long prep table.

"You should have said something to me," I said, my self-righteousness waning.

"I did, several times," he said before turning his back to me. I'd been dismissed, first by Candace and now by George. I counted to ten again.

I had Eloise and Henry coming in a few hours, and I needed to be in a better mood. I grumbled at George and retreated to my workstation to begin my work on the cake tasting. I tried to keep the area clear and stay out of his way. By three o'clock, I had several samples ready and readied myself for the couple. I prepared a small table in the back of the restaurant for privacy. Candace gave me a scathing glance when I took the table. I knew this was *O So Sweet Cake* business, but the Blue Moon would get the catering. I tried to ignore her, but between Candace's comments and George's space issues, it began to bother me.

At four-thirty, Henry and Eloise entered the Blue Moon restaurant. Henry was handsome. He reminded me of Matt Damon only taller and darker. Eloise strolled in on his arm looking like an appendage every woman in the place wanted to cut off with a hacksaw. She wasn't an unattractive woman, but you wondered what he saw in her.

Eloise introduced us, and Henry grinned back at me with perfect white teeth. When I worked in advertising, I would have hired someone like Henry to be a spokes model, generically handsome and non-threatening. He shook my hand firmly and held eye contact until our hands released. He wore his sincerity like his Brooks Brother shirt. Eloise glowed and appeared proud of her acquisition, like a new pair of shoes. You never thought girls like her ever got men like Henry, but somehow she had. Secretly, I hoped Henry was the real thing, because if he loved her and wanted to marry her, one would go in the win column for the ordinary girls who never went out for cheerleading, never became homecoming queen, and never got the prince.

"Mrs. Swift said you were a genius with cakes," Henry said as he took a bite of chocolate cake filled with butterscotch icing.

"Tomorrow Maggie's going to help me find a dress. Mom said I could get anything I want. Isn't that wonderful, Henry?" Eloise cooed. Henry stroked her hand. She blushed and shuddered, an orgasmic moment shared between the two of them. It left me a little uncomfortable.

"I wish she'd allow me to pay for something," he complained. Eloise shook her head.

"No, Henry, you're paying for the honeymoon," she protested.

"Still, honey –"

Eloise stopped him with a finger to his lips, leaned, and kissed him without removing her finger. Henry stopped protesting, and I silently moaned.

"She promised me the perfect wedding." Eloise disengaged herself from Henry's gaze and turned to me.

I stared at them both wondering what the hell was going on. I proudly admitted I was a cynic. I'd been one since my father tried to convince me the Tooth Fairy exchanged money for teeth. I didn't buy it at five, and I didn't buy what Henry and Eloise were selling now, because they were trying too hard. I knew what Maggie thought of them. Typically hopeful, she wanted to believe Henry loved a dumpy plant store manager and love was indeed blind. On the other hand, she wanted me to see them together, talk to Henry in particular. She needed her optimistic belief in their love knocked into reality by a cynic.

"What's the next flavor?" Eloise asked, as she regained her focus long enough for me to complete the tasting. When they finally agreed on a flavor, Eloise threw me for a loop when she pulled out the photograph of an elaborate wedding cake. It had too many tiny red roses to count, six tiers, and intricate piping. The detail work was ridiculous. I stared at the photograph and her, a little dumbfounded. I hated saying no but I needed to bring some reality to the table.

"This is a lot of work. I may not have time for this. Why not try something simpler," I said. Eloise's whole body seemed to close in on itself, and her large eyes moistened.

I braced myself for her tears.

"We would appreciate if you did the best you can. I want to give her everything," Henry said, his eyes pleading. He genuinely wanted to make her happy, which surprised me.

"It must be perfect," Eloise chirped. I couldn't believe it, but I felt myself nod. I had to stop hanging around Maggie; she affected my ability to say no. Eloise clapped like some trained seal and Henry grinned. Everyone was happy, except me. I got a respite from the delusion when Eloise excused herself to go the ladies room. I finally had Henry alone.

"Eloise is something else," he said proudly.

I smiled. "Where did you two meet?"

"At Verde Nursery. I went to buy plants for my new house and we started talking. She made me laugh, and she was sweet. I brought the plants, and they died within a week. I went back. Before I knew it, she had brought some to the house, showing me how not to kill them. Sweetest girl I ever met, honest and kind," he said. I studied him. If he were acting, he was good.

"Eloise... isn't the kind of girl you normally date?" I said tentatively, hoping not to offend.

Henry laughed.

"I know it seems odd, but I've traveled a lot, meet all kinds of women, models, corporate types, very high maintenance. I'm burnt out on them. I never had a real relationship with any of them I didn't miss five minutes after we parted ways. Eloise is a breath of fresh air. She's genuine, kind, and giving. I couldn't say the same of my last relationship." He sounded sincere.

"Too intense?" I asked.

Henry laughed.

"After the last one, I had to check to see if I still had my manhood," he said, with a hint of disgust, which left me to believe someone burned him bad.

"She's perfect," Henry said, using Eloise's favorite word as we watched her returned to the table. She was as graceful as a harbor deal. Yeah, she was perfect alright, but perfect for what?

chapter 6

MRS. VERDE HAD summoned Maggie to Verde Nursery. Maggie wanted me to come along. I didn't think she needed the company but someone to watch her back. Mrs. Verde had the warmth of a reptile and the disposition to match. Personally, I didn't trust her. Who would sabotage their own daughter's happiness? Even if Henry turned out to be a serial killer, Mrs. Verde's cool indifference to her daughter wouldn't nominate her for mother of the year. I've seen strangers on a subway with more emotional connections than the Verdes.

When we arrived at Verde's Nursery, I expected a sleepy little Long Island nursery catering to weekend gardeners. I was wrong. The place was massive, with scattered outer buildings and greenhouses surrounding a main brick structure. A large illuminated roadside sign guided you to a huge parking lot in front of the main building's entrance. Several cars filled the lot. For a weekday, the nursery was full of people pushing carts to their car trunks and pickups bringing and hauling landscaping material. The scope of the place impressed me.

We parked in the back of the main building near the loading dock where an office door stood open. I followed Maggie into a small reception area. File cabinets and bulletin boards lined the room. A small desk sat empty next to an office door labeled *A. Verde*. As we approached, we heard the sound of two women arguing. Their words were muffled by the closed door and the thick walls. I turned to Maggie, who seemed as uncomfortable as I did. I wanted to leave but then everything went silent. A heartbeat later, an annoyed looking Jenny Esposito pushed through the office door. Her surprise at seeing us didn't dissipate her anger.

"Bitch," Jenny said beneath her breath as she stomped passed us on three-inch heels. Her hips swayed angrily out the door in a dress that left little to the imagination. A stone-faced Mrs. Verde stood in the office doorway.

"You're late," Mrs. Verde arched an eyebrow and retreated back into her office.

Maggie sighed and took a deep breath as if she were about to jump off a cliff and walked into the office. I stood there for a moment unsure if I should follow or wait outside. Jenny's hurried exit and Mrs. Verde's dour expression didn't spell warm and inviting for me. Maggie realized I wasn't by her side; she glared at me and that was answer enough. I followed.

As I entered, I became aware of a man sitting on a small couch opposite Mrs. Verde's desk. He had dark curly hair and olive skin with features that reminded me of Eloise. He was in his late twenties to early thirties. His broad shoulders and massive chest reminded me of a bodybuilder who'd gone fat. The potential for muscle definition headed toward pudgy.

"Sit," Mrs. Verde said as she sat behind her desk and lit up a thin brown cigarette. The office reeked of strong cigarettes and a hint of fertilizer. She took a deep drag and exhaled pungent smoke in our direction. Maggie and I didn't move. Our eyes were locked on the man.

"Sit!" Mrs. Verde commanded. Maggie and I shared a glance at each other before taking the two seats in front of the desk, with our backs to the stranger.

"Jenny seemed upset," I said. Mrs. Verde took another deep drag. I noticed a faded no smoking sign hung above her, no doubt a reminder that some rules didn't apply to her.

"You brought the cake-maker with you," a disapproving Mrs. Verde said to Maggie. "What kind of business are you running?"

"Odessa helps me on occasion with my work," Maggie said. "She is incredibly astute, and I wanted to get an objective opinion about Henry." Maggie made me sound like a human lie detector. Mrs. Verde didn't seem impressed and cocked an upraised eyebrow at me.

"Well, what do you think of Henry?" She stared at me, her tone cool and dismissive. Besides the possibility of my getting lung cancer by proximity to this woman, the silent stranger at my back bothered me more. I turned to stare at him and he gave me a crooked grin.

"Unless your daughter has photographs of Henry having sex with an underage circus clown, something else is holding his affection, and I don't think it's love," I said as I turned back to Mrs. Verde. I fanned away a plume of smoke she aimed at me.

"Excuse me, Mrs. Verde, but would you like to tell us who this is?" Maggie turned around to gaze at the stranger as well.

Mrs. Verde gave us a throaty laugh. "This is my insurance," she said.

"Insurance for what?" I asked. I didn't have to turn around to know the stranger's eyes were on me.

"You're the expert at reading people, you tell me," she said snidely.

I didn't like this game, and I suspected Maggie didn't either. However, I took the opportunity to get a better look at Mrs. Verde's *insurance.*

Dating my ex-boyfriend, Davis, had its benefits. He lived by the adage that clothes made the man. The man wouldn't go out the house unless he was impeccably dressed. He believed people judged you a minute after they met you based on your appearance. His theory: what you wore told everyone who you were. Judging from the stranger's off-the-rack clothes from the big and tall men's store, his worn, rubber-soled shoes, and the thick and rough hands, this man was a laborer. A heavy gold chain hung around his neck, telling anyone who cared what he wasted his money on. Also, he was appreciating the attention

I gave him; his smug smile convincing me he thought much too highly of himself. Other things caught my attention, but I'd had enough.

I turned back to Mrs. Verde, who sucked on her cigarette and grinned.

"Relative of yours," I said and her smile faded a bit.

He had Eloise's dark skin tone and the same stupid grin.

"My cousin's son, Apolo," Mrs. Verde said.

"Like in the Greek god?" Maggie said in disbelief.

"Apolo Zeno, one L," he said, grinning at her.

"What do you mean insurance?" Maggie asked.

"Either you stop the wedding or I do," she said and stared at Zeno. He gave her an adoring smile.

"You paid me to do a job, Mrs. Verde." Maggie didn't hide her irritation. "Let me do it."

"And what have you done, except waste my money and order expensive cakes from your friend's restaurant?" Mrs. Verde said snidely.

I didn't like this woman.

"I'm working on Henry and doing an intensive background search on him. There isn't much, Mrs. Verde. He is a successful real estate developer, has been for the last ten years. If Henry doesn't love her, what could he possibly want from your daughter?" Maggie said.

"Eloise has nothing. She lives in my house, eats my food, and is employed by me. Whatever she has, I give her. Oh yes, I forgot, she's still has her My Little Pony doll collection. Henry might want that," she said, her tone turned impertinent.

"There must be more," Maggie insisted.

The old lady shook her head.

"Sorry to ask this, but what if you die? Wouldn't Eloise inherit everything?" I asked, but I wasn't that sorry.

Mrs. Verde angrily stubbed out her cigarette.

"Ninety-five percent will go to my church. The rest goes to Eloise, only if she has a college degree from a reputable school. I told her if she marries Henry, she won't even get that." A crooked smile slipped back onto the old woman's lips.

"School?" Maggie asked.

"Eloise has attempted three colleges in the last eight years and is still a freshman. She knows nothing and does nothing. Besides being fat and lazy, she's spoiled."

"Mothers tend to spoil their children." This only intensified Mrs. Verde's ire.

"Not me, you fool, her father," Mrs. Verde replied, her tone hostile. "I had Eloise late in my life, unexpected. My husband was ecstatic at her arrival. He spoiled her, giving her everything, and then he died. He left me to deal with the business and a twelve-year-old who thought the world revolved around her," Mrs. Verde said. I got the feeling she was proud of the fact she survived her husband, built up the business, and alienated her daughter.

"You've done a wonderful job with the place," Maggie said, smiling at the old lady. Only I recognized Maggie's insincerity.

"My Vincent started with nothing. His father came over from Sicily and worked landscaping for the rich families on Long Island. Sometimes Vinny would work with him, but my Vinny wanted more. He opened up a small neighborhood nursery in Bensonhurst, Brooklyn. He did well, but the neighborhood limited him. He sold his nursery and brought land out here. For forty years, he toiled until he made Verde's Nursery one of the finest on the Long Island. Then one day he keeled over onto the compost heap out back and died. I found him three hours later. Even at the funeral, you couldn't quite get the odor out." Her nose wrinkled.

"I'm sorry, Mrs. Verde, I am," Maggie said, and I knew she meant it. I, on the other hand, couldn't work up a bit of compassion for the steel-plated witch. I found myself rooting for Henry to be Eloise's prince so he could save her from this woman.

"Sorry doesn't help me. What are you going to do?" Mrs. Verde snapped.

"We're going to do some surveillance on Henry. His past is clean, but he could be up to something now," Maggie said. This seemed to appease Mrs. Verde.

"Good. You've got less than three weeks or else," she said.

Mrs. Verde liked pushing people.

"Three weeks or what?" Maggie turned to Zeno, who grinned at her.

"Apolo is going to talk to Henry," she said.

"And Henry will just go away?" I said.

"Why don't you stick with cakes, dear," Mrs. Verde said. Her voice left me cold. "Or maybe Apolo needs to talk to you."

"Mrs. Verde!" Maggie yelled, understanding the threat.

"No worries, Maggie," I said and stood up. "I'll stick to cakes and Mrs. Verde will stick to the best compost in the tri-state area."

Zeno suppressed a laugh. Mrs. Verde glared at him and the amusement vanished from his face.

"We better go," I said nearly pulling Maggie out of her chair.

"See you around, girls," Zeno said, grinning.

"I doubt it," I said, taking Maggie by the arm and leading her out the door. Once outside, we both took a deep breath of smoke-free air. After our encounter with Mrs. Verde and Zeno, I needed a shower.

"Well!" a voice said from behind us. Jenny stood by a small compact car. "She wants you to stop the wedding, right?"

"No," Maggie said.

"Seriously?" Jenny smiled.

"No, the wedding is fine," I said.

"Great. For once that woman doesn't get what she wants," she said.

"Do you know the guy in her office, Mr. Zeno?" I asked.

She scowled.

"He's no mister. That pig. He's Eloise's cousin." Jenny had obviously experienced Zeno's charm.

"Zeno is Greek, right?" I asked, assuming the Verde family was Italian.

"Yeah, so is Mrs. Verde. Her family is from Astoria. They're butchers." Jenny wrinkled her nose.

"You make it sound like being a butcher is a bad thing," Maggie said.

Jenny smirked and rolled her eyes.

"There are butchers and then there are the Zenos," she said as if we should know the difference.

"You're a little too cryptic for me, Jenny," I said. Considering Mrs. Verde threatened me with a talk with her cousin, I wanted clarification.

"Let's say I would be suspicious of any of their meats," she said in a hushed tone.

This didn't help. Either I worried Zeno might turn me into hamburger or sell me tainted lambchops.

"And?" I prompted.

"That family is greedy and devious, including Mrs. Verde. She got lucky when she married Mr. Verde, but that doesn't make her better than me. Even though Henry's a bit of a snob, at least he has the class and history to back it up. Mrs. Verde married into it. She was just a butcher's daughter when she married Mr. Verde," Jenny said.

"You don't like her much," Maggie said. Jenny's face twisted in disgust.

"It just kills her that Henry is marrying Eloise. I'm glad I'm here to see it. The minute they say I do, I'm going to jump up and down just to see the look on her face." Jenny's lips curled up in a wicked grin. I wondered what motivated Jenny to push Eloise's marriage to Henry and the answer seemed clear. She hated Mrs. Verde.

"The woman had the nerve to look down on me when I was a kid, when half of her family are criminals. In fact, Apolo is on parole. He has screwed up so much, I think his family shipped him out of the city to keep out of trouble."

"What kind of trouble?" I asked.

Jenny shrugged.

"He's a butcher. The last time I was around him, he was carrying knives and covered in blood," she said, as if that were evidence of some crime. Jenny was no Sherlock Holmes, but even she sensed Zeno's malevolence.

"Butchering meat doesn't make you a criminal," Maggie said.

Jenny shot her a dour expression.

"The man enjoys his work." Her eyes widened. "Since he's been here, he hasn't done a thing. He's supposed to be working in one of the greenhouses, but I've never seen him lift a thing." Jenny's gaze returned to the office door.

How could I explain to her Mrs. Verde didn't need him for lifting? Unless he had to get rid of Henry's body after he had a *talk* with him. This time I stared at the office door, expecting Zeno to step out of the office dressed in a bloody butcher's apron, carrying sharp knives and cleavers and singing show tunes from *Sweeney Todd*.

Just what I needed, I thought.

chapter 7

TWO DAYS AFTER Eloise handed me the picture of her dream cake, I sat at the Blue Moon's bar frustrated. The photograph of a six-tier cake with elaborate piping, hundreds of perfectly made gum paste roses stared back at me, laughing, smug in its superiority. I needed to modify the design to make doing the cake manageable. There were too many damn flowers, too much detail work, and too many damn tiers. Did the girl think she was about to feed an army? Did she think I had a staff of twenty? In truth, the cake wouldn't be an issue if Maggie found something on Henry. Something big, like being—dare I say the words—a serial killer. I crumbled up the photo and tossed the thing in the garbage. I called Maggie in the hope of better news.

She had problems of her own. Her role as wedding planner was taking more time than she wanted. Eloise was no help, considering she didn't know what the hell she was doing. Their trip to a local bridal shop failed miserably. Eloise couldn't or wouldn't make up her mind. Mrs. Verde ditched the bridal party after the first hour, stating pressing business at Verde's Nursery. Possibly a new shipment of manure had come in and she had to inspect the lot personally.

"With each dress, it got worse. The girl doesn't have a clue to what she wants. Jenny didn't help. She kept pushing Eloise to elope. She does it to piss off Mrs. Verde, but it's getting old," Maggie said in exasperation.

"Get any information on Henry?" I asked. Maggie said no. Everyone she talked with praised his work.

"Nobody's that perfect," I said.

"He's developed three properties in the area, and no one has a bad thing to say about him, even his former partners."

"What former partners?" I asked.

"Henry belonged with this development group for the last eight years or so. They were successful and worked mostly on the east coast. They were written up in magazines and were well-respected."

"Why former if things were going well?"

"There were three of them: Henry Duschumel, Robert Costa, and Irwin Stein. Stein was the original owner of the business and took on Henry and Costa as partners. Stein was in his seventies and near retirement when he took on the other two. They did well for several years until Costa became ill and around June of last year, he died. Stein decided to retire, leaving Henry to go on his own. In fact, his first solo project is right here on the island, called Bella Vista."

"Bella what?"

"One of those ritzy planned communities. You've seen them. They're popping up all over the place," she said.

"So, he comes to New York, starts his first solo venture, and finds true love?" Weirder things had happened, I thought.

"I'm curious about his new development, aren't you?" she said. "Why don't we take a look at it?"

Between the lunch and dinner crowd, things were slow at the restaurant. Going home held no interest because Lee wouldn't be there. Candace didn't demand I make desserts, check the books, or clean out the bathrooms. I could stay and work on Eloise's cake some more. I opted for a drive instead. I needed to clear my head.

"Yeah," I said before I disengaged the phone. Now I was curious.

When I went to get my handbag and car keys from the office, George appeared from nowhere and blocked my way. He accomplished this because he stood over six feet tall, solid as a brick wall, and just as big.

"What, George?" I was impatient and ready to leave.

George terrified most staff with his dictatorial temperament, yet he was an excellent cook, ex-military, ex-taxi driver, and God only knew what else. His effect on me varied. Some days he could be a teddy bear. Other days, I feared for my life.

"Stop asking everyone about your sister's friend," he said between clenched teeth.

I'd cornered one of the waitresses earlier in the day about the elusive Mr. Pendarvist. Fearful of Candace's retribution, she said nothing. When I tried Bebe again, he just walked away.

"You must know something about him," I said, hoping to get some details. George's face darkened as he took a step toward me. This wasn't one of his teddy bear moments.

"He's occupying Candace's time and keeping her out of my kitchen. She is bearable to work with lately, or haven't you noticed?" he accused. I realized he was right. My sister acted—happier.

"Hey, she's my sister and I'm concerned," I said, much too defensively.

"She's fine. The restaurant's fine, don't mess it up." He had his finger in my face. His dark face glistened with the heat of the kitchen. Finding a little of my nerve, I pushed his finger out of the way.

"Don't mess it up," he warned and stepped aside. I left the Blue Moon with George's words in my head.

Don't mess it up!

By the time I got to Maggie's house, my irritation from the lack of a cake design and George's insistence I stay out of my own sister's business had annoyed me. Maggie picked up on my foul mood immediately. When I told her about Candace, she agreed with George, which only aggravated me more.

"Leon might be like Henry, a serial killer," I said as we drove to Henry's new housing development.

"I doubt that." Maggie did her best to ignore my complaints by reading a street map. We were searching for Crescent Lane with no luck.

"Why not?"

"Because Candace isn't Eloise. Your sister isn't a naïve girl, easily swayed by some smooth talking Casanova. Give her some credit, O. She's your sister. Turn here." She pointed left, and I made the turn. I pushed my thoughts about Candace and Leon away, but not too far. She was still my sister, and I was equally protective of her as she was of me.

When we arrived at the site, a high chain link fence walled off the place. An enormous billboard stood high above the development. Bella Vista promised attractive condominium-style townhouses, a lavish community center, and stores. The photographic rendering of a perfect community filled with attractive and responsible neighbors might appeal to the empty nesters and retirees who wanted the luxury of a house without the inconvenience of maintenance. The houses were in different stages of construction, at least seventy-five percent completed. We found Henry standing by a prefabricated guard booth talking to a guard.

"Isn't he going to wonder why we're here?" I asked.

"We're here on the pretense that we need his help with Eloise, and it's not that far from the truth. The girl changes her mind every five minutes. She can't decide on a dress, the food, the music, or anything else," Maggie said, disgusted.

"I know you're frustrated with Eloise and you feel you're wasting too much time on dealing with her ever-changing wedding plans, but that's kind of weak," I said. Did she think Henry was stupid?

"She doesn't understand there isn't much time and an elaborate wedding might be out of the question. I really need Henry's help to explain that to her," she said.

"Yeah, but—" I began, but realized something was distracting Maggie. I followed her gaze across the street from the construction site where a man stood by a dark, late model sedan. He was short and stocky, with graying hair and a ruddy face. His focus was fixed on Henry.

"What's this about?" a curious Maggie said, pulling out a small digital camera she had in her bag and snapping a picture. Ever since she started this P.I. thing, she often whipped out a camera. In the middle of conversation, dinner, or shopping, out came the camera. Unfortunately, I looked straight at her when the flash went off.

"Why are your eyes closed?"

I glared at her, snatched the camera, and showed her she had the camera's setting on flash. There were little white spots floating in front of me.

"Sorry," she said.

When my vision came back, we got out of the car and headed toward Henry. We stopped when the guard came out to approach the stranger. They talked briefly, but the conversation intensified when the guard grabbed the man's jacket. The stranger stumbled trying to twist away. He broke free, got into his car, and drove away.

Henry appeared relieved. He said some words to the guard upon his return, and both men shook hands. We paused a moment before we continued. When Henry caught sight of us, his attention turned in the direction the stranger had gone. It was obvious we'd seen the entire incident. He plastered an awkward smile on his face when he turned back to us.

"Ladies, what a surprise." He walked over with his arms out-stretched in greeting. Maggie took the lead.

"I'm sorry to bother you at work; I'm desperate for some help." Maggie poured on the charm. She had a way of going soft and girlie, a persona of both vulnerable and sexy. Men ate it up, and Maggie threw her charm at Henry like the opening pitch at a Yankees game. An instinctual inner reflex kicked in and allowed her to embody Jessica Rabbit and Little Bo Peep. If I tried that, I'd hurt myself.

"How can I help you?" he said, a little concern dancing in his eyes, probably wondering how much of the incident we'd seen.

"If this wedding is to happen in less than three weeks, I need a little cooperation from the groom. Eloise seems to be in a constant state of—how should I put this—flux. I would ask her mother's help, but their relationship is a bit...." Maggie tried to find a nice way of saying his future mother-in-law was an overbearing, manipulative, control freak.

"Strained," Henry said. "She doesn't want to give up her little girl."

"Well, yes. Despite that, this wedding is going to happen. I'll make sure you and Eloise walk down the aisle on time," Maggie said, matching Henry's smile wattage. Between the two of them, I almost went blind.

"Wonderful, I had my doubts since Mrs. Verde hired you," Henry said, his smile slightly fading.

"My reputation is at stake. Trust me, I've dealt with mothers-in-law," Maggie said. If her own mother-in-law was any indication of her resilience, Mrs. Verde didn't have a chance.

"Great! So what brings you here?" he said, his smile revving up.

"Eloise has changed the menu on me twice and hasn't yet brought a dress. She can't decide on the theme and flowers need to be ordered. Time is running out, and I need to get things moving." Earlier in the day, Maggie had called Candace about some wedding tips and now she actually sounded competent.

"Oh dear, sounds like my girl. Let me give her a call," an apologetic Henry said. He pulled out his cell phone and punched in numbers. We listened as he appeased, apologized, and begged Eloise to cooperate. When he finished, he seemed a little whipped.

"She promises she will try," he said. I thought he believed it, but I sure didn't.

"We hate to bother you with such trivial things," Maggie said. She pretended to notice the development's construction area for the first time. "Wow, this is something."

Henry's smile widened and he seemed proud of his accomplishment.

"Yes, this one's special. There is already a guaranteed eighty-five percent fill rate. Considering the current market, that's good," he said.

"That's wonderful. In fact, my husband and I were thinking about moving," Maggie said with a straight face. Henry's glee at the prospect of another sale was orgasmic. He turned an eager eye to me, but I politely shook my head. One fish on the line was enough.

"I'd love to give you a personal tour later. I have a meeting elsewhere but let's set a date," he insisted. Maggie agreed. We thanked him for his help with his fiancé. Henry got into a new, shiny, black Mercedes parked out front and drove away.

"You want me to break the news to Roger that you're moving?" I teased as we headed back toward my car. My humor faded when I caught sight of the dark sedan parked at the end of the street. The man, who we'd seen run off earlier, had returned. Maggie saw him too.

"Perhaps we should talk to him," she suggested.

"Are you crazy? We don't know who he is. He could be a —"

"Please don't say serial killer. You have serial killers on the brain." She waved off my concerns and started walking down the street.

"What would a wedding planner and a cake maker have to say to a stalker?" I said as I followed. She smiled at me.

"I am a prospective buyer. Maybe he knows something about the Bella Vista or at least about Henry." Maggie had a tendency to talk to anybody, anywhere, at any time thinking that her fairy godmother would protect her. Positive she had left her magic wand at home and my pepper spray was in my other purse, I wasn't too keen on the idea.

"I have to pick up Rocket at his camp later, so let's stick to coffee."

"I don't have to pick him up," I said as we drove away from Bella Vista.

***

Maggie's house in Hicksville was on a quiet street where there were no cops or serial killers. Her 1950's ranch-style house lay nestled on the manicured lawn, flower boxes in the window, and newly painted trim. A modest house by most standards, a sanctuary from the day's events, I sat content with a fresh cup of coffee and a Tylenol for my emerging headache. For a brief moment, the incident triggered the beginning of an anxiety attack. I fought the attack off with deep breathing and the belief nothing else bad was going to happen. This was a lie I could embrace.

The family dog, a five-year-old dachshund named Mr. McGregor, came waddling up toward me for his usual sniff and greet. An intelligent beast, with large, wet black eyes and a constant perplexed gaze on his auburn face, he took a seat beneath my feet and promptly fell asleep.

"I have a half hour before I pick up Rocket from day camp. I want to print out these pictures before he comes home," she said.

"Not again," I said. Recently, Maggie had a home office built for a little added privacy for when she brought work home. The point was to keep her husband from snooping. Roger hadn't been thrilled with Maggie's new career choice. She soon realized the problem wasn't her husband, but her 8-year-old son, Rocket. Lately, he had taken an interest in his mother's work, possibly due to the many hours he spent at the McAvoy Investigation office with his mom when she couldn't find a babysitter.

"How'd he get in this time?"

Maggie sipped her coffee and shook her head.

"I left the window open. Luckily, I had the files locked in the cabinet. He might crack that one day. I don't know what's gotten into .him."

"Christ, Maggie, his dad sells insurance for a living and his mom plays at being a private eye. Let me guess which out of the two sounds more interesting." I pretended to think about it.

"He needs a hobby," she said.

I laughed at the thought. The last hobby Rocket had was with a Mr. Wizard chemistry kit that helped burn the eyebrows off his best friend. To hide his crime, Rocket stole his mother's eyebrow pencil from her cosmetic case and attempted to draw new eyebrows on his luckless friend. His ruse was discovered when his friend's mother noticed the kid's eyebrows didn't match. His interest in archeology made him dig up the backyard of three neighbors. His interest in astronomy got him a view of Mrs. Willington showering next door. He didn't need a hobby. He needed a lawyer on retainer.

"Maybe I'm a bad influence on him," Maggie said. I hated the doubt I saw in her.

"Please, I'm worse than you." I dismissively waved away her concerns.

"Seriously, O, lately all I can think about is this case." Maggie shook her head. "The other night I burned the dinner because I was doing a background trace on Henry."

"Did Roger say anything?"

She shrugged her shoulders and stared down at her coffee mug.

"He wouldn't," she said.

"Because he knows this is important to you. He understands," I said. "If he doesn't, you remind him that you saved his butt and his job because of what you do."

"I saved him because I love him, O," she said sweetly.

"Yeah, and because you could. I know sometimes I worry about this private eye thing, but you're really good at it." I covered my hand over hers and squeezed.

"It shouldn't affect my family, especially Rocket."

"Rocket is fine. Roger is fine," I reassured.

Maggie smiled at me.

"I hope I'm not fooling myself with all of this," she said.

I started to answer her, but the house phone rang. Maggie got up to answer.

"Hi, Eloise," Maggie said. She listened as the bride-to-be talked and with each passing minute, her worry lines on her forehead deepened.

"In fact, she's right here. Let me talk to her first." Maggie covered the receiver and took a deep breath. Her lips clenched. Whatever Eloise was proposing couldn't be good.

"Eloise wants us to come to the bridal shop in Hewlett. She says she's found a dress, and she wants you to base the cake on the dress."

"What!" I said.

"Give me a half an hour and we'll be there," Maggie said before she hung up the phone.

"I'll wait right here for Rocket," I said. "You can placate Eloise all you want." I sat back in my chair and sipped my coffee. Maggie shook her head, took my coffee mug, and dumped the contents in the sink.

"I have to pick up Rocket at the day camp, and you are coming with me," she said. I snorted in disgust and followed her out of the house, remembering I was Robin to her Batman, Ethel to her Lucy.

Exactly thirty minutes later, we were in front of the Sweet Heart Bridal Shop in Hewlett, Long Island. Rocket sat in the backseat working his way through a peanut butter and jelly sandwich his mother hastily made for his afternoon snack. I insisted on a sandwich as well. Being a sidekick made me hungry. Before we got out of the car, Maggie compelled her son not to divulge the fact that she worked for McAvoy Investigations, a fact Rocket was extremely proud of and told anyone who would listen.

"I'm like your assistant," he said, negotiating a deal to keep his silence. Smeared jelly decorated his smiling mouth and fingers, which he promptly wiped on his camp tee-shirt.

"Yeah, like Robin," I said, shaking my head, knowing that Rocket the Sidekick was an accident waiting to happen.

"A good assistant is quiet and observant," Maggie said, hoping to get cooperation from an 8-year-old. Rocket promised he'd behave. Good luck with that.

A minute in the Sweet Heart Bridal Shop, I was on estrogen overload. Besides the perfumed air, hyperactive sales associates, and the perpetual cheeriness, the place reeked of females. Everyone fluttered about like bees in a hive. The atmosphere was as relaxed as a jury deliberation at a murder trial; life and death hung on a decision of the right or wrong dress. The associate hustled us into a backroom fitting area to view the bride-to-be trying on dresses. The bridesmaids and Jenny were in the tiny space, and nobody smiled.

"Eloise swears she's found the dress. She went looking on her own, early this morning." Jenny sounded skeptical. The women's trapped expression said everything. Maggie explained that the anxious looking women were workers from Verde Nursery and forced to be Eloise's bridesmaids. I'm sure Eloise or her mother made their appearances mandatory. We sat on uncomfortable folding chairs awaiting Eloise's emergence from the changing room.

Rocket's first time in the inner sanctum of estrogen ecstasy made him sit on the edge of his seat expecting a three-headed moose to come from behind the closed changing room door. He ate the last of his peanut butter and jelly sandwich like some spectator at the circus. Maybe he knew something I didn't.

chapter 9

SOME SCIENTISTS BELIEVED that animals sensed pending disasters, like earthquakes or tidal waves, an inner radar that detects when an earth-shaking catastrophe was about to happen. I sat next to Rocket thinking I didn't need a flock of geese or dogs chasing their tails. I had an anxious 8-year-old whose frightened face made me wonder what might emerge from behind the dressing screen. I held my breath when Eloise stepped out.

"Mommy," Rocket whimpered at the sight. A collective gasp filled the room. Everyone held their breaths and thankfully their tongues.

Eloise's dress of choice, a champagne-colored monstrosity, had enough taffeta to clothe a small nation. Bows were everywhere, mostly in places where bows shouldn't be. Not a small girl by any means, the extra material only made her appear like a glob of melting vanilla ice cream. With each step she took, the stiff material and the crinoline petticoat sounded like popping corn. The wide hoop skirt extended out at least two feet. Henry would have to hover off the ground and float in to kiss his bride. A chagrined saleswoman followed behind, fluffing up the dress, as Eloise climbed on a small pedestal. I assumed she thought we needed a better view of this disaster. If Eloise expected inspiration from her selection, she succeeded. I'd make a cake and leave it out in the rain for a week—perfect.

"Oh my," one of the bridesmaids said.

"So, what do you think?" a beaming Eloise asked. She turned slowly. I stared at a dumbstruck Maggie. Rocket's audible gasp was heard by everyone.

"Don't you think my dress is pretty?" a chirpy Eloise said to him. To my surprise, Rocket thoughtfully appraised her.

"Like princess pretty or..." his eyes narrowed in contemplation, "...or ogre pretty?"

I stopped breathing.

"Rocket," Maggie admonished.

"What do you mean?" a confused Eloise said, jumping off the pedestal to face him.

"He didn't...." Maggie tried to intervene but Eloise seemed intent on getting Rocket's meaning.

"What did he mean?" Eloise asked Rocket's hapless mother.

Nothing came out of her mouth.

"You know, ogre pretty," Rocket said, standing up and spreading his tiny arms. "Big and fat, but you're not green." In the same way someone would have asked him to explain a dinosaur, he'd tried to explain the wonderful delight of Eloise's humongous, hideous dress.

I couldn't stop myself. "What's princess pretty?"

An angry Maggie glared at me.

"Cinderella and Sleeping Beauty." Rocket started ticking off names on his fingers. "You know... pretty." Rocket held out his hands in front of him slightly spread apart.

"Small....tiny." Rocket scanned the room of shocked faces for confirmation, when he got none he continued. "Not green."

"What do you mean ogre pretty?" Eloise sputtered in disbelief.

Before Maggie or I could reach for him, Rocket ran around Eloise with his arms outstretched to demonstrate her girth. He disappeared behind the skirt's massive structure and reappeared on the other side. To Rocket, this was show and tell.

"You know big and fat and kind of scary," an excited Rocket explained.

Eloise's faced flushed as her eyes watered. A meowing sound emanated from her chest as her shoulders shook.

"Oh my God," Jenny said.

Eloise glared down at the small boy.

"Yeah, like that." Rocket pointed to Eloise's distraught face, reddened with embarrassment "Big and scary." Maggie gasped in disbelief. Without saying a word, I grabbed Rocket—sticky fingers and all—and headed for the door.

"I'm going to clean him up," I said not turning around to face anyone. Maggie probably cursed herself for not thinking to do the same thing and escape. I went through the door with Rocket and closed it quickly behind me. Eloise began to bawl. She sounded like a whale dying. Wonderful, I thought, just great. I glared down at my godson. Rocket stared up at me with his mother's blue eyes and innocence on his face.

"Did you have to say ogre pretty?" I said.

Rocket hunched his shoulders.

"She asked," he said dryly.

"Next time a woman asks you if they're pretty, lie."

He glared at me.

"Mommy told me never to lie," he said.

"Trust, this will come in handy one day," I reassured him. I didn't think he believed me.

"Lying is good?"

"No," I said.

Rocket crossed his arms in exasperation.

"So lying is bad?" He sounded serious.

"Except when women ask you if they're pretty." Rocket's blue eyes narrowed in confusion and I knew I'd lost him.

"Including Grandma?" he said. Just like an 8-year-old to throw me for a hypothetical loophole. I needed to make an exception.

"Except Grandma. Always tell her the truth about how she looks," I said. "Especially when she dresses really bad."

"I don't understand." He crinkled up his face. Then I remembered what Maggie said a few hours ago in her kitchen about being a bad influence on Rocket. I stared down at my godson, knowing that if he took my advice with women, he'd save himself a lot of aggravation. Maybe not his grandmother, who could use a reality check every now and then, but he'd score points with most of the female population.

"Neither does most of the male population. Don't worry about it. Come on, let's find a bathroom," I said as I stopped a passing saleswoman, who pointed me toward the other side of the store. I made sure Rocket's sticky fingers didn't touch anything as we headed toward the lavatory.

"I can do it," Rocket protested as I tried to go in to the small bathroom with him. I didn't trust him to clean himself properly, but he blocked my way.

"I have to pee," he said as if the sight of his miniaturized penis would scare me. I sighed and let him go in on his own.

"Don't forget to wash your hands twice or I'll follow you into the bathroom until you're eighteen," I said through the door. A saleswoman carrying a gown glanced at me briefly before moving on down the narrow hallway. Self-conscious, I stepped away to give Rocket some privacy.

My attention drifted to an open fitting room, where a dress hung on a rack. At first glance, the dress seemed like any other. However, the closer I got, the more the beauty of the gown shone. The simplicity of the silhouette, the sweep of the elegant train that pooled onto the floor like liquid, drew me nearer. The cream silken material had a richness and depth. I must have been drooling because I didn't notice the saleswoman sidling up next to me.

"It's gorgeous, isn't it?" she said. I nodded, barely acknowledging her presence. There were no words to explain why the dress pulled at my soul. The sales clerk walked over to the rack, took the dress down, and brought it over to me. I stroked the soft material, and it looked as beautiful as it seemed.

"The material is lovely against your skin," she said as she draped a piece of the fabric over my arm.

"Yes," I said. The woman could have told me I'd grown a tail, and I would have said thank you.

"You'd be perfect for it. You have the height and lines to pull this off," she cooed.

"I've never seen anything so..."

"Do you have someone special in your life?" she asked.

"Yes," I said without thinking.

"I'm sure he'd love this."

The thought of Lee seeing me in the dress made me smile. "He'd love this."

"You should try the dress on, Auntie O. Or do we have to go back with Mommy?" Rocket said. Entranced by the dress, I didn't realize he'd come out of the bathroom. I didn't want to go back to Eloise's fitting room or return Rocket to it. Eloise had traumatized the kid enough. What would be the harm in trying on a dress? I turned to the saleswoman, whose eager face pushed me over the edge. The woman must have read my mind because she hustled Rocket and me inside an empty fitting room. I protested, but the saleswoman refused to listen.

"You're just trying it on," she said as she guided me behind a tall screen. I peered out from behind the screen. Rocket sat patiently waiting. His face showed no sense of a pending disaster, thank God. I slipped out of my clothes and the sales lady helped me into the dress.

"Now that's princess pretty." Rocket beamed.

"Perfect," the saleswoman said. No doubt, she wanted a sale, but I didn't care. I stared at myself in the three-way mirror and fell in love with the idea of me in this dress. The image of Lee in a tux wasn't too far off and for the first time, the idea didn't scare the crap out of me.

"That is a pretty dress." I turned to see Jenny standing in the doorway. The haughty stare she gave me made her almost seem carnivorous—the way a woman wanted something she couldn't have. My chagrin at being caught only intensified her predatory gaze. I kicked myself for getting lost in the dress.

"She's pretty, right?" Rocket said. Jenny nodded, as if reluctant to do so.

"Maggie sent me in search of you two. She thought you'd gotten lost. She's calming Eloise's nerves," Jenny said, not once taking her eyes off the dress.

"Shouldn't you be with Eloise? She's your friend," I said. She shrugged.

"Eloise doesn't need a friend; she needs a mommy. Since Mrs. Verde refuses the part, your friend Maggie will do," she said with a smile I didn't quite believe. She reached out to rub the gown's material, but I stepped off the pedestal and away from her in time. I headed to the changing room.

"The guy at the bar, right?" she said. I turned to face her.

"Excuse me?" I said.

"The guy at the bar—the one in the suit and glasses." She grinned. I said nothing. She'd guessed right about Lee and I didn't like that either.

"Does he know you want a *white* wedding?" Her eyes crinkled with delight. "Life must be good; first Eloise and now you."

"Not me, I'm just trying on a dress," I said.

"Sure, okay." Her lips curled into a smug smile.

I needed her to change the subject.

"You should be happy for Eloise, her finding Henry. He's a good man…isn't he?" I asked, wanting to redirect her attention.

"Good and boring," she said, losing her smile.

"Too boring for you," I said.

Jenny's eyes darkened slightly before she gave me a disingenuous smile.

"Let me tell you about Henry." She crossed her arms "The only thing he loves is that damn Bella Vista."

"And Eloise," I added. Her smile widened.

"Yes, of course Eloise. She's prefect for him. She'll worship the ground he walks on," she said and rolled her eyes in disgust.

"You're not the worshiping type?" I said.

"I prefer to be the object of worship," she joked, but I thought she was serious.

"If Eloise marries Henry, her mother will cut her off?" I asked.

Jenny rolled her eyes. "Don't worry about dear old Eloise. She'll get her perfect wedding and the last laugh," Jenny said.

"I couldn't imagine Mrs. Verde laughing at anything, let alone Eloise's wedding. She's not too fond of Henry, and if she doesn't change her attitude she'll lose her daughter."

"Please, that would be the least of Mrs. Verde's problems. Trust me; she wants to keep Eloise in the family, at least for awhile. As for Henry, the woman would hate anyone who'd take Eloise away from her. The last man that came sniffing around her daughter she fired."

"Fired? Who was that?" I asked. Finally, I actually wanted to hear what she had to say.

"Tommy Millhouse. He worked in maintenance at the nursery. He walked around making moon faces at Eloise. Christ, he still lived with his parents. Trust me; he would have turned your stomach. Eloise loved it. Tom was her frog; you know, the one you settle for when your prince doesn't show." Jenny laughed. I didn't find her words funny. I glanced at Rocket who didn't either. The child remained silent, thank God.

"But her prince did show. Henry came along," I said. Jenny nodded, and her smile returned.

"Tommy didn't like that, got angry, and broke a few things before the police had to escort him off the property. That was the last of Tommy. You ask Eloise about Tom now and she'll say Tommy who? She's all about Henry now." She brushed her hands together as if she were slapping off dirt.

Without warning, a camera flash went off and we both turned to see the sales woman taking my picture.

"If you're not ready now, possibly later. I'll print this out and get it to you before you go." She gushed. I ran my hands along the silken material and caught myself in a sigh.

"Odessa!" Maggie stood in the doorway with this stupid expression on her face. I thought she was going to cry.

"O, you look beautiful," she said as she stared at me in shock. Embarrassed by the attention, I nearly ran behind the changing screen.

"I guess you thought we'd all fallen into a black hole. Here they are safe and sound. I better go back to Eloise and do the maid of honor thing," Jenny said before her footsteps took her out of the room. I dressed quickly, feeling stupid for trying on the dress. I stepped out from behind the screen. Maggie kept smiling. I gave her a scorching look before I headed for the door.

"Odessa," she called out to me in a capitulatory tone, perhaps sensing my mortification. I stopped, turned on my heels, and pointed at her.

"If you breathe a word of this to Lee, so help me, I will hurt you," I said. This only made her smile widen.

chapter 10

WHEN I RETURNED to Queens, I didn't want to go to the Blue Moon. I'd had enough of George and Candace's criticism. I needed to concentrate on my own life and business. I wanted to forget about Maggie, the Verdes, the dress, and especially Horace Fouke, the Bug King. I had cake orders to complete and bills to pay. I came home, turned on some music, put on my apron, and went to the work area I had set up in my dining room.

With the music playing, I pulled out two lightly frosted cakes from an extra refrigerator I put in the room. Due in a few days for a bridal shower, I had to cover them in fondant before decorating. The fondant had to be flavored and colored to match the décor of the event—a pretty Wedgwood blue. I coated the stainless steel table with confectioners' sugar, then added several drops of food coloring into the center and began kneading the block like dough. The labor-intensive work took all my effort to get the rich, deep hue that I wanted. Afterward, I added vanilla extract to the mix for flavoring. The music played, and I worked. By the time I finished, I'd covered both cakes, my arms ached, and I hadn't given anyone or anything a second thought.

I needed to make blue gum paste orchids; each shaped by hand and painted. They had to dry a day or so before I placed them on the cakes. I rolled, colored, and sectioned off pieces to begin. I had completed only one flower when the doorbell rang. The wall clock read six-fifteen. I washed my hands but couldn't remove some of the blue food coloring from my fingertips. From the living room window, I saw the familiar UPS truck sitting out front and the driver standing by the door.

I recognized the UPS driver who delivered packages on this route. We exchanged quick greetings, and I signed for a small package wrapped in brown paper. As he said goodbye, I saw Lee's car coming down the block. He pulled his SUV behind my three-year-old Volvo and got out. He greeted our neighbor, Mrs. Poojari, and talked to her briefly before he came up the small walkway. Dressed in a blue sari that almost matched the blue color of my hands, she waved at me. I waved back. She was a sweet tempered woman with a lovely musical voice and wonderful East Indian dessert recipes. Lee loved her tandoori chicken.

"What have you been up to?" He pushed his glasses down his nose to scrutinize my hands.

"Blue orchids," I said, giving him a kiss and stepping aside to let him into the house.

"Mrs. Poojari said I should stop taking advantage of you." He slipped off his suit jacket and pulled at his tie, dropping his over-stuffed leather briefcase next to the living room sofa. He rolled his shoulders, stretched out his arms, and walked into the kitchen. He returned with a bottle of beer in his hand and took a long, satisfying swallow. Leaning up against the door jamb, he appeared both delicious and exhausted.

"Of me?" I raised an eyebrow at him.

Lee put down the beer, came over, and slipped an arm around my waist to pull me close. His hand rubbed the center of my back, which had gotten stiff from working all day. It felt great.

"She said," he began with a playful glint in his eyes, "women are not cars you can lease. It's time to buy," he said, mocking Mrs. Poojari's East Indian accent.

I laughed, and Lee silenced my laughter with a kiss. When he pulled away, he held me in a hug and whispered in my ear.

"Does the woman want to be bought?" he said softly. This time I pulled away and stared into his eyes. They looked tired from too much work but seemed expectant. I stroked his cheek and the hint of whiskers tickled, but his question had a stronger effect.

"Are you interested in buying?" I asked, trying to hide the uneasiness in my voice.

In the last few weeks, Lee had been hinting at a more permanent commitment from me. He'd given up his Manhattan apartment and settled into my house and life. Unlike most women who wanted a husband, children, and the picket fences, I hesitated. I'd been burned before and was still uneasy when it came to committing the rest of my life to one man.

Before Lee, I'd thought I had loved someone with all my heart, only to discover they hadn't loved me the same way. My ex-boyfriend Davis' abrupt departure from my life left me skittish. When Lee arrived, the wound was still fresh and too raw to allow any talk of a serious commitment. We'd been together for over a year, and yet the fear remained... just a little. Perhaps that's what Lee had picked up on.

"Always," he said and kissed me again. He smelled of musk and wanting. He invaded my skin, and I couldn't image him not being in my life. In truth, I'd been this way before with Davis and got royally screwed by him. I knew Lee was a different type of man. Yet, he'd been married before and that hadn't worked out. How would this be different? I stepped away, taking a deep breath in an attempt to regain my equilibrium.

"I have to finish these flowers." I tried to make excuses for my sudden shift in emotion.

"I'm sorry if....." Uncertainty plagued his face.

I shook my head, not wanting him to consider himself responsible for my own insecurities.

"You're perfect," I said.

He shook his head. "Don't say that. No one is perfect."

His forceful tone surprised me.

"You are," I insisted. Anyone who could put up with me was damn near saint-like. He reached for me and pulled me close again. He clasped my hands within his and held them to his chest.

"I'm not, but with you," he said, "I am close." His seriousness confused me because he seemed almost apprehensive. I watched as he struggled to find words.

"Close to what?" I asked.

"I love this," he said, looking around the small house we shared. "I want to keep it."

It occurred to me—maybe for the first time in our relation-ship—that Lee had his own insecurities. I was too busy worrying about him leaving me as Davis had. I didn't think my leaving him was an issue. I would never leave him by choice. I kicked myself for not recognizing this. I rested my head on his shoulder as he pulled me into a tight hug.

"I need to tell you something," he whispered to me. It sounded like a confession, and I wasn't ready. I didn't want to talk anymore, so I kissed him. I put such urgency into the kiss and Lee couldn't resist responding to me.

The phone rang and interrupted us. I broke the kiss.

"Answer the phone and I'll get out of this suit," he said, smiling at me wistfully.

"Okay." I watched him go upstairs. I wanted to follow, but I headed to the kitchen to answer the phone. It was Maggie.

"Hey," I said.

"You okay?" she asked, reading my mood perfectly.

"Yeah, what's up?" I said not wanting to get into a discussion.

"I want to find the guy who Mrs. Verde fired," she said.

"Why? He got jealous, acted like an ass over Eloise, and Mrs. Verde let him go."

"Maybe he has some insight on Eloise and Henry," she said.

I sighed. She was grasping at straws.

"What could he possibly tell you? Henry is the perfect man for Eloise and he's more than happy to step aside," I said.

"He was disgruntled," she said as if that was an answer.

"When I lost my job at Eastman/Kendrick, I was disgruntled too. You know what I had to say?"

Maggie said nothing.

"Nothing good or worthwhile," I said.

"O, you're not helping." Her tone was annoyingly patient.

"Sorry, I'm...nothing," I said, trying to shake off the mood I had found myself in after talking to Lee.

"Something's bothering you?"

I kept silent.

"Perhaps you're right about Tommy and he's a waste of time. It's just that I'm getting nowhere with this case. I'm doing more work as a wedding planner than a detective." The frustration in her voice was palpable.

"Why don't you drop it? Let Mrs. Verde manage her own mess."

"No. I can do this," she insisted.

"Then ask Frank for help."

"No," she insisted. She'd said before she thought Frank didn't believe she would ever be a private investigator.

"I know you want to do this but—"

"I will. I can." Her voice was determined and unmovable.

"Okay," I said. "Why don't we meet tomorrow after you drop Rocket off at day camp? We'll have coffee and brainstorm," I said.

"O, thanks," she said.

A barefoot Lee walked into the kitchen, dressed in sweats and a tee-shirt, carrying the box I'd left in the living room. He handed it to me and pointed to the phone.

"Maggie," I mouthed silently.

He gave me a wicked smile, stood behind me, and wrapped his arms around my waist. He nuzzled my neck, interested in finishing up where we left off.

"Don't worry, we'll figure something out," I said, as I let Lee trail kisses along my neck. I prided myself on being able to multi-task. I kept trying to open the small box while talking to Maggie and letting Lee seduce me. I only stopped when his hand found its way beneath my work apron and under my shirt. My mind went to one thing. Lee pinched me in a particularly sensitive place.

I yelped

"What's wrong?" Maggie said.

I took a deep breath. Lee's attention became more insistent. He was trying to work my apron off.

"Nothing," I said breathless, trying to gain control.

"Odessa, are you paying attention to me?" Now she sounded annoyed.

Being driven crazy by Lee's hands and mouth, my multitask-ing skills were fading fast. Something had to give. I gave Lee a gentle bump away, turned and faced him. I covered the phone with my hand.

"Let me get off the phone with Maggie," I pleaded. He didn't seem interested.

"Please," I begged and he stopped. He'd given me a lecherous look before he headed toward the refrigerator.

I took a deep breath.

"Sorry," I said. I took the opportunity to open the box. I'd given it a little shake. Something inside thudded softly. I checked the address again. Someone had written my name in neat block letters.

"So tomorrow?" Maggie said.

I ripped off the tape and opened the box. I started taking out the shredded newspaper that covered what was inside.

"We'll talk...." I stopped, dropped the box, and screamed.

Inside the box, little black beady eyes stared back at me. Some-one had sent me a dead rat.

"Odessa! Odessa!" Maggie's voice called out.

Suddenly, Lee was by my side.

"What the...." He glared in disbelief at the sight of the rat on the floor.

"Odessa, are you all right? What's going on?" Maggie's frantic voice screamed from the dropped receiver.

"You're okay, you're okay," Lee said, reaching for me. I was getting as far away as possible.

"Lee...Odessa?" I could hear Maggie shouting.

Lee frantically searched the kitchen and found the dustpan, scooped the dead animal back in the box, and closed the lid. He took the box to the mudroom and put it by the door.

"Throw it away," I yelled, pointing to the trash.

"Odessa." Lee came over with his arms outstretch to engulf me and I held on tight.

"Damn it! Will someone tell me what's happening?" Maggie demanded. Lee grabbed the receiver from the floor.

"Someone sent Dessa a... a dead rat in the mail," he said. The realization of what he said brought everything into clarity for me. That someone had to be Horace Fouke.

"In the morning, I'll call the detective on the case. They're going to find this guy." He tried to reassure me, but it wasn't working.

"Odessa, are you all right?" I heard Maggie ask. I wanted to say yes, that I was fine, and I wasn't letting Horace get to me, but I couldn't. I held on to Lee as the steel butterflies danced through my stomach and the pressure of an 800-pound gorilla pressed on my chest. The event had triggered an anxiety attack, something I hadn't experienced in months. I knew Lee sensed it and he held me tighter.

He said, "I've got you."

chapter 11

THE NEXT DAY, Lee worried about me staying home alone. In truth, my anxiety attack had been brief. Its reemergence caught me off guard. My reassurances that I was okay didn't pacify him, but I convinced him to go to work anyway. He promised the detectives working on the case would find the elusive exterminator. However, I understood the reality of the situation. Fouke was a nuisance to them. They had real criminals to arrest. They considered his little stunt a mild form of harassment. Unless the man came at me with a tank, I wasn't a high priority.

I needed to do something. Of course, telling Lee I wanted to go after Fouke myself wasn't an option. If he knew what I wanted to do, he'd sit on me until the Bug King was behind bars. I needed someone who understood my dilemma, someone who understood my extreme need to find the biggest can of bug spray to rid myself of Horace Fouke. I needed a comrade in arms. I needed Maggie. I headed for Hicksville.

"After last night, I think I know what to do," she said. We sat in her kitchen and she poured me a cup of coffee. We'd spent much of the morning rehashing the night before and the gift Fouke left for me. Reluctant to tell her about the anxiety attack, I did. Maggie reacted by pulling me into a much needed hug.

"You're okay," she said. "But, we'll need help on Fouke."

"Like who?"

"Frank," she said.

"What about the insurance case for Roger?"

"Please." She rolled her eyes. "He's on day twelve of a two-hour job."

"So, why is Frank still doing the surveillance if it takes only two hours to solve?" I asked.

"I needed him preoccupied while I worked for the Verdes. Now I need him to find Horace Fouke for you." Maggie's smile hid her shrewdness. She sat at her kitchen table, the picture perfect image of the American mom. Yet, this red-headed pixie had latent Machiavellian tendencies when it came to manipulating her boss. I gave her an approving grin.

What could one say about Frank McAvoy, private investigator? He might have been a hotshot New York City detective once, but his glory train had left the station. For a man who often regaled us with stories of his daredevil exploits, his current incarnation existed on take-out food, cursing too much, and a much needed introduction to Jenny Craig. Twice-divorced and a cautious man by nature, he morphed into a maniac when a blackjack table was nearby. An avid gambler, the man had a tendency to throw his money away at anything with odds.

Maggie and I went to talk to Frank.

We found him sitting in his late model Crown Victoria, spying through binoculars at a house a block away from the house he was spying on. I had no reservations about ruining his day. He sat staring out of the driver's side window, holding a twenty-four ounce 7-Eleven Big Gulp cup perched precariously on the steering wheel. He never heard me sneak up along the passenger side and bang on the car hood. As expected, Frank's catlike reflexes failed him. He fumbled the binoculars and crushed the Big Gulp in a reflexive spasm. He let out a litany of profanities as the drink gushed all over him. I quickly slipped into the passenger seat.

"Hey, Frank." I smiled at him.

The crushed Big Gulp cup trembled in his hand. A vein snaking up his neck began to throb as his grip on the cup tightened. He probably imagined it was my neck.

"What the...?" he growled, turning towards me.

"Maggie sent me," I said. I dangled a bag of food in front of him.

"Get the fuck out of my car." A vein in his throat throbbed.

"I bring you sustenance," I said.

The furrow in Frank's brow deepened, as he wiped at the spill with his tie and nearly growled at me.

"Threaten me and I'll leave with my food, or I can stay and let you clog your arteries," I said. Frank froze in indecision. Unsure of whether a cheeseburger was enough to stop him from strangling me, I pulled out a French fry. He growled and grabbed the bag. For a moment, I worried he thought strangling me might be a better option.

"One day, Odessa," he warned before taking a sizeable bite from the burger. Bits of food fell. He picked up each piece and dropped them in his mouth like a human vacuum.

"One day I'll watch you eat without losing my appetite," I said. Frank grunted.

While he shoved more food into his mouth, I scanned the messy car. An assortment of empty coffee cups and a day-old newspaper lay strewn across the backseat. Behind the driver's seat, I found what I needed, a large digital camera. The dashboard clock told me I had five minutes to explain everything to Frank.

"I need a favor," I said. He turned to me, chewing his food like a cow. He smiled at me and took another bite.

"You'll need more than a burger, honey," he said, popping a French fry into his mouth.

"Listen, Frank, you owe me," I complained.

He laughed and nearly choked. "What the hell do I owe you?"

"The last two cases you had, I sent to you." I pointed a finger at him. I didn't have time to argue, but I needed to make my deal quick.

"You did it for Maggie, not me, so get off that high-horse, princess." He shoved the last of the burger in his mouth.

"She works for you, Frank, so I'm helping you. Remember, those little trips to Atlantic City aren't paid with your hopes and dreams," I shot back.

"I don't go to Atlantic City anymore," he said.

"What?"

"The Indian casinos are much better." He sounded proud of the fact, almost altruistic. I guessed losing your money to Native American entrepreneurs didn't bother him.

"Whatever, you owe me. If you don't, I'll tell Maggie you showed Rocket your gun," I said.

Frank flinched. He looked like a kid caught with his hand in the cookie jar.

"The kid was curious," he said, much too defensively.

"Rocket is curious about hotwiring a car; you going to show him that?" I cocked an eyebrow at him.

"It wasn't loaded," he said, his irritation growing.

"It will be when Maggie finds out you showed her eight-year-old your Smith and Wesson," I said.

Frank frowned and grumbled something.

"Yes, Frank, I didn't hear you," I said.

"I can't, I'm on a case," he said, sighing.

I shook my head and handed him the camera. I pointed to the house he'd been spying on for the last several days.

"What the...." Frank stared at the commotion in front of the house and began snapping pictures.

"Is that Maggie's mother-in-law?" he asked, peering through the binoculars.

"Yes, and those blue-haired women next to her are her Grey Avengers," I said.

"What the hell are they..." Before Frank finished, a man came out of the house wearing a neck brace and walked with a cane. That was the elusive Jeremy Reese.

Ever since Maggie decided to become a private investigator, she'd become a skillful researcher. She liked digging through old court records, making inquires, and searching for the truth in between doing laundry and fixing dinner for her family. If you wanted to know if your daughter's new boyfriend had any outstanding warrants, or wondered why someone just brought a wide screen TV with your credit card, call Maggie. It took her fifteen minutes to find out that George's middle name was Percy. Finding out about Jeremy Reese's criminal history took a little more time.

Over the past ten years, Reese had left a trail of nuisance lawsuits, insurance scams, and petty larceny in his wake. The man had more name changes than Prince did. Reese's recent incarnation demanded that he use his given name considering the house he now resided in belonged to his Uncle Leo. Maggie found the seventy-nine year old Leo residing at a rehabilitation center in New Mexico recovering from hip surgery while nephew Reese cared for his house. Uncle Leo hadn't been gone a month before Jeremy started running scams.

Maggie broke the news as gently as possible about Jeremy's current insurance scam. A veteran and retired Long Island railroad worker, Uncle Leo didn't take it well when she explained to him what his nephew had been up to in his house.

I craned my neck past Frank's huge shoulder to see several older women in pink sweat pants. They stood in front of the house yelling at Reese. At the center of the melee, Mrs. Swift stood in a matching pink headband, giving the hapless Jeremy a piece of her mind. The dazed man tried to back away, but the women swarmed around like attacking bees. One of the old ladies kicked away Jeremy's cane beneath him almost causing him to fall. Mrs. Swift pointed at his neck braced and tried to rip it off, but Jeremy successfully dodged her.

"What the hell is going on?" Frank asked in disbelief.

Reese evaded the senior citizen hit squad. He maneuvered around them like a seasoned tight end for the New York Giants. This wasn't a man who was suing a local restaurant over a slip and fall.

Reese would have broken the hundred-yard dash back to his front door if two old ladies hadn't blocked his way.

"The next time Maggie wants to help, just let her. Instead of sitting in this car for days, smelling like ripe cheese, would it have killed you to let her do a stakeout?" I said.

Frank stopped snapping pictures and turned to me. "Odessa, tell me now," he growled.

"Okay, our Mr. Reese has been away for a few months because he was serving time in a Philadelphia city jail lockup for running petty scams. He told the family he'd been working in California as a shoe salesman," I said.

Frank stared at me impatiently.

"Did you know if you sell stolen goods across state lines it's a felony?" I said.

"Of course."

"Well, it's news to me. Anyway, Reese stayed in his uncle's house selling stolen goods on one of those eBay type websites. You know the one, where you clean out your closet filled with junk and expect some poor idiot to buy it and eventually put in his own closet," I said.

"What stuff? He's been in that house for days, no visitors, nothing, nada, zilch. Everything was delivered to the house—food, newspaper, everything."

Frank looked uncertain knowing he missed something.

"Those delivery trucks go both ways. Jeremy set up an account with them."

Frank's eyes darted back and forth, trying to search the caverns of his memory.

"What stolen goods?"

"You know the story of the guy at the construction site who every day went out the front gate with a wheel barrel filled with dirt. The guard never stopped him because who cares about dirt." I waited for Frank to get a clue.

"Yeah, he was stealing wheel barrels," he said, giving me a blank stare.

"He sold his uncle's stuff. Maggie found the website and delivery accounts. The uncle confirmed the pieces listed were his. Maggie promised him she'd take care of it," I said, pointing to the scene at the house.

"How?"

"Well first, she unleashed the Grey Avengers on him, a group from Mrs. Swift's senior center. They help other seniors against fraud, abuse, and neglect. That lady over there with the blue hat, her son is a U.S. Marshall. You don't want to mess with her," I said. We both watched as the women surrounded Reese and had him on his knees.

Maggie appeared with a clipboard and spoke to Reese. He yelled at her. The Grey Avengers went into a tirade. Reese stopped. Maggie continued. When Reese nodded and stood up, the women stepped back. He did a few jumping jacks, deep knee bends, and ran in place. All the while, Frank clicked away on the camera.

"I don't believe this," Frank said.

"Reese will drop his case. Roger will be happy because Maggie will tell him it was all you and how you saved them a truckload of money. So I repeat. I need a favor," I said.

I had him. Unexpectedly, a smile played across his face that had me worried. A smile like a junkyard dog, he wanted something in return.

"A favor for a favor," he said.

"What?" I shifted away from him.

"You and I at the Blue Moon, a steak dinner," he said.

Was Frank asking me out? I leaned away from him and groped for the car door handle.

"You want a date?" I didn't hide the terror in my eyes.

Frank almost choked on his laughter.

"Hell no. You're going to serve me dinner," he said, grinning at me. I took a deep breath in relief.

"Fine, whatever. I need you to find someone for me?"

"Your boyfriend finally ran out on you?" he said, grinning.

"No!"

"I figured living with you might make a man miss his...you know." Frank waggled his eyebrows. Conversations with Frank were frustrating if not cryptic. He shot an unmistakable look to his lap and grinned, implying that living with me had emasculated Lee.

I rolled my eyes at him.

"I'm just saying." He smiled.

I held up a finger to stop him.

"I want you to find a guy."

His smile faded.

"Who is he?"

"He tried to kill me, and he wants to finish the job," I explained. A corner of his mouth went up in a half-grin.

"You didn't date him, did you?" he said.

chapter 12

WHEN I LEFT my advertising job in Manhattan, I thought I'd escaped a stress-filled life. Somehow, the pressures of dealing with large money accounts, demanding clients, and equally demanding bosses never reached the anxiety producing zenith I felt now. I'd been unceremoniously dumped by a no-good ex-boyfriend, had threats on my life, meddling family members, and life-changing events. I dreamt about bugs and serial killers. Perhaps I should call my old boss and ask for my job back.

I needed the rest.

"You going to sit in my kitchen all night?" George grumbled.

I sat at my workstation at the Blue Moon, unsure of what to do. Lee had a dinner meeting with a client in Brooklyn and wouldn't be home until late. Maggie was home with her family, doing what families did. Frank was somewhere having a celebratory drink after closing the insurance case. I would have preferred him hunkered down in the office reading the file Maggie gave him on Horace Fouke. I should be home making blue orchids, but the idea of being there alone freaked me out. I stared up at George, desperate to tell him how fearful Fouke had made me and about the anxiety attack he triggered, but his current territorial zeal made talking to him difficult.

"Yes," I said flatly and turned my back to him.

He walked in front of me and ruined my view of the wall calendar we got from a meat distributor. It had a cow standing in a tranquil pasture, thankfully unaware of its fate. Ignorance was bliss and I envied the feeling.

"You plan to bake something?"

"No. Don't you have someone to subjugate, George?" I asked. He shook his head.

"I guess they did not find the bug guy?"

"No, George. He's still out there hunting for me," I said and gave him a weak grin.

"That wife of his came by. She wanted to know about you pressing charges against him." George stared down at me with concern in his eyes. I knew he meant well.

"I asked Frank to find him," I said. George seemed to think this was a good idea. I didn't tell him anything about Frank's free meal.

"She talked to Candace for a while, and those two looked as if they were ready to build the scaffolding for the execution," he said. The idea of Mrs. Fouke and my sister collaborating worried me. I didn't need Candace harassing me to do something about Fouke. I wanted to do it in my own good time.

"Why is he picking on me, for Christ's sake?" I said, resting my forehead on the cool steel table. Between Frank, Reese, and the Grey Avengers, I was exhausted. I needed to go home and finish those damn orchids. I preferred to climb into bed and forget about all of them, blue orchids included.

"Why is a good question," he said.

I stared up at him, yawned, and tucked my arms beneath my head for a pillow.

"You going to sleep here?" he asked and I shook my head.

"No, George. God forbid I would take up space." I got up from my seat and sighed.

"Good," he said before returning to his prep area.

I grabbed my handbag and headed for the dining area. A clinking noise inside the bag made me stop. I checked inside and found two brand new cans of pepper spray. It had to be George. Somewhere he had an unending supply of the stuff. I gave him a thankful look, which he ignored. I was happy to know he still liked me. He just wanted me out of his kitchen.

I pushed through the double doors and headed for the bar. Candace stood by the front talking to Leon. Aware of my attention on them, she tensed. I made a show of ignoring them. I didn't care about Leon or anybody. I wanted a drink, preferably more than one. I took a seat by the bar and begged Trevor, the bartender, to make the strongest martini legally possible. His white teeth gleamed against his dark skin, which gave him an irresistible smile.

"Where is that sorry excuse of a boyfriend?" he said in a beautiful Bahamian accent.

"Working," I said.

"I'd be by your side twenty-four-seven protecting you from the bug guy," he said, shaking the cocktail shaker and flirting with me. Trevor's accent, a sweet concoction of his early West Indian island upbringing and living in Brooklyn, had a calming quality.

"I'm fine," I reassured him. He poured the drink in a large martini glass and leaned toward me.

"You certainly are. You tell me when you want to kick Opie to the curb and give a brother a shot," he said. I couldn't help but smile. Trevor was better than two martinis.

"You'll be the first," I said, getting up from the bar stool with my drink. If I stayed around and talked to Trevor, his flirting would kick into high gear, and I didn't have the energy to fend him off. I found an empty seat in the corner and tried to relish my drink in private. Candace's dagger-eyed glares shot my way made this impossible. I needed to tell her I no longer cared who she dated, serial killer or not.

"What is your problem?" I said, annoyed. Then I had a wicked idea. I pulled out my cell phone and dialed Frank. He picked up on the fifth ring. He sounded drunk.

"Odessa, what the hell do you want?" he grumbled.

"I'm adding something on to that little deal of ours," I said, watching Candace and Leon. She caught me staring. I plastered a disingenuous smile on my face.

"You can't add on things," Frank complained.

"Dinner for a week," I said. Silence. I thought Frank hung up on me.

"Can I bring a friend?" His request surprised me; I didn't think he had any friends.

"Sure, whatever. I need you to find out about someone. A guy named Leon Pendarvist. He's dating my sister, and I need to find out if he's a serial killer," I said. There was another long silence.

"What is with you Wilkes women? Do you always attract people who want to kill you?" he said with some amusement in his voice.

"Shut up, Frank. Just find out what you can," I said. He reluctantly agreed and told me not to call him anymore for the rest of the evening. Then he hung up on me. Despite Frank's rudeness, I smiled in earnest for the first time all day. Candace caught wind of it and ushered Leon into her small office behind the front register, as if I cared.

While I contemplated how little I cared, my phone rang. It was Eloise. Whatever possessed me to give the woman my number, I didn't know. She had me on speed dial. As the phone rang, I debated whether to answer when a customer sitting at the next table gave me a rueful glare. I answered the phone.

"Hi, Eloise," I said, my enthusiasm draining.

"Hi, Odessa. I'm sending you some images of cakes I found in a magazine and I wanted to get your opinion," Eloise said, her voice happy and irritating. My only opinion was for her to stop calling me every five minutes.

"Sure, Eloise," I said instead.

"Oh yeah, the other thing is, I've invited a few more people to the wedding." She almost sounded contrite.

"How many?"

"My high school reunion is the same week I'm getting married, so I invited a few of my old friends."

"How many?" I asked, my impatience growing.

"I can't wait for them to meet Henry," she said.

"How many?"

"Eight," she said.

"What? Have you told Maggie or your mother? "I asked.

Since Maggie continued to have issues finding things on Henry, the wedding was becoming a reality. Mrs. Verde might solve the problem by having Zeno deal with him. Not that I wanted Henry to be dealt with; I just preferred not seeing Eloise anymore.

"These are your friends, Eloise?" I questioned. I had lots of friends in high school, but I couldn't think of five people I'd invite to my wedding except Maggie. Perhaps while in high school, the student body had the same opinion of Eloise as her mother did. Her way of proving them wrong was to show up with a rich and handsome groom. I wasn't sure what was worse: the idea of Eloise showing up with Henry, or the idea that Henry might not show up at all.

"Sure, Eloise, sure," I said with resignation.

Before I hung up, she had given me more suggestions about the cake and wondered if I could tell someone at the Blue Moon about the additional guests. Sure, I said. I'd love to explained to Candace about the extra guests and watch her go ballistic. She'd already ordered the food from her suppliers for a menu that took Maggie two days of convincing Eloise to agree too. Relieved when she finally said goodbye, I snapped my phone shut and turned off the ringer.

I'd tell Candace in the morning about the changes and worry about the fallout later, I thought. I drained the last of my drink, gathered my things, and headed for my car. I went through the kitchen instead of the front because if Horace Fouke was out there hunting for me, I didn't want to make things easy.

"You're going home?" George asked as I headed for the exit.

"Yeah," I said.

He stopped stirring a pot and wiped his hands. "I'll walk you out."

It didn't sound like a choice.

Out in the parking lot, George scanned the vicinity as if he were doing recon for his old Marine unit. He told me to go straight home and call him when I arrived. He told me to call Lee to get his estimated time of arrival. He didn't want me accidentally spraying my boyfriend when he came home.

"If you scare him off, who would replace him?" he said deadpan. "He's worried about you."

I wanted to think he was joking, but I wasn't sure.

"He said he's worried?" I asked, realizing the two men talked about me.

"Yeah, but I told him not to worry. You can handle yourself when you pay attention to the situation around you. This Horace guy is a pussycat. I knew that the minute I laid my hands on him. He's afraid of his wife, and I bet he's afraid of you. "

I laughed. Were we talking about the same guy?

"Then why does he send me dead rats?" I said.

George shrugged.

"Maybe he's a crazy pussycat," he said and smiled.

"His wife probably drove him crazy and he's too gutless to confront her. Now she wants my help to put hubby under the jail," I said.

"She's working hard to make it happen; too bad you won't cooperate."

"I'm been busy," I said.

"You live with a lawyer. How hard is it?" he said.

"I've got a lot going on," I complained as I started the car. George stepped back.

"I'm not expecting you to wrestle him to the ground," he said. "Don't let him intimidate you. Hell, you're not afraid of me."

"No, George, you're a pussycat." I smiled, but how could I admit to George that Horace Fouke had scared the crap out of me. I said nothing except goodbye and drove out of the parking lot. In my rearview mirror, I kept scanning the cars behind me. Half of me expected nothing, but the other half expected a van with a bug on its roof.

chapter 13

THE FOLLOWING MORNING, Horace Fouke remained on the loose. However, with Frank and the New York police on the case, I breathed a little easier. At least, I tried to. I spent the rest of the time finishing my blue orchids, paid some bills, and reassured Lee over the phone for the hundredth time that I checked and locked every door. When Maggie asked me to meet her about the Verde case, I appreciated an excuse to get out of the house. I packed my pocketbook with the can of pepper spray George had given me. After checking the front door peephole to ensure the Bug King wasn't lurking outside my house, I exited and headed for Hicksville.

The uneventful trip to Maggie's took twenty minutes. I arrived at her doorstep and heard what sounded like a gaggle of geese or a Tupperware party gone badly. Maggie opened the door; I immediately recognized the look of complete exasperation on her face. In her living room, her mother-in-law, Mrs. Swift, was presiding over a group of elderly women dressed in similar pink velveteen sweat suits.

"Is that Mimi?" someone cried out.

"Who is it?" another one cackled. Maggie stared at me and rolled her eyes as her shoulders tensed.

"It's not Mimi," she said, her voice as tight as the rest of her.

The moment I stepped into the small ranch style house, every eye in the living room locked on me.

"What's going on? " I asked as Maggie headed for the kitchen.

"I'll tell you later," she said, shaking her head. Before we took another step, the doorbell had rung again. Maggie went to answer, cursing beneath her breath. With her on door duty, I headed toward the smell of freshly made coffee. I didn't get far because Mrs. Swift waylaid me.

"Olivia," she shouted and gestured me to join her and the ladies in the living room. I cringed as the woman screwed up my name again. If I didn't think she wasn't already at the first stages of dementia, I'd give Maggie's mother-in-law a piece of my mind—again.

"When did Maggie get a housekeeper?" one woman in thick glasses asked.

I glared at a blue haired lady with too much lipstick and not enough steady hand-eye coordination to do a decent job on her make-up. I guess nobody had the heart to tell her the circus wasn't in town.

"Roger can afford a maid?" another one asked.

I sighed. These were Mrs. Swift's Grey Avengers. The same radical bunch we set on Jeremy Reese. I understood his trepidation as Mrs. Swift's geriatric coven surrounded me.

"She's not a maid, she's a cook," Mrs. Swift proclaimed, even though I've told the woman a thousand times I was a dessert chef.

"Yes, Mrs. Swift." I figured the quicker I answered the quicker I could escape.

"Olivia here isn't married and she's living with a man," she said proudly as if she'd discovered some hidden truth. The women's eyes narrowed in disdain.

"Mrs. Delacroix's granddaughter moved in with her boyfriend, and she's beside herself," Mrs. Swift said.

"He's in a rock band," a woman sipping a can of soda said.

"Does your family accept these living arrangements?" the soda lady asked.

"I didn't ask," I said tightly. All the women gave me a disconcerting stare.

"I told her about the cow thing, and getting the milk for free," Mrs. Swift explained. I turned to her as if she'd just grown an extra head. Receiving advice from Mrs. Swift was like begging sympathy from the IRS. You just didn't want it in any form.

"Kids don't listen," someone said. I grew angrier by the second and took a deep breath to calm myself. I thought of Jeremy Reese and realized he didn't have a chance. What made me think I did? Thankfully, Maggie reemerged with a woman I assumed was Mimi, caught sight of what was happening, and pulled me out of the circle of death.

"Odessa and I have to go," she said, and we escaped to the kitchen.

"I thought her name was Olivia," someone said.

Away from the women, I poured myself a cup of coffee, went to a familiar cabinet next to the stove, and pulled out a bottle of whiskey Maggie had hidden.

"Those women are dangerous. I thought my Aunt Renne's church ladies were tough. I bet Jeremy Reese is somewhere blowing his brains out," I said. Before I had a chance to pour liquor into my cup, Maggie had grabbed the bottle.

"I need you sober," she said, putting the whiskey back in the cabinet.

"Why are they here?" I asked, disappointed with the lack of fortification.

"Lenora is babysitting Rocket for me. She also had a meeting, so she's having it here. Where we're going, I can't take Rocket," she said.

"Where is he?" I asked.

"Locked in his room with the dog."

"Smart kid," I said, eyeing the cabinet where the liquor resided.

"Let's go," she said and grabbed her shoulder bag off a hook in the kitchen.

"Can we go through the back and avoid the Spanish Inquisition?" I begged.

"Good idea." Before we could make it out the door Maggie's cell phone rang.

"Hi, Jenny... you what...when... you did... finally." Maggie breathed a sigh of relief, smiled and said, "Great, can you take a picture and send it to my cell phone? Thanks. I owe you a bunch."

"What did she do?" I asked.

"She found a dress for Eloise at the bridal shop we went to with Rocket. She swears that it's tasteful and even you would love the dress."

"Wonderful, now if she could only design a cake for me," I said.

Maggie's phone chirped again, no doubt the email from Jenny with a photo attachment. I was curious about Eloise's choice of wedding dress.

"Well, what does it look like?" I asked.

Maggie's surprised expression faded fast and was replaced with a stunned one.

"How bad could it be?" I went over to see. I stared down at the tiny image and realized it was pretty awful. Jenny was right; she found a great dress, a beautiful dress. She found *my* dress, the one I'd tried on at the bridal shop. The one I'd imagined myself walking down the aisle with and more importantly walking toward Lee.

"My dress," I croaked.

"I'll tell her to pick another," she said.

It took a moment for the fog in my head to clear, and I shook my head.

"She doesn't have time to find another dress and get alterations done," I said quietly. "You know how long it took for her to get this one. It's just a damn dress." I couldn't tell whether I was depressed or angry. Maggie put an arm around me and squeezed. I thought about the photograph that the sale clerk had given me that I still had.

"Witch," I said.

"I'm sorry, O," Maggie said as she released me.

"Let's go," I insisted. My elated mood had been pounded down by the Grey Avengers and a blonde, dress-stealing hag.

We got into Maggie's car, and I didn't ask where we were going, I didn't care. I sat in the passenger seat with the seat tilted back and shut my eyes. Lee would never see me in my dress, and it bothered me. It shouldn't because I wasn't ready to get married. Or was I?

I was officially confused.

We drove for fifteen minutes before Maggie finally spoke.

"There are other dresses," she said.

"I don't care," I reassured her, but I know she didn't believe me.

"Why would Jenny do such a thing, knowing how much you loved the dress?"

I glared at her as she drove—the answer to her question too easy to explain.

"Because I wanted *that* dress," I said flatly.

She turned to me, and then sighed, unsure of what to make of my current mood. I didn't know what to make of my mood; self-pity wrapped in anger, sprinkled with a dash of denial and finished off with thoughts of revenge.

"You sure you're okay about the dress?" she said. Her voice was sympathetic.

"I'm fine," I lied. I closed my eyes again, and we drove in silence.

Ten minutes later, I began paying attention to my surroundings and realized we were at the Nassau County correctional facility. I should have known if Rocket wasn't coming with us, the place had to be unsafe for kids and clueless friends. We parked.

"Why are we here?" I said.

"Barnaby Biddle," she said knowingly.

"Who is Barnaby Biddle?" I asked.

"You met him the day he got arrested in front of Bella Vista."

My mind flashed back to the scene on the street of the man who'd been hustled into the police car as if he were on the America's Most Wanted list. The fact Maggie knew his name didn't surprise me. The reason why we wanted to find him did. I stared up at the large uninviting building, which housed thieves and murderers.

"Biddle is being released on bond this morning around eleven. I think we need to talk to him about Bella Vista." Maggie's attention fixed on the entrance from which Mr. Biddle might emerge.

"Maggie, don't you think that might be dangerous?" I didn't want an introduction to Biddle.

"Something is going on between Henry and him, something serious. The police showing up and arresting him wasn't coincidental," she said.

"Maybe the guy is just a public nuisance," I said.

"He's a member of a local construction and building laborers union. He's had a few run in with the law."

This got my attention, and I poked her in her shoulder to get hers.

"The law," I said wearily.

"A few DUIs," she said.

Biddle was a drunk. What a surprise.

"So far, I do not like this guy," I said. Maggie gave me a noncommittal glance as if she hadn't made up her mind.

"He's the only lead I have right now." Her eyes set in determination.

A haggard looking Biddle appeared at the entrance, fifteen minutes later.

County jail hadn't been conductive to Biddle's well being, because he looked exhausted, angry, and in need of a drink. He appeared older than I remembered, dressed in the same clothes he wore several days before. He needed a shave and no doubt a shower. He walked stiffly down a path away from the jail and toward the street. A transit bus passed and stopped at the corner, and Biddle headed in that direction. I guessed county jail didn't have valet parking. Maggie started the car to intercept him.

So preoccupied by Biddle's arrival I almost missed a man standing outside the gate. His attention seemed focused solely on Biddle. The man had grayish hair and was tall and lean with a middle-age paunch. He was dressed in tan pants and a dark brown plaid suit jacket.

"Do you see..." My eyes locked on the approaching Biddle.

Biddle walked closer to the stranger.

"Yes," Maggie replied, her eyes trained on the two men. As Biddle approached, he seemed unaware of the attention. He stepped passed the gate, and the suited stranger abruptly took him by the forearm and pulled him down the street. Biddle protested but stopped when the man said something in his ear. They stopped walking and exchanged words. We were too far away to hear. When Biddle stepped away, the man got in his face again pointing a finger at him. The conversation went on for a few minutes before Biddle put some distance between them, turned, and ran down the street to the bus stop. The suited man pulled out a cigarette, lit up, and stared at Biddle as he went.

"Does anybody like this guy?" I asked.

"Obviously not," Maggie said. A county bus came down the street. Maggie didn't seem to care that Biddle got on the bus. Her attention turned to the stranger who pantomimed a gun with his finger at Biddle and fired. Biddle stumbled up the bus stairs as the doors closed behind him. With Biddle gone, the stranger turned and walked in the opposite direction. Without warning, Maggie made an illegal U-turn that nearly put my heart in my throat.

"What the hell are you doing?" I went for my seat belt.

"Following him," she said as she cut into traffic.

"What about Biddle?"

"Forget about Biddle for now. Who is this guy?" she asked. She pulled in behind a car and slowed down. The stranger headed for a late model dark sedan several feet from the jail's entrance.

"Maggie, you can't follow every person you meet," I said. She didn't listen and pulled in closer. When the car drove off, she slipped in between two cars behind and followed.

"Write down the license plate," she directed. At first, I resisted, unwilling to deal with yet another potential serial killer. I wrote the number down. I stared at her briefly, catching the zeal in her bright blue eyes. She was on the hunt, a soccer mom stalking her prey.

I once took her desire to be a private investigator as a distraction from a rather mundane life. It was something to spice up her day, between doing the laundry and grocery shopping. She'd embraced this new career with the same gusto I once did when I worked in advertising. I couldn't help but notice the change in her and wondered if this was a good thing. Maggie Swift, Private Eye. Who would have thought?

chapter 14

"You know he could be a serial killer," I said as Maggie parked her car across the street from a small, dull green Cape Cod style house. The man who had accosted Biddle outside of the county lockup, pulled his car into the house's narrow driveway and got out of the car. This was obviously his home.

"You have killers on the brain. That worries me," she said. She had a small pair of binoculars and stared as the man disappeared into the house.

"I worry about them because you keep trying to find one," I said.

"Don't you want to know who he is and why he met Biddle at the jail?" she asked, finally putting the binoculars down.

"No," I said. "Obviously, Henry doesn't like Biddle, why should anyone else? He's probably a menace or something and the guy did a public service by telling him to get out of town."

"Biddle seems harmless," she said.

"Ted Bundy seemed harmless too. So did the guy who dressed up like a clown and lured people to his basement and killed them." I cocked an eyebrow at her for effect.

Maggie put the binoculars down and stared at me, possibly wondering if I was serious. Maybe I did wonder too much about serial killers, but they were out there and searching for victims. If I imagined killers behind every tree, Maggie saw circus clowns. Can you say John Wayne Gacy?

She was about to say something when the front door opened, and the man walked out of the house. I took the binoculars to get a better view of him. Older than I expected, possibly mid-sixties, his facial features were frog-like, with wide, thin lips and large downward sloping eyes. The sallow hue to his skin made him appear sick. Since first setting eyes on him, he hadn't lost his scowl.

The stranger took out keys and opened the trunk of his car. He pulled out a small green plastic garbage bag. He scanned the street methodically as if he expected someone to spy on him. Maggie and I slipped down further into our seat to escape detection. He walked over to the trashcan in front of his small house, pulled off the lid and shoved the bag inside. He secured the lid back on the can and stood for a while, staring down the street.

"What is he waiting for?" I asked. My question was answered by the rumbling sound of a large garbage truck coming down the street. As if on cue, the man went back to his car, closed the trunk, and got into the driver's seat. He pulled out of his driveway and drove in our direction. We slumped down even further until his car passed. We waited until the deep rumbling sound of his car vanished.

"That was weird," I said to no one, because Maggie had hopped out of the car and ran across the street to the green house. Down the block, the garbage truck hurried down the street, as one man drove, and another dumped the trash in the back. They headed in her direction, picking up the pace as they went. Indecisive as to what to do, I sat in the car and stared in both mortification and panic as Maggie went to the trashcan and pulled out the plastic bag.

The bag must not have been tied properly, because it opened up as soon as she clutched it to her and bits of shredded paper came out. A sudden gush of wind pushed the slivers skyward. Winter was months away, and it was snowing in July.

"Maggie, get back here," I yelled as the garbage truck serviced a house two doors down. She ignored me and began picking up the bits of paper blowing across the lawn. She tried to chase after them. I got out of the car and ran to her.

"Maggie," I said between clenched teeth. "Let's go!"

The truck pulled up to the green house, and the men were checking out trashcans and Maggie. I understood their fascination, since she resembled a chicken with its head cut off, chasing after slivers of paper. She glanced up at me desperate with panic as the papers swirled about her feet. I grabbed her forearm and headed for the car.

"He'll know someone has been in his trashcan," she said.

I stopped and glared at her. She still held the near empty plastic bag and clutched a handful of paper.

"How? Do you plan to stay around and discuss it?" I said.

Maggie hesitated and blinked. I thought she was considering it.

"Let's go!" I demanded and pulled her to the car.

"You okay, lady?" one of the men said to her. Even he recognized crazy when he saw it.

"Yes, thank you," an apologetic Maggie said. She tried not to appear guilty as she walked back to the car. She shoved the handful of paper back in the bag, retied it, and placed it carefully on the backseat. We drove off as if we'd stolen the crown jewels of England.

"I won't even ask what that was about," I said. She shrugged her small shoulders and gave me a pitiful sigh.

"You know I hate leaving a mess," she said.

We drove in silence for a long time before we spoke again. I couldn't stay mad at her, despite her sudden recklessness. In our long friendship, Maggie had always been the voice of reason, telling me to stop and think before we went head first into some craziness I'd concocted. Now I was the sane one. What had the world come to?

"Frank would have never done that," I scolded, my annoyance still fresh. She frowned, and I regretted my words immediately. "But Frank couldn't find a clue if a clue wiggled on his lap and kissed him on the mouth."

Maggie smiled as the tension between us faded.

"This is so important to me, O," she said. "I can do the Verde case without Frank, but I don't think I can do the job without you."

"Next time, warn me," I pleaded.

"Okay, promise," she said as she drove. We were heading back to the office with a strange man's trash in the backseat. As we pulled into the strip mall's tiny parking lot, the site of Zeno standing next to a pristine cherry red Mustang made me groan. After the garbage incident, I didn't want any more drama.

"God, what does he want?" Maggie said, not pleased at the sight of Mrs. Verde's insurance. Leaning up against his car, he grinned at us as we parked next to him and got out.

"Is there a reason why you're here?" Maggie slammed her car door.

"I'm here to check up on you ladies," he said, losing his smile. His eyes went to what was in Maggie arms. She clutched the bag close to her.

"I'm working on it." She sounded like a scared child.

Zeno pushed himself off his car and walked over. His physicality seemed more bravado than threatening, at least I hoped so.

"I need more than that, sweetheart," he said, his voice absent of emotion.

"We're working hard, so why don't you bother someone else," I added, and Zeno's expression turned cold.

"You and that mouth of yours," Zeno said and smirked. "It's gonna get you in trouble one day." He took a step closer in an attempt to intimidate. He stood around five nine. I had at least an inch or two on him, and I could tell he didn't like the height difference. Zeno had a nasty temperament and a Napoleonic complex.

"Mr. Zeno, you're not helping." Maggie softened her tone in an effort to intervene. He pointed to her and gave her a crooked smile.

"You see how polite she is." He turned back to me. "You need to be polite." His words didn't sound like a request. Silently I sighed. This was a man who watched *The Godfather, Parts 1, 2,* and *3* more than once.

"She's sweet," Maggie said in my defense. I didn't feel sweet, I didn't even feel hospitable.

"Listen, ladies, I don't want no trouble here. You do as my Auntie V says and we'll be all right. So let me repeat myself, what do you have for me?" Zeno said.

"Hounding me for information won't help," Maggie insisted. "Mrs. Verde wants results, but I can't make things up."

"You're cute, sweetie, but I recognize bullshit when I hear it." He ran a finger along her cheek.

Maggie flinched. When Zeno turned to me, I glared back.

"My aunt wants results, and she'll get them one way or another," he said.

Maggie clutched the garbage bag we had gotten from the stranger's house tight to her chest. Zeno leaned in, pinched a piece of the bag with his finger and gave the bag a little tug. The bag was cheap, and I thought the plastic might rip. Then he tugged the bag again. In an attempt to pull away, Maggie caused the plastic to tear. Bits of paper floated to the ground.

"Why don't you keep your hands to yourself?" I stepped in front of Maggie.

Zeno eyes narrowed on me.

"Ladies, you're not taking me serious," he said, his grin returning. "You ever seen a cow butchered? The way you slice through meat and bone, it's an amazing thing."

Maggie gulped audible.

"Mr. Zeno, please," she begged.

"You don't actually kill it, do you?" I asked.

Zeno stared at me, as if unsure of what I meant.

"What?" he said.

"The cow," I said.

Maggie gave me an 'are you crazy' look.

"What the hell...." Zeno gave me the same appraising stare.

"Someone else kills the cow and then you butcher it," I said.

Flustered, Zeno said, "Woman, are you—"

"I mean the cow is already dead and you come in after with a knife and cut the meat up, right?" I said.

He blinked. "Yeah, but—"

"So it's not like you get into the ring with the thing, beat the cow into submission, and then go in with the knife," I said and feigned incomprehension.

"Odessa," Maggie warned, but I was past warning.

"Or it's not like you go hunting in the woods in search of the wild, elusive bovine," I continued. Zeno's face reddened in exasperation.

"That's not the point," he yelled.

"Even if you had to kill them, cows are pretty dumb, right? They'll stand there and let you whack them on the head, won't they?" I shrugged and turned to Maggie for consensus. She glared at me in disbelief. "Not much of a contest, is it?"

Zeno's hands clenched tight. I thought he wanted to hit me.

"That's not what I'm—" Zeno began but I stopped him.

"Unless you're saying something else and I'm missing it." I smiled at him and blinked.

Zeno' eyes narrowed on me. He turned to Maggie who shrugged and gave him a desperate smile of her own.

"Because I have a close friend who's a chef and he sometimes butchers the meat in my restaurant," I said with delight. "He is a master."

Maggie stared at me with a weak smile on her face and nodded.

"Huh—" Zeno's bravado was gone and replaced with total confusion.

"George, that's the chef, learned his skill in the military," I said, keeping my smile. "Did you learn to butcher in the service?"

Zeno shook his head slowly.

"He's very good with knives, skillful, almost artful," I said. "In fact, a couple of days ago someone came into the restaurant and tried to hurt me with a knife and George disarmed him just like that." I snapped my fingers. "The guy peed on himself. All his martial arts training I guess." I gave an insincere laugh.

"In fact, George was in the Marines' Special Forces or something. Perhaps I can introduce you and you can compare butchering techniques," I said as I lost my smile.

This time Zeno took a step back.

"Why don't you tell Mrs. Verde we have a few good leads," Maggie offered.

Zeno never took his eyes off me as he nodded. He turned and walked to his car. He'd given me one last menacing glare before he got in and drove way, his car's noisy engine disturbing the quiet.

"Odessa, sometimes I wonder about your common sense," Maggie said to me.

I shrugged and waved her concerns off.

"Oh please, I never heard so much bull in my life," I said.

Maggie shook her head and sighed.

"Next time, warn me, okay?" Maggie said, her worried face finally relaxing.

I shrugged.

"Okay."

chapter 15

"WHY CAN'T I have the blue ones?" Eloise asked. She seemed confused by Maggie's explanation of the obvious. You would have thought we tried to explain cold fusion to her.

"It's too late to make the tablecloths blue, they've already been ordered," Maggie said, exasperated. Eloise blinked every time she heard something she didn't like. The nervous twitch came off as Morse code. It read: *this does not compute.*

Eloise, Maggie, Jenny, and I had commandeered a small staff lounge in the main area of Verde Nursery to deal with the constant shifting landscape of Eloise's wedding. Maggie desperately needed to finalized details. With Eloise demanding changes every five minutes, it was impossible. We also contended with constant interruptions by staff getting their lunch from the communal refrigerator or retrieving drinks from a large, noisy soda vending machine. A zoo would have been quieter.

We couldn't use Mrs. Verde's office because she'd opted out of the meeting, stating she had another engagement, also making it clear her office was off limits. I'd never met a mother-of-the-bride so disengaged with the proceedings of her daughter's wedding. Surprisingly, Eloise seemed quite fine with the arrangement. The further they were from each other the better they behaved, at least to some extent.

I sat to the side keeping my mouth shut. I didn't want to make the cake or watch Eloise walk down the aisle in a dress I loved. My enthusiasm to help Maggie's investigation began to fade. I'd had enough of Eloise's wedding demands, finding the truth about Henry, and Mrs. Verde's threats of dire consequences. So disgusted by the entire situation, I tossed the picture of me in the dress the bridal shop sales person had taken in my kitchen trash. What was the point of keeping it?

"If she changed the tablecloths, then she would have to change the color of the flowers," Jenny said finally exasperated with her friend. Since the beginning, she'd encouraged and supported Eloise. Yet recently, her girlfriend's constant demands tested even her patience.

"I could change the flower order through the nursery." Eloise shrugged. Maggie had already ordered over three thousand dollars worth of flowers.

"It's my favorite color," Eloise whined. Maggie rubbed her temples. Jenny shook her head, and I kept silent as the acid in my stomach churned.

"I need something blue," Eloise continued as if the louder she whined the more convinced we might become.

The night before, I'd come home from Maggie's house annoyed with Lenora and her Grey Avengers and their ill-informed comments about my life and relationships. I was still annoyed with Frank, since he hadn't found Fouke and annoyed I didn't feel welcome at the Blue Moon. On the way home, I freaked out because I thought a dark van with a bug on top was following me. When I finally got home, I found a phone message from Lee saying he wouldn't make it to dinner. I was alone and miserable.

I sat at the kitchen table and opened a jar of peanut butter to eat for dinner. All the while, I stared at the photograph of me in the wedding dress, knowing Lee would never see me in it. Twenty minutes and a half a jar of peanut butter later, I tossed the photograph in the trash, went upstairs, took a hot shower, and went to bed. I wanted to forget about the Bug King, the Blue Moon, and even the stupid dress.

I'd almost accomplished that until Maggie called this morning about a meeting with Eloise.

"Why can't the placement cards be engraved?" Eloise asked. Her voice cut through the buzz in my head.

"Not enough time and too many additional guests," Maggie explained.

"Ellie, you need to stop inviting people," Maggie said.

Eloise acted wounded.

For over an hour, Maggie tried to rein in Eloise's changes for the wedding. She needed to find out the truth about Henry, and she was losing time. Even with Candace's help, things still needed to be finalized. The more Maggie tried to pin Eloise down, the more she demanded changes. This went from a quick wedding in three weeks to an event that was slowly turning into a spectacle, with Eloise at the center of it. The girl had found her voice and there were no plans of shutting down. She complained about everything, from her brides-maids' shoes, the selection of last minute musicians, and the size of the floral arrangements.

I'd had enough and stood up to leave.

"I'm sorry, I need to go," I said to no one in particular.

"O, where are you going?" Maggie said, getting up from her seat and joining me at the break room door. Jenny and Eloise stared at me.

"We haven't decided about the cake," Eloise cried. I gave the girl a murderous glare. Somewhere on my workstation at home was a completed sketch of Eloise's massive cake. The design had taken me hours to complete and she had the nerve to say the cake needed more work.

"I've decided. We settled the design two days ago, and I even accepted some small changes, but enough," I said. Maggie's eyes pleaded with me, but I ignored it.

"You can't just leave." Eloise stood as the surprise drained from her face and was replaced with something else, something, I'd never seen in the young woman—anger.

"Bye," I said and turned to leave, but Maggie caught me by the arm.

"O, please," she begged beneath her breath.

"I can't do this all day," I said.

"You can't just walk out and go," a smug Eloise said. Her eyes darkened and her lips pressed together in a tight grimace. She resembled her mother.

"Ladies," a nervous Jenny said, hoping to appease us.

"You promised me your cake. I told everyone it would be your cake. They know you've been on television," Eloise said with an edge of irritation creeping into her voice. A few months ago, I'd been invited to a local cooking show for a baking contest and won third place. It was my only claim to fame.

"Eloise, be fair. This is the fifth time you've asked her to change the design, the flavor, and the amount of tiers. Yours is not the only cake she's responsible for," Maggie said, ever the voice of reason. She still wouldn't change my mind because I wanted to get away from them. I'd put my business on hold for Eloise's grand wedding and enough was enough. I'd turned jobs away since this whole thing started.

"I should get what I want, shouldn't I? I'm the bride," Eloise screamed. Her face turned red and puffy. "This is my day, my day!"

Just as she spoke, a man wearing a green Verde Nursery maintenance uniform walked into the room. He stared at Eloise like a deer in headlights. She returned a dismissive glance, and he noticeably shrunk away from us. Hurriedly, he put change in the soda machine and waited for his soda. Nothing happened. He pressed another button and still nothing happened. We all stared at him, making his discomfort worse. When he chanced a glance at Eloise, his slight smile vanished when she ignored him. Without getting his soda, he turned and left.

"Bye, Tommy," Jenny said. I didn't appreciate the smirk she wore.

Was this the same Tommy tossed out by Mrs. Verde? Unless there was another person wearing his heart on his sleeve for Eloise, I couldn't imagine. He was back and working at the nursery again. I cocked an eyebrow at Maggie, whose curiosity piqued as well.

"I want my cake," Eloise demanded as if the awkwardness of Tommy's presence hadn't happened. The girl had lost her mind.

"No one said Odessa wouldn't do your cake. It's a week before the wedding, and you need to focus on other things instead of something that has already been settled," Maggie insisted.

Maggie silently pleaded with me, hoping the situation wouldn't go from bad to worse in a New York minute. I didn't need a minute. I stepped passed Maggie and faced Eloise.

"I've been accommodating, because I know this was a last-minute situation. Normally, I wouldn't take this job but Maggie asked me, and she's my friend," I said.

"I want the cake that I want," she nearly growled.

"Odessa, please," Maggie quietly begged. I turned to her pleading eyes, imploring me to stay.

"Come on, Ellie. The theme will be beautiful. The flowers and winery will be to die for," Jenny chimed in and put an arm around Eloise.

"Yes, Eloise, trust me. It will be perfect, just like you want," Maggie added.

"I know, but…" Eloise said, shaking her head as if the suggestions floating around in there didn't suit her.

"Henry loves the Tuscan theme. He said it reminded him of his trips to Europe with his parents," Jenny said, and that seemed to deflate Eloise's ire.

"It does?" Eloise softened as her conviction faltered.

"George, the chef at the Blue Moon, made up a wonderful, elegant menu, very stylish," Maggie said. Eloise let out a long, exasperated sigh before she took her seat again.

"Now everyone is happy," Jenny said, giving her girlfriend a hug. A smile returned to her face, but Eloise's eyes remained dark and focused on me.

"I'm happy. I'm the bride, right?" Eloise's smile brightened.

"We're okay," Maggie said, staring at the both of us. Her role as mediator complete, she took a seat, exhausted. Everyone seemed quite content except me. I still had to do the damn cake.

Eloise got up, came over, and held her arms out to me in a conciliatory gesture. I glanced at Maggie, who silently urged me to be pacified. My annoyance with Eloise lessened. When I worked in advertising, I'd met hundreds of Eloises, each of them brides for the day, demanding, insisting they get their way. I took a deep breath and steadied myself as I let Eloise give me a disingenuous hug.

"Friends again," she said, smiling at me. I forced my lips into a smile and nodded. She leaned in close, whispered into my ear, and said, "Jenny told me about the dress. I understand."

I stiffened and disengaged the embrace. I couldn't imagine what she understood, that I was so jealous that she had my dress I wanted to sabotage her wedding. I'd admit my opinion about Eloise had drastically changed since the first time we met. I no longer thought of her as a sweet, innocent girl being taken advantage of by Henry. Or that she was some poor, helpless woman-child bullied by an overbearing mother. I stared at her as if she were some new species of animal.

"We're good," a chipper Eloise said. Her smile broadened. Possibly satisfied that she'd won something from me I hadn't figured out what yet.

I seethed and stared at Maggie, whose apologetic eyes held mine.

"Great, because all this drama can make a girl hungry," Jenny said, grinning at us both.

"Who's in the mood for lunch?" Eloise asked, clapping and rubbing her hands together.

My stomach churned into high gear. Every time I caught sight of her cheerful face, a bucket of acid dumped into my belly.

"Since we're done, we have to get to work," Maggie said. She gathered up her pocketbook and handed me mine. She wanted a hasty retreat.

"Are we finished?" Eloise asked.

"Odessa?" Maggie peered up at me. The concern, which danced in her eyes, reminded me of a time long ago when I dealt with my anxiety disorder. That was then, and this was now. I wasn't having an attack. There were no steel butterflies flying in my stomach or a 300-pound gorilla sitting on my chest. Her apprehension had more to do with the anger that radiated off my skin. I wanted to tell Eloise where she could shove that certain shade of blue.

"O," Maggie whispered. I stared down at her and recalled something I'd forgotten. I remembered Maggie's real job was to find out the truth about Henry. Mrs. Verde planned to use that information to stop the wedding. The memory made me smile. No wedding, no need for a dress; my smile widened. If Maggie did everything right, with a little help from me, Eloise would be blue alright, blue and miserable.

"Yeah, were almost done," I said, making eye contact with Eloise and giving Maggie an exaggerated thumbs up.

Her look of concern turned to dread.

chapter 16

"So, you don't care about the dress?" Maggie asked. She turned off the car ignition, grabbed her oversized shoulder bag from the back seat, and kept her eyes on me the entire time.

"Oh, I care about the dress," I said with certainty. However, I knew when someone was measuring my level of crazy. My sanity had come into question just before we left Eloise and Jenny at Verde Nursery. Maggie watched me give the bride-to-be a heartfelt apology for my obstinate behavior. Maggie almost choked on her own spit at the sight of me asking Eloise's forgiveness.

"What are you up to?" she asked.

"What makes you think I'm up to something?" I said innocently.

"Eloise has been horrible recently. Look how she treated poor Tommy," Maggie said, as if she was annoyed at Eloise's behavior.

"I'm not one to talk. I always want to kill my ex-boyfriend," I said, following her out of the car. We were back at Bella Vista.

"Davis kind of deserved it," she said.

We walked along the high chain link fence surrounding Henry's construction site, on the backside of the property. Well away from the prying eyes of the security booth and the guard, we found ourselves behind the site. There was a slight downgrade that sloped into a large, empty weed-filled lot. On the left side across the street sat a large shopping center and on the opposite side, the parkway. No wonder Henry was so pleased; the site was prime real estate.

"You don't find Tommy working back at the nursery weird?" I asked.

"Yeah," she said "I didn't think Mrs. Verde was the forgiving type. Perhaps she had second thoughts about him."

"Tommy as competition for Henry," I joked and realized she wasn't paying attention to me. "Why are we here?"

"Something is wrong," she said.

"You said..." I stopped myself when Maggie shook her head.

"On the surface this place is fine, perfect, and everything is in order. I checked the licenses, permits, and anything I could find on the public record, but..." She held up a finger.

"I hate when you say but," I said. Her buts came with complications and sometime disasters.

"It's too perfect. Like Henry is trying too hard," she said and pulled out a folded piece of paper from her shoulder bag. Surprisingly thick and stiff, I opened it, careful not to tear the rigid paper. The stiffness came from small strips of paper glued onto full sheet.

"What is this?" Several large sections were missing.

"It's part of some kind of report. Most of the information is gone. Check out the address." She pointed to the top of the page, where I read a partial address. I looked up at her and then the street name.

"This address?"

She nodded.

"Where did you get this?" I asked and noticed for the first time the poor condition of the paper, but more importantly, the evenness of the cut strips of paper as if cut by a machine.

"The garbage from that man's house," she said.

"Gross, Maggie. Thank you so much." With my forefinger and thumb, I held the report out to her. She snatched the paper from me.

"Stop being a baby." She carefully put the report back in her bag.

"So who is he? I like to know whose trash I had my hands on," I said.

"Clement Drummond. He works for the county," she said.

"What did you do? Stay up all night gluing?" I asked. I'm sure Roger appreciated a romantic evening of puzzle pieces.

"Well you can thank your godson." She gave me a rueful smirk.

"Why?" I said curious about Rocket's involvement.

"He wanted to make amends for breaking into the office. I found the paper on the kitchen table this morning. He must have worked on putting the pieces together most of the night," she said.

"Why are there pieces missing?"

"He said he couldn't find them."

"I thought you locked the bag up in your office."

"I did," she said.

"So he got into your office—again."

Her smile faded.

"Yes, but…I know…he means well," a contrite Maggie said. She sighed, resigned to the fact her son wanted to follow in her footsteps. I smiled, because somewhere, Maggie's mother-in-law was convulsing.

"Accept the fact: Rocket does not want to sell insurance." I laughed.

"I have to figure out how my kid keeps getting into my office," a resigned Maggie said.

"Interrogate him later. What about this Drummond?" I said.

"A supervisor of some sort, I think. Things are missing and I can't figure everything out yet. I did a quick check on him but didn't find much. He pays taxes, worked for the county for twenty-eight years, and lives in the house we found him at for at least fifteen years. He acts like a standup guy," she said. Her attention went back to the construction site.

"If he's so standup, girlfriend, why are we here?"

"I said he acted like a standup, but what person dumps shredded material from work in his garbage at home?" The corner of Maggie's lip hooked up in a smile.

"Anything else in his treasure trash?" I mirrored her smile.

"Mostly reports I don't understand. The important thing is a county official has shredded material about this place," she said.

I stared through the chain link fence as the sound of construction trucks and men with automatic tools filled the air. There were half finished houses and some finished ones. Though the place resembled a disaster zone, I could imagine the completed product, like a thousand other gated and planned communities I'd seen before. I guessed to some, there was a sense of security from the sameness that attracted some people to places Henry built.

"What's the name of the guy again? The one Drummond met at the jail?" I asked.

"You mean the man he threatened, Barnaby Biddle," she said.

"Barnaby. Who names their child Barnaby?" I chided.

"He belongs to a local laborers union. I'm working on getting more information," she said.

"You think he worked on Henry's Bella Vista?" I pointed to the construction site.

"Maybe. I know Henry put out a restraining order on Mr. Biddle. I'd like to know why," she said.

"From Henry's reaction, whatever happened must have been pretty bad. You have Biddle's address?" I asked. She nodded and pulled out a spiral notebook she favored when she was on a case.

"Let's give Mr. Biddle a visit," she said and seemed quite happy at the prospect of finding a just-released criminal. I gave her a cautious glance and checked my pocketbook for the pepper spray George gave me.

***

In Barnaby Biddle's neighborhood, the corner bar anchored the partial commercial street of small storefront businesses. A few were boarded up, while others lay dark. Unlike some of the better stores and shopping malls that dotted much of Long Island, these establishments had seen better days. A working class neighborhood of tiny one-family houses, struggling commerce, and depreciating property values was in contrast to the luxury townhouses being built by Henry.

We found an inebriated Biddle outside of his apartment building. Let me correct myself: he was stupid drunk. Obviously, he wanted to make up for lost time in jail and decided to go find a bar. His inability to walk in a straight line or remain vertical confirmed his intoxicated state. Every few steps he fell down, got up, and struggled in an attempt to reach his front door. Maggie and I stared in awe as Biddle did a death-defying high-wire act on the sidewalk.

"We won't get much out of him," Maggie said, still amazed at Biddle's ability to stay on his feet.

I laughed.

"Are you kidding? Who's more talkative than a drunk," I said, opening the car door and getting out. Maggie quickly followed.

"He can't even stand up, O," she said.

Biddle tried to maneuver by an old lady with a shopping cart. In an attempt to appear sober, he straightened up and almost fell backwards. He teetered for a moment, listed to the right, stumbled, and collided with the shopping cart. The old lady shrieked in alarm as Maggie and I ran to her rescue.

"Let me help." Biddle's slurred words were almost incomprehensible. He tried to steady himself and grabbed the shopping cart handle, nearly pulling it over on top of him. I made the mistake of trying to stop his fall, and I got pulled down to the ground for my effort.

"Oh no!" I yelled when I nearly fell on Biddle. I got a full whiff of his three-day-old funk and almost gagged. He reeked of cheap liquor or lighter fluid; I couldn't tell which.

"Hey, honey," Biddle said, smiling up at me. As I tried to extricate myself from him, I felt his hand rub against my breast, lingering a bit too long.

"You want to keep that hand?" I warned as Maggie and the old lady helped me off of him.

It took us a moment to right the shopping cart filled with groceries and Biddle, who seemed intent on helping. The elderly woman tried to hold her breath as she wrestled a bag of frozen peas from him.

"Just trying to help a lady," Biddle said.

"Let go, Mr. Biddle," Maggie implored to no avail.

"Let me buy you a drink," Biddle said, pulling on my sleeve. He started laughing.

"No, you've had enough," Maggie scolded, as she picked up a can of corn rolling down the street."

"Come on." He struggled to get to his feet, only to fall on his butt.

"Oh dear," the old lady said as Biddle tried to make a pillow out of a sack of potatoes. Before he got too comfortable, I snatched the bag.

"Hey…" He stared up at me as if his vision finally cleared. "You're a tall drink of water, Cleopatra Jones." Biddle gave me a sloppy grin.

"What?" I said. I stood towering over him wondering how long Biddle would remain conscious. His eyes drooped. We wouldn't get anything if he passed out on the street.

"You want a beer?" I asked.

Biddle's eyes widened in delight and a smile spread across his face.

"Odessa!" Maggie scolded. She was too busy helping the old lady on her way to argue with me.

"A little Jack Daniels would be nice." Biddle's goofy smile beamed back at me. I certainly got his attention.

"You can't give him more liquor." Maggie stood between Biddle and me.

"Hey lady, Cleopatra here wants to buy me a drink," Biddle protested. He got to his feet unaided.

"Odessa," Maggie said, her tone warning me.

I reached around Maggie and grabbed the ever-shifting Biddle, and we headed for the bar. It was difficult to keep him moving and holding him up at the same time. Much to her dismay, Maggie took the other side.

"O, this is so wrong," she said.

I stopped and stared at her. She was right, of course, but she needed the information Biddle had in his alcohol-soaked head. I didn't think a sober Biddle would be forthcoming.

"Hey, ladies, why'd you stop?" Biddle said. He was losing the battle to stay upright.

"Great," I cursed and contemplated my options.

"Please, O, let's not do this," Maggie pleaded.

"Okay, okay. Listen up, Barnaby. I'm going to ask you a few questions, and you'll answer them. You understand?" I said forcefully. Biddle's eyes widened slightly.

"What about that drink?" he said.

"Unless it's coffee, no drink," I said. The light went out in Biddle's disappointed eyes.

"Oh, Cleo, why you doing this to me?" Biddle whined.

"You want to go back to jail, Barnaby?" I cocked a rueful eyebrow at him. This got his attention, and panic danced into his eyes. There was a little in Maggie's as well.

"I didn't do nothing, Cleo." Biddle tried to get free, but we had a firm grip on him.

"I have two witnesses who'll say you grabbed me inappropriately, Barnaby. That's a sexual assault." In truth, Biddle's slight-of-hand was more of happy accident than a full on grope. This accusation seemed to give him a little backbone and he straightened, perhaps sobering up at the seriousness of the charges.

"Didn't mean to touch your boobies, Cleo. They're a little small for me, but I'm sorry," he said in a sloppy apologetic tone that bordered on pathetic.

"They are not small," I said in exasperation. "Anyway, you did grope me. So why don't we talk and I'll forget about having you arrested," I offered.

"Sure, Cleo, sure." Biddle gave me a lustful smile.

I groaned, returned a stern look, and said, "That's Ms. Jones to you."

chapter 17

As an unemployed construction worker, Barnaby Biddle resided in a walkup studio apartment. His entire net worth equaled a toaster oven, a busted nineteen-inch television, dirty clothes, steel-toed work boots, and a worn tool belt. The place smelled of stale beer and Old Spice, a heady mix that almost made me gag. Barely ambulatory, Maggie and I maneuvered him through a minefield of newspapers, magazines, take-out cartons, and clothes to get him to a ratty looking Lazy Boy lounger. He fell into the seat like a sack of wet flour.

"Can't tell you the last time I had two pretty ladies up here. Even my preacher daddy would say, 'A man hath no better thing under the sun than to eat, and to drink, and to be merry.'" A sloshed Biddle grinned and showed us yellowing teeth in desperate need of a dental visit. Lately, I'd been finding myself with men who drank too much and cared little for oral hygiene.

"That's sweet, Mr. Biddle," Maggie said. She went to the small kitchenette and washed her hands, twice. I took a whiff of my clothes and knew no amount of hand washing was going to rid me of the eau-de-Biddle fragrance.

"Where's my drink?" Biddle demanded. His limbs moved more like Jell-O than muscle and his eyelids were heavy and failing him.

"I'm sure they serve a mean latte in county lock-up, sugar," I said, staring down at him with my hands on my hips, doing my best impersonation of Cleopatra Jones. His anger failed him.

"Here, Mr. Biddle," Maggie said as she held out a glass of water for him.

"Water." His nose crinkled in disgust. "If I had two nickels to rub together, I'd be back drinking with my friends. You got two nickels." He yawned and closed his eyes.

"Hey, this is no way for a preacher's son to act," I yelled.

"Amen!" he yelled as his bloodshot eyes sprang opened.

"He's going," Maggie warned as Biddle's eyes shut again like a creaky garage door. I leaned down and shook his shoulder. He stirred and opened one eye to stare at me. I guessed opening the other one was too much effort.

"Hey, Cleo, my old man said I'd amount to nothing but trouble," he said with a wicked grin. He placed a hand on my hip. I removed it.

"Well, Barnaby, he might have been right," I said. "I need you to listen, okay?" Biddle nodded stiffly as if his head might roll off.

"Cleo, anything for you, beautiful." He smiled and grinned at me. "Daddy said I could never resist a beautiful woman." His hand went for my hip again, but I slapped it away.

"They arrested you at Bella Vista." I had to raise my voice because Biddle kept on slipping in and out of consciousness. He grinned at us, not saying a word. He was probably having a delightful conversation in his head.

"Why did they arrest you?" Maggie said still holding the water out in front of him, hoping he might drink. I imagine Biddle's only interest in water was as ice cubes floating in scotch. He still said nothing, and I knew this was getting us nowhere. I took the glass from Maggie and tossed the water in his face. Startled, he shivered as he glared at me wide-eyed.

"Why'd you do that, Cleo? Ain't no way to get a man's attention," he said.

"Why did you get arrested at the Bella Vista construction site?" I asked, raising my voice.

Biddle blinked. "Said I was a troublemaker."

"Why?" Maggie asked, leaning next to him and placing a hand on his forearm.

"Ain't no trouble at all," he said. "Just did my job."

"What trouble?" I persisted.

"Ran my mouth too much but a man's gotta say what's on his mind." His day old beard and bloodshot eyes made him look tired and worn down. "Just took a nip now and then. Ain't no way to treat a man."

"Why can't you go back to Bella Vista, Mr. Biddle?" Maggie stroked his hand and came even closer. Biddle stared up at her bright blue eyes and shook his head. He frowned.

"Been in the business over fifty years, I do a decent job," he said as his voice waivered a bit.

"Why can't you go back?" I pushed.

Maggie scowled at me. She wanted to mother him, Christ, she wanted to mother everyone.

"Don't matter now, damn Duschumel blackballed me to every-one who'd listen. Can't get no job in this county. I saved his ass, and he does me like this. I'm done with this mess." Biddle pulled away from Maggie's hand and turned to me. His smile was both amusing and poignant.

"Why did Henry Duschumel kick you off the site, Barnaby?" I smiled back at him hoping to encourage some answers.

Biddle sighed and he closed his eyes. I shook his shoulders, and he pushed my hand away. Biddle shifted in the chair trying to get comfortable.

"Go away, Cleo," He yawned again and his voice trailed off. "Come back tomorrow."

"Will you tell me what I want to know about the construction site?" I asked. Biddle crossed his arms, slumped down in the chair, and nodded.

"Tomorrow, promise," he said and nearly curled into a ball. I didn't know if a sober Barnaby Biddle would be more helpful than a drunken one.

"Mr. Biddle," Maggie said, hoping to raise him from his slumber.

"He's gone," I said, standing up.

"Perfect, we got nothing." Maggie's disappointment mirrored my own.

He stirred a bit, opened his eyes briefly before closing them again. His resurrection vanished, and he started to snore. We watched him for a while, hoping he might get a second wind, but he slept peacefully. Maggie took the opportunity to do a cursory search of his room, and I helped, not knowing what to search for in the tiny studio apartment. Twice I had to stop Maggie from cleaning up.

"If you clean his house, he probably won't recognize where the hell he is when he wakes up," I said. This didn't stop her from folding clothes and putting them in a dresser. When I caught her staring at the dishes in the sink, I insisted we leave. However, when Maggie placed a blanket over Biddle, I didn't protest.

"We'll try tomorrow," I said, Maggie agreed, and we turned to leave.

"Hey, Cleo," Biddle yelled, scaring the crap out of me. Maggie yelped.

Biddle half-stood, half-leaned against the chair. He rooted around beneath the chair's cushion and nearly lost his balance. The way he teetered, I wondered how long this resurrection would last.

"Got something for ya," he said. His head bobbed up and down like one of those dolls. He barely had control of his other limbs as he held out something to me. It was the size of a plum wrapped in a newspaper.

"For you," Biddle said, smiling with his eyes almost shut.

"What is it?" I asked.

"A..." he began, swaying and righting himself, stiffening his back to stand. "A mote in that bastard's eye." I took the thing just as he fell backward onto the chair. His snoring began again. He sounded like a lawnmower starting up.

"What the hell is a mote?" I said, staring down at a sleeping Biddle.

"I think he's really gone this time," Maggie said. "We'd better go."

"What do I do with this?" I said and peeled off the paper to reveal a dark, porous stone.

"Is that a rock?" Maggie said, peering down at my hand.

A sleeping Biddle was no help, but a gift was a gift, I thought and shoved the stone into my pocketbook. We left him sleeping soundly and his apartment slightly cleaner. In the small kitchenette, I found a small yellow writing pad. Maggie handed me a pen from off the counter to write a note. I wrote my cell phone number and said I'd return in the morning. I playfully signed the note Love, Cleo. P.S. Thanks for the rock. I tacked the paper on a small bulletin board by a wall phone in the kitchenette. The note would be the first thing Biddle noticed when he woke up.

On the drive home, the image of Biddle asleep alone in his pitiable small apartment bothered me. Maggie would go home to Roger and Rocket, and I to Lee. Biddle had been blacklisted and arrested. He had no one. Despite being a falling down drunk, he didn't seem like a bad man. The fact that he seemed fixated on a 1970's icon of black exploitation films, I found both weird and charming. I couldn't imagine why Henry thought he was a threat.

When I arrived home, my answering machine's message light was blinking. One was from Eloise with more changes about the cake. I happily pressed the delete button. The second was from Jenny telling me about an invitation to Eloise's bachelorette party. I erased that, too. When pigs flew, I thought. The idea of being in a room with those two just made me want to kick somebody. I put the Verde wedding out of my head and called Lee.

"Are you working late?" I asked.

"Where are you?" He sounded concerned. This only meant they hadn't found Fouke yet.

"Home."

"Alone?" he said. "I thought you were with Maggie."

"She's not my babysitter," I complained. "Short of giving someone a harsh talking too, what do you think she can do?"

Lee said nothing.

"Dessa, I don't want you alone."

"Well, when you get home, I won't be," I said and sighed because I didn't want to argue with him. I wanted him to come home. I wanted to talk about Biddle. I wanted company.

"Come home," I said and hung up. I stared at the phone, knowing he wouldn't call back. Lee understood when I didn't want to fight. I understood he'd seen me frightened by the exterminator and that made him fearful my anxiety disorder had come back. He wouldn't admit that bothered him. My disorder worried me too but not as much as everyone thought. If Fouke showed up at my door, I wouldn't run screaming and hide beneath my bed. I didn't want to see him, but I wouldn't fall apart if I did. I had George's pepper spray, good locks on the doors and windows, and he was starting to piss me off, royally.

***

When Lee came home, he was still annoyed with my lack of concern regarding Fouke. I put him in a better mood with a home-cooked meal and lots of attention. We sat at the kitchen table eating and making small talk, avoiding the topic of Fouke and Lee's insistence on getting the restraining order. I asked him about his day, and I told him about Biddle.

"He gave you a rock," Lee said, amused at the idea.

"A nice rock," I said and got up from the table to show him. "In fact, he called it a mote, whatever that is."

"Should I be jealous?" he mocked. I placed the stone in front of him.

"He calls me Cleopatra. I think I'm in love." I batted my eyes. He didn't seem concerned about sharing my affection with someone else. He picked up the stone to examine and slid it back over to me.

"Hate to break the news to you, sweetly, it's not a rock," he said and went back to eating.

I picked up the stone.

"It's plain old concrete," Lee said.

"How do you know?" I said, disappointed.

"Trust me, it's a guy thing," he said, and I gave him a rueful look.

I rubbed my thumb along the surface and pieces crumbed. Lee was right, and I pouted.

"He called it a mote, like a mote stone," I said, feeling stupid.

"A mote...isn't that a line from the bible?"

I shrugged. I remembered something biblical about a mote, but I was a long way away from Sunday school.

"What did Maggie think of Mr. Biddle?" Lee said.

"She wanted to clean his apartment."

His mouth curled into a lopsided grin.

"He said it was the mote in the bastard's eye," I said, staring at the rock. "I wonder if he meant Henry."

"Maybe it's special or perhaps he just wants to throw the thing through Henry's living room window."

Why would Biddle carefully wrap it in paper? What was the point?

"Someone else's trash is his treasure," I said.

"I know someone who could find out," Lee said. "You remember the civil engineer who helped me with that landlord from Staten Island, Jake Nordmeyer?"

I remembered the case, where Jake's expert testimony found the landlord's maintenance of his building negligible. Lee won the case. I also remembered my first introduction to Jake. He nearly talked me to death with questions about baking, advertising, interracial dating, and the Yankees' chances for another championship. My encounter with him in Lee's office left me with a headache and a promise to stay clear of him. He reminded me of those kids in high school who took care of the audiovisual equipment. Either they grew up to be Bill Gates or a man determined to complete his comic book library before the age of forty.

"I'll ask him to take a look at it," Lee said.

"It could be junk," I said.

"Possibly not." He gave me a questioning look that was hard to read. "Maybe we should be careful about what we throw away." He leaned in and kissed me. He tasted like a pot roast.

"Wait here," he said and got up from his seat and left the kitchen. When he returned, I was still flaking off pieces of the concrete chunk, amazed at my own stupidity.

"I think this belongs to you." He held out something I recognized immediately, slightly crumpled—the photograph of me in the wedding dress.

chapter 18

THE CRUMPLED PHOTOGRAPH sat on the kitchen table like a ticking time bomb. Lee sat next to me and slid the picture closer. The candid picture caught me in a moment of complete happiness. The beautiful, simple lines of the dress, the soft cream color of the fabric against my brown skin, and the overhead lighting made both the dress and me glow somehow. I never thought I could look that pleased.

"I emptied the trash the other night and this fell out," he said, giving me a curious expression. "Let's just say, finding you in a wedding dress surprised me." He took my hand, turned my palm up, like some fortuneteller, and traced the length of my life line.

"Good surprise or bad surprise?" I asked.

"Depends," he said. Lee had the ability to go noncommittal on you, which was wonderful for being a lawyer but annoying when you tried to figure out what he thought.

"On what?" I tried to pull my hand away, but he held tight.

"On why you threw the photograph away," he said, and this surprised me. I remembered why I'd thrown the photograph away and my anger erupted.

"Eloise Verde."

Lee's brow furrowed in bewilderment. Maybe he anticipated something deeper or profound, but not because of a woman he'd barely met.

"Who?"

"That woman stole my damn dress." I made a face and tossed the photograph back onto the table. "Helped along by a skanky maid-of-honor."

"You've lost me." Lee shook his head and released my hand.

"You remember the woman who came up to you the other day at the Blue Moon? She whispered something in your ear?"

He eyes narrowed than widened in recognition. He nodded.

"Exactly what did she say to you?" This time I narrowed my gaze on him.

"Nothing. I want to talk about the dress," he insisted.

"What did she say?" I insisted.

"She's not important." He took my hand again. "You didn't throw the photograph away because you realized you didn't want to get married or just marry me?"

Could confusion be contagious? I stared at him, wondering how he'd jumped to such a far-reaching assumption. I cocked a discourteous eyebrow at him.

"My dress," I said, stressing the point. "The most prefect dress I'd ever seen. I wanted to be married in this dress, walk down the aisle in this dress."

Lee's mouth curled up in a playful smile.

"Am I waiting for you at the end of that aisle?" he said.

Lee's confusion finally became clear to me. Seeing me in a wedding dress signaled to him I was ready for a deeper commitment. Throwing the photograph away said another thing. Being a guy, he didn't understand sometimes it was about the dress and just the dress. He didn't care someone else might wear it. He only cared that I had an interest in putting one on me. He was clueless, and I patted his hand.

"Do you want to be at the end of that aisle?" I asked.

He smiled.

"Yes," he said with so much certainty. I held my breath.

"When did you decide this?"

Lee laughed.

"Five minutes after I met you."

I gave him a dismissive wave.

"First time you met me, Maggie knocked you in the head. The second time, you hit me in the face with a pie. When we went out for the first time, someone attacked you. Does pain and humiliation constitute affection and commitment?"

"I had to get your attention." He leaned forward and grinned at me.

"Leland Mackenzie, you had me when you hit me with my own dessert."

We laughed.

We'd never talked about our future together. We never went beyond the day-to-day existence we'd made for ourselves. However, the moment he moved in with me, things had changed. Our relationship became solid. Unable to verbalize what I thought the future held for us, Lee had less of a problem with expressing his need to solidify our relationship.

I leaned in and kissed him and he responded by pulling me off my chair onto his lap. I pushed the kiss deeper, wanting more. I drew away first, staring down at him smiling. I ran a finger along his lips and sighed.

"What?" He seemed disappointed.

"I loved that dress," I said, a little heartbroken.

"I love you," he said, pulling me down into another kiss.

***

I awoke the next morning and remembered a partial dream about Lee, the dress, and a walk down the aisle. When Lee left for work, he seemed relieved about why I wanted to get rid of the photograph. Our relationship was solid. He wanted to keep the picture to frame for his office. It sounded a little silly, but I didn't argue. My quarrel remained with Jenny and Eloise, dress-stealing Witch One and dress-wearing Witch Two.

With Lee off at work and Eloise and Jenny just annoying background noise in my head, my thoughts turned to Biddle. I wanted to see him. I had no doubt passing out drunk wasn't a unique experience for him. I still had my concerns. Did he have family or friends who checked up on him? The image of him sitting in his tattered lounger made a part of me ache a bit. I needed to reassure myself he was alright.

I called Maggie to arrange a return visit to Biddle's apartment.

"What's wrong?" I asked. She sounded annoyed when she answered the phone.

"Wedding venue has a problem," she said.

"So?" I said. My mind was preoccupied by Biddle and not some petty disaster cooked up by Eloise or Jenny.

"I have to fix it," she insisted.

"Why?" I didn't hide my incredulity.

"I'm the freaking wedding planner, remember?" she said, her impatience showing.

"I want to check up on Barnaby," I said, disinterested in her problems with the Verde wedding.

"After."

"Now," I insisted.

"No venue, no wedding. Which means I have to find another one," she said. I imagined her pulling out her hair. "I don't have time to find another one, even if I knew where to look."

"How long?" I didn't want to deal with Eloise.

"The morning, maybe if I can figure out what the heck is going on," she said.

"I hope you're not asking me to come," I said apprehensively. "Because I'm keeping my Eloise exposure quota down to a minimal today."

"Please," she begged.

"You want cheese with that whine?" I said.

Maggie didn't laugh.

"I don't want to be trapped with them all day," she said.

"Ask Candace," I suggested.

"O, please. If I call Candace, she'll just brush me off. Coming all the way out here, no way she'd do that for me." I heard the stress in her voice and sighed. My relatively good mood picked up speed in its descent when I finally agreed to call Candace and talk her into going to the winery.

"Love you, O," Maggie said. Maggie knew Candace would try to take over the wedding. If my girlfriend had any sense, she'd let her.

I gave a quick goodbye to Maggie and called Candace.

"What do you want?" Candace said. My sister wasn't a morning person or an afternoon person, and last time I checked, she didn't do too well at night.

"Remember you promised to help Maggie with this wedding stuff," I said, trying to sound as apologetic as possible. She said nothing and for a moment, I thought she might have hung up on me.

"Candy?"

"The dessert case is low." Impatience dripped from her tone. There would be no love from Candace.

"I'll do the desert case, double. I swear."

"The paper goods order hasn't been put in, and I need checks written for the meat vendor." Her list continued until she had me indentured for a month.

"Anything, Candace, anything." I sighed, and then I remembered something.

"One thing, Eloise Verde doesn't know about Maggie's... umm...other job," I said.

"What other job? You mean the one where she runs around sticking her nose in other people's business," my sister said. I felt her smugness even through the phone line.

"Yeah, the private investigator thing. So please don't mention it," I said.

"One condition, or otherwise I tell anyone who asks what Maggie does," she said.

She had me doing slave work for weeks, what more did she want?

"Tell Maggie's boss to stop hanging around the Blue Moon. He keeps staring at me," she complained. Confused at first, I remembered what I asked the rotund private detective to do for me.

"Sure, I'll put a leash on Frank. Promise about Maggie," I said and felt as if we were both kids again, doing pinky swears. I called Maggie back and told her Candace was on her way.

I had other plans.

"I'm going to talk to Biddle, and I'll meet up with you later," I said.

"You sure you want to do that on your own?" she asked.

"Unless he's a mean drunk, I think I'm okay," I said and told her goodbye. I got in my car and headed to Biddle's apartment. I left home with Candace and her Frank problem a fond memory and arrived at Biddle's apartment building on Merrick Road twenty minutes later. To facilitate my arrival, I stopped off at a local donut shop and bought breakfast. Not even Biddle could argue with sugar-glazed donuts and coffee.

Biddle lived on the second floor of the walkup, and I'd remembered how difficult it was to get him upstairs the night before. For a small man, alcohol made him as coordinated as a blind clown with one leg. I hoped his mood had improved for breakfast. Suddenly, the idea of meeting him on my own didn't sound smart. I proceeded anyway. Part of me wanted to make sure he was all right, and the other half, probably influenced by Maggie, still had a burning need to ask him about Henry Duschumel.

I walked up the stairs to a poorly lit hallway that smelled of stale air and a hint of mold. A broken light in one of the fluorescent fixtures caused the others to flicker, giving the place a creepy, bad horror movie sense. Despite the fact she was less than five feet four and looked like someone's doll, I wished Maggie was here. If there was a serial killer around, she would talk him out of his axe and into counseling.

I stood in front of Biddle's door, took a deep breath, and knocked. No one answered, so I knocked again.

"Mr. Biddle," I called out.

Silence.

"Barnaby, it's... Cleo from last night," I said, slightly embarrassed.

Silence.

I continued to knock a few moments more and louder. When one of the doors down the hall cracked opened, I swore an eye stared back at me. It didn't look like a very happy eye, and I tensed and stopped knocking. My knocking garnished me nothing but silence from the other side of the door and creepy attention from the tenant down the hall. Either a drunken Biddle couldn't answer or he left. I needed to take my noble intentions and breakfast and go. Anyone with two cents realized this was the part in the movie where the hapless girl became the first victim of a series killer. By the time he was on victim number twelve you wouldn't remember who the first victim was. I ran to the stairwell. The All Seeing Eye watched me go as I bounded down the stairs taking two at a time. I heard a door slam, to my relief.

chapter 19

OUTSIDE BIDDLE'S APARTMENT, the warm summer air came as a relief to the stifling hallway. I hadn't found Biddle, and I'd accomplished nothing but indenturing myself to my sister. The image of an eye peering out of the door staring back at me gave me a chill. The way my luck ran, some psycho resident of Biddle's apartment building would become enamored with me and join my stalking club.

I didn't know whether to wait for Biddle's return or come back later. I contemplated my options as I scanned the tired little neighborhood, which hadn't revived itself from the night before. An occasional car appeared and disappeared down the empty two-lane street. Some of the storefront businesses were in the process of opening. Others appeared to have gone out of business long ago. Like Biddle, the neighborhood had seen better days.

As I stood in the entrance of the apartment building wondering about his whereabouts, my cell phone rang. Maggie was probably calling to tell me my sister had killed Eloise or had made her cry or something equally annoying. I was anxious to tell her about Biddle. I dug into my pocketbook while I crossed the empty street and headed for my parked car.

The phone continued to ring.

"Give me a minute," I complained as I rooted through the junk I'd accumulated in my bag. I still had Biddle's breakfast in my hand, which made searching for the phone difficult. Distracted, I paid little attention to the oncoming traffic. Only when I heard the revved up motor of an approaching vehicle did I look up. A heartbeat later, the bug on the top of the roof of the oncoming van got my full attention. The glare from the early morning sun blocked my view of the driver. It didn't take a genius to guess who was behind the wheel—Horace Fouke, the little cockroach.

The van picked up speed and headed toward me. I barely had enough time to dive out of the way. The van whooshed past, barely missing me. I'd dropped my phone in the middle of the street and I landed on my pocketbook, the bag of donuts, and coffee. The warm wetness seeped through my blouse. As I sat up, a lone passerby shouted and pointed down the street. I turned and realized the bug van made a u-turn.

I felt immobilized with fear and disbelief and sat there. Finally, I scrambled to my knees and slipped between two parked cars as the van came roaring back. A blur of an oversized cockroach and wheels flew by and continued down the street. When I didn't hear any screeching tires or the sound of the van returning, I peered up from behind one of the cars. The remains of two donuts stuck to my shirt and coffee drenched my pants. The van disappeared down a street, screeching tires as it went. My phone lay in the middle of the street pulverized.

"What is your problem?" I screamed in the direction of the disappearing van. I noticed curtains parting in one of the windows on the second floor of Biddle's building. Mr. Crazy Eye probably had a fantastic view of the entire incident. I cursed. I cursed Fouke, Mr. Crazy Eye, and the mess that was my shirt.

I got in my car, slammed the door, and I headed for the safest place I knew—the Blue Moon. On the drive, I checked the rearview mirror every five seconds and tried not to drive like a maniac. I took long deep breaths. I tried to calm myself, because I refused to let Fouke get the better of me or get me arrested for driving without my sanity. Honestly, if Fouke stood in the middle of the street, I would run him down.

When I finally arrived at the restaurant, my coffee soaked blouse had stiffened, and I smelled of stale French roast. I entered through the kitchen, hoping to avoid the embarrassment of explaining my appearance. Unfortunately, I ran into George. The big man stared and gave me an appraising look that bordered on pathetic. He grumbled something and shook his head.

"Don't ask," I said and pushed past him. I went to the office and got one of the Blue Moon's tee-shirts the kitchen staff wore. Downstairs in the locker area in the small bathroom, I cleaned up and changed. The clothes helped but not by much. This thing with Fouke was getting old.

When I finished, I called Maggie. She'd been trying to reach me for over an hour. I told her about my phone and Fouke. It took her a moment to get around the idea that Fouke tried to run me down. It took me more than a moment. A dead rat was one thing, but trying to make me roadkill was a whole new level of crazy. What had I ever done to him, besides being a victim and a witness to the demise of his marriage?

"This thing with Fouke is getting dangerous," she said and I couldn't argue with her.

"I hope your day went a lot better."

"Candace and I are on our way back. She's finishing up with the manager," she said.

"I guess no one died?" I said.

"Surprisingly, no. Eloise tried to play prima donna for a minute before Candace shut her down," Maggie said.

"What do you mean?"

"This is your sister we're talking about," Maggie said in a reverent tone.

"Let me guess, Eloise whined about something stupid and Candace told her if she didn't behave, the universe as she knew it would change drastically," I said.

"Candace told Eloise to stop wasting her mother's money and her valuable time every instance a new idea floated into her head. She explained they abolished slavery and servitude comes at a cost in this country. If she needed to act like a twelve-year-old, she shouldn't be surprised if she was treated like one," Maggie said.

"Sounds like my sister." I grinned.

"She finished off with, if Eloise raised her voice to her again, her Tuscan-inspired wedding would resemble the New York City dump because that's where everything would end up." Maggie laughed.

"What did Eloise do?"

"Lowered her voice. I have to say, you sister has a way with her."

"Usually her way. Right now Eloise is the least of your problems. I couldn't find Barnaby," I said.

"He could be anywhere. If he decided to get his car and started drinking again, God help him, O. Maybe we should call the local hospitals in Barnaby's area," she suggested.

"More like the local jail," I said.

"He has to turn up somewhere." She didn't sound too hopeful.

"He could have gone back to the construction site, which would certainly get him arrested," I said.

"I hope not. I'm sure he's fine. Candace is almost finished, and we'll hurry back," she said before disconnecting.

I hated to think Biddle had gotten arrested again or landed in some hospital busted up. I started to make a few more phone calls. I called the local hospitals in the hope one of them had Biddle. Forty minutes later, I came up empty. No one had seen Barnaby Biddle.

I didn't know whom else to contact, so I decided to work on some desserts for the restaurant. I guessed my sister's sense of servitude didn't extend to her family.

In the kitchen, I set up my stations, preheated the oven, and pulled out my mixer and bowls. I did my best to avoid another tirade from George and kept my area as self-contained and clean as possible. He didn't grumble once. By the time Maggie and my sister arrived, I had cakes cooling and had started working on a peach cobbler and some fruit pies. Maggie found me in the kitchen, and from the expression on her face, she hadn't located Biddle either.

"He's probably in some bar," she said, but she didn't sound convincing.

"He's broke, remember?" I let out a groan of frustration. "I should have gotten the super or someone to let me in and check on him," I said.

"Finish up here and we'll go back together," she said. "We'll get someone to let us in."

"Sounds like a good idea." I could tell her thoughts weren't far from Biddle.

We quickly finished the last of the baking, cleaned up to George's liking, and headed for the parking lot through the back door. I stopped when one of the waitstaff told me Candace said I had a visitor. I groaned because it was just like my sister to set up a meeting with a new customer without telling me. The woman had more invested in my cake making business than I did. I thought about ducking out but she did me an enormous favor dealing with Eloise. I told Maggie to meet me by the car and I went to find my sister.

As expected, I found Candace at the front. To my surprise, Mrs. Fouke stood next to her. I hadn't seen the woman since the incident with her husband. Considering her family's dynamic, I didn't want to see her again either. She'd come looking for me, not once but twice and that made me curious. I guess the Fouke's family trait was persistence and irritation.

As I approached, Mrs. Fouke affected a caring smile. It made her appear uncomfortable.

"Ms. Wilkes, I was just explaining to your sister about Horace," she said.

"I hope they found your husband, because he almost ran me over this morning in that damn bug van," I said.

Candace's mouth dropped opened, and Mrs. Fouke shook her head.

"What? When?" Candace asked. She stared at my Blue Moon tee-shirt and pointed. "Why are you wearing that?" Pilfering tee-shirts had its priority with her psycho stalker, tee-shirt thief—no contest.

I ignored her.

"What did I tell you? He's insane," Mrs. Fouke said. "He's still out there. The police won't take him seriously. He called and threatened me yesterday too, but because I'm just his wife, they don't listen to me."

I gave the woman an appraising glance. She harangued her husband for years, had him arrested and barred from their house. He had a reason to run her over with the bug van. What had I done?

"Why are you here?" I wanted to bring this pity party to an end. If she wanted to commiserate over our mutual distaste for her crazy husband, she'd have to do it alone.

"I've checked with the detective on the case. He said you haven't talked to him." Her raised voice garnished a few glances from nearby tables.

"I've been busy. I'll get to it," I said.

"What is it going to take?" A hint of hostility crept into her voice.

"You need to calm down, Mrs. Fouke," Candace insisted.

"Then tell your sister to do the right thing. You have to make the cops believe Horace is a real threat or else." Mrs. Fouke glared at us.

Candace stiffened at the threat. Her cold eyes narrowed on Mrs. Fouke. This stare had turned lesser mortals to stone. Mrs. Fouke never noticed or was too intent on making her point.

"I'll take care of the police." I was willing to say anything to get the woman out of my face.

"Tomorrow. I'll tell the detective you'll see him tomorrow." The words sounded more like a command than a request. I didn't like her dictating my schedule. I barely tolerated when Candace tried it.

"Okay, Mrs. Fouke, she'll take care of it," Candace said in a placating tone, which surprised me. Perhaps she was measuring the level of Mrs. Fouke's crazy. Mrs. Fouke nodded, but glared at me as if she wanted to measure my resolve.

"I'm sorry, I'm so upset, but you don't know Horace like I do. He is a dangerous man. Our marriage was pure hell. I want him out of my life once and for all." She made a lashing motion with her hand in a show of cutting the Bug King out of her life. This didn't seem like the act of a fearful woman but a vengeful one.

chapter 20

I LEFT THE Blue Moon with the clear impression I wasn't one of Mrs. Fouke's favorite people. Short of walking me down to the police station and demanding a restraining order against her husband, nothing seemed to appease the woman. I didn't like being pushed into something. I didn't like when my sister did it, and I didn't like Mrs. Fouke's efforts to dictate my life. I preferred to solve my own bug problem.

On our drive to Biddle's apartment, I borrowed Maggie's phone to call the other man in my life—Frank. I knew I was only paying him in food, but I expected a little more from our ace private investigator. All he had to do was find Fouke.

"Do you care about this case?" I yelled at Frank.

"I don't have a crystal ball. This guy has fallen off the face of the earth. He's not using his credit cards. He hasn't been at his business, and he hasn't made a call in days." Frank spit out the word in frustration.

"The guy almost killed me," I said.

"Thankfully he's awful at it." It was hard to tell if he was serious or not.

"You've been a lot of help, Frank. Just remember, if he gets me, I will haunt you," I said and snapped the phone shut.

"You told him," Maggie mused.

"Frank is as helpful as a three-legged chair," I complained.

"He'll find him, don't worry," Maggie said as she drove. She always had more faith in Frank than I did. The biggest resource of Frank's detective agency was Maggie.

When we arrived at Biddle's building, I felt alert. The curtain from the window of Mr. Crazy Eye didn't move, thank God. Even with Maggie with me, my trepidation wouldn't fade as we climbed up the stairs to Biddle's apartment.

"You think he's inside?" I whispered.

She shrugged and knocked again.

"He could be passed out," I said. "Can't you pick the lock or something?" I wasn't sure if Maggie's eyes widened in surprise or righteous indignation.

"I can't pick a lock," she complained. This was the same woman who led me into so many strange houses I stopped counting.

"I bet Frank could," I said snidely.

"Frank has no morals." Maggie scowled at me. She was right of course.

"He can't even find a guy with a bug on his van," I said, realizing I had the wrong person searching for the Bug King.

She knocked again and called out Biddle's name with no response. She tried the doorknob and the door opened. We shared an intrepid glance before she gave the door a gentle push. The stench hit us first, a dank funky odor that made me blink. Maggie put her hand over her mouth as she almost gagged. I reached out for her a second too late as she took a step inside.

"No," I warned. The sound of a door opening made me turn to see Mr. Crazy Eye's door open, as the familiar orb peered out at me. My creep factor went up a few notches.

"O," I heard Maggie say in a quivering voice. Against my better judgment, I stepped inside. It took a moment to get Mr. Crazy Eye out of my head before I entered the room and found Maggie standing in front of Biddle's lounger. Behind her were Biddle's upraised feet.

"What is that smell?" I said as I approached, only to have my question answered at the sight of Biddle lying back in his lounger as if we'd interrupted a catnap. A wide-eyed Maggie stood frozen as her eyes fixed on the immobile Biddle.

"O, I think..." her voice trailed off.

"You think what?" I said, annoyed with her inability to talk. I stopped when I saw Biddle's still body laid out before me.

He was dressed in the same clothes from yesterday. His mouth was opened, eyes closed, and arms dangling at his sides. His face was slack and Grey. Stunned, I took a step back and almost tripped on a bottle.

"He's dead," Maggie said just above a whisper.

"No shit, Sherlock!" I screamed in panic. I'd never seen a dead person up close, and never without a casket. Biddle must have soiled himself, because the stink of putrid bodily fluids triggered a part of my brain that made me want to vomit and run.

"Oh, Barnaby," I said.

Maggie put a hand on my arm and squeezed as a steady stream of tears fell down her cheek. This triggered tears of my own. Why was I crying? I hardly knew the man. He was an alcoholic, a troublemaker, a...sweet soul. I wiped my cheeks with the back of my hand.

"O." Maggie pointed down at the bottom of the lounger where two empty liquor bottles lay. Another empty bottle nestled by my foot. After noticing the bottles, I took in the room. Clothing and dresser drawers lay on the floor. Closet doors were open, and their contents spilled out. My attention went back to Biddle.

"You're sure he's dead?" I said.

Maggie glared at me.

"You want to take his pulse?" she snapped uncharacteristically. "He's not breathing, O, and he's....bluish."

"Bluish?" I rolled my eyes. "Is that a technical term?"

"I'm doing the best I can here and you're not helping," she complained.

"Sorry," I said and we both took a deep breath.

"God, I can't believe he's dead," Maggie said, taking a step closer.

"Maybe he had a heart attack or something." I took a step closer too. He appeared peaceful in a dead sort of way.

"I don't think so," she said. She scanned the room, turning and taking in everything.

"What do you mean?" I tried to follow her line of sight.

"We didn't leave the place like this," she said. "As sloppy as Barnaby was, he wouldn't destroy his stuff."

Someone had been searching for something, someone in a hurry. Biddle wouldn't dump out the sugar or coffee tin to find something he had hidden.

"These bottles are everywhere." Maggie took a step back and moved one with her foot. I read the label. With the Blue Moon having its own bar, I got familiar with the types of alcohol the restaurant brought. I've signed and paid for a few liquor deliveries myself.

"It's not the cheap stuff," I said, reading the labels.

"Your note is gone." She pointed to the empty bulletin board. Someone had pulled the note off the board and left a thin sliver of paper behind.

"My phone number was on it," I said, feeling a little uneasy with the idea someone had purposely taken the note.

"We need to call the police. Someone obviously gave him all this liquor so he could drink himself to death," Maggie said as she pulled out her phone. I held up a hand to stop her.

"Should we be here when you do that?" I said.

"We need to be here, because if we're not, the police won't treat this as a murder." Maggie's small face filled with anger. I shook my head.

"How are you going to explain this to them?" I said, pointing at Biddle. "He's a drunk found with bottles of liquors."

"Wouldn't they want to find out he didn't have the money to buy a beer let alone three bottles of expensive liquor?" Her cheeks flushed with anger.

"He had generous friends," I said. "And another thing, are you going to tell them you're practicing without a license?" I folded my arms and stared at her. Her indignation dampened by the reality of a possible arrest.

"Okay...okay, but I'm still calling and I'm not leaving." She jutted out her tiny chin at me.

"Okay," I said, staring down at Biddle. My eyes moistened at the sight of him.

Maggie pulled out her phone and called.

"Hello, I'd like to report a death."

We waited just outside the apartment for the police to arrive. Two uniformed Nassau County patrolmen showed up fifteen minutes later. They were efficient, professional strangers who didn't know Barnaby Biddle, and jumped to the most obvious conclusions when they walked into the apartment. It took all my efforts to keep Maggie silent. They ignored the ransacked apartment, the expensive liquor, and a question I asked myself only when we were told to wait downstairs in the hallway.

"How do you know Barnaby has no money?" I whispered.

"I checked, of course," she said. Of course, she did. Maggie should be in the Guinness Book of World Records for her ability to do the fastest background check in history. "He was behind two months' rent and on his union dues."

"Who brought the liquor?" I asked.

"Bigger question here is who bailed him out?" she said. I hadn't thought about someone getting Biddle out of jail. I had another question for her, but said nothing when an officer stepped out of Biddle's apartment and headed toward us.

"Hi, ladies," he said with a smile. Maggie smiled back which held his attention briefly.

"We're extremely upset about Mr. Biddle," she said.

"Well...finding a dead body will do that," he said.

"Just the other day he seemed fine," she said with a great deal of concern in her voice.

"Yeah, that's the thing." He pointed to the door where Mr. Crazy Eye lived.

"One of Mr. Biddle's neighbors said you were here the other day helping him up the stairs to his apartment. How long had you known him?"

"Not long. We met by accident," Maggie said, beaming up at the taller man. "He had a collision with a woman in front of the building, and we tried to help them both. She walked away okay, but Barnaby could barely walk."

The officer wrote as Maggie talked.

"We got him upstairs, talked to him briefly to make sure he was alright. We even cleaned up a bit," I said.

He raised an eyebrow.

"She can't help it," I said, smiling at him, hoping to deflate his curiosity.

"Neighbor said you returned early this morning," he said to me. I glanced up at Mr. Crazy Eye's window and silently cursed him.

"I came to check on him, but I didn't get an answer," I said, remembering Lee's words about dealing with the law. If you have to lie, don't. If you do have to tell the truth, don't. Don't say anything without a lawyer, but if you had no choice, keep the truth to a minimum.

"When she told me, I insisted we come back and get the super to open up. Mr. Biddle wasn't a young man," she said.

"The door was opened, and we walked in and found him," I said and sighed for effect. Maggie sighed too and gave the officer a pitiful look.

He wrote in a little pad.

"He also said you were almost run down by a van....with a bug on it," he said in disbelief.

"I was on the phone crossing the street and didn't watch where I was going," I said. I didn't want to explain Horace Fouke, the Bug King.

"The guy said the van turned around and tried to hit you again." The officer's eyes narrowed in suspicion. I raised my eyebrows knowing a lie was about to come out my mouth.

"I said something unladylike and I guess he took offense," I said.

"What the hell did you say?" he said as he and Maggie stared at me.

"I don't want to repeat it," I said, feigning embarrassment.

They waited.

"I don't want to repeat it," I said adamantly.

The officer's eyes lingered on me.

"Well, be careful," he said.

"Yes, sir."

He wrote, and we waited.

"Do you know how he died?" Maggie asked. He shrugged and checked his notes.

"Probably alcohol poisoning or he asphyxiated on his own vomit," he said flatly as if he'd seen this kind of death a hundred times before. Maybe he had, but I hadn't, and neither had Maggie. It left us both speechless.

"Oh, Barnaby," I said wistfully.

chapter 21

MAGGIE AND I drove home barely saying a word. Biddle's death had affected us deeply. I never expected to care so much for a total stranger, but I did. I never expected to be so angry at the implication someone had been in the apartment with him and brought alcohol. A drunk, if not an alcoholic, Biddle wouldn't refuse a drink. They might as well have served him dynamite.

"Someone intentionally brought those bottles of scotch, knowing he might drink himself to death," I said, staring mindlessly at the passing traffic.

"Someone also paid his bail bond," Maggie added as she drove me home.

"Henry?" I asked.

Maggie shrugged. I thought about bringing up Drummond, but I didn't. Other than the altercation outside the jail, what relationship did he have with Biddle? We knew what he had with Henry.

"Barnaby was a problem that wouldn't go away," I said.

"Biddle was a construction worker, low man on the totem pole. What conflict did he have with a multimillion dollar developer?" she said.

We fell into another long silence.

"Also, whoever went into his apartment searched for something," she said. "But the most valuable things Barnaby owned were thrown on the floor like garbage—the tools he made his living with."

I thought about Biddle's ransacked apartment as the image of him came flooding back, with his goofy smile and outstretched hand holding a rock wrapped in newspaper, like a gift at Christmas. "The other night, Barnaby gave me the rock, remember?"

Maggie nodded.

"You think it came from Bella Vista?"

"Yes. From what I found out about his work history, Bella Vista was his last place of employment," she said.

"I showed the thing to Lee, and he said it was a piece of concrete," I said.

"Why would he...?" Maggie stopped herself and stared at me. "Has to be the concrete from Bella Vista."

"Lee sometimes works with this expert, a civil engineer. I could ask him to look at it," I said.

"You think it's important?" she asked.

I shrugged. I didn't know if the piece of concrete given to me by a drunken construction worker was important. When we finally pulled into my driveway, we had more questions than we had answers. Maggie had to go and be with her family. I had Lee. What did Biddle have?

"You think he can tell anything from one piece?" I said, not sounding hopeful.

"I wish we had more. Unfortunately, Biddle only gave you one. If there had been any more, they are gone by now," she said.

Yeah, I thought, along with my cell phone.

"What do you want to do?" I asked before getting out of the car.

"Let me think about it and I'll call you in the morning," she said. We both felt a little beat down by Biddle's death. I couldn't get the man's smiling face out of my head.

"I'm sure you'll come up with something," I reassured, but her expression was doubtful. Her only lead to Henry's secrets just died.

"O, you don't think talking with us had anything to do with Barnaby's death?" she asked. Her tone was soft and apologetic. With her impish face, she appeared childlike.

I shook my head. I didn't want to think we were the cause of anything, let alone someone's death. I closed the car door and watched as she drove off. Her mind was heavy with the events of the day, mine as well. Was Biddle alive when I arrived earlier? Could I have done something? I tried not to dwell on him and went inside.

There were messages on my voicemail from Jenny expecting me to come to Eloise's bridal shower. I didn't want to celebrate. The other messages from customers didn't get my heart racing until I heard the one from my Aunt Renne. The same aunt I promised cupcakes for her choir. I'd forgotten. God and the First Baptist Church were going to get me.

"Crap!" I said as I rushed to the kitchen and checked the time. I had one night to make over two hundred cupcakes. For half a minute, I thought about going to the Blue Moon with its immense ovens and counter space. Then George's scowling face popped into my head. I had to make the cupcakes in my small kitchen. The thought of baking and icing two hundred cupcakes nearly numbed me. In all the chaos, Jenny called again begging me to come to Eloise's bridal shower. Eloise's bridesmaids where bowing out and Jenny worried no one would show. Somehow, she convinced Maggie to attend. Just to get her off the phone, I agreed, regretting it the moment I hung up. Two hours later, Lee found me in the kitchen covered in flour, chocolate, and panic. He stood in the doorway, briefcase in hand staring at me petrified.

"Hi..." Lee scanned the kitchen and the mayhem. "...honey."

"I forgot about Anne Renne's cupcakes, and I can't do them at the Blue Moon because of George saying I'm always messing up his kitchen." I took a long, deep breath as my nerves began to rattle. "Candace agrees with him. She never agrees with him. I don't....have enough room." I took another breath, still in a near panic.

"Babe, slow down." Lee raised a hand to calm me.

"It's been a horrible day...first Fouke and..." Something angry and sad swelled up in me.

"What about Fouke?" Lee's eye's darkened at the sound of the Bug King's name.

"Forget Fouke, I don't care about him. I have these cupcakes and no space," I yelled. "And Barnaby..." His name caught in my throat and my eyes burned. I took a deep breath to steady myself, but nothing helped.

"Who?" Lee came to me, trying to find some semblance of calm and sanity, because hot tears rolled down my cheeks.

"Barnaby's dead!" I said and fell onto his chest as he embraced me. I felt hot tears run down my cheeks. He didn't care about the flour or chocolate and held on tight.

"Start from the beginning." His voice was even and calm as he rubbed the small of my back. I had a few false starts, but I told him about the bug van, Mr. Crazy Eye, and Barnaby. He listened, and I talked, rehashing a horrible day. We stood for at least five minute holding on to each other. I felt better, centered, and solid. I wiped my tear -stained cheeks, covering myself in flour. The sight made Lee smile.

"So how many do you have to make?" he asked and scanned the kitchen before taking off his jacket and rolling up his sleeves. I smiled at the sight of him, a man ready to help me make cupcakes. I knew this was Superman.

Luckily for Lee, he didn't have to give up his day job because his baking skills were nonexistent, though he did learn how to ice a mean cupcake. We both fell into bed around one thirty in the morning, exhausted and happy the First Baptist Church Choir had cupcakes.

The next day, an exhausted Lee helped me load the boxes filled with cupcakes into my car, both of us still tired from the night before. Lee had an early court appearance and wasn't able to stay home even though he needed more sleep. I'd hate to think he lost a case because he couldn't keep his eyes open. Before he had left for work, he reminded me to be careful about Fouke and got my promise I'd put in a restraining order against the exterminator. I got into my car and headed for the church.

First Baptist Church was an impressive structure of brick and stained glass. It had a thriving congregation with a youthful minister and active community services. Like most black churches, First Baptist was one part religion, one part social network, and one part political; and to keep your membership you had to come most Sundays and be a card-carrying Democrat. The choirs mirrored the church's social structure. The old guard and senior choir was anyone over the age of sixty. The adult choir had anyone past the age of thirty. The youth ensemble, which also included the children's choir, started at birth and ended at twenty-one. There were grandmothers and great-grandchildren singing in the same choir stand, a generational thing with mothers and daughters, fathers and sons.

First Baptist had been my parents' church. As a child, I sang in the youth ensemble until school and other activities outside the church overshadowed my interest in singing. Though I didn't attend church as often as my Aunt Renne would like, I tried. Candace went every Sunday and sang in the adult choir in her burgundy and gold robe, praising God and singing like an angel. I always wondered how anyone with such a cantankerous disposition could have such a sweet voice. I took Lee to hear her sing once and it totally dumbfounded him.

When I arrived at church, I found my Aunt Renne in the large basement area that housed a small kitchen. As usual, by her side was her gang of four: Ruth, Queenie, Gladys, and Sister Charles. None of them was under the age of seventy, Sister Charles being the youngest at seventy-one. They were readying for the coming celebration. Members from the youth ensemble and children's choir helped out with decorating the place. Barely making five feet, my Aunt Renne spit out orders like a general on D-Day as she instructed the hapless teenagers to carry the cupcakes to the reception area.

"Thank you so much, baby girl." She proudly displayed her brand new dentures with a huge smile as she pulled me into a hug.

"You look tired," she said.

"Two hundred cupcakes will do that to me," I mused.

"Praise the Lord for you. Oh, before I forget, Mrs. Mansfield's daughter will call you about her wedding cake. Poor child is finally getting married," she said with some lament.

"That's a good thing, right?" I didn't remember Mrs. Mansfield daughter.

"Well, she's been living with her boyfriend for eight years." Through the large lens of her glasses, she rolled her eyes. "The baby is due in six months. The fool is about seven years and three months late," she said contemptuously and gave me a scrutinizing glance.

"I'm happy for her," I said with a forced smile, because I still didn't remember Mrs. Mansfield's daughter.

"How's Lee?" she said, cutting through my early morning fog and weariness. I stared down into her rich dark chocolate face and realized she was making a point using Mrs. Mansfield's daughter's current situation.

"Not a fool," I said, and this seemed to appease her.

"That's good," she said, patting my hand. We were interrupted by Sister Charles who munched on one of the cupcakes.

"These are delicious, Odessa," she said, licking her lips. Aunt Renne gave her a withering look.

"You want to save some for the choir, Sister," Aunt Renne admonished.

"Oh, I just wanted a little taste," a guilty-looking Sister Charles confessed. Considering she weighed over two hundred pounds, a little taste wasn't her problem.

"Glad you like it," I said. Then I remembered something about Sister Charles. She knew her Bible better than any Sunday preacher. An encyclopedia of Bible quotes and references, the woman was a Biblical Google.

"Sister, can I ask you a question?"

"Anything, honey." She took another bite and smiled at me.

"There is a verse about a mote or something, I think. I've been trying to remember, but I—"

Sister Charles held up a finger and closed her eyes.

"Either how can you say to your brother, Brother, let me pull out the mote that is in your eye, when you yourself behold not the beam that is in your own eye? You hypocrite, cast out first the beam out of your own eye, and then shall you see clearly to pull out the mote that is in your brother's eye," she said, taking the last bite of cupcake. "That's Matthew 7:4-5 if you must know"

"King James," Aunt Renne said.

"Thank you. Why don't you have another cupcake," I said, smiling at her. She grinned and went back in search for another treat. Aunt Renne stared at me, curious.

"Someone I met the other day just died. He said something about a mote. I tried to figure out why he said it. Now I guess I know," I said.

"Sorry, honey. Was he a nice man?" she asked, and I nodded.

"I liked to think so."

"We'll pray for him," she said. I was pleased with the idea the First Baptist Church congregation would say a prayer for him.

Oh, Barnaby Biddle.

chapter 22

I DROVE AWAY from the church wondering why Biddle thought Henry was a hypocrite. The two were so different: Henry, with his laced-up control; and Biddle, with none whatsoever. What at Bella Vista made the men judge each other so harshly? If Mrs. Verde was right, and if Henry's intentions toward Eloise were less than loving, then he deserved some judgment. Biddle was no poster boy for perfection and the virtuous life. I thought about the two men, and they had already judged each other severely. First Henry, whose restraining order against Biddle said everything about what he thought of the now-dead construction worker; and Biddle, who treated a piece of concrete from Bella Vista like some damning evidence.

The question nagged at me for much of the morning as I ran a few errands, which included replacing my phone. Without a cell phone, I felt disconnected. The sales clerk at the local mega-mart electronics store loaded me up with accessories and programmed my phone with the same phone number. The purchase buoyed my mood, and I decided to continue the sensation by shopping for some clothes. A raspberry silk blouse and a pair of jeans later, Biddle's death still bothered me, but the shopping therapy did ease my gloom. After two hours, I sat in my car, unplugging my brand new cell phone from charging in the cigarette lighter. I turned on the phone, happy to get an "in service" signal again. I noticed I already had a voicemail icon on the tiny screen. Considering I'd been without a phone for a while, I connected to my voicemail service.

"I don't know what you're up to, Jones, but you're not going to rock my boat. Stay out of this or else," a gruff male voice said. I stared at the phone, stunned, and then quickly scrolled to the phone's call log—a blocked number.

"What the..." I began and realized the caller called me Jones. I wanted to think the call was a wrong number and Jones was a common enough name. I wanted to believe there was no coincidence between the note taken from Biddle's apartment and me. I took a deep breath and rubbed the center of my chest, because a tiny seed of trepidation was growing. I rubbed at the spot and tried to push the emotion back. When it didn't work, I called Maggie. She was out at the Verde Nursery dealing with another of Eloise's wedding issues. I didn't care; I needed a little reassurance.

"Did it sound like Henry?" she asked.

"I didn't recognize the voice," I said, worried now that I had someone else beside Fouke harassing me.

"Don't freak out, O," Maggie insisted. She didn't have half the Serial Killers Knitting Club after her.

"Maybe I need to change my perfume or something," I said, frustrated I had yet another maniac after me.

"Barnaby talked about you to this guy," she said.

"Prefect, just wonderful." I checked around for the bug mobile and anyone else interested in me.

"You think he knows Barnaby gave you the piece of cement?"

"If he read the note he does," I said. "Where are you?"

"Heading to the office. After the Verdes, I need to go back to bed and start over," she complained.

"Meet me at the Blue Moon," I said. Talking to Maggie always calmed me down.

"What's there?" she asked.

"Safety," I said. "George, Bebe, and a few of the family court officers have their usual lunch group today."

"Sounds pretty safe to me," she said and promised to meet me in an hour.

When I got to the restaurant, the afternoon lunch crowd had taken up every table. As expected, five family court officers sat in a corner booth in their crisp white shirts eating sandwiches and hamburgers. Happily to the left of them were two NYPD officers having lunch as well. I felt pretty safe. Also, Candace stood by the door guarding her domain like a hungry pit-bull.

"Don't forget the cake for Mrs. Deforest's retirement party," she scolded. The woman left messages on my answering machine at home and told Lee, George, and Bebe to remind me as well. Did she think I was senile or something?

"Didn't forget," I said, slightly annoyed.

"You've been distracted lately and I want that cake," she said her tone firm and insistent.

"This is another last minute thing you threw at me," I said.

Candace rolled her eyes.

"Mrs. Deforest has been around since Mommy owned the restaurant and you don't want to make a little cake for her," she said.

"You always try to guilt me into things, Candy," I said, not appreciating her manipulation.

"I can always buy a cake at the supermarket," she said dryly.

"Any particular flavor?" Of course I would make the cake for Mrs. Deforest the same way I'd made all the those cupcakes for my Aunt Renne. Sensing she had won the argument, Candace smiled.

"No, but make sure the cake's theme has something to do with travel," she said and I looked at her as if she'd lost her mind.

"You want a theme?" I said incredulously.

"Yeah," she said firmly and gave me a dismissive nod.

I sighed. I could argue the point about how much it would take to do a themed cake but what was the point. I walked away from Candace and headed toward the kitchen.

Before I went into the kitchen, I checked the large dessert case in the back of the restaurant. A monstrosity of glass shelves and lights, the case had been the bane of my dessert-making life since I started working with my sister at the Blue Moon. Sometimes I believed Candace sneaked in at night and emptied the case just to piss me off. I opened the glass door, pushed a few of the fruit tarts out in front and took out the remaining peach cobbler. By the time I straightened everything out and rearranged the desserts to make them more appealing, Maggie came walking through the door. She talked to Candace briefly before heading toward me. From the scowl she had on her face, her encounter didn't seem to go any better than mine.

"If she tells me one more time I'm doing something wrong about the wedding, I'm going to scream," Maggie said between clenched teeth.

"Remember you wanted her help," I chided.

"Between Mrs. Verde and Candace, I will scream," she said. I gave her a reassuring pat on the shoulder and told her to follow me into the kitchen.

Lunch service at the Blue Moon could be called organized pandemonium. Since most diners were on a time restraint to get back to work or court or some midday appointment, the orders were pretty rushed. Maggie and I barely slipped into the kitchen before George gave a withering stare.

"I'm doing Mrs. Deforest's cake so power down," I said. George growled and went back to slicing something.

Maggie took a seat by my station as I slipped on an apron. I took out ingredients for the cake, deciding to make a chocolate raspberry cake. Mrs. Deforest always favored the cake when she had meals at the restaurant. Since it was her party, I'd give her what she liked.

"When I stopped by the Verdes this morning to get Eloise's new changes on the wedding," Maggie said as she helped me crack eggs, "I caught her and her mother arguing."

This surprised me.

"Mrs. Verde complained about the cost of the wedding and Eloise threatened to elope again."

"What did Mrs. Verde say?" I asked as I measured out flour and sugar for my dry ingredients.

"Nothing. That's the strange thing. She just backed off." The thought of Mrs. Verde backing away from anyone made me pause.

"That's hard to believe." I'd written up some of the invoices Candace had given Mrs. Verde, and the woman had a right to complain.

"I thought the woman would choke. Then Eloise said something about a church in Brooklyn her mother is pouring her money in and that shut her mother up."

"What church in Brooklyn?" I asked. I measured the cocoa powder and added to my other dry ingredients.

"Remember Mrs. Verde said if she died all her money would go to her church in Brooklyn and not to Eloise. Well, from what I gathered from Eloise, her mother has given thousands of dollars toward the church's restoration," Maggie said, finishing up with eggs and scooping out some shell pieces. I narrowed my eyes disapprovingly.

"Well that's mighty Christian of her," I said, checking the bowl for more egg shells.

"Not really," she said. "After her mother stormed off, I asked Eloise a few more questions about it. I got the impression her mother poured money into the church to impress everyone in the old neighborhood."

"That woman looks down on everyone. I hate to meet the people she has to impress," I said.

"Mrs. Verde grew up poor and wasn't welcomed in Mr. Verde's family right away. You know the whole mixed-marriage thing."

I gave her a confused look as to what was mixed about Mr. and Mrs. Verde. As if reading my mind, she explained.

"Mrs. Verde was a Greek Orthodox before she converted to the Verde family's Roman Catholic religion. Eloise told me her mother tried to buy her way into their good graces for over forty years. When the neighborhood church needed restoration, her mother stepped in."

I stared at her and shook my head.

"I'm thinking she's trying to be a good Christian and all she wants is a little respect," I chided.

"Eloise told her mother if she found it easy to waste money on a church where no one liked her, then she can spare a few dimes for he only child," Maggie said.

"Good for her," I said, surprised that I was rooting for Eloise.

"Anyway, Eloise won the argument and now I had the unpleasant luck of telling Candace that Eloise has added a seafood station to the menu," Maggie said.

This explained Candace's scowl.

"God knows what all this has to do with Barnaby," I said.

Maggie shrugged.

"Maybe when we know why the concrete was so important to Barnaby, we'll find out the truth," she said, and I agreed.

"What about getting more samples from Bella Vista without Henry getting suspicious?" I asked as I poured my cake batter into pans.

"I'm thinking about it," she mused, and then she made a face.

"What?" I asked.

"Zeno was at the nursery." Her mouth curled into a sneer. "He asked about you." I glared at her in disbelief. What did Zeno want with me?

"I'm glad I missed him," I said curtly.

Maggie leaned forward.

"O, I'd be careful around Zeno. Let's not antagonize him," she said.

"If he leaves me alone, I'll leave him alone." I could say this because officers from the nearby family court surrounded me. There was also Bebe, George, and Candace.

"Zeno's on probation remember?" she whispered as if his probation officer sat outside the kitchen door. "Eloise thinks his family sent him to the nursery to keep him out of trouble for awhile."

"Do you know what he's on probation for?" I asked. Maggie shook her head. "Probably for threatening a cow," I mused but Maggie didn't laugh.

"Please don't mess with him, O," Maggie pleaded. "I think he thinks you disrespected him."

I sighed and shook my head.

"He thinks....that's a concept." I slipped the pans into a hot oven. "I don't need any more people in my fan club, trust me." Especially some crazy Greek butcher who thought I needed an attitude adjustment.

chapter 23

THE NEXT DAY, I asked Maggie if she had any ideas about getting more samples for Lee's friend. She told me to pick her up at Rocket's day camp. Certain she had the solution to the problem, I didn't ask for details. I just went and got her. I wasn't surprised to find Rocket at her side in a blue and green Quinnipiac Day Camp tee-shirt. The idea of my godson in the middle of a construction site made me pause a moment.

When he got into the car, he barely said hello before he proceeded to tell me about his latest escapade. Maggie sighed; obviously she already knew the story. Rocket explained how he and Jimmy Maldonado made chocolate milk come out of their noses during lunch. Jimmy's older brother had taught it to him, and Jimmy taught it to Rocket, passing on the tradition of boys behaving badly.

"Willie Cunningham tried it, and he almost choked to death," he said, with hands flaying in the air. Clearly, this was a serious miscalculation on Willie's part. They had to call in the camp nurse when the milk went down the wrong way as Willie began to choke, causing him to vomit. This caused a chain reaction of vomiting throughout the entire lunchroom.

"No more milk through the nose," Maggie scolded.

In the rearview mirror, Rocket smiled, happy now that he and Jimmy had become legends at Quinnipiac Day Camp.

"Rocket, didn't you get into trouble tying up Mrs. Murphy?" I said as we drove to Bella Vista.

"I wanted to show her the new knot I learned." As a Cub Scout, Rocket had a fondness for knots. Somehow, the hapless camp instructor allowed an 8-year-old to demonstrate his latest discovery, the boa knot. Once restrained, Rocket and a few other mischievous 8-year-olds released all the small pets in the camp, which included three turtles, one long eared rabbit, and two iguanas.

"I'm still hearing about that little stunt," Maggie lamented. "They never found one of those iguanas."

I turned to look at Rocket and knew mayhem and chaos would follow him wherever he went. I pulled up to the Bella Vista construction site.

"Wow, we're going inside?" Rocket said as he strained against his seatbelt to see. His eyes widened in delight. Just like most men, dirt and power tools were Rocket's drug of choice.

"I called Henry this morning to ask about a tour of Bella Vista. He seemed more than happy to give me the grand tour," Maggie said. The idea of seeing Henry so soon after Biddle concerned me. Did he go to Biddle's apartment looking for the piece of concrete and ply him with alcohol?

Maggie and I both suspected the chunk of concrete Biddle gave me came from Bella Vista. She found the last salary Biddle received came from the construction company currently building the residential complex. He'd been unemployed ever since. Biddle felt the piece of concrete was important. Did Henry?

After parking the car, we headed to the front gate where we first encountered Biddle. Henry stood at the gate now, smiling back at us, warm and inviting. He didn't appear to be a scheming manipulator. I walked toward him with trepidation, and I sensed the same thing radiating off of Maggie. Rocket appeared oblivious of our concerns, because all he saw was dirt and bulldozers.

"Finally, I've got you here," Henry said, his slickness making me edgy. "You won't leave until I have you into one of my houses."

"That's what I'm here for," Maggie said, producing a hundred-watt smile. I mastered only twenty-five watt.

Henry guided us to the spacious doublewide trailer, decked out in green awnings, and two large outdoor flower pots. The inside had office space for two sales representatives, a small conference room, and a large office for Henry. He introduced us to harried salespeople, busy with clients of their own.

"The team is busy, so I'll be your tour guide today," Henry said. I tried not to like him, to find some hint of evil in his eyes or a turn of words which might reveal his true nature. I couldn't. His friendly, warm manner put all at ease around him. He gave us the glossy brochures and an impressive advertising package. Obvious to anyone around him, Henry's passion for Bella Vista radiated from him. What threw me was his attention to Rocket, who he included in every conversation, never once ignoring his presence and his importance. Bella Vista planned to be a family-oriented community. Nothing spelled family like eight-year-old boys.

"Wouldn't you like to live here, young man?" Henry said to Rocket. To my surprise, Rocket nodded and put on the biggest disingenuous smile I'd ever seen.

"Rocket can tell his dad how wonderful Bella Vista is," Maggie said. Her eager smile mirrored that of her son.

"It will be a magnificent community," Henry said proudly.

"Will you and Eloise live here after you're married?" I interjected into Henry's sale pitch and Henry noticeably stiffened.

"I guess my house," he said, his discomfort palpable.

I pushed.

"The wedding is days away. What are your plans exactly? Eloise seemed to be caught up in the wedding and hadn't talked about anything else," I said.

"She wants the wedding to be perfect. I promised her that much," Henry said with a forced smile.

"When this is finished, you'll move on to something else, no doubt," Maggie said. We stood in the kitchen of one of the model houses. Maggie checked out the appliances as if she actually thought about buying one of Henry's cookie cutter homes.

"There is always a new project. Though the market is pretty tight now and new construction has slowed. Bella Vista is my priority. I have a lot invested in her success. I won't take on any new projects until she's off the ground and running the way I want," Henry said.

We continued on with the tour—Maggie playing the role of the interested party and me asking Henry probing questions about his development. Whatever Henry's shortcomings, he was emotionally and financially invested in making Bella Vista a success. There was an intensity and passion in him I thought was missing when I met him with Eloise.

As the tour began to wind down, Maggie continued to work on Henry. Rocket and I stared at her, amazed at her level of bull. She went on to tell him how marvelous Bella Vista would be to live. She hit all of Henry's self–gratifying buttons. The schmooze-fest went on and on until I thought I'd barf from the sugar overload. I sighed in relief when we finished and Henry walked us back to his office. Maggie took Henry's hand in both of hers, beamed up at him with her baby blues, and I knew whatever she was up to was about to happen. Here it comes, I thought.

"Can I ask one little, tiny favor of you?" she said, her voice coquettish.

"Of course, anything. You've been wonderful with Eloise," he said, sounding almost apologetic.

"Well, my son…," Maggie said, grabbing Rocket in a hug, "loves trucks, and cranes, and anything that digs."

Henry gave Rocket an appreciative glance. Rocket returned a weak smile and a thumbs-up.

"The thing is I wonder… I know it's too much trouble," Maggie said coyly.

"Anything," Henry said.

"Rocket wants to visit the construction site," she blurted out. "I'll take a few pictures he can take to camp tomorrow and show off,"

Maggie said. Rocket nodded vigorously as if someone had turned on his happy switch. Henry stared at them both, uncertain. I took my cue to help push him along. I stood next to him and whispered.

"The thing is, Henry, Rocket isn't popular at camp. He's small for his size and the kids kinda pick on him. This would make him awfully cool."

"Well, I'm not sure... the insurance, you know and liability," a wary Henry said.

"Can I put on a hard hat?" Rocket said enthusiastically.

Henry stared down at the small boy, unaware of his manipulation by more than one Swift. Rocket might have been interested in touring the construction site at Bella Vista, but I was sure the idea didn't exist until his mother put the notion into his little head.

"Come on, Henry, how would a quick visit hurt? A few minutes in front of a truck, snap, snap, take a picture, it's done. You'd make a small boy happy and the star of camp," I said, encouraging this deception. Henry thought for a moment, staring into Rocket's blue eyes and wavered. He reluctantly agreed. As if on cue, Rocket displayed his happiness by jumping up and down.

Henry took us out to the construction site and introduced us to one of his foreman, a pleasantly looking man named Bill. He gave everyone a hard hat and took us on a tour of Bella Vista's construction site. We stood in the area of almost completed houses. Maggie took pictures, and Rocket posed. He posed in front of men putting on siding, posed in front of a large dump truck, posed with a two men hauling tarring material, and posed with a brick in front of a pile of bricks. When they headed for an area not fully constructed, I begged off. Henry did the same. His expensive loafers and tailored suit wouldn't appreciate mucking through the dirt. We watched Maggie and the foreman trail after a happy Rocket.

"This is sweet of you, Henry. Rocket will be the star of the Quinnipiac Day Camp," I said, hoping to make small talk.

"He seems like a great kid," he said. I had to agree that Rocket played his role perfectly.

"Were you thinking about having kids soon?" The question flustered Henry for a moment before he packed on a tight smile.

"I'm just handling the idea of getting married. One step at a time," he said.

"Things happen," I said.

"There is a lot on my plate. Bella Vista is my baby now. Having children will have to wait," he said, his tone turned cool.

"It's a pretty big baby. I don't envy you," I said.

"Bella Vista will succeed. People will want to live here. I've poured everything in it and failure is not an option I can live with," he said, scanning the finished and unfinished houses that stood before us.

"It's a grand endeavor. You're responsible for so much. I don't think I could do it," I confessed, and this drew him back to me, focused and determined.

"Don't be surprised about what you might do if you want something bad enough," he said.

I tried to read him. Was he still the Prince Charming of Eloise's dreams? Did he do anything to Biddle? No doubt, the man had secrets. Just when I thought I had an idea about who he was, my certainty slipped away as easy as Henry's quick smile.

"Auntie O!" Rocket came running toward me, covered in dirt like a Tasmanian Dirt Devil. He carried the hard hat given to him by Henry, covered with signatures. Somehow, he'd gotten some of the workers to autograph the hat. I guessed to Rocket, they were better than rock stars.

"Say thank you to Mr. Duschumel," Maggie said, following behind her son.

Rocket thanked Henry before we all left. It was an admirable thing for him to do despite what I thought he might have done to Biddle, if he did anything at all. As we drove away from the construction site, Henry stood surrounded by what appeared to be his only passion.

chapter 24

ROCKET'S JUNIOR SUPER spy duties were over. When the tour ended, we took him home, where Maggie bagged and tagged the clothing he'd worn at the Bella Vista construction site. She printed out pictures she'd taken of him and the various places they'd toured. He came away with samples of his own, shoved into his pocket. The kid could put the Mars land rover to shame. Maggie rewarded him with his favorite lunch, chili hot dogs and a root beer soda. While he ate, Maggie finished bagging the last of the items we collected from Bella Vista to place in my car. I called Jake Nordmeyer and arranged to drop off the samples.

Sometimes I caught her staring at her son as if she were both amazed and frightened for him. I understood her guilt over using him so blatantly to get the samples from Bella Vista. I thought the idea ingenious, but I didn't need to worry about my child's moral character. Rocket, oblivious of this scrutiny, took the trip to Bella Vista as a game. He had fun, played in the dirt, and had left the moral ambiguity to the adults.

"What's wrong?" I asked.

"Nothing," she said much too defensively.

"Rocket had fun." I tried to reassure her.

"God if Roger found out." She shook her head.

"What have you been telling him about all of this?" I asked. Maggie finally looked away from her son. She looked conflicted.

"Roger still thinks all I do for Frank is filing," she said.

That made me pause. For months, Maggie had been helping Frank with his cases and doing a little more than filing. Even if Frank wasn't keen on her doing fieldwork, Maggie was an intricate part of the business. Given a name and a social security number, Maggie could find your life history in an afternoon. If Roger thought Maggie wasn't anything more than a secretary, the truth might give him pause.

"So what about the home office you have?" I asked.

She shrugged.

"He doesn't ask, I don't tell."

"So between your boss and your husband, the only man in your life who knows what you really do is your eight-year-old son?" I said.

We both looked at Rocket, who was draining the last of his soda. His face was a mixture of curiosity and devilment.

"So what about the wedding planner bit? How did you explain that to Roger?"

She shrugged her small shoulders.

"He just thinks it's another interest I've fallen into." Maggie stared back at me, her angelic face ingenuous. I looked at her for a time, amused that covert super agent Cleopatra Jones had nothing on her.

***

I left Maggie's to go to Jake Nordmeyer's in the Bronx, with the samples in my car trunk. Biddle's death still bothered me, and I was determined to find out what really happened to him. Whether Biddle thought of me as his avenging black super agent angel, I wasn't sure. If there were something wrong with Henry's Bella Vista and Biddle knew about it, how far would the developer go to cover the problem up? After our tour at Bella Vista, there was no doubt in my mind the place was Henry's passion; such emotions drove the sanest man to do horrible things.

With Fouke always in the back of my mind, I checked the traffic all the way to the Cross Bronx expressway searching for his bug van. Traffic moved quickly as I reached the northeastern part of the borough and didn't see anything resembling a bug in my rearview window. My paranoia made me wonder if anyone had followed me. I tried to put the thought out of my head as I drove onto Jake's street.

Jake lived alone in a house he'd inherited from his parents, who avoided the New York winters by moving to Florida. He used to teach high school science but quit because children made him nervous. He preferred making a living doing consulting work. As weird as he acted sometimes, Lee thought of him as an excellent engineer and a decent guy. Luckily for me, he was beholden to Lee because of a civil suit he did on Jake's behalf. Lee never told me the details, but the settlement awarded Jake enough money so that he never had to work in the city's school system again.

I parked my car in front of Jake's house and grabbed the samples out of the trunk. Before I had a chance to knock on the door, it opened suddenly. Jake stood in a worn Fordham University tee-shirt, sandals, and Bermuda shorts. He'd grown a beard and still hadn't learned to comb his hair.

"Hi, Jake," I said. He took no notice of me because he seemed preoccupied with the street outside his door.

"Something wrong?" I asked. He shut the door behind me just as I stepped inside the house.

"No, not really, just some neighborhood kids playing pranks." I followed him down a long, narrow hallway into what used to be a living room. Now it resembled a high school science classroom. I guess Jake didn't socialize much unless he socialized with a lot of science geeks.

"They have a thing with my garbage cans, always tossing them or stealing them," he said. Considering my recent garbage escapade, I sympathized.

"No worries, I got something for them," he said, giving me a crooked smile. He pointed to a small monitor sitting on one of his workbenches. It had a view of the front lawn, his garbage cans, and my car.

"Cameras." I couldn't hide my surprise.

"Threats of arrest might deter those delinquents." He sounded proud of his efforts. Perhaps getting out of teaching had been a smart idea.

"I guess you've got to have a hobby," I said, a little wary of Jake's enthusiasm.

"What do you have for me?" Jake eyed the large bag and photographs I laid on the table.

"We think there is something wrong with the concrete," I said. Maggie had carefully labeled everything and Jake seemed to appreciate her efforts, one control freak to another. He took out a sample and pieces crumbled in his fingertips.

"Where did you get this?" he said.

"From a new housing development on Long Island," I said. He turned to me, the amusement on his face gone.

"Homes?" he asked, sounding curious.

I nodded.

"How many?"

"Twenty five, possibly more. I was there this morning, and most are already completed."

"Most," he said and zipped the bag closed.

I nodded. His silence lingered too long for my liking, and I began to worry.

"What!" I yelled.

"Do you want suspicion or facts?" Jake said with practiced condescension I'm sure his former students didn't appreciate.

Annoyed, I said, "You must confuse me with Lee. I'm not a lawyer so give me an educated guess." From the frown he gave me, you'd thought I'd insulted his mother.

"Educated guess," he said, his indignation blatant.

"Come on, Jake, give me something," I pleaded but the damage was already done.

He laughed mockingly.

"How soon then?" I asked.

"A week, maybe." He put the last of the samples in various boxes.

"I need the results sooner," I insisted.

He laughed again.

I folded my arms and glared at him.

"You're sure not like her," he said, shaking his head.

"Who?" The only common bond we shared was Lee.

"His ex-wife, Julia," he said, his eyes giving me a quick once over.

At the mention of Julia's name, my annoyance turned a little darker. His relationship with Lee began at a time when he was still married to Julia, hence the opportunity to compare. Bad enough I thought Lee compared me to her, now Jake. Did I want to hear his play by play? Sure, why not.

"Yeah, different in what way, Jake?" I said tightly.

"Just…different." He sounded apologetic as he picked up the shift in my mood.

"I repeat, how?"

"Different…" a nervous Jake said. "…pardon the pun, as night and day."

I didn't like his pun or the comparison to blue-eyed and blonde Julia.

The photographs I brought sat on a worktable and I grabbed the one of Rocket covered in dirt holding a brick. I showed the photograph to Jake.

"Say hello to my little friend," I said, in a bad imitation of Al Pacino's character, Tony Montana, from *Scarface*. "I know an eight-year-old who would love to visit this place."

Jake stared at the photograph and frowned.

"Okay, okay…all the time she was married to Lee I could never read her. She was like a sphinx, cool as a cucumber. Five minutes after I first met you, I knew you liked me," he said with a failing smile.

"I like you?" My tone was dubious.

Jake struggled to hold his grin.

"You've got two days Jake, or I'll bring Rocket by for a visit," I said, scanning the room filled with equipment that looked expensive.

"Rocket!" he said as if Rocket's name explained everything.

"How about three, sooner if I can," he offered. Three days sounded better than a week, I thought.

"Thank you, Jake," I said, smiling. There was a little remorse about threatening Jake with a visit from Rocket, but not much. My remorse morphed into annoyance when I remembered I had to go to Eloise's bachelorette party. I wanted an evening with Lee and no bride, bridesmaids, slutty best friends, or stalkers.

When I stepped outside of Jake's house, my annoyance went to full on aggravation at the sight of Zeno standing next to my car.

"Hey there, Oprah," he said with a malicious grin.

"What do you want?" I said. Zeno stepped in front of my car door when I pushed my remote.

"You weren't friendly before, so I figure I'd try again," he said.

"You followed me?"

"Almost lost you on the Cross Island Parkway, Oprah." He sounded proud of himself.

"Stop calling me Oprah," I said. "Is that the only other black person you know?"

Zeno's smile faded like ice on a skillet, quick and angry.

"You got some mouth on you. Anyone ever tried to shut you up?" Zeno's black eyes burned into me, his intent clear and threatening.

"What do you want?" I said, remembering Maggie's warning.

"I want what you know." He took a step toward me. When I tried to reach for the car door handle, he grabbed me by the forearm, his fingers squeezing hard. I winced.

"Let go." I tried to get free of him. He jerked me hard to face him and slammed me against my car almost knocking the wind out of me. I tried to push him away, but he grabbed me by the throat.

"Got your attention now," he whispered, his breath hot on my face. Tears ran down my face as his grip tightened. I nodded because I couldn't speak.

"Good," he said, his smile returning. "Whatever you are gonna get on this Henry guy, you're going to tell me before you even think about telling my Auntie V. It's worth a lot to her, but it's worth a lot more to me."

He released his grip, and I rubbed my throat. I glared at him angry and furious, but I said nothing.

"I plan to get a payday from this," he said, sounding proud.

It dawned on me what Zeno wanted.

"You're going to blackmail Mrs. Verde?" I asked in disbelief.

His grinned widened.

"Smart too." Zeno shook his head. "See if you could just keep that mouth of yours shut. That woman wants this wedding stopped one way or another, and I aim to please. I rather she pays me than you."

"You could talk to Henry, the way you just talked to me." I rubbed my throat.

"Yeah, but Eloise might find out and Auntie V insists Eloise stay happy," he said. "Anyway I got you, don't I, sweetheart?" He gave me a lecherous smirk. His eyes went dark again, and I nodded.

"I'll keep in touch." He stepped away and headed toward his car. "Hey, maybe when this is over, we can go have a drink. I'm a great guy." He put his hand on his heart, grinned, and got into his car.

I waited until his car turned the corner down the block. I rubbed my neck and I headed back to Jake's front door. I'd never been so happy that someone else's paranoia was going to help me deal with Apolo Zeno. I hoped Jake's camera caught his good side.

chapter 25

LUCKY'S TEXAS BAR and Grill in Bayside, Queens wasn't what I had in mind when I thought of a bachelorette party. The bar's specialty was barbecue, cold beer, and ten different flavored margaritas. I wasn't expecting Chippendale dancers, but God help me, not country and western. I sat in a small, stinky leatherette booth dumbfounded by the New Yorkers and transplanted southerners who frequented the place. Who would have guessed Nashville was alive and well in New York City? What was next, NASCAR in the Bronx at Yankee Stadium? The music was loud and angst ridden about somebody breaking somebody's heart or maybe someone kicking somebody's dog. I couldn't tell. The decor and memorabilia on the walls hinted at someone cleaning out a deluxe double wide trailer and pickup truck.

The bachelorette party consisted of Maggie, Jenny, Eloise, two hapless bridesmaids, and me. The other bridesmaids were missing in action, each supplying Eloise with believable excuses, which didn't incur her wrath. We were a sorry group of women, surrounded by people who genuinely wanted to be there. The night consisted of drinking watered down margaritas made with cheap tequila, telling Eloise how lovely she looked and how great the wedding will be. Lying kept everyone happy.

Every now and then, Jenny would encourage everyone to get up and do some convoluted dance which required you to form a chorus line and dance like an idiot. I told her I didn't know how to dance. This was a lie, of course, but she wasn't going to call me on it. Maggie made her excuses as well and sat most of the night sipping on a virgin blueberry margarita that looked like window cleaner.

"Who picked this place?" I yelled over the music into Maggie's ear.

"Eloise, she's a fan," she said. We stared out at the dance floor as the bridal party tried their hand or at least their feet at line dancing. I shook my head.

"Well you have me until ten o'clock, and I'm out of here," I said. A disappointed Maggie's brows knitted.

"Come on, O. I don't go out much. I had Rocket and his friends most of the afternoon, and I need some adult activity," she whined.

I gave her an unsympathetic smile.

"At eleven-thirty, I expect to be home. At eleven forty-five, I expect to be in bed with Lee doing adult activity."

"You scheduled your sex?" Maggie giggled.

"No," I said. This insult coming from a woman who had to work around Rocket's Cub Scout troop meetings and Roger's bowling night.

"You have to schedule your sex?" a voice from behind me said. Jenny leaned over the booth.

I groaned. A waiter happened to pass by, and I stopped him to order.

"We have, lime, strawberry, raspberry..." I held up a hand to stop him before he went through all fifty favors. I didn't have time.

"Take out the margarita and just give me the tequila," I said. He took the order and left. Jenny sat by me and collected a yellowish margarita she'd been drinking.

"Is Eloise having a good time?" Maggie asked. Eloise danced between her hapless bridesmaids.

"She's as happy as a dog with a bone," Jenny said in a horrible southern accent.

"Henry being the bone, of course," Maggie said. Jenny shrugged and sipped her drink.

"You've known Eloise a long time?" I asked.

"Since kindergarten, two peas in a pod," Jenny said, crossing her fingers. A lively song came on the jukebox, and she started bouncing to the beat while she sipped her drink.

"You were from the old neighborhood?" I asked.

Jenny sipped and nodded.

"When did the family move out to the Island?" Maggie said.

"When Eloise was about ten. Mr. Verde made enough money to move out of Brooklyn."

"You haven't seen Eloise since she was a kid and now you're two peas in a pod?" I said not hiding my surprise.

"Girlfriends forever," Jenny said in mock salute.

Maggie and I glanced at each other.

"How did you two hook back up?" Maggie asked.

"You two ask a lot of questions," Jenny said, eyeing us both.

"Just curious," Maggie said with a perfected playful smile. Another song came on, and the music seemed to distract Jenny. Eloise and one of the bridesmaids waved her over to the dance floor. She took a long sip of her yellowish drink before getting up to join them.

"Come on, ladies, dance." She did a small dance in front of the booth. This got a few of the bar's male patrons' attention. I guessed that was the point.

"I don't know how to do line dancing," Maggie said meekly. Jenny turned to me.

I shook my head.

"I'm saving my energy for later," I said smugly.

Jenny giggled and shimmed away.

The girls danced to another song before they returned to our table. A giddy Eloise ordered another round of drinks and food. Immediately the topic of the conversation went to the wedding and the preparations. Eloise wore a silly hat that read "Bride to Be." Jenny had given her a plastic wand which Eloise waved dangerously as she threw out demands. As the night wore on, she got louder as the alcohol lessened her inhibitions.

"I don't feel so well," she said and wavered at bit. She grabbed her stomach and then her mouth.

"Oh no," Jenny yelled and grabbed her by the arm and pulled her out of the booth. Maggie quickly followed as Eloise and Jenny dashed to the bathroom. The bridesmaids, I labeled Number one and Number Two because I couldn't remember their names, stared in awe.

"Should we go help?" Number One said, her eyes straining through the crowd.

"Jenny can handle it," I said and sipped my tequila. Bridesmaid Number Two made a face.

"You've known Jenny long?" I asked.

Bridesmaid Number Two shook her head no.

"Melissa, from accounting, told me Jenny hadn't seen Eloise in years. A couple of months ago she came around and started working for the old lady. Then all of sudden, Eloise is engaged, and everything is topsy-turvy," Bridesmaid Number One said.

"So they hadn't seen each before a few months ago?" I said. Both women nodded.

"She shows up. Tommy gets arrested. Eloise starts back talking to her mom, which she never did, and now she's marrying some guy who just showed up," a confused Bridesmaid Number One said.

"He's back, you know," Bridesmaid Number One said.

"I know," I said.

"Mrs. Verde took him back, just like that." She snapped her fingers.

"She says all is forgiven," Bridesmaid Number Two said.

"That's a first," Bridesmaid Number One said snidely.

"Well, Tommy always helped her with her church thing," Bridesmaid Number Two said.

"The one Mrs. Verde is restoring in Brooklyn?" I asked.

Bridesmaid Number Two rolled her eyes.

"The way Tommy tells it, Mrs. Verde is building them a new one. He used to go to Brooklyn all the time fixing everything. Before he left, he complained the woman wouldn't even replaced the sprinkler system in one of the greenhouses, but she puts in a new fountain at the church in Brooklyn," Bridesmaid Number Two said.

"Tommy did the tile work in the bathrooms so they could be just like the Vatican," Bridesmaid Number One said.

"Please don't repeat what we said, please. Mrs. Verde is a wonderful boss, honestly," she said sheepishly.

"Your secret is safe with me. So let me get this straight. Jenny comes around the nursery a couple of months ago, works for Mrs. Verde for a hot minute, and leaves. Then Mr. Tall, Dark, and Handsome shows up and gets busy with Eloise," I said.

A laugh escaped from Bridesmaid Number Two, and she covered her mouth in embarrassment. "Sorry, it's just...what is that about? He's like Brad Pitt and Eloise is...."

"Eloise is Eloise," I said not missing her point.

"He didn't look at me twice," Bridesmaid Number One said, and I had to admit she was attractive.

"What about Jenny?" I was searching for a connection. They both shook their heads.

"I don't think she likes him much," Bridesmaid Number One said. "She's always saying something catty about him. How stuck up he is and how he thinks he is too good for anybody."

Our conversation about Jenny died with her return from the bathroom. Maggie and a pale Eloise were close behind. The rest of the evening didn't improve as Eloise possibly sensing this wasn't the girls night out she'd envisioned. Even Maggie got a little testy. Eloise insisted she dance with some drunken stranger who'd come to our table trying to pick one of us up.

"Come on, it would be funny," Eloise said with her own embarrassing moment still fresh in everyone's mind. Maggie refused. Eloise turned my way for a hot minute, but I gave her a *'don't even ask me'* look. Bridesmaid Number One and Two started making eye contact with the ceiling. When Jenny happily volunteered, she turned the awkward moment into provocative teasing. She handled the drunk and his friends with the aplomb of a master of ceremony. She laughed, wiggled, and jiggled her way into their hearts or someplace further south. She left them to want more as she returned to the table out of breath and laughing.

"Jenny has a way with people," Eloise said. I doubted her sincerity.

I noticed a growing resentment had started to emerge between the women. Maggie sensed the tension as well. She kept on glancing my way every time Eloise made a partially veiled insult aimed at Jenny's sometime flirtatious behavior. Jenny reciprocated with hits of her own aiming at Eloise's weight and dowdiness. This playful banter between two friends grew. When they tired of sniping at each other, they aimed their cattiness at Bridesmaid Number One and Two.

"Come on, Odessa, lighten up and have a good time," Eloise bellowed. She waved her wand at me. In what universe was being trapped in a country and western nightmare with two of the most disagreeable women I've ever met consisting of a good time?

The clock over the bar read ten-fifteen. Maggie leaned over to me and whispered in my ear. "You can't leave me here with these women."

I laughed.

"Oh, yes I can." I pulled out my cell phone and dialed home. Lee picked up on the second ring. I heard the television in the background.

"Hey, how's the party?" he said.

"I'm leaving in about ten minutes, so turn off the television and change the sheets," I said.

"The Knicks are going into double overtime; let me think about it," he said.

"I don't think the Knicks will keep you warm tonight," I said before disconnecting. Everyone at the table stared at me. I gave them a lecherous smile and stood up.

"Thanks, Eloise. It's been fun," I said and slipped out of the booth.

"You can't leave now," a petulant Eloise commanded. She waved the wand at me.

"If she's leaving, I'm going," a happy bridesmaid Number Two said.

"A half an hour more, O." Maggie's baby blue eyes pleaded. They had no effect on me.

"Sorry, as much fun as I'm having, I've got to go." I grinned at Eloise.

"She scheduled sex with her boyfriend," Jenny said with a smirk.

"Yes, indeed I have, and it will be glorious, head-banging sex." I said, ignoring Jenny's snipe at me.

Maggie groaned. Bridesmaids One and Two giggled.

"But this is my night," Eloise whined.

"In about half an hour, it will be mine. Goodnight, ladies." I waved goodbye and left the bar with a spring in my step and a grin in my heart.

I got in my car and headed for the Van Wyck Expressway back home. Traffic was light for a Thursday night, and I merged onto the highway with the memory of the women at Lucky's fading fast. I turned on the radio and found a classic R&B station. I needed to get the honky-tonk rhythm out of my head. I cut into a vintage Gladys Knight's song, and I hummed along, promising never to drink tequila mixed with fruit again. So preoccupied with the song, Lee, and sex I never saw the van come up from behind me.

I looked in my side view mirror as the van approached. The huge cockroach on the hood was a dead giveaway that I was in trouble. Driving in the far lane by the center guardrail, I tried to speed up. The van sped up, inching its way closer. I wanted to get off the expressway onto a side street, but I was too far over to cut across oncoming traffic. For a half a mile, our speed increased. I slipped into a gap in traffic and recklessly cut across two lanes with horns blaring angrily at me.

Gladys left and was replaced by the Temptations, singing something about papa being a rolling stone.

My angle for the next exit was off about ten degrees, and I missed it. Driving at the speed I was on the express lane shoulder was a disaster waiting to happen. The van drove in the right lane, and it wouldn't let me back into the lane. I had nowhere to go but into a stone overpass looming ahead. I thought I had enough space to stop, but I wasn't sure. I stepped hard on the brakes, griped the wheel, and closed my eyes. I had heard the crunch before I felt my three-year-old Volvo's right front end smashed and scrape along the stone overpass. My head hit the side window and my left hand smacked hard into the steering wheel. The airbag deployed, pushing me hard back into the seat before the car came to a stop. Something wet trickled down my head and my ears rang.

I was alive and thanked God and Volvo for making a damn good car. I didn't have time to be relieved because my driver's side window shattered and glass exploded around me. Through the window, a dark figure held a tire iron.

chapter 26

FLASHING POLICE CARS, the odd aroma of roses, and a vague image of a black-clad figure running away swirled in my muddled memory about the crash. My head throbbed, and my hand hurt. I appreciated the police and the emergency services workers as they helped me out of my damaged car. When I sat on a gurney in the back of an ambulance, an EMS worker took care of the small cuts on my face, a bruise on my forehead, and my left wrist. Through my foggy haze, flashing lights illuminated the police officers taking statements from people who had stopped to help. The whole ordeal was surreal.

My last adventure in an ambulance came when I got fired from my advertising job in Manhattan. On the subway ride home, I got caught in a tunnel fire, leaving me with minor smoke inhalation. The second time around didn't improve my appreciation of riding in ambulances. My head hurt and my face burned from the antiseptic used by the EMS worker. His constant reassurance turned annoying after the twelfth time, and the tequila in my stomach wanted out.

Two hours in the emergency room didn't improve my mood, but the Vicodin helped nicely. Lee came in ten minutes after I'd arrived, and the sight of him allowed me to take the real first deep breath since the accident. He looked both half-terrified and relieved at the sight of me. He stayed by my side the entire time, listened to the instructions from the doctor about my care, and promised him I'd follow them.

I left the ER after being scanned, probed, and medicated. They taped my wrist and gave me a prescription for pain.

I didn't realize how tired I was until I got home. Lee ushered me up to bed and the nice, clean sheets beneath me made me smile. The evening could have ended better. I appreciated being alive and home with Lee. His concern didn't fade, though. He started making men noises about catching Fouke, gun control, and capital punishment. He wanted to squash the Bug King. I would have found his concern very sexy, if my body didn't hurt so much. He calmed down enough to tuck me into bed and sleep by my side without hurting me.

I slept through much of the morning. Lee stayed by my side, taking care of me. When my head finally cleared the by the afternoon, I didn't expect to hear arguing coming from downstairs. The noise seeped into my dream and stirred me awake. The Vicodin had worn off, and the night of the accident came roaring back—pain, the crash, and the man in black. There was a thickness in my head I couldn't shake. The sound of arguing cut through like a knife. I inched my way out of bed like an old woman, and I moaned like one. When I reached the top of the stairs, I heard familiar voices.

"She needs to come home," Candace said, her voice hot and demanding.

"She is home," an indignant Lee said. By the strain in his voice, he struggled to keep control.

"The maniac tried to kill her, and she's not safe," Candace shot back.

I thought about joining them, but I didn't. My sister and my boyfriend needed their alone time and I preferred not being their referee.

"How will she be safe with you? Do you plan to scowl at Fouke? That seems to be your weapon of choice," Lee said, his anger finally showing.

Whoa!

"What did you say?"

I almost squealed with delight at the surprise in her voice.

"If I had a wound for every dirty look you've given me, you would be doing twenty to life," Lee said. "Go home, Candace. I only called you because you're her sister. Now if you can't help, go home."

He had always shown her deference, ignored her bad moods and slights toward him. He made every effort to connect with her even when she refused him at every turn. This Lee didn't care what Candace thought.

"She's my—" Candace began.

"And you are not the only one who loves her. I love her, too. I understand it's impossible for you to believe me, being the evil white devil," Lee said.

Double whoa!

"White? You could be Casper for all I care," she snapped back. "It's just you're not—"

"Davis," he bit back. "You know he's married."

Candace laughed.

"Yeah, and your first marriage was permanent," she said with too much satisfaction.

There was a long moment of silence as if Lee were gathering his thoughts or contemplating murder.

"Go home, Candace." The fight had drained from his voice.

"I love her, too, you know," Candace said, her tone finally softening.

"I know she knows, and she'll call you the moment she can." Lee sounded whipped.

"Okay...okay, I'm going," she said. "Next time I'm bringing Aunt Renne."

The door slammed behind her.

"You can come down now," Lee said. He peered up from the first floor.

I took the steps slowly, and he met me halfway. He kissed me gently on the lips as if I might break.

"Weapon of choice?" I teased. "Evil white devil."

"If she brings your Aunt Renne next time, I'm screwed," he said.

"I'll call Candace," I promised, and he truly seemed relieved.

"I'm sure this will set me back a hundred brownie points with her," he said, walking me toward the kitchen.

"Don't worry, honey, I will always have the high score," I said. Hearing Candace, I suddenly remembered I'd forgotten to call Frank about stopping his investigation on Leon. I had second thoughts about it now. A couple of days with Frank harassing her should mellow her out about Lee. One irritating overweight white devil trumped a cute one.

Happily, Lee spent the rest of the morning away from work pampering me. I can say without a doubt the man can't cook to save his life, but I didn't love him for his cooking. Over bad eggs and burnt toast, I talked about the accident, trying to remember more details, but everything happened too fast.

After my incident, Lee made two important phone calls. First, he called the police in the hope they would take Fouke's apprehension more seriously. Afterward, he called Maggie. She wanted to come to the hospital, but Lee convinced her not too. It took a lot of convincing. He only called Candace when I was already home in my bed doped up with medication. Considering my sister's most recent response, I'm sure Lee wished he had a little medication of his own.

When Maggie came over later that morning, I felt a lot better. My wrist didn't hurt too bad, but my head still ached. I appreciated her gentle hugs and concern.

"I'm going to do something about Fouke," she swore.

"Frank's on the case," I said.

"I told him what happened, and he's truly upset, O. He said Fouke has fallen off the face of the earth," she said.

"Well, he was on the Grand Central Parkway two nights ago. He's like a bug ninja," I said.

"Don't worry, we'll find him." Maggie crossed her arms and stood before me like an angry sprite. I wanted to believe her.

"I did find out more about Drummond," she said.

"Who's Drummond?" Lee asked.

"He works as a building inspector for the county," she said. "I found his name on some of the shredded reports."

"A building inspector shredding reports... what a novel idea," Lee mocked.

"Is he connected to Henry?" I asked. Before she could answer, the doorbell rang. Lee got up and went to the door. He reappeared in the kitchen with a dozen perfect red roses.

"They're beautiful," Maggie said, fawning over the bouquet in his arms.

"You checked it for rodents?" I asked Lee cautiously.

"No rodents. I know where these came from," he said. I sat in one of the kitchen chairs, and he placed them on my lap. I read the card. Aaron sent roses with apologies and best wishes. The aroma of the roses was intoxicating. I called Aaron.

"They're beautiful, Aaron. Thank you," I said.

"You welcome, darling. I'm just sorry my mess has spilled on to you," he said warmly.

"Next time pick clients with not-so-crazy spouses," I said, and he laughed.

"Truth be told, I would have pegged Mrs. Fouke for the crazy one. The divorce got ugly. She'd gone a little nutty after finding out Horace had an affair," he said.

As his words sank in, something struck me as odd. I pushed the speaker button on the kitchen phone.

"What about Horace? The man attacked me," I said.

"To be honest the only time he'd done anything as crazy was at the restaurant. She owned half his business anyway, but she wanted the rest. Nothing like a woman scorned. Perhaps it drove him over the edge," Aaron said with a hint of regret in his voice.

"Maybe you had the wrong client," Maggie said, whose interest in the conversation perked up.

"She came by the restaurant insisting I press charges against him. She feared for her safety. She was more than pushy about it," I said as my mind whirled around the facts.

"I don't care about Mrs. Fouke. It's Mr. Fouke who needs to be stopped," Lee interjected.

"Frank can't find him," Maggie said.

"Police can't either," I said.

"So he's a sneaky guy," Lee said.

"I wouldn't exactly categorize him as sneaky. To be honest, Fouke was good with bugs, but his wife ran the business. Personally, I thought he was afraid of her," Aaron said.

"Maybe he's having a nervous breakdown," Maggie said.

"Did he say anything to you that night?" Aaron asked. I said no. He hadn't said anything to me the other times, except for the meeting in the back of the Blue Moon, when Bebe chased him off. I recalled how he stood unmasked and wanted to say something to me before he ran. Then memories of the accident and the black-clad assailant popped into my head. The recollection made me dizzy, but the image of someone dressed in black and smelling of roses, running away was clear. I turned at Maggie who, by the look on her face, was already drawing conclusions of her own.

"Everyone would assume Mr. Fouke has lost his marbles. The attack at the restaurant was unfortunate but he'd been drinking since the divorce proceedings. As his first offense, he might have gotten community service..." Aaron's voice trailed off. He was coming to a similar conclusion.

"With attempts on Odessa's life, there would be real jail time to face," Maggie said.

"What are you saying?" Lee asked.

We all stared at each other. I still held Aaron's roses and the fragrance filled the room. The aroma reminded me of the crash. The familiar scent lingered long after Fouke had gone. At the tip of my memory, I had a thought, which wouldn't emerge.

"Dessa," Lee said, coming close and wrapping an arm around me. I barely even noticed, the scent of flowers triggering something. It was the same fragrance I remembered from the night of the crash but—perfume.

"At the car crash, I smelled perfume," I said.

"Horace Fouke wears perfume?" Aaron said in surprise.

"No, silly, but I bet Mrs. Fouke does. I also know where Mr. Fouke could be," Maggie said.

I'd already made the humongous leap of clues, which pointed to a self-serving Mrs. Fouke. I didn't have a clue as to where Horace was.

"Excuse me," Lee said.

"Frank said Horace had fallen off the earth. He's not at work, not using his credit cards, and has not been seen by anyone except supposedly, Odessa," Maggie said, pointing at me.

"Except for the time Bebe chased him, I haven't seen him. He's been in that damn bug mobile," I said.

"Which belongs to the business, which Mrs. Fouke has access to," Aaron added.

"You can't be serious," Lee said in surprise.

"It's a convoluted way of getting rid of her husband and gaining full access to the business. He'll be too busy dealing with his new buddy in the shower and dropping his soap to worry about his profit margin," I said.

"What new buddy?" a clueless Maggie asked.

I groaned at Maggie's naïveté.

"Where is he?" Lee demanded. We all turned to her.

"Where is the last place you'd look?" she said.

"Under my bed," I replied.

"Who is he afraid of more than you?" she said. I thought about it for a hot minute.

I smiled at her and said, "The Bug Queen."

chapter 27

"No," Lee said.

"Give me your car keys." I held out my hand. He shoved them into his front jeans pocket. As fun as getting them out of his pocket might be, I preferred him to cooperate.

"No," he said.

I stood in disbelief. Lee rarely said no to me. Yet, he'd already put one Wilkes woman in her place today; why not go for a record?

"Fine, Maggie will take me," I said.

Maggie had a terrified *I don't want to be in the middle of this* face.

"Lee might be right, O," she began, but I held up a finger to stop her. I was tired of people jumping ship on me.

"She's not taking you anywhere," he said with certainty. He was angry, and so was I. I recognized the universal signs of being extremely pissed off. My hands were on my hips. My incredulous glare was perfect, and I was up in Lee's face.

"You just got out of the hospital," he said.

I mockingly gave myself a pat down.

"I have all my body parts," I said. He laughed and pointed at my head.

"You're missing one if you think I'm letting you anywhere near her."

Maggie tried to back away into the living room. I turned and glared at her.

"Stay," I commanded, and she stopped.

"If you're right, Mrs. Fouke is trying to kill you, and you think she's hiding her husband at her house. Do you think it's a good idea to go over there and talk to her? It's not happening. We'll call the police," he said, his voice rising. If there was a button for Lee's anger, I was about to jump on it.

"Let me?" My eyes widened in incredulity. "The last man I had to ask to go anywhere was my father, and trust me, honey, you are not him."

"Don't want to be him. Right now, I don't even want to be your friend. I want to be the rational mind in this room who knows this is a disaster waiting to happen," he said, showing a few of the universal signs of his own. We were in each other's faces.

"What should I tell the police? I think Mrs. Fouke is trying to kill me to frame her husband?" I hunched my shoulders mocking confusion. "I was sure because after she slammed me into an overpass, she smelled awfully nice!" I shrieked. This only made my head hurt.

"Does sound weird," Maggie said in a small voice. Lee scowled at her.

"Why did you think I sent Frank after him? Just to help the police?" I said. "I need a little payback."

Without warning, Lee grabbed me by my shoulders, and I thought he might shake me. Perhaps remembering my bruised state, he slightly loosened his hold, but didn't let go.

"The other night scared the living shit out of me when they called me about your accident. Don't you get that? Then I had to tell your sister, which made my day ten times worse," he said, as his anger faded and was replaced with dread.

I sighed and smiled at him.

"Oh, baby, you should be used to this by now," I said, happy he wasn't going to kill me. He released me, exasperated by my thick head, and pulled me into a cautious hug.

"Dessa." My name sounded like a plea, and I empathized with his distress, but he needed a reality check. Maggie insisted my ability to cut through other people's delusional thinking was my superpower.

"Lee, honey, this is me, Odessa Marie Wilkes. I come from a long line of unforgiving women." I smiled at him, and his frown lines deepened. "If I don't deal with Mrs. Fouke, it will fester and come out in bad places and to the wrong people." I gave him a knowing look.

"I'm trying to be serious," Lee said. He rubbed his temple as I wrapped my arms around his neck and kissed him on the cheek.

"You see Maggie over there." I pointed to my friend. She looked like a child caught in the middle of her parents' argument. An exhausted Lee sighed and nodded.

"Maggie is Hershey milk chocolate, delicious, sweet, and every-body loves her," I said, smiling at her. She stood with her red hair tied in a ponytail—wearing jeans and a pink tee-shirt—and as threatening as a cupcake.

"You're coming to a point, aren't you?" a weary Lee said.

"Yes, of course. People like Eloise, Jenny, and Candace are another type of chocolate. They are bitter chocolate, impossible to eat. It's only good when you add the sweetening too them," I said, explaining carefully.

His body relaxed slightly, but not much.

"And which one are you?" he said, the playfulness coming back to his eyes. I leaned in to whisper in his ear.

"Semisweet, of course. Just enough bite to make the chocolate interesting—an acquired taste," I said.

He grinned.

"How do you think this stuff up?" he said.

"I worked in advertising for years," I joked.

Lee took a deep breath and sighed.

"First, I'm going with you," he began, but I shook my head. He nodded in reply. "Second, you will not break any law."

"Federal or state?" I asked.

Lee didn't laugh.

"Third, and most important, the moment we find anything the police can use, we call them. Do you comprehend?" he said slowly, as if I were some imbecile. I nodded slowly because idiots did that.

***

The Foukes' house was a testimony to delusions of grandeur and crude style. The house had columns; I kid you not. *Gone With the Wind* columns, a miniaturized plantation house. The home stood out in a modest Staten Island neighborhood like a middle finger. I guess the Bug King and Queen needed a palatial manor. We sat in Lee's SUV staring up at the place as if it were an attraction at Disneyland.

"God, what an ugly house," Maggie said in wonderment as she peered out the passenger side window.

"Well, if you've seen the Foukes, you'd understand," I said and started to open my car door. Before I could step out, Lee reached over and stopped me.

"What's your plan?" he asked.

"We're here for some compensation," I said.

Lee's eyes narrowed.

"We are?" Maggie said.

"I'd wished you'd worn a suit," I said to Lee, who was dressed too casually in a tee-shirt and jeans.

"Why?" he asked, the mistrust in his eyes again.

"Because you're not dressed like my lawyer. I want Mrs. Fouke to take you seriously," I said.

"I can speak legalese in jeans," he said with a hint of smugness.

"I plan to sue her for damage and mental distress," I said.

"What?" a surprised Maggie said.

"What the hell are you talking about?" Lee said.

I released his hand from me and opened the car door.

"Do you think she'd believe we wanted to talk to her about our mutual misery over her husband? No way. I need her attention, and since she's all about the business, I'll start there," I said, stepping out of the car. Lee quickly followed.

"What are you talking about, Odessa?" He only used my full name when he wanted to let me know he was serious.

"Her husband and business partner tried to kill me not once, but twice in their company van, which holds not only Horace libel, but the business as well," I said, walking up the driveway to Mrs. Fouke's version of Tara on Hudson. Before I could continue, Lee stepped in front of me.

"So you're here to threaten her in the hope she will reveal something?" he asked. I nodded. He closed his eyes, took a deep breath, and stepped aside.

"This might work," he said with some surprise, as we continued up to the front door. I rang the bell.

A surprised Mrs. Fouke answered. The rose perfume I'd remembered at the accident triggered my anger again, but I controlled myself from yanking every strand of hair in her over-coiffed head. At first, she was reluctant to let us in, but I insisted, and stepped inside without waiting for a response.

The Foukes' mini-mansion exterior was antebellum, while the interior looked like a set of one of those 1960s Italian muscle movies with Steve Reeves playing Hercules. Lots of ornate Italian furniture too bulky for the space intended. A white lava rock wall took one entire side of the living room. White polished marble floors and a pristine fireplace left me cold.

"You have a lovely house," Maggie said with not much warmth.

"Who are you?" Mrs. Fouke pointed to Lee and Maggie.

"She's my best friend, and Lee is my boyfriend," I said, only slightly smiling. She regarded them with cold speculation as one of her eyebrow slowly rose.

"He's also my lawyer," I said to level out her eyebrows.

"Lawyer?" she said. Lee pulled out a business card from his wallet and handed it to her.

I walked to what I assumed was the living room and took a seat on a cream-colored tufted couch. Maggie and Lee followed me. Mrs. Fouke made a slow descent to an adjacent chair.

"What's this about?" she asked tentatively.

"The other night, your husband tried to kill Odessa," Lee said, his eyes burrowing in on Mrs. Fouke.

"He did?" Her eyes widened in surprise. "Well you should tell the police this, and perhaps they'll finally do something about him."

"We did, and they will," he said. His demeanor turned chilly.

"It's been upsetting." I made my voice quiver a bit. "I had a medical condition that has returned because of this entire incident with your husband."

As if on cue, Lee put an arm around me.

"Her business has suffered," Maggie said.

"Horace has ruined my life. I've had to deal with the business on my own," Mrs. Fouke said.

"Your business partner terrorized me." I rested my head on Lee's shoulder for effect.

"I have no control over my husband. He's gone insane," Mrs. Fouke said. A twitch formed at the corner of her mouth.

Lee squeezed me tighter. Mrs. Fouke was starting to piss him off.

"Can I use your bathroom?" Maggie asked abruptly. Her words cut through the building tension. Everyone stared at her.

Mrs. Fouke sat silently.

"I have to go, bad lunch." Maggie rubbed her stomach and stood up. Mrs. Fouke hesitated.

"Mrs. Fouke," Maggie said and did a little hop, trying to sell the sense of urgency to Mrs. Fouke.

"Huh....huh...use the one upstairs," she said and pointed up at the stairs behind her.

"Thank you," Maggie said and dashed out of the living room.

"Some people can't eat Indian food," I said, smiling as I watched Maggie sneak down a hallway instead of up the stairs. Lee watched her too, but to his credit, said nothing. An anxious Mrs. Fouke was about to turn around when Lee spoke up.

"The reason why we're here, Mrs. Fouke, is because twice your company van was used to attack my girlfriend, and my client." This pulled Mrs. Fouke's attention back.

"Client?" she said.

"You are currently the co-owner of the business. You are then partially responsible for some of the damages incurred by your ex-husband's use of a company vehicle," Lee said, sounding like the smart lawyer he was.

Mrs. Fouke blinked.

"Her car is wrecked. There are medical issues, of course. Since we don't have your husband to deal with, we'll deal with you." Lee gave her a cursory smile.

"What? No... Horace. He has keys to the company, and the cars," an anxious Mrs. Fouke said.

"Part your company, part your responsibility. You never reported the van stolen, did you?" he said.

A wide-eyed Mrs. Fouke shook her head. "Are you suing me?" she said.

Lee leaned forward as the intensity radiated off him.

"Your ex-husband and current partner tried to commit vehicular manslaughter, which I don't much appreciate," Lee said.

Mrs. Fouke flinched.

"You can't blame me...."

"I can't?" He stood up and glared down at her.

"I'm a victim, too," she cried.

"Did he go after you? No, but for some reason, he went after Odessa."

"Who would believe me if he did? Married to Horace was nothing but abuse. I'm just his wife," she cried, as she tried to squeeze out tears.

"There were police reports, I called and checked. A domestic disturbance is what they call it," Lee said. "To the officers' surprise, they had to save Mr. Fouke from you. There was even a trip to the ER, including several stitches for Horace, but he wouldn't press charges, would he?"

"That's a lie." She nearly spat at him, getting some of her fury back.

"You're right; no one would believe Horace going after you. However, if he attacked Odessa, things would be different, wouldn't it?" He folded his arms and glared at her.

"What are you saying?" a defensive Mrs. Fouke said.

"You needed a better victim," Maggie said, standing in the hallway with a gaunt Horace Fouke.

chapter 28

A FURIOUS LEE'S forearm had Horace pressed hard against the wall. The pressure must have been substantial since Horace acted like a rag doll and appeared as pale as one. He wept like a baby. Maggie and I stood on both sides of Lee, trying to pull him off. I'd never seen him this angry.

"You had a knife to her throat, you drunken son-of-a-bitch," Lee barked.

"It's not his fault, Lee," Maggie said. We both had our arms wrapped around each of his. We had little effect; the man climbed rock walls for fun.

"You could have killed her," Lee said.

"I'm sorry. I'm sorry," Horace said, wheezing out each word. Lee pushed harder.

"He came to the restaurant to say sorry, right?" I gave up on pulling on his arms and grabbed his face and turned it to me. "He wanted to apologize. Of course, I freaked out and didn't let him." I remembered Fouke standing by the Blue Moon dumpster. I mistook his obvious embarrassment as murderous rage. He'd gotten drunk and done a foolish thing.

Fouke tried to nod but Lee restricted his mobility.

"Let go," Maggie begged.

"I'm sure this covers one of those federal laws, or at least a state one, honey. Let the bug man go," I said.

Lee released his hold and stepped away from Horace. The exterminator crumpled into a pile on the floor, gasping for air. I noticed a dark spot growing around his crotch. The man should invest in some adult diapers. Since Fouke wasn't going anywhere, we turned our attention to Mrs. Fouke. From her panicked expression, she needed an adult diaper of her own.

***

The New York City police weren't fans of Mrs. Miriam Fouke. To show their lack of appreciation, they arrested her for threatening me and holding her clueless husband hostage in the basement family room. Somehow, the woman convinced the Bug King she wanted to help him. She told him she would convince me to drop the charges so he wouldn't go to prison. Desperate and obviously stupid, Horace believed her. The fact she doped his food didn't help her. The woman made me think twice about the institution of marriage, but then I remembered Lee and Horace had nothing in common.

After dealing with the Foukes and the police, Lee drove us to the Blue Moon for a quick celebratory drink. I also wanted to tell Candace the good news in person. I had to admit, driving to the restaurant and not checking the rearview mirror for a giant bug worked for me.

"I knew the woman was up to something," Candace said as she stood over our table.

"Why didn't you say anything?" I asked.

Candace folded her arm.

"If you wanted a detective, you should ask your friend. She sure isn't a wedding planner," she said, glaring at Maggie.

Maggie cringed.

"Don't worry, I took care of everything, even the rehearsal dinner," an exasperated Candace said.

"Thanks, Candace, you're wonderful," a grateful Maggie said. The corner of Candace lips curled slightly but quickly faded.

"I must have victim written all over me," I sighed, staring at my bandaged arm.

"Lucky he didn't grab me." Candace cut Lee a nasty glance. "I'm sure my evil eyes would have turned him to ashes."

Lee suppressed a smile, possibly remembering Wilkes women loved revenge.

My phone rang and saved him from any more of Candace's quips. The display read Jake Nordmeyer.

"Hey Jake…" I began before Lee took the phone away. He told Jake to call me in the morning and disconnected.

"I can't believe you did that." I reached for the phone, but he held it away from me.

"You need to stop and slow down," he said, his words filled with concern. "I told Aaron I was taking a few days off to take care of you."

"He's pushy too," Candace said beneath her breath, but loud enough for us to hear.

"Dinner and bed," he said firmly, ignoring my sister.

"I need a real drink." I stared down at my iced tea. I felt like crap, and my hand throbbed as if someone took a mallet to it.

"No liquor," Lee said.

"You are pushy but right," Maggie said, smiling at him in admiration.

"I should work on Eloise's cake," I said as my sense of urgency was ruined by my yawning.

"How are you going to manage?" Lee pointed to my hand.

"Don't worry about it." George's voice came up from behind me. I turned to see the chef wiping his brow, his dark skin glistening.

"Why shouldn't I worry?" I asked.

"My friend teaches at a culinary school, and he's going to send you one of his recent graduates to help you finish any outstanding work, and do the baking for the restaurant until your hand gets better." He sounded dispassionate when he said it.

"I don't need help," I said. I wasn't going to help them replace me.

In unison, everyone said I did. I slumped back in my chair, with my aching hand, wondering how I was going to row my boat alone. Someone would replace me as the dessert chef at the Blue Moon, and I'd just handed them the perfect excuse to do it. I groaned.

"I need to lie down," I said.

Lee took me home.

***

Jake, being the anal retentive person he was, showed up at my house the next morning five minutes before Lee told him too. I awoke late to the sound of Jake's loud voice coming from my kitchen. What I hadn't expected to find was Maggie drinking coffee, eating muffins, and listening intently. The party had started without me. When I entered the kitchen, Lee pointed to an empty chair, commanding me to sit. I gave everyone a sleepy hello and sat.

"You told Jake you'd send Rocket to his house," Maggie said, glaring at me.

"I wanted the report right away, and a gun wasn't available," I said and smiled when Lee put a plate of eggs and toast before me. He might have been bossy, but I liked the service.

"You make him sound like a menace," Maggie said.

"Roger Junior, aka Rocket, removed the eyebrows off his best friend because he wanted to know how hair removal cream worked. He's rewired every clock in your house." I shook my head. "He has a file at the local police department because he unscrewed everyone's license plates on your block and switched them for laughs and giggles."

An indignant Maggie glared at me. Jake's eyes widened, and Lee shook his head.

"Is this a P.I. case or wedding?" Lee said, pouring himself a cup of coffee before joining us at the kitchen table.

"It's both," Maggie said.

"This is extremely exciting." Jake's eyes brightened. He'd been working his way through some cranberry corn muffins covered in orange marmalade. He also didn't seem too concerned about sitting next to the woman who gave birth to someone I used to threatened to destroy his house. Every now and then, Maggie smiled at him. She'd won him over.

"So what's going on?" I asked, hoping to get the Cliffs Notes.

Jake pulled out several photographs of Bella Vista from his briefcase. He slid one in front of me. The picture of a large pile of rubble I assumed was the dubious concrete.

"This is…?" I said and yawned

"From this section here, I could tell they poured new foundations for some of the houses," Jake said.

"So this isn't just a wedding?" Lee asked. He gave them a closer examination. "Why is Rocket in these pictures and why is he covered in dirt?" He turned to Maggie.

I cocked an eyebrow at my best friend.

"Why don't you ask the Mother of the Year?" I said.

"He…was…helping me collect samples," Maggie said.

Lee laughed.

"For that, you deserve some coffee," he said, getting up and pouring me a mug of my best French Roast. I grumbled as he handed me the half-empty cup. I wasn't an optimist.

"How long will this nursemaid thing last?" I complained.

"Doctor said for you not to exert yourself for a few days, limit caffeine, no alcohol, and plenty of rest." With his glasses perched at the tip of his nose, he smiled at me as he retook his seat and happily sipped his coffee. He looked like a demented Clark Kent.

"We have good news and bad news," Maggie said, breaking open a muffin and buttering it.

"Give me the bad news first," I said.

"The bad news is the first concrete firm Henry hired did shoddy work and went out of business halfway through the project. Jake made some calls with people he knows in the construction business," Maggie said, smiling at the hapless man. He was being seduced by a red-headed pixie, and he didn't even know it.

"On paper, the company appeared solid, but not in practice. Lee would have sued and beat them into submission if he had a client," Jake said, proud to be associated with Superman.

"Trouble is, Henry's contractors used this company, and the concrete went bad or something. Jake can tell you the technical stuff," Maggie said. Jake smiled at her.

"It set the project way back, and I'm sure the developer lost a pretty penny. The samples you gave me were problematic," Jake began. "Mixing concrete is like baking one of your cakes. There are exact circumstances to consider. A truck doesn't just show up and dump out concrete for the foundation."

That was what I thought happened.

"It's awfully fascinating." Maggie hung on Jake's every word. I put sugar in my coffee, stirred, and tried to appear interested.

"You make concrete by mixing water, aggregates, cement, and some additives," Jake said.

"Cement, concrete, what's the difference, and what the hell are aggregates?" I asked. Jake seemed to bounce in his chair from excitement of a captive audience.

"Aggregates can be crushed rocks or sand, depending on how smooth or coarse you want it. Cement is like the glue which holds the aggregates together. Like the eggs in a cake." He seemed proud of the analogy.

"So what went wrong with Henry's foundations?" Lee asked.

"I don't know who did the compression test," Jake said and got a blank stare from all of us.

"A test shows the compressive strength of hardened concrete. Any reputable lab would fail it. I suspect someone switched the samples or doctored the report. The poor concrete caused major foundation problems with honeycombing." Jake stopped when I held up a hand.

"Should I even ask what honeycombing means?" I said and drained the last of my coffee. I eyed Lee who stared back at me slowly shaking his head.

"How about some juice?" he said cheerfully.

"Honeycombing occurs when the cement mortar and aggregate particles fail to mix properly, forming gaps or voids. This makes the concrete highly unstable. Do you understand?" Jake said as he reached for another muffin. I marveled at his appetite.

"Truthfully, you lost me at concrete is like making a cake, but the gist is the foundation failed. That's the bad news. What is the good news?" I asked.

Maggie sighed.

"The truth is the bad news and good news are the same," Maggie said, trying to avoid eye contact with me.

"Sounds like a horrible sandwich," Jake said mostly to himself.

"Well, the bad news is the faulty concrete. The good news is Jake thinks they corrected the problem. The original cement company went out of business, and Henry's contractor found a more reputable one. The ripped out all the old foundations and poured new ones," she said, smiling.

"I'm assuming correcting the problem is the good news. Mr. and Mrs. Jones' house won't collapse in the middle of the night," I said.

"The truth is he could have done a cosmetic fix. Nobody would have been the wiser until years later when the concrete started to deteriorate," Jake said.

"What's the bad news?" I asked. Lee touched my hand, and I turned to him.

"He's a good guy if he fixed the problem. The fix cost him a lot of money. Trust me, honey, not many developers would solve the problem by replacing all those foundations. He did the right thing," he said. He seemed to admire Henry for it.

"A problem which is no problem...is no problem," Jake said, sounding like Mr. Spock.

I groaned and knew we had a problem.

chapter 29

I WANTED AN evil guy, someone in a black hat, greasy moustache to twirl, and a cackle for a laugh. Mrs. Fouke didn't have a moustache or even a black hat, but her heart was as dark as they came. She drugged her husband, stole his business, and tried to run me down. This was clear and easy to understand. However, real life wasn't simple or easily understood. Henry Duschumel was not a simple man. I had to force myself to remember he might be involved in Biddle's death. Could he be a murderer and altruist?

Lee drove Maggie and me to Verde's Nursery to explain to Mrs. Verde why Henry might become her future son-in-law. Maggie said she could tell her on her own, but I thought she needed the backup. Lee came along because he'd morphed into my sidekick. I was a sidekick with a sidekick. I bet Robin or Kato didn't share these problems.

When we got to the nursery Lee parked the car, and we headed for Mrs. Verde's office in the back of the building. Twenty-feet away from the building I stopped him. His presence was just too awkward. He was like a three-ton legal gorilla in the room.

"I promise to refuse any caffeine drinks or arm wrestle if you take a hike." I waved my bandaged left hand at him.

Lee folded his arms, stared at me briefly, and zeroed in on the large window display offering sales on gardening items. Verde Nursery was offering a weekend special on plants and fertilizer.

"I'm going to get some fertilizer for the lawn. Call me when you're ready to leave," he said.

"What lawn?" I said with a lot of skepticism. I envisioned the front of the house and couldn't remember anything green.

"It's that brown thing you're constantly walking across from the garage." He shook his head.

"Oh, I guess," I said perplexed with Lee's preoccupation with a patch of dirt.

"Ever notice other people's lawn in the neighborhood? How nice and green they are," he said.

"Mrs. Poojari has a wonderful lawn," I said.

Lee nodded.

"She suggested I bring the neighborhood's property value up by seeding the lawn." His lips curled into a knowing smile.

"Oh!" I said, slightly chagrined that my neighbors thought my lawn brought down their property values.

"Don't worry, in a few weeks, she'll be envious." He promised.

"You don't mind?" I asked.

Lee shrugged.

"I live here too, right?" He eyes searched mine as I faltered on responding.

"Yeah," I said much too enthusiastically. "You go, baby, and seed our lawn."

Lee's mouth shifted into a slight grin before he turned and headed for the large sliding glass doors of the nursery.

"With Roger, it's power tools," Maggie said.

"Either I underestimated how domesticated he is, or he's up to something," I said with some concern.

Maggie gave me a look of disbelief.

"The man is living with you, sharing your bed, eating your food. Now he's seeding your lawn. For heaven sake, Odessa, what does the man need to do short of standing on top of your roof and shouting he'd make a good husband?"

I stared at Maggie.

"Oh crap." I moaned.

"When he starts going to Home Depot's power tool aisle, begin to worry," she warned.

We headed for Mrs. Verde office. When we rounded the corner to the back, to our surprise, we found Tommy talking to Mrs. Verde. He stood close, listening intently as the old woman spoke. Perhaps she forgave his transgressions toward her, or she'd finally come to realized Tommy was the son-in-law she preferred.

"Strange bedfellows," I said.

"Maybe she forgave him," Maggie said. "If we're lucky, she will be in a forgiving mood when I tell her about Henry."

"Don't hold your breath." I gently pushed Maggie forward.

When we approached, Tommy smiled and waved before Mrs. Verde said something to him. He lost his smile and left in the opposite direction, avoiding us.

"I guess you've mended fences," I said, never taking my eyes off Tommy as he entered one of the greenhouses.

"He's a good boy. Things went a bit too far," Mrs. Verde said.

We all went into the office where Mrs. Verde lit a cigarette. We took our usual seats. My bandaged left hand caught her attention.

"I guess the cake will be a no-show. How about the groom?" she said. She inhaled deeply and blew out a long plume of smoke in my direction.

"The cake will be there." I waved away the smoke.

"Unfortunately, so will the groom." Maggie's tone was too submissive for my liking.

Mrs. Verde's eyes narrowed and she stubbed out her cigarette in a small ceramic flowerpot littered with other cigarette butts. Her mouth crimped in annoyance.

"Can you guess how much I've put out for this circus called a wedding?" She stepped from around the desk and came toward us.

"I'm sorry, Mrs. Verde, but there's nothing to find. His business is clean. He hasn't broken any laws. To tell you the truth, he turning out to be a pretty nice..." Maggie stopped herself. This wasn't what Mrs. Verde wanted to hear.

"He's marrying Eloise, for Christ sake. You don't find his proposal in the least bit suspicious?" she said.

"Honestly, after dealing with your daughter, I do question Henry's...choices," I said and Maggie scowled at me.

"The truth is, Mrs. Verde, Henry is bringing more to this marriage than Eloise. She has more to gain marrying him," Maggie said.

Mrs. Verde's face flushed, and her mouth twitched.

"You better make something up. I don't care. Henry will not be at the wedding on Saturday," she said.

"I can't make up something," an indignant Maggie said. Even Tinker Bell had her standards.

"I've shelled out a lot of money, and I demand results, girlie." Mrs. Verde hands balled into a fist, and the thin blue veins on her skin pulsed. Her eyes narrowed in contempt.

"I won't invent anything, Mrs. Verde." Maggie said, showing conviction of her own.

The files at the edge of her desk went flying as the woman sputtered her disapproval at Maggie's morals. Maggie's face went white as Mrs. Verde pointed a finger at her. For a moment, I thought Maggie might need an adult diaper.

"You will find something and do the job I paid for!" Mrs. Verde screamed. "He cannot marry Eloise!"

Little blue veins inched up Mrs. Verde face. Her nostrils flared as she glared at Maggie. Her mouth contorted in anger and fury. Maggie sat silent, frozen in her seat with either fear or shock.

"It could be true love," I said, hoping to break the tension. The humor didn't help. Mrs. Verde turned her attention and wrath on me.

"You've gotten a lot of money out this—the catering, the cake," she said. Her lip curled into a smile conveying something I didn't like.

"I paid for you to find dirt on Henry Duschumel and I got nothing but an overpriced party."

"You paid me to make a cake, and my family's restaurant to do the catering." I pointed to myself and then at Maggie. "You paid her to find dirt on Henry. Your issue is with her."

A wounded Maggie glared at me, hurt, her sense of betrayal palpable. Mrs. Verde had accused her of not doing her job. Maggie did her best, but Mrs. Verde was doing a better job of intimidating her. I turned to my friend whose blue eyes seemed a little red around the edges as she bit her lower lip. She was either going to cry or yell. I prayed for yelling. If she wanted to play detective, she'd meet worst people than Mrs. Verde. She needed to put on the Big Girl Dress and stand up for herself.

"I did my job, Mrs. Verde. I checked out Henry Duschumel. He's clean, and a whole lot nicer than you," Maggie snapped.

"Tell me he loves Eloise," Mrs. Verde said snidely.

"I'll tell you this, if he wants Eloise it's not because she's rich; you'll make sure she doesn't have a dime to her name." Maggie stood up to face Mrs. Verde. "You don't want your daughter to marry Henry then have the guts to tell her. She's a grown woman."

Mrs. Verde gave us a dismissive wave.

"Grown–up, my fanny. For fourteen years, my husband spoiled her and told her she was a princess. She's lazy. Without me, the girl doesn't have the common sense to blow her nose," Mrs. Verde said.

"Well, I guess working in servitude will show her," Maggie said, matching Mrs. Verde's ferocity.

"Oh please. She lives rent-free, and she has a job," Mrs. Verde said.

Maggie shook her head, disappointed in a mother who measured her love by her force of will.

"Eventually, even my husband thought Eloise couldn't take care of herself. That's why he put me in charge of everything, even our daughter," Mrs. Verde snapped.

"You don't think much of her," I said.

Mrs. Verde laughed.

"You don't think much of her either, do you?" she said her words biting.

I remembered Henry at Bella Vista, and there was the excitement and passion in his eyes. It wasn't there when he looked at Eloise. Mrs. Verde was right; I didn't think much of her daughter. One thing I did know: whether or not she stayed with her mother or married Henry, she would end up in a house with no love.

"There is time to find the truth, Mrs. Verde. I haven't stopped searching or closed this case," Maggie said, more determined than ever.

"I guess you are wasting time sitting here, aren't you? Or should I get someone else to do the job for you?" she said.

"Please don't tell us you're going to send Zeno after him," I said.

"Listen, cake girl, if Eloise is too blind to see she's being made a fool of, so be it. I wouldn't expect less from the girl, but no one takes anything from me," she said between clenched teeth. "Now get out of here and find something Eloise will believe to stop this wedding."

"What if the truth breaks her heart?" Maggie said, and I read the concern on her face, even if Mrs. Verde didn't.

"What are you, the love detective?" Mrs. Verde said. "A broken heart never killed anyone. Now get out of my office."

We left, none too pleased with Mrs. Verde or ourselves.

Outside of Mrs. Verde's office Maggie punched me in the arm.

"What?" I rubbed my shoulder.

"I'm just the caterer. Thanks so much," Maggie said, stomping away from me.

"Oh, come on. You told her, didn't you? Nobody pushes Maggie Swift around," I shouted after her, knowing she couldn't stay pissed at me long. For Maggie, staying angry was like holding her breath. When we got to the car, Lee had the back door open and dumped a large shopping bag into the back. He must have brought out the store because several bags sat in the cargo bay of the SUV. The patch of grass in front of my house just got extremely expensive.

"Hey," he said, opening the back door for Maggie. She almost got in, but stopped, turned to me as I approached, and held out a finger.

"I'm sorry," I said.

Lee stared at us.

"What did she say?" Maggie asked.

"Who, the Wicked Witch of the West?" I asked.

"About taking stuff," Maggie said.

"What are you talking about?" I said.

"Are we going home?" Lee asked, already in the driver's seat. I imagined he was anxious to play with his new gardening tools.

"She said no one takes *anything* from me?" Maggie said.

"Earth to Maggie." I snapped my fingers in front of her face.

"She said anything, not anyone. Not Eloise. Eloise is a person, not a thing," Maggie said.

I put both hands on her shoulders and gave her a little shake. Her mind was someplace else, and I needed her to land.

"Earth to Maggie, NASA needs its spaceship," I said.

"Are we going or not?" Lee got out of the car.

Maggie spun away from me and started doing her happy dance she did when she reached some conclusion before anyone else.

"What's wrong with her?" a wary Lee said.

"I wish I knew," I said with some lament. Maggie had walked in circles for about a minute before she stopped in front of us.

"She knows what it is." Maggie smiled.

"Who?" Lee asked.

"Mrs. Verde. She knows what Henry wants from Eloise," Maggie said, grinning.

"She does?" I said surprised at the notion Eloise had anything anyone wanted.

"What is it?" Lee asked.

Maggie shrugged. "I'm not sure, but I think it's this."

She pointed to the nursery main building. Henry wanted Verde Nursery.

chapter 30

WE ALL LOOKED up at the large, impressive green and gold Verde Nursery sign sitting at the entrance of the driveway leading to the main building. Many local mom and pop stores fell to the corporate chain stores and outlets. Verde's remained standing, providing personal service and high-quality goods. Customers and tradesmen from the surrounding area thought of Verde's as a fixture to the community, a landmark, a rite of passage each season. The nursery was a gold mine. More importantly, it was a thing.

"If Henry marries Eloise, how would she lose this place?" Lee said.

"Why doesn't Mrs. Verde just tell Eloise?" I said.

"This woman told Eloise all her life she was worthless and lazy. Now her mother is going to tell her the man she's about to marry only wants her because somehow he'll have access to this." Maggie gestured to the Verde's main building.

"I'd marry him out of spite. In fact, I'd elope just to piss her off," I said. Lee gave me a long appraising look and tried to suppress a smile.

"What?" I asked him.

"What if I told Candace I wanted you for your house? Would you run off and marry me?" he said.

"No," I said flatly. "That's a weak proposal."

Lee slid his glasses up the bridge of his nose, and his smile widened.

"Mrs. Verde said the minute she confronted Eloise about Henry, her daughter threatened to run off," Maggie said.

"Then she offers to do the wedding, pay for everything. She had three weeks to find out Henry's real intentions, because it's not her daughter," I said.

Maggie suggested we leave Verde's Nursery, and she directed us to a nearby pizza parlor. We sat down over a pepperoni pizza and drinks. We ate and told Lee about the Verdes and our dilemma. He didn't think Mrs. Verde would have Henry killed, but she might do something desperate or stupid. For Lee, desperate and stupid often went hand in hand.

"For Mrs. Verde, it's about money," Lee said as he ate his pizza. He'd been eating and asking a thousand questions. He understood Maggie's dilemma. She had a difficult client who only gave her partial information and expected miracles.

"Welcome to my world," he complained, taking another huge bite from the slice. Sauce dripped onto his tee-shirt, and he stared at the spot as if it were a science experiment, unsure of what to do about the stain. Without asking, I dipped a napkin in my glass of club soda, reached over, grabbed his shirt, and wiped the stain away with the napkin. When I finished with my handiwork, both Lee and Maggie stared at me, smiling.

"Tomato sauce is hard to get out," I said in my defense, embarrassed by my own domesticity.

Maggie's smile widened.

"Why do I suddenly feel like Rocket?" Lee said, staring at the large wet spot on his shirt.

"Oh, be quiet," I said. "Can we get back to the problem?"

"The problem is Mrs. Verde is holding back information you need to stop the wedding," Lee said, scrutinizing the spot. "Also, she needs someone else to play the bad guy in this."

"He's right. Mrs. Verde is bending over backwards to accommodate Eloise's every whim. If I'd found anything on Henry, she wouldn't be the one to tell her," Maggie said. I agreed.

"What does Eloise get out of this besides a freaking perfect wedding to a man that probably doesn't love her?" I said.

"She gets away from her mother," Lee said. I shook my head, not satisfied with the excuse.

"So does a bus ticket and a membership in The Big Girls Club," I said.

"I trust my instincts. Eloise has something Henry wants, and Mrs. Verde would like to keep," Maggie said.

"The nursery seems the only thing Mrs. Verde wants," Lee said. Maggie and I nodded. "You said Mrs. Verde inherited the property after the death of her husband. At the time, Eloise was a minor, so her mother probably became the executor of the Will. Mrs. Verde would be responsible for taking care of property, assets, bills, and taxes."

"Can we back up a bit?" I asked. There were other things to consider. "How do faulty foundations connect with all of this?"

"A simple coincidence," Lee said. "Don't make this more complicated than it is."

"What about Barnaby? Where is he in all of this?" I asked.

"His connection might be only the foundation problem. If you said that Henry had him arrested, maybe your friend harassed the jobsite. Making too much noise, simple as that," Lee said.

I had no doubt Biddle was a nuisance to Henry. He had millions tied up in a fancy development and didn't need unfavorable publicity. With a shaky real estate market, Henry didn't need waves. He needed a hundred percent fill rate. A drunken Biddle complaining about shoddy concrete, no matter how well Henry corrected the problem, wasn't a good thing.

"Do you think Henry might have done something to this Barnaby guy?" Lee said.

"I didn't read him as a bad person. He was sweet to Rocket." Maggie sounded conflicted. She had a client, a lying, duplicitous client, but still her client. Lee's presence gave her some perspective.

"You've been charged to do a service. Find out the truth about Henry. The same way lawyers have to deal with the truth their clients give them to present their case. If their clients withhold the truth, they would be doing their lawyer and themselves a disservice and lessening their lawyer's ability to do a good job," he said.

"Why would a client withhold the truth?" Maggie asked.

"Because they know the truth would hurt them in some way. Maybe Mrs. Verde is no different," he said.

"So you're saying that my job is to find out the entire truth to do a good job?" Maggie said.

Lee nodded.

"Sometimes, the truth hurts, but it's necessary," he said.

Maggie sat silent for a long time. She wanted to do the right thing, the best thing for everyone. More importantly, she wanted to be a good, private investigator and sometimes what she wanted had very little to do with that.

"What are you going to do?" I asked.

She looked up at me, her wide blue eyes sad and conflicted.

"My job," she said.

***

The next day, Esperanza Gonzales stood at my front door. She stood just over five feet, with shiny black hair braided into two thick braids that hung past her shoulders. She had expressive black eyes in a moon-shaped face the color of caramel. She proudly came to my house dressed in her culinary school chef's jacket, ready to work. I leaned that she was born twenty-one years ago on Staten Island, and her parents emigrated from Bolivia. The youngest of four children, she always wanted to be a dessert chef. When her teacher recommended her to George, she jumped at the chance.

Though hiring Esperanza hadn't been my idea, once meeting her, I couldn't resist her charm and willingness to please. Lee took a liking to her instantly and even spoke to her in Spanish, which surprised me. I wondered how well I knew him. Within an hour, she and I fell into a comfortable routine of working together. Unfortunately, my house was small and Lee's presence and constant interruption was hindering our progress with some of the jobs we had to do. I begged him to go to the office for a few hours. Reluctant to leave, he did when I promised I wouldn't overdo it. The moment he left, Esperanza and I tackled Eloise's massive cake. Even with my dicey hand, we managed.

An hour and a half later, Esperanza completed the decorative pieces. Hand painting the remaining gum paste flower was tedious, but the girl seemed to enjoy it. We worked and talked about her family and dreams to open her own shop one day. I told her how I came to become the Blue Moon dessert chef. She seemed amazed. I guess losing my high-paying job, imploding on a Manhattan street, surviving a subway fire, being dumped by my boyfriend on the same day, and then reduced to being a dessert chef was better than a Spanish television novella.

"God's way of telling you that you were in the wrong life," Esperanza said. I'd never thought of my life's most distressing moment explained that way. It made me smile.

Esperanza explained while her parents worked her grandmother took care of her. In between learning how to make Bolivian desserts and teaching her grandmother English, they watched the soap opera *All My Children* dutifully.

"She should compare notes with my Aunt Renne, though I think she's a *General Hospital* fan," I joked.

My 80-year-old aunt was convinced God had a plan for everyone, even me. After my career had imploded, I was very shaky and certain God's plan was written in crayon. My aunt would stop by the restaurant and we'd talk about my downward-spiraling life expectations. She sat patiently, while I complained.

"My life was ruined," I'd said.

"You seem happy now." Aunt Renne had said. Her well-worn Bible would be close by to pull out some appropriate quotation for me.

"I got fired from my job."

"It wasn't the right job." She'd smiled.

"What about the subway fire? I could have died," I'd said, getting annoyed with her lack of empathy.

"Misfortune makes you realize life is short, so pay attention, and usually there's an exit sign," she'd said with certainty.

"My boyfriend dumped me on the worst day of my life." I was yelling by now.

"Why are you complaining? You have someone better." By then, I was sure I'd annoyed her with my self-pitying. Instead, she'd patted my hand and given me a perceptive gaze as if she had the answer to everything. Aunt Renne would love Esperanza. They both believed there was a plan.

Finishing earlier than expected, I wanted to take Esperanza to the Blue Moon and get her acquainted with everyone. With no car to drive, I had to call a cab. Before we left, I wrote down a few of my basic recipes and some of the Blue Moon favorites. We talked some more about her duties, the Verde wedding, the restaurant, and how well Lee spoke Spanish.

I called Lee to tell him about our plans and wanted him to pick me up at the restaurant later. He suggested we eat an early dinner. He wanted to invite Aaron. The rotund lawyer was still apologizing to me about the whole Fouke debacle. A dinner together would reassure him I was all right.

At the restaurant, a surprised Candace looked about as welcoming as the Spanish Inquisition. When I introduced her to Esperanza, Candace asked for identification. Knowing my sister, I'm sure she wanted to see a green card. Before Candace checked her teeth, I took Esperanza to the kitchen to meet George and show her my workstation. Thankfully, George was happy to see her. They spoke about her teacher and her training at the school. Esperanza seemed to relax, and so did I.

"Unlike some people, I like the area kept spotless. I expect you to do the same." George glared at me.

"Yes, chef," Esperanza said in a strong voice that he appreciated. I shook my head in disgust.

"Bite me, George," I said, leaving Esperanza to warm herself in the glow of George's large ego. I left the kitchen, grabbed a full cup of coffee, and found an empty seat at the bar. I wanted to enjoy my solitude. It wouldn't be long before Lee would arrive with Aaron or Eloise calling about her cake or Maggie wanting me to help her save the world.

I was halfway through my coffee when a nightmare from my past walked through the front door. Davis Frazier, my ex-boyfriend and world-class jerk. Tall, lean, and the color of polished mahogany, dressed impeccably in a hand-tailored suit, many of the restaurant's female patrons turned to stare. He was a GQ cover boy for corporate America and every mother's wet dream: a successful man with a steady job.

He locked eyes on me and flinched. I had that effect on him since I threatened to kill him several times. I hadn't seen him for a couple of months, so my dislike for him had waned. Seeing him after so long rekindled the sour taste in the pit of my stomach I'd forgotten. My reservations about marrying Lee, no doubt stemmed from my disastrous relationship with Davis. The cretin made me question myself every time I told someone I loved them, especially Lee. I pushed my coffee aside. Candace appeared from the office, as if on cue, to greet him. She loved Davis.

I could tell Davis wasn't expecting me to be at the restaurant. This made me smile. To complete my sense of triumph over tragedy that was my relationship with him, my smile widened. He said something to Candace. She turned in my direction. My smile faded a little but not much. When I got up and walked over to them, Davis took a step behind my sister, the gutless weasel.

"Hey, Davis," I said, stepping around Candace and giving him a disingenuous hug. Stiff in my arms, he broke the embrace first to stare at me.

"Still an asshole?" I asked.

"Still on medication?" he replied.

chapter 31

DAVIS FRAZIER WAS a handsome man, a successful investment banker, and married to an unbelievably sweet woman. Taquinda Johnson Frazier was a pleasant surprise when I first met her. Intelligent, friendly, beautiful, and willing to take Davis' crap and make him a better man, a task I was unable to achieve or even attempt. The Will and Jada Smith of the corporate world, they made an attractive couple. Five years ago, Taquinda and I had the same ambitions, the same dreams, and at different times, the same man. While my career derailed along with my self-confidence, Taquinda's as an entrepreneur and business-woman took off.

When Davis couldn't handle the extreme shift in my life, he bailed on me. He came back at the behest of his fiancé, Taquinda. She tested his character by urging him to obtain my forgiveness. I admired her for putting Davis to the herculean task of obtaining it, since I was unwilling to forget or forgive him. At the time, I managed my anxiety disorder with little blue pills and martinis. I preferred killing him. Then I met Taquinda, and to both of our surprise, we liked each other, despite our choice of men. While I tried to forgive Davis, I made friends with his wife. This arrangement worked for me, as long as he stayed out my line of sight. My sister made this difficult because she always kept in contact with him. Her delusional thinking had to do with Davis and me getting back together. The whole breaking up thing never registered.

"Odessa, why are you always so horrible to Davis?" my sister complained.

I smiled at him. "Because he refuses to go away and die."

"You said she wouldn't be here." He adjusted his tie, a nervous habit he still had.

"She just showed up," Candace said, disappointed with my presence.

"You need to get over me, Dessa," Davis said. He liked to think he was the love of my life, and I snapped when the relationship fell apart. I found it ironic that he thought I was delusional.

Candace gave us both a satisfied look. "She still has feelings for you."

I laughed.

"Yeah, rage and resentment," I said.

"Odessa, get a grip," Candace said and began to led Davis away from me. "Anyway, he's not here for you. He's here for me."

My past relationship with Davis had garnered my sister access to his skills as an investment banker. I guess Candace didn't feel loyal enough to break ties with him after our relationship had ended. I guess finding a new investment banker was harder than being a loyal sister.

"He's all yours," I said and watched them head toward her office. Then I thought of something and went after them.

"What now?" His face began to tense.

"How's Goldberg?" I asked.

"Fine?" a suspicious Davis said.

"Does he still work for you or have you thrown him under a bus too?" I said.

Davis sighed.

"He's an associate now and has his own assistant," he said. "You send him cookies for Christ's sake."

"He is sweet, and he did me a big favor. Anyway, I need some help with something," I said.

Davis groaned in exasperation.

"You can't use my staff as if they were 911 operators," he protested.

"Oh please, my last request gave you the inside scoop on a killer investment for your clients. So please, get off the cross; somebody else needs the wood," I said, tired of his sense of importance.

Once I'd asked him to help research the firm that fired me. This made him privy to some private information. He used what he knew and made a fortune. I never called him on his self-serving behavior. What I expected in return was a little help now and then. When he stood in front of me and feigned high standards and morality, it made me want to choke him.

"So before you get all indignant about this, you might get something useful," I said.

Davis took a deep breath and thought about it, the same way a vulture thought about feeding off dead carcass, white meat, or dark.

"What is it?" he said, pulling out his cell phone, reluctantly making his call. After a few minutes, he handed his cell phone to me. Goldberg seemed delighted to talk to me. I explained to Goldberg what I wanted, and he was more than willing to oblige. When the call ended, I gave Davis back his phone and he nearly ran into Candace's office.

"You're taking advantage of him," Candace scolded.

"He speculates on the misfortunes of others, finds companies' weaknesses, and uses them for his benefit, and I'm taking advantage of him," I scoffed.

Candace rolled her eyes, turned, and walked away from me. She continued to have a higher opinion of Davis than I did.

"Hey, Odessa, you got a phone call." Trevor, the bartender, held up the house phone. I went to answer the call.

"Thanks for not telling me," the familiar voice of Frank barked.

"Hi, Frank," I said, trying to sound cheerful but clueless about his new rant.

"The Bug guy, he's in jail."

I realized no one told him about Mrs. Fouke's arrest.

"No, but his wife is. She was the one trying to run me down," I explained

"It would have been nice if someone would have told me. Did you do this to me to make me crazy?" Frank said tightly.

"No, Frank. I'm truly sorry. The car crash shook me up," I said and tried to sound remorseful.

"Yeah, I heard about that too. You hit a retaining wall, and the wall almost won," he said.

"Your concern is touching," I said dryly.

"That's not the only thing I'll touch. You owe me a dinner for two and drinks included. I'll need a drink to ward off the twitchy looks from you sister."

I started to protest, but he did deserve a decent meal.

"Speaking of Candace, the other part of this deal is still on—to find anything about Leon." I stared at Candace's closed office door.

"I'll tell you after I have a very expensive steak dinner," he said and slammed down the phone.

***

After dinner with an extremely apologetic Aaron, Lee and I returned home. He decided to putter around with his new garden tools. I went to the kitchen, made some tea, and called Maggie. I told her about Goldberg, and she appreciated the help. She planned to go to the county courthouse early in the morning to search the public records for Mr. Verde's will. When I asked her about the rehearsal dinner, she groaned.

"Despite Candace's irritation with me, she arranged everything. It's at a restaurant near the winery, and hopefully, nothing crazy will happen. It's at six. Can you come?" she said.

I wanted to stay home in bed and sleep for about a week, but I agreed to join her on crazy patrol at Eloise's rehearsal dinner.

"May my home care attendant accompany me?" I asked. A determined Lee wanted to make sure I didn't do any handstands.

"That's fine. I like having him around," she said brightly and I knew she meant it. Unlike my sister, Maggie loved Lee.

"Where is he?" she asked.

"Outside trying to save the lawn," I said.

A long silence hung between us.

"Ever thought about marrying the man?" My girlfriend wanted a happy ending that included a house and white picket fences.

"O, are you there?" she said.

"I'm thinking about it," I lied.

"What's to think about?"

If I didn't give her the answer she wanted, she wouldn't let it go.

"I have an issue about the whole marriage thing," I confessed.

"What?" She pushed.

"A few things." I tried to hint to her that I didn't want to get into a lengthy discussion while Lee was outside puttering on the lawn.

"What things?" Like a dog with a bone, Maggie wouldn't let this go.

I took a deep breath and sighed. If I couldn't tell Maggie about my doubts, who could I tell? Definitely not Candace; she'd jump up for joy at the news.

"He's been married before. I never asked him about what broke up his marriage or anything. He's failed before, and he might fail again," I said.

"People get divorced, O. Maybe he wasn't ready then, but now he is," she said.

"I'm not sure, Maggie," I said.

"Do you expect someone better, another Davis?"

"Hell no," I said, distressed with the idea of meeting another self-centered jerk.

"Then stop waiting for something else to come along. You know you have what you want right there already," she said.

How could I explain to her every time I thought about taking the next step with Lee, I wondered if I made the best choice for myself. He wasn't what I'd planned. Hell, I hadn't planned to lose my career in advertising or work with my sister. I hadn't expected any of my recent life-changing events. I knew the world around me was chaos, but I was happy, and Lee loved me.

"Can you imagine me married to him?" I said. Just as I said the words Lee walked into the kitchen looking like he dug up the entire front lawn. He stopped, stared at me for a moment, and continued to the refrigerator. He took a bottle of water and left. I didn't like the expectant look he gave me.

"Odessa."

"What?" I said, distracted by Lee's attention.

"Tomorrow, will it be a problem?" she asked.

"As long as everyone behaves, I'll be there," I said.

After talking with Maggie, I spent the rest of the evening talking to new customers. With Esperanza, I could accept more orders. These referrals from other customers were opportunities I couldn't let slip away, despite my injury. I wanted to keep Esperanza longer but needed more room to work with someone else in my workspace at home and at the restaurant. Unfortunately, the restaurant was no longer an option for me. Lee had commandeered the tiny guest room on the ground floor for his stuff from his Manhattan apartment. Thinking about the whole thing gave me a headache. Since I had no immediate solution, I decided to shower and go to bed.

I crawled into bed around eleven-thirty. Lee sat on his side of the bed working his way through some of the paperwork he'd brought home. Shirtless and his hair still damp from his shower, he sat cross-legged looking serious. As if on cue, he gathered up his papers and placed them alongside the nightstand on his side of the bed. He'd taken off his glasses, turned off his bedside lamp, and slipped in next to me.

"I need to tell you something," he said, his voice barely above a whisper.

"Now?" I said, knowing whatever it was I wasn't going to like it. Lee was too serious.

"I've been putting off telling you." His face lit from the glow of my bedside lamp.

"You're running away to join the circus," I said, hoping to lightened the mood.

He laughed.

"You and Maggie are circus enough," he said as he wrapped an arm around my waist to pull me close.

"What's this about?" I asked.

"I need you to be quiet, Dessa. This only works if you don't talk," he explained.

I sighed and nodded.

"First, I want to say I love you," he said, laying the groundwork for something bad.

Unease began to seep through me and I realized I didn't want to hear anything he had to say. His word might change everything.

"Lee, we don't..." I began, but he kissed me more to shut me up than anything else.

When he was sure I wouldn't interrupt him, he took a deep breath.

"My marriage to Julia fell apart because my ambition got in the way," he blurted out. "When thing got bad, she had an affair with one of my clients. We got past her infidelity for a while, but the marriage fell apart eventually, and we divorced. I left the law firm and didn't practice for nearly six months, until Aaron called me to work for him."

"Lee..." Surprised by his confession, I couldn't continue.

"You wouldn't have liked me then." His eyes held some hidden truth. "I'm not that person anymore."

I shook my head, unconcerned with his past life or mistakes. He seemed more than willing to embrace mine. I ignored the regret in the eyes that stared back at me. I kissed him thoroughly.

"It's okay; you were just in the wrong life," I said and turned off the lights.

.

chapter 32

EARLY NEXT MORNING, I sat in Maggie's car headed to Glen Cove, Long Island and the Verde home. The morning sun hung high on the horizon, ready to bring the summer's heat. Before Maggie arrived at my house, I'd convinced Lee not to tag along. I promised not to join the circus as the high-wire act or exert myself too much. Our talk the night before convinced him I was of sound mind and at least rational. His voluntary confession of his failings and Julia's infidelities only reaffirmed my belief that he was a decent man. I'd put his mind at ease by explaining I liked my men a little semisweet as well. I told Maggie about Lee's admission. She thought it was commendable he and Julia could remain civil toward each other. Until last night, Lee never said one unpleasant thing about her; he probably thought he was responsible for driving the woman into another man's arms. I thought he gave himself too much credit for that one.

"Why aren't you happy he's telling you this?" Maggie said, as she drove.

"I'm not sure," I lied. This new level of intimacy between Lee and I pulled at my insecurities. There was a familiar panic at the uncertainty of our relationship. I pushed the feeling away and concentrated on the road, the good weather, and going to see the Verde home.

The backseat of her minivan held bridesmaids' gifts. Eloise opted to go to a tanning salon with Jenny instead of tending to her bridesmaids. Maggie took the task upon herself to find some small tokens of appreciation for the unfortunate bridesmaids. She'd gotten ideas of what to buy from Candace who had decidedly taken over the reins as the wedding planner. I wasn't surprised. My sister had a tendency of taking things over. If she'd been on the Titanic, the boat wouldn't have sunk or at least everyone would have been in a lifeboat rowing in unison.

"Get anywhere with the will?" I said as Maggie parked in front of the Verde house, a modest colonial, situated in a quiet neighborhood.

"No. I went to the county courthouse and didn't find anything on Mr. Verde's will," she said with disappointment. "Since Mr. Verde's death, someone named Greene and Dougherty has paid the nursery's sales and property taxes. They sound like a law firm."

"Maybe Lee knows them," I said, pulling out my cell phone to call him. He picked up on the second ring.

"Hey, how are those circus tryouts going?" he said.

"Didn't get the high-wire act, but the lion taming might be promising," I said.

"Why do I worry for the lions," he said dryly. The seriousness of our talk last night hadn't dampened his humor.

"Maggie's here and we want to ask if you know a law firm called Greene and Dougherty." I pressed the speaker button on my cell phone.

Lee chuckled. "All lawyers don't know each other."

"Hi, Lee," Maggie said. "Since you're our resident legal expert I have a question. Are all Wills supposed to be public records?"

"Yes," he said.

"Maggie went to the courthouse and couldn't find anything," I said.

"If there's no will, how would someone inherit?" Maggie asked.

"This is about the Verdes?" he said, sounding more like a lawyer than the man who talked about the failure of his marriage until two in the morning. "It would be split between the remaining relatives."

"But Mrs. Verde said she was the only beneficiary," I said.

"Then Mr. Verde must have left instructions about his estate before his death. In the absence of a will, I'd look for a trust. An executor would manage the trust for the family," he said.

"So if Mr. Verde left the entire thing to Mrs. Verde, how would you find out about it?" I asked.

"Either through Mrs. Verde or the estate's executor. The executor can be anyone, but probably is a lawyer specializing in estate trust, maybe Greene and Dougherty," he said.

"How would we get a copy?" Maggie asked.

"You can't," he said.

"Why not?" I asked.

"Because the document isn't for the public consumption, not like a will. Why don't you just ask Mrs. Verde the terms of her husband's estate? She is your client, isn't she?" he said.

"Why would she tell us?" Maggie said.

"Is there a way we can get a copy of Mr. Verde's papers without Mrs. Verde finding out?" I asked.

"Not legally," he said.

"Oh, that won't work," Maggie said.

"Thanks, babe," I said.

"Do you still want me to take you to the rehearsal dinner tonight?" Lee asked me.

"If you don't mind," I said. Lee didn't mind at all. If I asked him to take me on a date to a Klu Klux Klan rally, he'd ask what time should he pick me up. He'd also be the one to try and talk me out of it.

I told him I loved him, and we said our goodbyes.

Maggie parked the car in the driveway. We reluctantly got out and carried the boxes of gifts to the front door. Maggie rang the doorbell, and we waited. When the door opened, a smiling Eloise greeted us. Maggie and I stared because she had unnaturally orange skin. She looked like a nacho chip.

"Do you like it?" Eloise beamed and spun around for a better view. There was no better view.

Maggie and I remained speechless for a moment. Shock did that.

"It adds color to your skin," I said, because what else could I say?

"Jenny thinks so too. She said I was too pale," she said, stepping aside to let us come into the house. "I'll stand out," she said.

Yeah, you'll stand out like a safety cone in the middle of a disaster area, I thought. She closed the front door, and we followed her into the kitchen, where we found Jenny sipping soda.

"Hey ladies," Jenny said cheerfully. I noticed Jenny's skin appeared tanned and normal. A mute Maggie stood with her mouth opened. I nudged her with my elbow, and she closed it.

"We brought the bridesmaids' gifts," Maggie said. "Eloise, have you ever gone to a tanning salon before?"

"No, Jenny took me to her favorite place." Eloise sounded grateful. Maggie shot Jenny a nasty glance. Jenny smiled back at her.

"That's what friends are for," I said, giving the woman a nasty glare of my own.

"Well...okay, hum...the stylist will do your makeup and hair and...it will be perfect," Maggie said, as the assurance in her voice faltered.

"Let's put these away," Eloise said and took the box from me as Maggie followed her out of the kitchen.

"Don't you think Eloise over did the tanning?" I said to Jenny.

"Oh, don't worry. Makeup will cover it," Jenny said. At that moment, I appreciated having Maggie as a friend, because having Jenny as one would send me to murder.

When Eloise and Maggie came back, she was still orange and still smiling. As annoying as she had been, I felt sorry for her.

"Is your mother in? I need a check for the limousine service," Maggie said.

"Mom's at the nursery," she said.

"Can you write the check for me?" Maggie asked, and Eloise shook her head.

"I don't write checks," she said, grabbing a cookie from a half-eaten box. Eloise sucked the cookie down in one bite.

"You don't have a checkbook?" I said, surprised.

"Mom does all the bills," she said, sounding unconcerned.

"What do you do with your salary from the nursery?" I asked. Eloise shrugged.

"Mom takes care of everything. She gives me money for the week and extra if I need it," she said.

"Mrs. Verde has always been that way. She does everything from the office at Verde—household and company accounts. She likes everything in one place. I should know; I used to work for her," Jenny complained.

"You've worked for everybody," Eloise joked.

"I work for a temp agency," Jenny said, irritated.

"She even worked for Henry for a time..." Eloise started laughing, "...but they didn't get along."

As if on cue, Maggie and I turned and stared at Jenny. She'd only been back a short time in Eloise's life, and she worked for both her mother and her fiancé.

"Ever date him?" I had to ask. Jenny's look of incredulity was priceless.

"No," she said emphatically.

"I have to remind Jenny to be sweet to Henry," Eloise complained.

"Why, did he fire you?" I asked.

"No." Jenny glared at me.

"Did Mrs. Verde?" Maggie asked, and this flustered Jenny for a moment, but she recovered quickly.

"No, I left," she said, sticking out her chin. "I like to be the one who leaves."

I stared at her, amazed. The girl treated jobs as if they were relationships.

"I guess a temp agency is perfect for you then," Maggie said.

Jenny's eyes darkened.

"My two favorite people," a voice from behind us said.

Maggie and I turned around to find Zeno staring at us. Dressed in a ratty bathrobe and possibly nothing else, I noticed his hairy legs and imagined the rest of his body was equally furry. I heard Jenny groan. Maggie turned away, and Eloise shoved another cookie in her mouth. Zeno stared at me and smiled.

"Your cousin is staying with you?" a surprised Maggie asked.

"Auntie V thought me staying here would be a good idea, us being family and all," Zeno said, walking into the kitchen and scratching his stomach. "Hey Eloise, you think I can get some eggs?"

Without complaint, Eloise began fixing her cousin breakfast.

Jenny vacated her seat as if it were on fire.

"Maggie, let me show you the shoes I brought for my dress," Jenny said, excusing herself as if she smelled something rotten.

"Yeah, that would be wonderful," Maggie said. I couldn't blame her for wanting to put some distance between her and Zeno and envied her as she followed Jenny out of the kitchen.

"You want to stay and chat?" he asked smugly. Eloise placed a cup of coffee in front of him like a servant.

"No," I said flatly, remembering the last time we'd met.

"I like talking to you," Zeno said, his eyes hard on me. I watched as Zeno treated Eloise like a housekeeper and I didn't like it.

"You got something to say, Oprah?" Zeno said. Eloise acted like she hadn't heard him and shoved another cookie into her mouth.

"No," I said.

Zeno gave a snort and turned to Eloise.

"Hey girl, your mom says you'd do a load of laundry for me," he said, tugging at the collar of his bathrobe. "Got nothing to put on but my birthday suit, got things to do today."

I could tell Eloise wanted to complain, but she held her tongue and left us alone.

"I better go," I said and turned to walk away from him.

"Not so fast, girlfriend." He got up from the table and walked toward me. I took a step back, not giving him the opportunity to grab me again.

"You got something I can give to Auntie V?" He smiled, making my stomach turn again. I hoped he wouldn't try something in the house, but I didn't want to find out. I held out a hand to stop him.

"Why don't you come by my restaurant this Friday? I'll have something for you," I said.

Zeno smiled, pleased.

"Why can't you tell me now?" he said.

I sighed deeply, shook, and bowed my head. This was about as contrite as I could be without throwing up.

"Maggie's my friend and she doesn't need to find out," I said.

"Yeah, you're right. Why screw up a good friendship?" Zeno laughed.

"She'll be busy with wedding preparation all day, and I can get you copies of what she has to show Mrs. Verde. It's what she needs to get rid of Henry," I said.

"Good. I'm sure my Auntie V will be generous when I bring her the goods—nice and generous." Zeno's lips curled up in a dangerous smile that gave me second thoughts about what I had planned for him.

Luckily, Maggie and Jenny returned. They stared at Zeno and then me. I took the opportunity to get as far away from him as I could.

"We better go," I said and pulled Maggie out the Verde's front door.

"What was that about?" she said, obviously confused by my behavior.

"You don't want to know," I said and got into her car.

chapter 33

BETWEEN MRS. VERDE'S taciturn mood, Eloise's over the top enthusiasm, the bridesmaids turning hostile, and a desperate groom trying to keep everyone happy, the wedding rehearsal at the winery was just a prelude to the night to come. The dinner at a nearby seafood restaurant started fine but went downhill quickly. Mrs. Verde came dressed in black from head to toe, as if she were attending a funeral. Eloise downed too many pre-dinner cocktails. The bridesmaids went into revolt the moment the bride-to-be insisted they should limit what they eat. Eloise implied they had put on a few pounds and wouldn't fit into their gowns. Somehow, Jenny maneuvered herself next to Lee at the beginning of the evening and clung on to him like toilet paper on your shoe. She trailed after him wherever he went. Maggie had to restrain me from slam-dunking her butt into the parking lot.

I'd come to this horrid event to help Maggie, but spent much of the evenings watching Mrs. Verde ignore her future son-in-law, Eloise paw on her fiancé, and Jenny throwing Henry dagger-like glances. What was that about? Lee came to play my nursemaid and ended up as part of the wedding party. He stood in when Henry's best man got stuck in traffic on the Long Island Expressway. Lee spent most of the evening eating appetizers and avoiding Jenny. When she corralled him at the large dining table the restaurant set up for the rehearsal dinner, the poor man looked trapped.

"Lee's not going to do anything," Maggie assured, as Jenny playfully whispered something in Lee's ear. Jenny laughed, but Lee didn't. Lee's eyes met mine and silently pleaded for me to rescue him.

"The woman is unbelievable," I said in disgust. "If she didn't dislike Henry so much, I bet she would be doing a lap dance on him right in front of Eloise. The woman likes other people's things."

"Yeah, I don't know what that's about," Maggie said. We were both staring at Jenny now.

"Maybe because Henry chose Eloise instead of her," I said. "If you were Henry, who would you choose: a compliant, grateful, star-struck girl or an oversexed, socially limited bimbo?"

"I did a background check on Jenny after I dropped you off. Eloise was right; she doesn't keep jobs for too long. She's gone through three in the last year. She worked for Mrs. Verde for about six months and also in the management office at Bella Vista for three months. Currently she's unemployed," Maggie said.

"Right now it pays to be Eloise's friend. I'm sure the perks of being the maid of honor comes in handy, especially if Mrs. Verde is paying for everything," I said.

Maggie and I sat at the furthest end of the dining table. I wanted to sit next to Lee, but the bridesmaids and Jenny surrounded him like a hungry pack of wolves. Henry sat next to Eloise playing the role of attentive fiancé. He did this under the scornful eyes of his future mother-in-law. The two bridesmaids I met at Eloise's bachelorette party sat on the opposite side of the table, eating anything and everything in front of them as Eloise seethed. Bridesmaid Number One made a point of buttering a large slice of bread right in front of her. Bridesmaid Number Two worked her way through half of the appetizers with a smile on her face.

At our end of the table sat Mr. Grimbel, the nursery's head groundskeeper. He had the dubious pleasure of standing in for Eloise's father. Somehow, Eloise coerced the unassuming man to walk her down the aisle. From what I gathered from Maggie, Mr. Grimbel escorted three of his four daughters for their weddings. This made him

Verde Nursery's resident wedding expert and a perfect stand-in for Mr. Verde. A sweet-natured person, I found him easy to talk to about the Verdes. At the dinner, he delighted in telling stories about Mr. Verde, whom he obviously liked and worked with for many years.

"A fine man and good friend," he said wistfully.

"You think he would be happy for Eloise?" Maggie asked.

"Yes, indeed. He loved that girl," he said. "I know he spoiled her, but that's what you do with daughters."

"My dad was that way," Maggie said. They talked a bit more about children, and Maggie showed him a picture of Rocket.

"I wanted a boy," Grimbel said, staring down at the wallet size photograph. The photograph had Rocket in his Pee Wee football uniform covered in mud. From the expression on Grimbel's face, I didn't think he wanted that particular boy.

"I always hear how Mr. Verde loved Eloise but left everything to his wife." Maggie leaned close to whisper. "That surprised me."

Grimbel nodded.

"Never understood that one either. Mr. Verde loved bringing Eloise to work with him. She loved being around the place. He always said that one day all this would be hers, but I guess he changed his mind," Grimbel said. Maggie and I turned and stared down the table at Mrs. Verde. Henry tried to talk to her, but she sat stone-faced.

"Perhaps someone did change his mind," I said.

Down the long table, Henry's smile faded as Mrs. Verde ignored him. A solemn Henry shifted away and our eyes met. He took a moment to plaster on a strained smile which shattered the edges of his perfection. He looked vulnerable and a little more human. He held my gaze until his phone rang. He excused himself and got up from the table to answer. My eyes stayed on him as the desolation I recognized on his face morphed into restrained anger. Possibly realizing where he was, he regained control. He said a few words to Eloise before hurrying out of the dining area.

While Maggie talked to Grimbel and the rest of the table pre-occupied themselves with their own drama, I got up to follow Henry.

Before I had a chance to, Lee reached over Bridesmaid Number Three and grabbed me.

"Where are you going?" he said, desperation dancing in his eyes.

"The bathroom," I lied. Lee would sit on me if I told him the truth.

"Are you coming back?" he said between clenched teeth.

I smiled at him.

"The circus is in town, honey, I don't know." I pulled away to go after Henry. I left a woeful Lee and the rest of the zoo to find Eloise's Prince Charming.

I found Henry in the small parking lot just outside the restaurant. The poorly lit lot sat on a side road, with equally poor lighting. I could make out Henry's silhouette standing next to his shiny black car. He'd waited for over five minutes before another car rolled up into the lot. Just at the entryway of the restaurant, the familiar car of Clement Drummond parked next to Henry. The moment Drummond got out of his car Henry blocked him. The action took Drummond by surprise. Henry grabbed him by his suit jacket collar roughly and slammed him hard up against his car door. Henry slammed Drummond again.

"Enough, enough!" Henry shouted and pointed a finger in Drummond's face. Visibly shaken, Drummond shoved Henry off him. For a moment, I thought the two men would come to blows.

"You better give me what I want," Drummond shouted.

"The hell with you," Henry said.

As quickly as it began, the encounter was over, with Drummond getting back into his car. As he peeled out of the parking lot, he saw me. His car slowed and like an idiot I stood beneath the restaurant's bright signage as clear as day as he drove out of the lot. The hint of recognition, which played across his face, worried me as he disappeared into the night.

From the other end of the parking lot, Henry came walking back. I stepped back into the restaurant and slammed right into Maggie.

"We've got a problem," she said, her face pale and frightened. I didn't have a chance to ask her what was wrong because she pulled me into the main dining room area. The restaurant wasn't crowded for a weekday. I immediately noticed why Maggie was in such a state. Several diners appeared ill.

"Did you have the clams?" she shouted at me. Other people yelled too—waiters, patrons, and a few kitchen staff who'd come out to witness the mayhem.

"No, I hate clams," I said confused but then my heart froze. I remembered they served stuff mushroom with clams as appetizers. Lee ate them, in fact, he loved them. I broke into a run toward the back of the restaurant.

A pale Lee sat comforting Bridesmaid Number Three. Bridesmaid Number Two vomited in the lap of Number One, who clutched her mouth in reflex. Mr. Grimbel stood by Mrs. Verde's side as the woman looked deathly ill. Eloise seemed green around the edges, but at least she was mobile.

"I'm calling 911," Maggie shouted, and she pulled out her phone.

Jenny stood up against the wall averting her eyes. You would have thought the Black Plague had come to Long Island.

"You had the clams?" I asked. Lee gave a weak smile and nodded.

"This has been a wonderful evening." His face contorted in agony and his pale skin was damp to my touch as I placed my hand on his cheek.

"What's happening?" Henry said.

A wild-eyed Maggie grabbed him by his suit collar and yelled, "Did you have the clams?"

It was the mantra of the evening.

***

Three hours later, I ate a stale candy bar from a hospital vending machine. The place was overwhelmed from the food poisoning cases coming from the North Harbor Restaurant. I sat on a hard plastic chair and waited while the emergency room staff worked on Lee.

He claimed he was fine, but he couldn't stop throwing up. Besides the wedding party, six other diners needed treatment at the hospital. Mr. Grimbel, who was a godsend, took care of the two bridesmaids who received treatment at the scene and made sure they made it home.

Maggie sat holding Mrs. Verde's personal belongings. She'd gathered them up when the EMS workers came to work on the woman. Despite Mrs. Verde's cantankerous ways, Maggie stayed by her side. As for Eloise, Maggie instructed Henry to take his fiancé home. She demanded Jenny stay with her. Jenny complained, but Maggie was in menacing mommy mode, so nobody messed with her. Someone needed to remind Jenny that a good girlfriend held your hair while you barfed in the toilet bowl.

"Well, this has been wonderful," I said dryly. I kept my eye on the drawn curtains where Lee lay.

"They're going to hold Mrs. Verde overnight for observation, her blood pressure, or something," an exhausted Maggie said.

"The next time I ask Lee out, the man will run and hide." I sighed.

"He's okay," she reassured.

I glared at her incredulously, annoyed with her lackadaisical attitude to an unsettling night. I would have said something to her, but she clutched Mrs. Verde's pocketbook so tight I thought she might snap the strap.

"Maggie," I said, and she turned to me with trepidation in her eyes.

"What would Frank do if he had the answers to a case in his hands?" she said meekly.

"You know Frank, he'd go for it. Why?" I asked my attention fully on her.

She stared down at Mrs. Verde's large patent leather pocket book.

My eyes followed hers.

"Maggie, what are you thinking?" I said, concerned. "Because whatever it is, you stop it."

She nodded, but she didn't hear me. I worried about Lee. I wouldn't leave him, but the psycho glaze-eyed stare Maggie gave the emergency room exit had me worried. Her trance was shattered by a cell phone ringing. The ringing came from Mrs. Verde's bag. The phone rang several times and stopped. It rang again. It was twelve forty-five and someone needed to talk to Mrs. Verde.

"Maybe it's Eloise," Maggie said and opened the bag and pulled out the cell phone. She checked the LED screen and made a face. The phone kept ringing loudly and a passing nurse shot us a disapproving look. Maggie answered it with a tentative hello. Her eyes widened as she listened before disengaging the call.

"Who was it?" I asked.

"It wasn't Eloise….it sounded like Tommy," she said and stood up. "I have to go."

"Go where?" I asked as she nearly ran to the emergency room exit. I stood torn between following her and staying with Lee.

"Go where?" I shouted, but she'd already disappeared through the large automatic glass sliding doors.

"Maggie, damn you," I said. I turned back to the drawn curtain and knew I needed to decide. I wanted to stay by Lee's side, but I knew if I didn't go after Maggie, there would be trouble. I took a deep breath and put on my Big Girl Dress, grabbed my bag, and ran out the door.

chapter 34

"HELLO, CLEO," A man's voice said. I turned to face Clement Drummond staring at me. He had a thing for parking lots because he caught me between Lee's SUV and another large truck in the hospital's lot. I never heard him sneak up, too concerned with finding Maggie and trying to stop her from doing something stupid. He took a step toward me, and I felt like a victim sandwich as he squeezed me further in toward the garage wall.

"I'll scream," I said, realizing how stupid that sounded. Just scream you idiot. I opened my mouth to let out a good one when Drummond opened up his suit jacket. A small gun was tucked into his pants waistband. I lost my scream, lost my nerve, and almost lost the candy bar.

"Got your attention now, don't I, Cleo?" he said. I nodded. Trapped between two cars in an isolated parking lot and there was a gun. You had me at hello.

Drummond reeked of stale cigarettes and cheap aftershave. Taller than I had expected, he wore a bad suit he could have stolen from Frank's closet. His slicked back salt and pepper hair looked stiff and unnatural. Even in the dark, his eyes seemed dull and yellow.

"Where's Duschumel, Cleo?" he said, coming close and grabbing me by the arm. He gave me a hard yank.

"My name isn't Cleo," I said, trying to get a sense of reality to the conversation.

"That's what Barney called you, so don't lie to me." He reached into his pocket and pulled out a tattered piece of yellow legal paper. It had my cell phone number written on it.

"Cleopatra Jones!" I said in disbelief that he wasn't making the connection between the movie icon and me.

"I saw you at his apartment. I got your number," he said. "He gave you the concrete sample."

"He gave me a rock," I said, trying to play off the significance.

Drummond's eyes narrowed and the smirk on his lips expanded into a wicked grin.

"And Duschumel, tonight," he said and pulled my arm again.

"You're hurting me." My pain seemed to please him.

"Are you making a deal with him?" he said.

"What deal?" I said. "I was at his rehearsal dinner for his wedding."

Drummond snorted in disbelief.

"He thought he'd give you what's mine?" He barred his teeth at me, and my heart stopped.

"I'm just making the wedding cake," I said.

"Yeah, right. Let's go, cake maker, and find a quiet place to talk." Drummond pulled me by the arm from between the parked cars. I searched the empty lot for someone to notice us. If I screamed, would he shoot me?

"I can't go with you. I need to help my friend. She's in trouble," I said and twisted my arm in the hope I'd get free. Drummond held fast.

"We're going someplace private," he said, his words menacing. I went from scared too terrified in a heartbeat.

"Ask Henry. He'll tell you I had nothing to do with anything," I blurted out.

"Can't find Henry, but I got you," he said, growling at me like some junkyard dog.

Drummond's car sat at the far end of the lot, near the main road. I tried to push the panic down but it kept on rising up in my throat. Drummond's grip on my arm tightened, and he didn't care. My fear got the better of me as my eyes burned from oncoming tears.

This man would kill me and throw my body in a New Jersey landfill, like some bad episode from *The Sopranos*. I thought about the people I loved. Candace would cry in between booking reservations. Lee would forgive his ex-wife and go back to her. George would give my job to Esperanza. I thought about George again and how he told me to handle Horace Fouke. I took another deep breath.

"Now get in the car," Drummond said and patted his side where he holstered the gun. He'd opened the driver's side door and expected me to slide over to the passenger side seat.

I willed myself to do something and pushed back my fear. I'd dealt with the Verdes, Horace Fouke, and his crazy wife. I found my calm somewhere around pissed off and angry.

"The sample is in my bag," I said. I didn't have to fake the fear in my voice as I reached inside my pocketbook.

"That's good." Drummond grinned.

"Here, you can have it," I said, finding the small canister at the bottom of my pocketbook. I wrapped my hand around the pepper spray George had given me for Fouke. I flipped off the safety switch with my thumb before pulling it out. In a quick move, I sprayed him across the eyes on the first pass and got him again on the second. Drummond screamed and cursed. He clawed at his face in agony as the pepper spray did its job. He fumbled for something in his pocket—the gun maybe or a handkerchief. I took the opportunity to shove him as hard as I could. He stumbled backwards. He lost his footing and fell, cursing all the way. I heard a sudden pop, like a firecracker that echoed in the silence of the night. I jumped.

"I'm shot!" Drummond screamed. He grabbed his left foot.

An odd burning aroma hit my nose, and I cringed. A fallen Drummond lay sprawled at my feet. Something oozed between his hands as he clutched his foot. It was blood. His gun had gone off, and he shot himself. With his eyes shut tight from the pepper spray, he gyrated on the ground screaming. I took a closer look at his foot, and a small area by his big toe was gone, shoe and all.

"I'm dying," he wailed.

I'd never seen anyone shot, or that much blood. My stomach went a little queasy as I stepped away from him and hoped my stomach would catch up with me.

"Don't leave me here," he begged. I almost laughed at the irony. He wanted me to save him.

"You're not dying, you moron," I said to him, my anger emerging. I backed away.

"Get me a doctor or something," he said.

I stopped. I didn't have time for this, or the police. Maggie needed me. I could stay and deal with Drummond, or I could go help my friend. I thought about what he would have done to me if he forced me into his car. It sent a chill down my spine.

"Entrance is that way about a hundred feet. I'm sure if you scream loud enough someone might come." I pointed to the emergency room entrance.

"You bitch!" he yelled.

Drummond started screaming again, begging for help. No part of me had any sympathy for him. He'd done something to Biddle, and he'd wanted to do something to me.

"He died from his own vomit alone," I said, staring down at him. "That liquor was poison to him."

"What?" Drummond screamed. I started walking away and headed for my car in search of my friend. Drummond was the least of my concerns. If he wanted help, he'd have to crawl on his belly to reach the emergency room entrance. I didn't worry, because snakes could do that.

***

At one-thirty in the morning, I pulled up to the large, empty parking lot of Verde Nursery. I didn't want to take any chances, so I turned off my headlights and slowed down. The half moon gave me very little light as I approached the main building, but not much. Through the darkened windows, the eerie shapes of some of the larger plants made them looked like people, which freaked me out. On the drive to the nursery, the beginnings of an anxiety attack started, and I thought I might have to pull over. My encounter with Drummond triggered the episode, and my anticipation of finding Maggie in handcuffs added fuel. I didn't want to think Maggie would use Mrs. Verde's keys to get into her office. Alone in another parking lot, I wanted to be wrong.

I wasn't wrong.

Well hidden from the road, I found Maggie's minivan hidden between two small work sheds in the back. My tires crunched on the gravel, making more noise than I wanted as I parked behind her minivan. Going to the rehearsal dinner gave me an opportunity to dress up and have a night out with Lee. I wore a short silk dress and heels which weren't meant to walk on gravel. I liked these shoes, and if they were ruined, I was going to kill Maggie.

At the hospital, she'd gotten that mad gleam in her eyes, which meant she had the chance to do something stupid. With Mrs. Verde in the hospital and Eloise out of the way, Maggie had an opportunity to search Mrs. Verde's office. The Sam Spade in her couldn't resist it.

Cursing every gravel-shoe-destroying step I took, I approached a steel security door. I pressed my face against a small window to the outer office. The venetian blinds were down but slightly open. I peered through the slants. There was just darkness. I tried the door handle, but it didn't budge; it was locked. Where was she?

Unexpectedly, a hint of light moved back and forth deep inside the dark office. I pressed my ear to the window. I've worked in enough offices to recognize the sound of a copy machine. God help us, I groaned. She was in there making copies. Now I knew she was crazy. She stole Mrs. Verde's key, broke into her office, and used her copy machine to seal the deal on the crime. For about half a minute, I contemplated leaving her there, calling 911, and collecting Lee and going home. It was only the idea of Maggie in the Nassau County Lockup that cooled my temper. I'd just finished fending off Drummond, and now I was saving her. Hell, when was someone going come to my rescue and save me? Then I thought of everyone who cares for me and got over myself.

The sudden sound of gravel crunching beneath tires coming toward me tempered my anger. I had to hide. I ran to the far side of the building by what appeared to be a trash dump. I knelt between stacked wooden crates and a pile of something that seemed like dirt but smelled worse.

A truck drove up slowly with its lights off and parked next to the office entrance. I didn't recognize the truck, but I recognized Tommy when he stepped out. He cautiously approached the office window and peered inside. I held my breath and felt helpless. I worried Maggie would come out to investigate the noise. Without thinking, I stood up, grabbed a small rock near the pile of debris, and flung it just behind Tommy in the thicket of tall grass and thin trees. He turned in the direction of the sound, scanning into the tangled brush.

"Who's there?" he said. He sounded scared. Good, that made the two of us.

The moment he turned his back again and headed for the office, I threw another. He nearly jumped out of his skin turning around searching for the source of the sound. I waited. When I threw another rock that binged of his front fender, he ran back to his car. Clutching the wheel like a crazed manic, he drove away kicking up gravel as he went. Chicken, I thought. I took a deep breath because my heart finally started up again. My relief was short-lived because the office door slowly opened. Maggie's red hair glistened in the dull moonlight. She stared in the direction of Tommy's car and hadn't seen me standing behind her.

"Have you lost your mind?" I yelled.

Maggie yelped and nearly dropped the papers she was holding as she turned to see me. I stomped over to her, grabbed the papers before she had a chance to protest. I headed for the cars with her following close behind.

I glared at her in disbelief and said, "You owe me a pair of shoes."

chapter 35

THE NEXT DAY, the bedside clock read eleven-thirty. After my little escapade with Maggie, I had to return to the hospital and collected Lee. Luckily, he was ready to go five minutes after I arrived, none the wiser that I'd almost been shot and assisted Maggie with a crime. All he wanted was to climb into bed and die a peaceful death. Maggie, the Verdes, and Drummond were the last people on my mind when I took him home and poured us both into bed at three o'clock in the morning.

I trudged downstairs with my throbbing head and hoped the Tylenol I'd just taken worked. My headache didn't improve with the site of Lee reading the copied documents I'd swiped from Maggie. I'd insisted I take them home with me to cool her overzealous curiosity. She needed a time out.

Lee sat at the old Formica kitchen table with his elbow on the table and his head propped in his hand reading. He was still in his pajamas and a bathrobe. He needed a shave and about twelve hours more sleep.

"Hungry?" I asked as I came into the kitchen and sat down next to him. I placed a hand on his stubble cheek, but he pulled away to give me a serious look.

"Should I ask where you got these?" he said.

I didn't like his coloring or his tone and arched an eyebrow at him.

"Should I ask you?" I didn't think I left the file out in the open. Knowing Lee, if he saw anything that looked legal it made him curious.

"Tell me you got this legally," he said.

I sighed.

"I got them from Maggie," I said, which explained everything.

"Where did she get them?" he asked.

"I plead the fifth." I put my hand over my heart and raised my other hand. He gave me a scrutinizing expression, which I mockingly returned. I got up to make some tea and put on the kettle.

Possibly convinced there was no more to be said about the source of the papers, Lee rested his head on the table. The night before had taken a lot out of him. I dropped the bread in the toaster, walked over to him, placed my hand on the back of his neck, and rubbed. He sighed deeply.

"Have some tea and toast. You'll feel better," I said.

Slowly he sat up. I bent and kissed him on his forehead. He shut his eyes briefly, as if coming to some resolution about something. Then his familiar grin came back.

"If you marry me, I can't testify against you," he said.

The toaster popped and the kettle began to whistle.

"If that's your idea of a proposal, I'll take my chances," I said, stepping away from him to fix breakfast.

"To be honest, that was as much as I can muster at the moment," he said. I'd put the tea and toast on the table and moved the copies out of his way.

"I'm not going to worry about those now," he said and began to eat.

"That's good, sweetie," I said and sat down to eat my own breakfast.

"Maybe we should get married, so when they arrest you, they'll give me conjugal visits." He pointed his toast at me.

"That's strike two, Leland McKenzie. If you give me another weak-ass proposal, I swear the only thing I'll say is, Lee who," I said.

He grinned but his smile faded a bit. He stared at me for a long time.

"What?" I said.

"I'm O positive. I have an organ donor card in my wallet. I give to Audubon Society and City Harvest. When I was twelve, I got hit by a car on my way to school. I broke my leg in two places."

"Lee," I said slightly confused.

He held up a hand to stop me before I could finish.

"I lost my virginity to Patty Maldonado at seventeen. She was nineteen. I should have saved it." He rolled his eyes. "My sister's nickname for me was Lele because she couldn't pronounce Leland as a kid."

"Why are you telling me this?"

"My favorite color is—"

"Blue. You love the hot dogs at Yankee stadium. You started rock climbing because a college buddy dared you to try and you love it. Your sister is older than you by eleven months and insists you two are twins. You snore when you're sick and hum when no one is listening." I stopped and held his hand in my hand. "I know you."

"I know you," he said and pulled me onto his lap.

"You're still not well." I wrapped an arm around his neck. He buried his head in the crook of my neck. His warm breath tickled my skin.

"Well enough," he said as he held me tighter.

"Don't worry about what you think I should know about you or who you were before you met me." I pulled away to stare down at him. "I love you because you are the man you are right now, that's enough." I stroked his cheek and kissed him.

I wanted to stay in his arms forever, but the phone rang. I cursed and got up to answer. It was Maggie.

"I'm sorry about last night. If I had known Drummond was around, I wouldn't have left," she said. For a half second, I thought about hanging up.

"You remember the story about a white whale and a crazy captain," I said. She didn't like the analogy.

"I'm still sorry, O." She sounded pathetic.

"Don't worry. It's not you, it's me. I worried about serial killers when I should worry that I've turned into a serial victim," I said.

"That's an odd way to look at it," she said. "How's Lee?"

"He's okay. He's reading the copies you gave me," I said.

"I didn't exactly give them to you, you took them," she said with a little annoyance.

"Whatever," I said, dismissing her complaints. "What's going on with the Verdes?"

"Mrs. Verde is being released from the hospital this afternoon. Eloise has recovered. The wedding is going to happen. When I returned her pocketbook this morning, she thanked me. I could tell she was still annoyed. I told her I was working on something, except I might not have the evidence in time for the wedding. She wasn't happy," Maggie said.

"Lee might find something in the papers. So what's next?" I asked.

"I need to pick up Rocket's suit from the dry cleaners. Roger conveniently has an out-of-town appointment on the day of the wedding, so Rocket will be with me. Is Lee planning to come with you?" she asked.

"He said he would, but the last time he met the Verdes, they almost killed him." This garnished me an apprehensive stare from Lee.

"I'll stop by later, okay?"

"I need to do something at the restaurant, and then I'm coming back home. I should be finished around one o'clock," I said.

"I thought Esperanza was taking care of everything," she said.

"This is something else. I'll tell you about the whole thing later."

We said goodbye and my attention went back to Lee. He had finished going over the papers and seemed anxious to talk. In fact, he appeared a little concerned.

"What's wrong?" I said. He held out the papers.

"I'm going to explain this to you and then I'm going to destroy these," he said firmly. I didn't find anything wrong with that considering how Maggie had gotten them.

"Okay, let's start with Mr. Verde, who was a very smart and generous man," he began and pulled out one of the sheets of paper. "He had a good head for business, and he left a small fortune to this family."

"You mean Mrs. Verde," I corrected.

He shook his head.

"He provided for them both," Lee insisted. "I don't understand what was going through his head, but I guess he expected his wife and daughter to have a better relationship than they do now."

"I'm confused," I confessed.

"Mr. Verde tied them together by the assets."

"Mrs. Verde said she owned everything—the house, the nursery, everything," I explained.

Lee nodded as if he understood this already.

"She does. She owns the building, the home, except one thing." He grinned at me.

"What's left?"

"The land. She doesn't own the land." His eyes widened.

"That doesn't make sense," I said. "So Eloise owns it?"

"The land is held in trust for Eloise, tying them both together. Mrs. Verde could sell off the assets, the buildings, the house, and she'd make a nice bit of change. However, the land is worth more. It's prime Long Island real estate," he said, smiling.

"Eloise acts like she doesn't own a thing. All her money comes through her mother. She resents it, I think," I said.

"Well, if she meets the proviso of the trust, she won't resent her any more. The trust allows her to use the land any way she wishes, even sell it."

"Whoa," I said as I wrapped my mind around the idea. "She could kick Verde Nursery out if she wanted or charge them rent."

"Yeah, but there's a catch," he said, still smiling at me.

"Don't tell me, Mrs. Verde has to turn into a human being before she can do anything," I said, and Lee laughed.

"Mr. Verde wanted to make sure Eloise could handle all the responsibilities the money would grant her. Remember, she was only a teenager when her father died. He wanted to provide for her, but he didn't want just to give her money. Maybe she'd blow the entire inheritance on a sport car or fancy clothes."

"Or a freeloading, no-good, dress-stealing, fake girlfriend," I said, remembering Jenny.

"Stay focused, honey." He leaned over and gave me a peak on the cheek. "Mr. Verde wanted to make sure Eloise was mature enough to handle the responsibility of her inheritance. He figured she would be if she were married or owned a business."

"So what stopped her from getting married when she was eighteen or starting a cat walking business?" I said.

"Eloise wouldn't receive land just because she married. She has to be at least twenty-two years old. I guess her father didn't want her to go into marriage too young. The problem is the age stipulation ends at thirty." Lee shoved a paper in front of me and pointed to a section. I read.

"He thought if she didn't marry by thirty, she'd be an old maid," I said in disgust. "He didn't have much faith in his daughter."

"He gave her a nine-year window," Lee said.

"What about the cat walking business?" I asked.

"The time frame is the same, but worse. Any business Eloise ventures into, its assets need to match the net worth of the land. You'd need to walk a lot of cats to equal the value of the land the nursery is sitting on," Lee said.

"This sounds crazy," I said.

"It's called an incentive trust. People make them because they want to elicit a particular behavior from the beneficiary by using the assets from the trust as motivation. The bad part about this is it can backfire on you." Lee gathered up the papers and put them aside. "You can't encourage people to behave a certain way by using money as an incentive. It can bring out the worse in them."

"Why would he do this to his own daughter?" I asked. I thought Eloise's father adored her.

"He probably thought he was doing the right thing. You can't blame him," Lee said. I cocked an eyebrow at him.

"Yes, you can. You can't spoil a child for years and then expect her to act like Mother Theresa and Donald Trump," I said, exasperated by good intentions gone wrong.

"I know. The bad thing for Eloise is she doesn't know this. Her mother is the executor of the trust. She is within her right not to tell her about the provisos. I guess she expects Eloise to do this on her own," Lee said.

"No, she didn't. Mrs. Verde has undermined her daughter since the day this thing was written. In fact, the woman goes out of her way to belittle her every chance she gets," I said. "I should tell that girl."

"You can't." Lee grabbed me by the shoulders. "How will you explain it? Oh excuse me, my girlfriend broke into your mother's office and that's how I found out the truth."

"I can give the girl some advice, can't I?" I leaned over and kissed him because he was cute and smart and a damn good kisser. The kiss turned into something more as I tried to catch my breath.

The Verdes were far from my mind.

"Won't this tire you out?" I said with some concern. He gave me an exasperated look and laughed.

"If I do this right, I hope so," he said.

chapter 36

LATER THAT DAY, I went to the Blue Moon. Besides other things I had to do, I wanted to check on Esperanza and the catering for the wedding. I'd taken a small table in the back to enjoy a piece of Esperanza's cherry pie that Candace couldn't stop raving about. Its crust was light, flaky and bursting with tart cherries. The pie was good, in fact, excellent. Candace seemed happy with the young girl. I was both relieved and miserable about the idea. I didn't think Esperanza would usurp my place as her sister, but she did an admirable job of replacing me as the Blue Moon dessert chef. My hand felt better, but I didn't think that would make too much of a difference to anyone who cared.

Tempted to talk to Candace about how I was feeling, I found her at the far end of the bar chatting with Leon Pendarvist. Together they were an attractive couple, talking, laughing, and at ease with each other. George was right. She seemed happier. She smiled more and irritated everyone less. Happily, I no longer thought Leon was a serial killer. Why should I rock the boat? There would be another time to talk to Candace about how I felt. I just didn't want my Blue Moon family to kick me to the curb. I was content with the idea Leon was a part of my sister's life, until I saw Frank walking in the restaurant's front door. Like radar, Candace's eyes locked on him and then me. So much for happy times.

Frank gave my sister a cheery hello and a stone-faced Candace pointed at me, like one of the village people searching for the monster. Frank tried to make small talk with Leon, but Candace went back to pointing. A hesitant Frank left them and headed in my direction. Behind his back, Candace scowled at me and promised retribution with her eyes. I smiled back hoping to diffuse her displeasure.

"Your sister is a hard woman," Frank griped and dropped his bulky body in a chair across from me.

"She's not hard, Frank; you're just soft." I stared at his bulging stomach.

Frank scowled in annoyance.

"I don't like being summoned, Odessa," he said.

"I appreciate you coming, Frank, honest, I do," I said.

Frank stared at my pie as if he wanted to have sex with it.

"Can I get you a slice of that?"

He nodded in exuberance.

I begrudgingly got him his pie.

"This would go good with a cup of coffee." He contorted his face into a pitiable expression.

I got him coffee.

"I'm surprised you didn't get the munchkin to help you with this," he said as he took a healthy bite.

"She's a little overwhelmed right now," I said. Frank glared at me ruefully. Like Maggie, I wanted to do this on my own.

"Yeah, someone needs to remind that little redhead she works for me, not the other way around." Frank spooned four teaspoons of sugar into his coffee.

"She knows, Frank," I said.

"No, she doesn't. She's got me running around searching for this Henry guy for a case I knew nothing about." Frank sipped his coffee.

"She's just a little worked up," I said.

"A little is her height. She's consumed," Frank said. "I wouldn't have touched the Verdes or taken their money. Besides, she isn't doing anything else. There are other clients, you know."

"You know Maggie." I tried to play off Frank's concerns.

"I know her. She's too smart for her own good. She forgets this is a job, not a religion," he said, the playfulness gone from his eyes.

"She wants to do her best," I insisted.

"I'll even admit the little redhead has good instincts most of the time when she isn't trying to keep everyone happy." Frank set his cup aside, rested his elbows on the table, and leaned forward. "She could get hurt, and I won't let that happen."

I smiled at Frank's concern for Maggie and his protectiveness of her. I thought of Maggie breaking in the Verde office, and I cringed. A year ago, she would have never thought about doing something so foolish.

"Maybe you should tell her this," I said. Frank leaned back in his chair and sighed.

"The only person she seems to listen to is a tall, black, crazy woman who makes a killer cherry pie." He gave me a warm smile. I didn't have the heart to tell him I hadn't made it.

"Lately, she's not listening to me," I said and sighed. "But I'll talk to her, I swear."

He laughed.

"Lighten up, Odessa, things will work out," he said and stopped and caught himself. "Geez, I sound like her."

I smiled at him because he did; Maggie's contagious optimism had infected him.

"Oh and another thing, drop the thing about Candace," I said, staring over to my sister and Leon. "I'm going to trust her judgment."

"You're sure?" Frank seemed wary.

"He's not a serial killer, is he?" I asked, now worried.

Frank shook his head. "No Odessa, he's not." He went back to finishing his pie.

At one-thirty, Frank greeted a tall, black man in dark shades and a Mets baseball cap and jacket. He was either a baseball scout or one of Frank's cop friends failing at trying to appear inconspicuous. Frank had little time for introduction as I put them at a secluded table, which had an excellent view of the restaurant.

A confident Zeno walked in fifteen minutes late for our meeting.

Obviously Eloise laundered and ironed his clothes because he appeared halfway decent, which had nothing to do with his character. Candace walked him over to my table and gave me a questioning glance as Zeno took a seat across from me. She lingered a bit, giving Zeno a cold appraisal with her eyes. Lee was right; the look was lethal because Zeno shifted uncomfortably in his seat.

"If you need me, I'll be in the kitchen with George," she said, to my surprise.

"What's her problem?" Zeno complained. He seemed relieved when she left.

"She doesn't like people messing with her sister," I said.

"Saw some resemblance there," he said, finding his smile. He scanned the restaurant and seemed impressed.

"This is nice." He nodded as if calculating some advantage for himself. "I'm pretty hungry; you think I can get something to eat?" It didn't sound like a request. It was the same tone he used with Eloise.

"No," I said flatly. Zeno caught the edge in my voice.

"I thought you promised to behave, Oprah." His eyes narrowed as a tight smirk played across his lips. He wore his bravado like a bad suit.

"Don't call me Oprah, Zeno," I said.

He leaned forward and smiled.

"Don't think because you're on home turf I won't do something. I told you about that mouth of yours. You cows always got to have the last word." His face hardened. For a brief moment, he rattled me, but I remembered this was my home and he didn't stand a chance.

"You're right; I should shut my mouth," I said and gave him a wry smile. "But not today."

"What?"

"You're disgusting and a pig," I said and sat back in my seat and crossed my arms.

"Listen, you bitch!" A patron sitting at the next table turned and frowned at him. Zeno sneered back. From beneath my seat, I took out a large manila envelope and slid it over to him.

"This is for you, Zeno," I said.

"About damn time. This better be what I asked for, because I need a payday," he said.

"Don't know about that, but it will do the job," I said, staring at him as he opened the envelope and took out a series of high-resolution photographs of his attack on me in front of Jake Nordmeyer's house. This wasn't what he expected. When he stared up at me, his chest heaved like a freight train.

"Before you think about wrapping your fingers around my neck, turn around," I insisted. He seemed too angry to listen. I repeated the request. Zeno took a slow turn, only to see Frank and his table guest. The color drained from his face. When he turned back to me, his anger returned.

"I'm going to kill you," he growled.

"I guess you recognize your parole officer, Mr. Warren Searles," I said. Searles held a manila envelope of his own and sat flipping through the photographs. He didn't appear happy.

"How stupid can you be? You sold bad meat out of the back of your car, Zeno," I said, disgusted. "Not only did you screw up the family business and reputation, your uncle was so pissed he had you arrested."

"How do you..." His eyes widened.

"The man sitting with Searles is Maggie's boss. He's good at what he does, and he has friends and connections in the probation department. He brought Mr. Searles here."

Zeno seethed.

"I thought about telling Mrs. Verde about what you tried to do, but I enjoy doing this more," I said.

With the presence of Searles, Zeno seemed to shrink in his seat. For the first time since I met him, he appeared a little frightened.

"I wouldn't have done nothing to you," he said beneath his breath.

"Christ, Zeno, you sold bad meat to people, disrespected and tried to blackmail your own family, and then you threaten me."

"Hey, I got a little carried away," he said, as his eyes searched for some sympathy from me.

I had none.

"I don't like people like you. You take and take and take. You need to go away," I said and stood up. In a flash, the rage returned into Zeno eyes. For a moment, I thought he might try something. He clutched the knife from the place setting on the table, and I had a flashback of Horace Fouke. I froze. Out of nowhere, Candace appeared by my side glaring down at Zeno.

"Is there a problem?" she asked calmly, her eyes still locked on Zeno. His attention turned to her.

"Mr. Zeno can't stay. He has a pressing engagement," I said. Frank and Mr. Searles started to walk over to our table.

"That's good, because someone just showed me some disturbing pictures," she said, leaning over him, placing one hand and all her weight on his wrist and the other on the knife.

Surprised by her quickness, Zeno froze as my sister snatched the knife away and scooped up the rest of the table's utensils. George would have been proud. A dumbfounded Zeno stared at her. I smiled at his perplexed expression, knowing Candace wouldn't tolerate another hostage situation at the Blue Moon.

"Hello, Apolo," Searles said as he stood next to him. Zeno and Candace glared at each other. Then she turned her attention to Frank, and surprisingly her face softened.

"What about some lunch, Mr. McAvoy?" Candace said her tone sweet and apologetic.

Frank blinked.

"I'm just gonna make sure Searles here is situated, and I'll be right back," a grateful Frank said. Candace turned to Searles.

"I hope you'll return, Mr. Searles. The Blue Moon has the best food in town," she said. Searles nodded. Candace stared at Zeno, who Searles pulled up from his seat by his forearm. She leaned toward him.

"You put another hand on my sister and you'll end up in a meat pie, like that." She snapped her fingers and Zeno jumped. Her face softened with a smile as she said goodbye and walked way.

"Is she single?" I heard Searles whisper to Frank.

"Thank you, Frank," I said, turning back to them.

"Are we telling the munchkin about this?" he asked.

"Later," I said and stared at a dejected Zeno.

"Let's go, Zeno," Searles commanded and pulled the reluctant man away from me. An unhappy Zeno cursed me.

I smiled and said, "Moo."

chapter 37

WHEN I ARRIVED home, I found Lee, Maggie, Rocket, and the Swift's family dog in my living room. Rocket and Mr. McGregor sat in front of the television watching cartoons. Maggie held a small plastic garbage bag and gave Lee dirty looks. He stood with his arms folded glaring back at Maggie.

"What's going on?" I asked.

"Hey, Auntie O," Rocket said without turning around to greet me. Mr. McGregor licked his hindquarters and ignored me all together.

"Why is Rocket not at camp? I asked.

"One of the kids came down with lice, and they're delousing the camp," she said. Cautiously, Lee and I glanced down at Rocket.

"He's fine," an annoyed Maggie said.

"Hey, babe" Lee said to me, never taking his eyes off Maggie and Rocket.

"He shredded everything," an irritated Maggie said. She held out the small plastic bag. I took the bag from her and opened it. Lee did a terrific job destroying the documents. Unfortunately, Maggie's anger blinded her to the fact that he did it to protect her. I had a little more clarity than her and headed toward the kitchen.

"Where are you going?" Maggie said as she followed me. She stared in disbelief as I dumped the bag into our trashcan.

"Hey!" she yelled and tried to retrieve the bag, but I held out my hand to stop her.

"It's worthless now." Lee stood in the kitchen doorway.

I shook my head.

"Not with P.I. junior around. He'll splice every piece together for the fun of it," I said, pointing at the little redhead mesmerized by the television. Lee eyed the boy suspiciously.

"It's genetic," I said. Lee's eyebrows rose in understanding.

"I can't believe you did that," she said.

"This coming from a woman who is horrified at the idea her son can break into her locked office at will," I said. Maggie's eye softened at the realization. "What's gotten in to you?"

"You don't need the papers. I can tell what you need to know," Lee said.

"The Cliffs Notes are that Mrs. Verde is a manipulative witch who knows the minute Eloise finds out that she owns the land the nursery sits on, her daughter will sell it right from under her mother's cold heart," I said.

"She owns the land?" Maggie said in disbelief.

"That's a little simplified, Dessa," Lee scolded.

"I leave the big legal words to you, sweetheart," I said, throwing him a kiss.

"Henry is marrying her for the land," Maggie said, walking away from me and back into the living room.

We found her standing next to Rocket. When she turned back to us, her eyes fixated on a spot on the floor.

Lee turned to me. "What is she doing?"

"Thinking," I said.

"It's been right in front of our faces," Maggie said to herself.

"Should I say something?" Lee whispered.

"No, don't worry, she'll land eventually," I said.

Maggie yelped and pointed at me.

"Henry's a real estate developer and Eloise has land. He marries her, kills her." Maggie threw up her hands in triumph.

"That's a little much, don't you think?" I said. Even I didn't think Henry would physically hurt Eloise.

Maggie sighed.

"He'll make her sell the land and build tacky houses on it," she said in disgust.

"Maybe he's desperate," I said.

"Dessa might be right," Lee said.

Maggie sighed again, still unhappy with him.

"What did your friend Goldberg say?" Maggie said.

I'd forgotten about the email Goldberg promised to send me. When I told Maggie I hadn't checked it, she glared at me impatiently.

"I think you should check your email," a concerned Lee said, afraid a crazed Maggie might pounce.

"Watch her," I warned, as I went to the workshop area where I kept my computer. Printing out the email and the attachment took me a few minutes. When I returned to the living room, Maggie snatched the papers out of my hands.

"Maggie," I complained.

"What!" she shot back. She still had a deranged expression on her face and I took a step back.

"You're like two halves of the same brain," Lee said, staring in amazement.

In unison, Maggie and I turned to him. Maggie's annoyance only deepened and I just sighed. Maggie dismissively turned her back on him and returned to Goldberg's report.

"Oh my God!" she cried out.

I took the paper from her and read the detailed report of Henry's finances.

"Oh my God and amen," I said and handed them to Lee. He read a few lines before his eyebrows shot up.

The report stated that Henry's dream of Bella Vista was bleeding him dry. He'd sold his lucrative partnership in his other firm to go on his own, and the move cost him millions. He had no support and no resources to fall back on. He'd taken out loans, took out a second mortgage on his house, begged, and borrowed. Was his next step stealing?

"He wants the land," Maggie said.

"You assume he knew about the stipulations in the trust," Lee said. "How would he have access to it?"

"We got access to it," I said, staring at a contrite Maggie.

"Eloise is the victim in all of this. Obviously, Henry is using her. Mrs. Verde purposely withheld information to control her," Lee said.

"Eloise invested so much into this wedding; this will break her heart," a disappointed Maggie said. The reality of her job finally hit her. She had to make Eloise's perfect day go from bad to worse. She sat on the couch. Her shoulders slumped, dejected, finally understanding what would happen.

"He's a weasel, pure and simple. Eloise's prefect wedding isn't worth marrying a sleazebag," I said.

"I have to tell her," Maggie said.

"Don't you think Mrs. Verde should tell her?" Lee said.

"Until Eloise's birthday, Mrs. Verde has to keep her daughter clueless. She'll even put up with Henry and pay for an expensive wedding that will never happen to keep her in the dark," I said.

Maggie looked confused. I'd forgotten to tell her the rest of the happy news.

"If Eloise reaches thirty without being married or owns a business worth the price of the land, the entire trust goes to her mother," I explained.

"What?" Maggie said, shaking her head in disbelief.

"Verde's Nursery is worth millions, and I'm not even talking about the land," I said. "The woman is loopy, but serious. She's using the money from the business to build Saint Patrick's Cathedral in Brooklyn."

"Oh my God, poor Eloise. I can't leave the truth for her mother to tell." Maggie stood up.

"What about Henry?" Lee said.

"You're right. He should tell her before tomorrow. He made this mess," Maggie said. Her eyes narrowed as anger darkened her pretty face. She would guilt him into telling the truth by making the report known. I would tell Davis and Goldberg as an added incentive. Their company would gobble up Bella Vista like freshly made sushi.

Without warning, Maggie's face brightened. She gave Lee her best hundred-watt smile. Lee smiled back but it didn't hold much conviction. When I realized what she was up to, I smiled at him.

"What?" Lee's smile vanished.

"Can you do me a favor?" Maggie came over, took Lee's arm, and pulled him over to Rocket. Still engrossed in the television show, Rocket was oblivious of his mother's attention. Something registered in Lee's eyes, replaced with unease. I immediately went to his other side and planted a kiss on his cheek.

"Maybe I should come with you," he offered, but Maggie shook her head.

"I started this case. I need to do this on my own," she said.

He turned back to me and said, "Why are you going?"

"I'm Robin, Kato, and Ethel, honey," I said. "I'm the sidekick, and I have to go." I pulled him away from Maggie and led him to the kitchen for privacy. Lee was happy to go because his discomfort turned to panic.

"I can't babysit Rocket," Lee said. You would have thought I'd asked him to guard the launch keys to nuclear missiles.

"He's not a baby. He's a small boy with a dog. Order pizza or Chinese until we get back," I said and gave a gentle pat on the back.

"Don't do this to me, Dessa," he pleaded. I'd never seen him so unnerved.

"Honey, think of this as a test," I said with a smile. "You want to be serious about our relationship; show me you can manage a prepubescent boy and his midget of a dog."

Lee sighed and rubbed his temple.

"Dessa!" He shook his head.

"Christ, Lee, you deal with criminals every day," I said. I threw up my hands in exasperation.

"Fine! Go! Leave me here with the kid, but if something happen, don't blame me," he said, folding his arms.

I glared at him.

"Of course I'm going to blame you; you're the adult," I said.

Lee said nothing.

"I thought so." I grabbed his chin and gave him a kiss before returning to the living room and Maggie.

A few minutes later, we said our goodbyes to an apprehensive Lee. Maggie told Rocket to behave. He gave her a thumbs-up without even acknowledging us. Mr. McGregor wagged his tail. I grabbed the sample reports for leverage, and we were on the road five minutes later. I took the time to go over the report from Jake again.

"Those new foundations were the beginning of the end for Henry," I said, as Maggie drove.

"You want me to feel sorry for him?" Maggie said indignantly. She had regulated Henry to the role of villain.

"He could have gotten away with them not being done."

"Not with Biddle walking around with rocks in his pockets," Maggie said.

"Biddle was a drunk and more of a nuisance," I insisted.

Maggie shook her head. "Are you defending Henry?"

"No, but I was ready to string up Horace Fouke because Mrs. Fouke lied," I said.

"We'll talk to Henry and then we'll lynch him," she said. She parked in front of a beautiful two-story home, with a well-tended lawn and a two-car garage, where Henry's car sat.

"Let's not go psycho on him, please," I said. "That is why I'm here, because every now and then, the Boy Wonder has to tell Batman to dial down the retribution a notch."

Maggie cocked an eyebrow at me.

I cocked one of my own.

"Okay, okay," she said and we got out of the car.

At the front door, Maggie almost rang the doorbell when we found the front door ajar. She looked at me before pushing the door open with her foot. She peered inside and stuck her head inside. I didn't even ask if that was a nifty idea to go inside because she'd already stepped through the door.

"Henry," Maggie shouted. No one answered as we stepped inside Henry's immaculate home, all chrome, leather, and extremely masculine.

"Car still here?" I asked.

"I'll check upstairs; check down here," Maggie said, and headed upstairs to the second floor. I went toward the kitchen and stopped when I noticed the answering machine's call light blinking. I pressed the button.

"Hi, honey, wanted to let you know I'm all right and can't wait for tomorrow," a happy sounding Eloise said.

A few calls came from the sales reps at Bella Vista talking about a bachelor party they had planned and someone would come by and pick him up. This explained Henry's absence but not the opened door.

"Odessa!"

Maggie came down the stairs with the last person I expected to see: Drummond. He had Maggie forcefully by the arm. He limped because of a heavily bandaged foot.

"Cleo. Didn't expect to see me again, did you?" he said, his voice strained with anger.

I said nothing as he gestured for me to come back into the living room. He pushed Maggie hard over to me, causing her nearly to fall. I caught her just in time.

"Because of you, I'm missing a toe," he growled and pulled out the small gun.

Maggie gasped.

"I'm sorry about the toe," I said as calmly as I could. His wild eyes danced between Maggie and me.

"If I didn't need you to find Henry, I'd shoot you right now," he said and pointed the gun at me. My heart jumped into my throat as it tried to escape.

"Henry hasn't returned from his bachelor party," I said, because I couldn't think of anything else.

"Then we're all gonna stay here and wait," Drummond said. He wiped the beads of sweat from his forehead and grimaced as he tried to balance himself.

"Are you all right, Mr. Drummond?" Maggie asked with more concern than I appreciated.

As he held the gun out at us, he dug into his pocket and pulled out a bottle of pills. His hand shook as he tried to open the lid with no success.

"Shit…shit," he cursed.

"Do you need help?" a placid-sounding Maggie offered, her hand outstretched, a kind and considerate expression on her face.

Drummond stared at her confused, but his face relaxed. Maggie took another step toward him.

"Maggie." I reached out to stop her.

"I'm okay. I just want to help," she said, keeping her focus on Drummond's tortured face. To my surprise, he held out the bottle to her and she took it.

"My foot is killing me," he cursed as if his own stupidity were my fault. Maggie read the label.

"You can't take this without something—juice or water. Let me get some for you," she said. She waited for an unsteady Drummond to say yes. When he did, she smiled and headed toward the kitchen. I glared at her incredulously as she passed, then I realized her smile had vanished when her eyes met mine. They were filled with alarm.

Silently Maggie mouthed the words. "Talk to him." She was up to something. She wanted me to make small talk with a psychopath with a gun—and they said I was crazy.

My attention went back to Drummond. His face grimaced in pain with every movement. I took a deep breath and tried to find my happy place.

"Sorry about your foot," I said, taking Maggie's cue to be compliant.

"Shut up, bitch," he barked.

So much for being kind, I thought.

"Okay, I'm not sorry," I said and folded my arms. "P.S., stupid. My name is not Cleopatra; it's not even Jones."

chapter 38

SOMETIMES, I NEVER took my own advice about poking snakes and striking matches at gas stations and dangerous men with weapons. However, when Maggie asked me to keep Drummond distracted, I didn't think small talk would do it. Maggie was the master of benign small talk; I wasn't. I was a Wilkes woman, so by our nature we were born to vex. He had a gun, and I had my mouth. It wasn't a fair fight, but you use what you got.

"You're a piece of work," Drummond said, snarling at me.

"I'm not the one threatening innocent people," I said.

"Nobody's innocent here, not you, not Duschumel, or even that little shit Barney." Drummond's face flushed with anger and something else.

"You killed Barnaby," I said with anger I didn't want to hide.

"The drunk killed himself, the fool. I just needed to know what he told you. He wanted to warn Duschumel. Even Duschumel thought he was crazy." He swayed and braced himself against the wall.

On closer inspection, Drummond seemed older than I remembered. I guessed a missing toe might age a man. Mostly, he looked exhausted, broken around the edges, as if he'd been running all night trying to catch a break. This was a man who hadn't bought a new suit in a decade. He drove an old car and worked for the county. Outwardly, he and Henry were opposites, inwardly they were both desperate men trying to find an edge.

"Henry's broke," I said, eager to break the news to him. I watched Drummond struggle to register the words. He shook his head as if something didn't compute.

"What?" He blinked.

"Broke, without funds, scrapped for cash—pick one," I said.

"This house, Bella Vista—he's loaded." I saw doubt creep into his eyes.

"Bella Vista is sucking him dry. He needs money, so if you want your payday, you'll have to wait," I said.

"No...no, he's rich." His eyes took in the expensive house and thought otherwise.

"Okay, if you say so." I didn't want to push him too far because he still had a gun.

"I say so, you stupid bitch. He thought he was smarter than me, but I've been around." He waved the gun in the air. "I've seen every trick in the book. I've used every trick."

"What tricks?"

Drummond laughed.

"I changed the inspection records, switched up the numbers. I had him over a barrel," he said, proud of his deceit.

"I don't understand," I said.

He laughed again, a little out of control.

"He poured those foundations and didn't have a clue the company he hired had a lot of citations against them. Somehow, the information never got out, and Duschumel hired them anyway. I knew the company was an accident waiting to happen, and I waited. When the reports came back, I changed them and got rid of the originals," he said, smiling. I thought of Maggie's pile of shredded paper and Drummond attempting to get rid of the evidence.

"Just long enough for Henry to dig himself into a hole, but he didn't do the entire development. He caught on, maybe because of Barnaby. He fired the company and hired someone else before too much damage was done."

"You can thank old Barney for that. Kept on complaining to Duschumel about the quality of the concrete," Drummond said.

"At first Duschumel thought Barney was nuts. Even when he tried to fix the problem, Barney wouldn't leave it alone." Drummond's head swayed a bit.

"Henry fixed the problem, but now Barney was making too much noise and drawing too much attention to Bella Vista," I said.

"You can't have bad publicity when you're trying to sell million dollar homes." Drummond laughed.

"Why hurt Barney?" I asked.

Drummond waved the gun.

"Told him to wait, and we'd both be rich," he said.

"I liked him." The image of Barnaby's goofy face came to me.

Drummond laughed again.

"After the second bottle, he started talking about his ebony Venus. Said you let him feel you up." He gave me a nasty grin.

"Don't get any ideas." I narrowed my gaze on him.

"You are not my type," he said in disgust. "I like women who are sweet." He stared in the direction of the kitchen where Maggie went.

"I know, sweet like Hershey's chocolate," I said and rolled my eyes.

"Yeah, Cleo, sweet like candy."

"That's not my name," I said annoyed.

"What the hell is your name?" Drummond said.

"It's not Cleo," I said.

"Well what is it?"

"Foxy Brown," I said with a straight face.

"What kind of name is that?" he said.

"My parents had low expectations," I said.

"You're lying," Drummond said.

"Here we are," a cheerful Maggie announced. In her hand, she held a large glass of orange juice and the open pill bottle. "Everything alright here?"

"Peachy," I said dryly. Maggie was acting like a stewardess on Looney Air, and I was trying not to get shot.

"Here you go," she said. She tapped out one pill, which he took without protest. She handed him the juice. "Drink the entire glass, I think you're dehydrated." Surprisingly, Drummond obeyed; perhaps it was a mommy thing or Drummond found it hard to say no to someone under five-four that looked like a wood nymph. He drained the juice down. Maggie took the juice glass and came over to me.

"You'll feel better soon," she said her tone reassuring.

"We're going to wait for Henry," he said.

"Okay, sit down. You must be tired," she said in a voice that was part-Dorothy and part-Glenda the Good Witch. She sat on the couch and patted the space next to her, and I took a seat. She motioned him to sit, and Drummond sat in an adjacent chair. Maggie startled me when she jumped off the couch and brought a small footstool over to him. He gently placed his injured foot on the stool and gave Maggie an appreciative smile. Maggie retook her seat.

"He thinks you're his type of woman," I said annoyed.

Maggie gave him a loopy smile.

"Like milk chocolate," I added snidely.

She stopped smiling.

"Well that's...nice," she said.

"Cleo...I mean Foxy....who did you tell about...the uh...samples Biddle stole?" Drummond asked, his speech slurred.

Maggie stared at me confused, probably wondering who the hell was Foxy.

"No one," I lied.

"What sample?" Maggie said. I looked at her dumbfounded. She was so in character the woman deserved an Academy Award.

Drummond waved the gun as if it were a hundred pounds.

"Don't you worry yourself about it," he said to her. He pointed the gun at me and smiled at her. How fair was that?

"I bet blackmailing Henry would have gotten you a hefty sum," I said.

Drummond went silent and glared at me. I guessed the truth hurt. The truth might hurt a lot more than, if he shot me. Drummond's head drooped and he tried to right himself. His gun hand rested on his lap and then slid to his side. The gun fell out of his hand and thudded to the floor. Maggie and I sat motionlessly.

"The son...of ...a bitch wouldn't...pay me my money." Drummond didn't even realize he no longer had the gun. His eyes closed, opened, and then closed again. His head dipped to his chest and didn't move. I heard the sound of snoring.

Maggie stood up abruptly. Her sudden moments were testing my nerves.

"Wait," I said, afraid he might awaken and shoot her by mistake.

"Don't worry; he's out for the night. I put enough pills into his juice to numb a horse," she said.

"What!"

***

"You could have killed him," I whispered. Maggie and I sat in yet another emergency room watching Drummond's attending doctor talk to the police. Maggie sighed, looking restless. She wanted to find Henry and time was running out.

"Nah," she said dismissively. "I read the label on the prescription bottle, counted the pills left, and guessed how many he'd taken already. Anyway, while I was in the kitchen fixing Drummond's cocktail, I called the ambulance. Didn't you wonder why they came so quickly?"

I shook my head. I was too busy getting over the shock of having a gun in my face for the second time and Maggie drugging Drummond into a stupor.

"You think they believed us?" she asked. The conversation between the physician and the police seemed to go on forever.

"That Drummond, a delusional, overmedicated and disgruntled county worker stalked Henry and was in desperate need of some rubber room time? It's true; what's not to believe?" I said.

The doctor talked. The cop took notes, and we waited.

"No, the thing about Biddle," she said, rolling her eyes.

"Don't know," I shrugged. I leaned back into the uncomfortable plastic chair. "If they believe he's crazy, getting someone like Biddle to drink himself to death couldn't be far off. Maybe if they check Drummond's files on the job, they may find something."

"I hope so. I'd hate to think he'll spend a couple of days in a padded room and go home," Maggie said.

"Amen to that," I said.

We had to be careful how we explained Biddle's death and the circumstances around it. Maggie's first official solo case came without a private investigator's license. We tried to tie everything to Bella Vista. I took creative license and expanded on Drummond's confession about falsifying inspection reports at the development site. I explained how Henry wouldn't cooperate with Drummond's blackmail. The officer seemed interested in the details, and I think I convinced him. At least for Biddle's sake I hoped so. While the police and the doctor conferred, Maggie and I sat, trapped in yet another emergency room as the hours ticked by.

"Ladies." Finally, an officer came over to us. "Not having a great night, are we?" he said.

"You don't know the half of it," I said wearily.

"Well, the doc's setting up a psych consult for Drummond and we'll go from there," he said.

"Can we go home?" Maggie said, pleading with her big waif-like eyes. "It's been an awfully long day." The officer thanked us for our cooperation and said someone would be in touch about the case.

"What about Mr. Barnaby Biddle?" I asked.

The man checked his notes from a small pad and nodded.

"A detective will call you about the case," he said, and I thanked him.

It was past midnight when we left the county hospital, exhausted. We hadn't found Henry and didn't have the energy to search every bar or strip joint in the tri-state area. I wanted to go home. Maggie needed to take Rocket to his own bed.

When we pulled into my driveway, my house was dark. Mr. McGregor greeted us as I opened the front door. Maggie gave him a gentle pat on the head, and he waddled back to his spot on the floor, next to his master. A sleeping Rocket lay wrapped in a pile of blankets in the middle of the living room, curled up in a fetal position. An exhausted Lee lay sprawled on the coach, gently snoring.

"They look sweet," Maggie said, as she stared down at them.

I scanned the room and took in the half-eaten cookies, an unfinished cupcake, and cartons of Chinese take-out.

"They're comatose," I declared.

"It's late. I'm tired, and I need to get Rocket home. With his Dad away, I'll have my hands full tomorrow." Maggie sighed.

"If you do confront Henry tomorrow, it is gonna be ugly," I warned.

"What choice do I have, O? I can't let Eloise marry the man," she said. Maggie carefully picked up her sleeping son. I walked her to the door and helped her to her car.

"The way the girl has been behaving lately, perhaps she and Henry deserve each other," I said, but Maggie shook her head.

"O, get over being upset with Eloise; she's just wearing the dress. Be mad with Jenny. You know how impressionable Eloise is. She sees anything on that wedding show she watches and she has to have it. Jenny told her about the dress," Maggie said.

"Okay, be nice to Eloise, check." I made a checking gesture with my finger. "Jenny is fair game, check." I repeated the gesture.

"Jenny is fair game. You know, ever since this wedding stuff happened, she's been really close to Eloise. Like it was her mission for Eloise to marry," she said.

"I think she hates Mrs. Verde more than she cares about Eloise marrying Henry. The woman probably did fire her," I said.

Maggie carefully placed Rocket in the car and buckled him in his seat.

"If I can't reach Henry, I'll talk to Eloise before the wedding," she said.

I said goodbye and watched her drive off. I went back inside to find Lee sitting up stretching and yawning.

"The dead has arisen," I said. "How much sugar and MSG did you feed him?" I began picking up food cartons and dishes. Lee pushed himself off the couch, and one by one, took the items from my hand and put them down. He held my hand as he shut off lights and locked up.

"I need to clean up," I complained. He shook his head and walked me upstairs to the bedroom.

"You owe me so much," he said.

"How bad was he?" I asked. He stopped, turned, and gave me a rueful stare.

"That kid has a lot of energy," he said dryly. Obviously, the nap on the sofa revitalized him. When we got to the bedroom, a mute Lee started unbuttoning my blouse and jeans. I didn't help because he seemed intent on doing the job himself. I stood in my underwear as he kissed me and guided me toward the bed. He never broke the kiss as we fell onto it. His need seemed to overshadow his patience. If I planned to enjoy any of this, I needed to slow him down.

"You know this is how they make little Rockets," I said, trying not to laugh. I guessed images of more Rockets pierced through his lust because he stopped and glared at me. I saw his mind work for half a second.

"There's always a catch," he said before he started kissing me again.

chapter 39

ON THE DAY of the wedding, everything was set. With no news to tell us otherwise, the Blue Moon catering staff readied the wedding venue. Bebe delivered the cake with the assistance of Esperanza. I supervised its assembly. Esperanza did an excellent job attaching the last of the cake decorations. I had to admit the cake was beautiful. Candace worked her usual magic and did a fantastic job decorating. Flowers appeared everywhere. A buffet-style food station sat beneath a long white tent with the wait staff dressed in Blue Moon's catering uniforms. Candace radiated with satisfaction. She'd done an excellent job. I didn't have the heart to tell her the wedding might implode at any moment.

Somewhere, Lee roamed the grounds with the assistant winery manager. When the manager found out he practiced law, the conversation volleyed between wines and litigation. Lee would come away from the meeting with a few bottles of the vineyard's best wine and a new client. Both men seemed quite happy with themselves.

Weddings are controlled chaos. Ultimately, they are about one thing and one thing only—the bride. The groom could come up in a monkey suit; hell, he could be a monkey, because everyone's eyes are on the bride. A wedding became a fairy tale, an illusion wrapped in delusion and fueled by money. If you had enough, your fairy tale/ illusion/delusion might be nice. As long as the bride happily stayed delusional, the wedding would be perfect. Unfortunately, Eloise's fairy tale/illusion/delusion would die a horrible death by a heavy dose of reality with the news about Henry.

Since Candace had turned into the wedding planner, Maggie was suspiciously absent. Several of my phone calls to her went directly to voicemail. When Eloise and Jenny showed up with the rest of her bridal party, Maggie still hadn't arrived. Some of the bridesmaids still seemed a little green around the edges from the food poisoning incident, but functional. Eloise's happy demeanor told me Maggie hadn't told her about Henry. I let her go on being happy when the entire bridal party went to get dressed in a room set up for them at the winery's main house.

I tried Maggie again, and again my call went to her voicemail. I began to worry. My concerned deepened when Mrs. Verde walked past the food tent dressed in a beautiful silk floral dress and wearing a smug look. This was the same woman who wore black to her daughter's rehearsal dinner. This was not a good sign.

"Hello, Mrs. Verde," I said, catching her attention. She stopped to face me.

"It's beautiful," Mrs. Verde said, taking in Candace's handiwork. "You're worth every penny."

"Mrs. Verde, have you talked to Maggie?" I asked, making the assumption Maggie had told her about what we'd found about Henry.

"No," she said. She opened up her small handbag, pulled out a cigarette, and lit up. She took a long drag and appeared pleased with herself.

"When did you last talk to her?" I asked my unease growing.

"The other day when I handed you the last check for the wedding. Now where do I sit? I don't want to miss a thing." Her anticipatory tone turned gleeful.

"So she hasn't talked you about Henry?" I asked.

Her eyebrow went up slowly.

"What about him?" she said. She gave me a frigid stare.

"Never mind," I said. I didn't want to talk about Henry, Zeno, or Maggie's absence with this woman. I went in search of Candace. She was overseeing the stocking of the bar area.

"Have you talked to Maggie?" The panic in my voice belayed her usual snotty retort.

"Early this morning, she asked me if I talked to Henry. I told her I hadn't. I wasn't too happy about it..." I didn't let her finish. I headed back to where we set up the dining area to find Bebe fussing with one of the cake stands. Esperanza stood by him watching him work.

"I'm leaving," I said as I peeled off my *O So Sweet Cakes* chef jacket.

"What!" a panicked Esperanza said. Bebe gave me a sardonic smile.

"Sometimes she does this," he said, ignoring me.

"What about the wedding?" Esperanza wrung her hands.

"Don't worry," I said, as I searched for my pocketbook from underneath the skirted table where the cakes sat. "If we're lucky there won't be a wedding."

Her eyes widened.

"How long will you be gone?" she asked.

"I need to find Maggie; she's missing." I tried to hide my fear.

"No, she's not," Bebe said as he stared out onto the open field.

"What?" I said, half-listening to him. I found my pocketbook wedged between some boxes.

"Who's Maggie?" a panicked Esperanza said, her eyes dancing between us.

"Trust me, don't ask," Bebe said and pointed in the direction just over my left shoulder. I turned to see Maggie stomping through the winery's grassy field. Rocket trailed behind, trying to keep up. I breathed a sigh of relief and replaced it with annoyance. The closer she got to me, I noticed the front of the beautiful silk wrap dress I'd given her for her recent birthday caked in mud and torn at the sleeve. Rocket hadn't fared any better. He wore his best suit, minus his tie, and the jacket had a ripped breast pocket.

"What the hell happened to you?" I said, running towards them.

"Where is she?" Maggie screamed between clenched teeth.

"Who, Eloise?" I asked.

"No, Jenny!" she yelled.

"Told you," Bebe said to Esperanza. I didn't want to guess how he would explain things.

"What happened?" I said and bent down to examine Rocket. I tried to brush off some of the dirt, but the jacket couldn't be saved.

"That witch...that ...." Maggie sputtered and stared down at her son. "Baby, go stand over by that bush." She softened her voice and pointed to an open area, several feet away from us. Rocket obeyed, walking away in a mangled suit, looking like a little businessman who'd just been mugged. When Maggie thought he was far enough away she went crazy.

"That woman locked me and Rocket in the basement of the Verde's house," she said and pointed to her son. "That...that..."

"Bitch," I offered and Maggie's eyes widened in agreement and nodded.

"I went over there because I couldn't find Henry to talk to him. So I wanted to tell Eloise. I didn't want her to show up here and have Henry break her heart." She took a deep breath to calm herself.

"What does Jenny ..." I started, but Maggie held up a finger to stop me.

"I wanted Jenny to help me break the news to Eloise, because her mother wouldn't care. As selfish as Jenny can be sometimes, they are friends, right?" Maggie tried to brush off the dirt from her dress as she tried to explain. "I told Jenny the wedding might not happen because of something I found out about Henry." Maggie stared at her ruined dress and threw up her hands in defeat.

"I should have known something was up when she told me to wait in the basement."

"Why would you..." I stopped because her finger went up again.

"All of Eloise's bridesmaids were at the house, and Jenny thought we should talk somewhere private, away from everyone. Like the idiot I am, I went with Rocket to the basement and waited, and waited."

"She locked you in?" I said.

"She locked me in and didn't tell anyone. They all left for the winery. I couldn't call anyone because on the way down to the basement she said she'd forgotten her phone and had to make a quick call. Before I could say boo, she took my phone. Then she locked the basement door. I'm such a jerk."

"How were you to know?" I said.

"The answer was staring me right in the face. I was too distracted by this crazy wedding. Jenny was the link between Henry and Eloise. She worked for the nursery and Bella Vista. She told Henry about the trust and had access to Mrs. Verde's files as her secretary."

"She hates him." I said, coming to the same conclusion.

"That's what threw me off. Evil witch," Maggie said from beneath her breath and out of earshot of Rocket who found something fascinating in the grass.

"Evil squared," I said.

"How did you get out of the house?" I asked.

Maggie pointed to Rocket who had something in his hand that squirmed.

"Put that down, baby," Maggie said sweetly. Rocket promptly dropped it and wiped his hand on the only clean spot on his shirt.

"Rocket found a way out?" I said, amazed at the boy's Houdini-like abilities.

"Laundry chute," she said.

I stared at her dress.

"I tripped and fell running to the car." Her face flushed with embarrassment.

"Why don't we go find Jenny," I said with a malicious grin.

"No, I need to talk to Henry first," she insisted.

"He's not here," I said. "It's getting late, and guests are arriving. I talked to Henry's best man. He said he dropped Henry at his house around two in the morning and hasn't seen him since." I thought of Henry's whereabouts, and then I remembered my conversation with Mrs. Verde.

"Speaking of female canines, I just talked to Mrs. Verde, and she's a little too happy. Like she knows this wedding isn't going to happen," I said.

"Where is she?" Maggie said, fire returning to her eyes. I steered her in the direction of the gazebo where Mrs. Verde sat beneath a large tree. Maggie stomped off with me close behind. We told Rocket to stay with Bebe and Esperanza.

We found Mrs. Verde sitting in a folding chair beneath a large shaded tree, smoking a cigarette and looking like a dowager queen. When she saw Maggie, she stubbed out her cigarette on the tree's trunk and tossed the butt away in the grass.

"Why is your dress dirty?" she asked coolly.

"Where's Henry?" Maggie said, her voice equally chilly.

"Excuse me," Mrs. Verde said.

"Tell me or I'll go talk to Eloise..." Maggie pointed to the winery's main house. "...and explain in detail about your husband's trust."

The color drained from Mrs. Verde as her face twisted in a snarl. "How..."

"Don't worry about how, because I will...damn it, I will tell." Maggie took a step toward her, her face hot with anger and indignation. I loved it.

"You broke into my office," a snarling Mrs. Verde declared.

"You think Eloise will even care how I got the information?" Maggie shot back. "Or that you hired me to break up her wedding?"

"Or that you've been keeping her father's inheritance from her?" I added. Mrs. Verde glared at me angrily.

"You don't know what you're talking about," Mrs. Verde said between clenched teeth.

"Let's go ask Eloise," Maggie said and turned.

"Don't you dare." Mrs. Verde stood up and grabbed Maggie's arm. Maggie twisted away. Then Mrs. Verde fumbled with her purse and pulled out a phone.

"What difference does it make? Monday is Eloise birthday. She won't marry Henry today or suddenly start a multimillion-dollar corporation. So your money's safe, Mrs. Verde," Maggie said. "To celebrate, why don't you add on a new rectory at Saint Anne's?"

Mrs. Verde winced, as her eyes searched the grounds.

"I hope you're not looking for Zeno," I said dryly. "He wanted me to tell you he'll miss the wedding. He's busy with his parole officer."

"What?" She shuddered.

"He has assault charges pending, and they take priority over kidnapping, blackmail, and his overriding stupidity," I said.

"Where's Henry?" Maggie shouted, drawing many of the arriving guests' attention to the mother of the bride and the cute little wedding planner.

"Ladies, what's happening?" Lee asked as he joined us.

"Where's Henry?" Maggie repeated.

"Odessa?" Lee said and caught sight of Maggie's dress.

"Mrs. Verde has Henry, and we're trying to shake the truth out of her without calling the police," I said sweetly.

Lee stared at Mrs. Verde.

"Last time..." Maggie warned.

Mrs. Verde remained silent.

Just when I thought Maggie might strangle the woman, she stopped, turned, and scanned the gathering crowd.

"Everyone is here from the nursery, aren't they?" Maggie said. I recognized the familiar faces of some of the workers.

"You closed the nursery for the wedding." Most of the guests stood milling around in small groups staring back at us.

"Where's Tommy?" Maggie said as she turned back to a fuming Mrs. Verde.

"Why would he come? He hates Henry," she said.

"Oh, he'd be here. He's a valued Verde's employee, and no matter how he felt, you'd make him come. Hell, even Eloise would have because she is that clueless. Zeno's preoccupied with his upcoming court date and all you have is little lovesick Tommy," I said.

Maggie snatched Mrs. Verde's phone. Lee started to protest, but Maggie didn't care. She took out the cell phone battery and tossed it to him.

"She might call someone and tell them to do something stupid," I said so he understood. For the first time since I met her, Mrs. Verde's tough veneer cracked, as worry filled her face.

Maggie turned and stomped away from her.

"Stop her," Mrs. Verde demanded of me.

I laughed and said, "I'm going to help her."

chapter 40

I CALLED FRANK to join us at Verde's Nursery. I thought we needed some muscle and someone with a clearer head than Maggie. She was still upset over what Jenny did to her and Rocket, which only compounded the anger she felt for Mrs. Verde. This was her first real solo case and everything was out of control—the client, the situation, and her focus. She needed a little guidance and experience; something she couldn't get from me. Personally, I was ready to pack the whole thing in and move on to a whole new drama.

"Why are you here?" Frank grumbled at my presence as we stood in the empty lot of Verde's Nursery. Maggie stood by the front door peering through the tinted glass.

"I'm Kato," I said flatly, and he stared at me for a long time.

"What am I?" he said sourly.

I gave him an appraising glance. He wore his usual rumpled polyester suit, the one he should have burned when he entered the nineties. I smiled and patted him on the back.

"You're the trusted manservant," I said and left him to talk to Maggie.

"I'll go check out the back," I heard Frank say. I watched him disappear around the corner of the main building.

"Do you think an alarm is on?" I asked as I stood next to Maggie.

"The back lights are on," she said and stood up.

Frank stepped from around the corner.

"There's a pickup truck back here."

"That's Tommy's. Can you make sure he doesn't go anywhere?" Maggie asked.

Frank glowered at her, shook his head, and disappeared again.

"I don't think he likes being a sidekick," I said.

"I don't think I like being a superhero," Maggie said. She sounded disheartened. I touched her shoulder, and she stared up at me.

"Sometimes, Maggie, I make a cake and I wonder about the people who pay for them. I'm pouring my heart and soul into the work, and these couples have a 50/50 chance of ending in divorce," I said, as she listened. "Some are good, some are not. I can't judge. I just make the best cake I can and get out of their way. You just do the best you can and get out of their way." Maggie squeezed my hand. Her eyes told me thank you. She wanted and expected people to behave better. She was my superhero, who saved me from lost jobs, crappy ex-boyfriends, anxieties about my life choices and my own indecision. She always wore the Big Girl Dress.

"Let's get this party started," I said and banged on the door with my fist.

Tommy tentatively came from the back of the store. He recognized us and his eyes narrowed in confusion. He pointed to the closed sign on the door.

"We're closed," he said. Maggie and I ignored him. I continued to bang as he came closer. Afraid I might break the glass he held up his hands in the hopes I might stop.

"We're closed," he repeated a few feet from the front door.

"Open the door, Tommy," Maggie demanded. Tommy's anxious eyes stared back at us as he slowly shook he head from side to side.

He wasn't cooperating. I searched around one of the decorative flowerbeds that edged the building and picked up a smooth, polished stone. It was the size and weight of a hockey puck. I tossed the stone in my hands. A panicked Tommy glared back at me.

"Go away," he demanded.

"Open the door," Maggie yelled.

I brought my arm back in a gesture to throw the rock when Tommy rushed to open the door. The moment he did, Maggie pushed through, with all her anger focused on getting inside.

"Where is he?" she said, glaring at Tommy, whose concerned face was dissolving into terror. He hadn't counted on this.

"Who?" His voice quavered.

"What did she promise you —Eloise, the nursery...a brain?" I asked.

"Henry's here, Tommy, so drop the act," Maggie said, standing even closer to him.

"I don't know who..." he stopped when Maggie put a finger in his face.

"I don't want your mother and father to have to bail you out of jail again," an angry Maggie said. "What you're doing is a federal crime. I don't care what Mrs. Verde told you. This is serious, extremely serious."

Tommy's eyes widened. He was a kid, just a kid in love with the wrong girl. Frank's entrance into the nursery startled him. He carried an engine part. He tossed it on a nearby counter with a thud.

"You told me to make sure he didn't go anywhere." He sounded bored as he folded his arms and glared at Tommy.

"My truck," Tommy said, starring at what seemed to be an important piece to his engine.

"Where is he?" Maggie demanded.

"I'm...I'm in real trouble," Tommy said, his voice cracking.

I rolled my eyes in disbelief.

"Zeno was supposed to be here..." Tommy slowly scanned the empty nursery.

"He's busy," Maggie said.

"He's in jail," I added.

Tommy seemed to stop breathing.

"Zeno went missing, and Mrs. Verde told you to do his dirty work," I said.

Tommy said nothing but slowly nodded.

"Where is he?" Maggie asked.

"In the machine shop." Tommy pointed to the back of the store.

"Lead the way, kid," Frank said, pushing Tommy forward.

We found Henry hogtied in a large storage room screaming his head off. When he heard us open the door, he begged someone to save him.

"Easy there," Frank said as he cut the bindings away from Henry's leg and arms. Henry snatched the pillowcase off his head. He looked as if he'd been manhandled by a gorilla. He seemed both relieved and confused when he saw Maggie and me. Then he saw Frank and Tommy and his eyes widened in alarm.

"Don't worry, they won't bite," I said. I wasn't so sure about Frank, who look displeased with each passing moment.

"Someone kidnapped me from my house." All the words came out in a rush.

"That would be Tommy over there." Maggie pointed at Tommy, who tried to move behind Frank. Frank pushed him away.

"For Christ's sake, man up," Frank said.

"Call the police. He attacked me. He's crazy," Henry said, with a wary eye on Tommy and the exit.

"Let's hold up on the police," Maggie said, raising a hand to calm him.

"Are you insane?" Henry's eyes went a little wild for a moment. I thought he was ready to bolt.

"Of course not, Henry, calm down. We need to talk," Maggie said and gestured Henry to follow her out of the room.

In the bright light, Henry shielded his eyes. Maggie helped him to an area that held patio furniture display. We all took a seat. It looked like some weird garden party.

"Are you thirsty, hungry?" Maggie asked. A wide-eyed Henry shook his head. "Okay, first, let us start with an apology." She glared at Tommy.

"He's not totally to blame; he just has a weak mind," I said sharply.

"Hey," Tommy protested but Maggie glowered at him until he apologized to Henry.

"Sorry, man," Tommy said, staring at his feet.

"You need to blame Mrs. Verde for his part in this," I said.

"Why would she…" Henry's voice trailed off as his mind worked the possibilities.

"She's upset about you trying to get your hands on Eloise's inheritance," Maggie said.

Henry said nothing.

"We know Jenny told you about the trust when she worked for you. She had access to Mrs. Verde's office. I'm sure her sneaky and conniving skills came in handy," I said.

"What money?" an interested Tommy asked. Frank told him to shut up.

"Henry's broke and he needs money." Maggie stared into Henry's eyes. "Here was a girl sitting on a fortune, and she didn't even know it."

"I don't…" Henry's voice wavered.

"You worked so hard on Bella Vista, only to have it undermined by bad concrete and a corrupt building inspector," Maggie continued.

Henry closed his eyes and sighed, maybe relieved the truth was finally revealed. His head fell into his hand and he took long, deep breaths. When he sat up, he looked defeated. He reminded me of Biddle and Drummond—broken.

"If you hadn't fixed those foundations, you might have gotten away with it," I said.

Henry's eyes darkened with a flash of anger as he shook his head.

"I couldn't leave *my houses* like that," he said.

I liked his answer.

"Somehow Drummond found out about it and tried to blackmail you," Maggie said. Henry nodded.

"He caused it, that son-of-a-bitch," Henry said, as a newfound anger rose up in him. "Somehow he was connected to that company.

He knew they did shoddy work and let me pour those foundations anyway. He watched and signed off on everything. He changed reports and smiled in my face as he did it."

"Biddle came to you and told you something was wrong. But why didn't you listen to him?" I asked.

"Biddle wasn't the most reliable source. He'd been sent home a few times for drinking. I couldn't trust him or know he wasn't working with Drummond. After what I found out, I couldn't trust anyone. He was persistent, though," he said.

"Who came up with the idea to go after Eloise?" Maggie said.

Henry turned away but turned back and shook his head.

"Jenny. She told me about the trust. Once Eloise and I were married, Jenny thought she could convince Eloise to sell the land," he said.

"What about the nursery and the people who worked there?" Maggie said.

"Jenny said Eloise really didn't care about the place anymore because of her mother," Henry said.

"Whoa, that's cold," Tommy said, and we all glared at him.

"The way Mrs. Verde treated Eloise, even I didn't think it would take that much convincing," Henry said.

"Eloise didn't want a husband, she wanted a rescuer," Maggie said to no one in particular.

Henry's eyes narrowed on her. "You don't sound like a wedding planner," he said.

"Sorry. I work for McAvoy Investigations, and Mrs. Verde hired me to find something on you so I would stop your wedding to Eloise," Maggie said. I caught Frank smiling.

Henry rubbed his face hard, possibly to hide his embarrassment.

"Mrs. Verde never liked me," he said.

"I thought she was protecting her daughter when the whole thing was about the land and her loss of income," Maggie said.

"Did you sleep with Jenny?" I blurted out, and Henry blushed.

"In the beginning. I stopped soon afterward. She became demanding and even angry when things weren't going fast enough." He sounded disappointed in himself. "When I finally came to my senses and told her the scheme wouldn't work, she threatened me with the information about the foundation. Somehow, she found out about it while working for me and threatened to expose me and make a fuss. She was worse than Drummond."

"Jenny, the gift that keeps on giving," I said.

"You asshole," Tommy said, getting a little of his courage back. I cut my eyes at him and he backed off.

"This coming from a man who let an old lady talk him into kidnapping someone," I said. A sheepish Tommy shifted his feet.

"Tommy wasn't the only one talked into something stupid." Maggie stared at a contrite Henry.

Frank shook his head.

"Eloise is a sweet girl," Henry said, and I thought he meant it. "I found that I liked her and really didn't want to hurt her. But Jenny kept pushing and making noises about going to the newspapers and exposing everything."

"You need to make this right, Henry. You have to tell Eloise the truth," Maggie said.

Panic filled Henry's eyes. "I can't. It would destroy her," Henry said, but Maggie's nose wrinkled in disgust.

"And marrying someone you don't love would as well. As a friend always reminds me, it's time to put on the Big Girl Dress. So let's do it." She gestured for him to get up. Henry hesitated.

"I hate to admit I dated someone who worked as a VP at a well-respected New York investment firm," I said. "I asked him to do a report on your financials. It wasn't pretty. If you don't do the right thing, Henry, in a heartbeat, your little money troubles will be on the six o'clock news."

Henry blinked.

"You think Jenny going to the local papers would ruin your day? Honey, I used to do this for a living. I'd disseminate such a spin on this to every media reporter I still have contacts with, you'll beg me to kill you," I said in an unforgiving, sharp tone.

A confused Henry stared at me.

"I thought you baked cakes," he said.

"I do, but in my spare time I'm a sidekick, and I used to work in advertising." I smiled at him.

"I'd be ruined," he said. "First Jenny and Drummond, now you."

"Don't worry about Drummond, he's in enough trouble," Maggie said.

"He's in a psych ward right now, holding up his pants because they took away his belt and shoelaces," I added.

"What?" Henry's eyes narrowed in confusion.

"Drummond has to convince the doctors he's not crazy," Maggie said.

"Yeah, he had a pretty emotional meltdown at your house earlier. He'll also have to explain his involvement in Barnaby Biddle's death," I said.

"He killed Biddle?" a surprised Henry asked.

"We think he had a hand in his death," I said. "After your rehearsal dinner, he tried to kidnap me and got his toe shot off for his efforts. Then we found him at your house when we went looking for you. He held a gun on Maggie and me and waited for you to come home. Luckily, Maggie nearly overdosed him on his pains meds so we could get away."

Frank stared at Maggie in amazement.

"So how much is an apology worth to you?" Maggie asked.

"Considering what you might do to me, not much. I'll talk to Eloise," Henry said as he got up.

A pleased Maggie clapped her hands and said, "So, let's go say I'm sorry, everybody."

chapter 41

I WAS ALWAYS suspicious of fairy tales and happy endings. I surprised myself by wanting one for Eloise. This was Maggie's influence on me, of course. Annoying as Eloise was at times, she deserved a little happiness. She had a fiancé who didn't love her, a girlfriend who I wanted to drop six feet deep into the Hudson River, and a mother who should give back her membership card from the human race. Why did I complain about Eloise's desire for a perfect wedding or even my dress? She was just looking for her own happiness.

I sat in the hallway of the winery's main house holding Lee's hand so tight I thought I might break it. If I hadn't, I'd be wiping tears away like Maggie. She cried buckets. We stared down the long, narrow hallway through the open door of the manager's office, watching Henry break Eloise's heart. We were the only ones there. Maggie had banished the bridal party to the reception area where Candace decided to open the bar and serve the hor d'oeuvres to appease the restless guests. Frank had Tommy, Mrs. Verde, and Jenny in a small parlor, keeping them away from Eloise. Each of them wanted to explain their part in the disaster.

Maggie, Lee, and I sat quietly as Henry talked to his former fiancé. To be honest, I didn't want to hear what he was saying to her. Eloise's sobs were enough. She sat in her wedding dress, as her soft, round shoulders heaved as she cried. Henry kneeled next to her, a comforting hand on her arm. His gentleness didn't make up for the heartache he caused, but his tenderness helped.

I held Lee tighter.

"Maybe I should get her mother," Maggie said, wiping her runny nose with a balled up tissue.

"Are you crazy?" I said and leaned into Lee, trying to steal some of his warmth. As if sensing my distress, he put an arm around me and pulled me closer.

"When she finishes crying, she's going to be angry, especially at her mother," Lee said.

"She has a right to be," Maggie said, glaring at the closed door on the opposite side of the hallway where Mrs. Verde, Jenny, and Tommy waited to explain.

"I thought Mrs. Verde was going to have a heart attack when Tommy and Henry came walking in together," I said and smiled at the memory.

"I took a picture," a smiling Maggie said, patting her handbag where her trusty camera lay.

"Are we calling the police on anyone?" Lee asked. He stared at us. I turned to Maggie because this was her show.

"Well...," she put a finger to her lips and thought about it. "Who broke the law?"

Lee laughed.

"Well, you did by breaking into Mrs. Verde's office," he said.

I slapped his thigh as he feigned pain, and I laughed at the face he made. My laughter died when Henry stood up. He bent down, kissed Eloise on the forehead, and headed toward us.

"Maybe we should go talk to her," Maggie said.

"What do you mean, we?" I said, panicked at the idea of comforting Eloise. She was like a car wreck, best seen from a distance and behind yellow police tape.

"Come on, O," Maggie pleaded.

"Go help the girl," Lee said, his eyes encouraging. He reminded me who I had in my life and who loved me. I got up and followed Maggie down the narrow hallway. Henry stopped us as we passed.

"She knew," Henry said.

"Knew what?" I asked.

"Eloise has known about the trust since she was nineteen." Henry stared back at Eloise, whose body still quaked with sobs.

"What do you mean, she knew?" I said.

"Eloise said she found out one day by accident. She overheard her mother talking to a lawyer." Henry's confusion matched my own.

"Why don't you wait with Lee," Maggie said, touching his shoulder to spur him on down the hall. We turned our attention to Eloise.

Inside the small office, Eloise stared up at us as we entered. Her red-rimmed eyes were teeming with tears. She looked like a broken-down doll. Maggie knelt down and pulled her into a hug only mothers could give, and Eloise clung on for dear life. When Maggie pulled away, she searched Eloise's eyes.

"You knew about the trust?" Maggie said.

Eloise nodded.

"You still wanted to marry Henry anyway?" I asked, somewhat in disbelief.

Eloise nodded.

"Why, honey?" Maggie asked.

"Because…." Eloise gulped for air, and her body shuddered as she wailed.

"Because?" I prompted.

"Because…."She sniffled and took a deep breath. "I'd be away from my mother." She began crying again.

"You'd marry a man who doesn't love you just to get out of your mother's house?" a skeptical Maggie said.

"She's horrible." Eloise sounded like a child.

"Henry doesn't love…." Maggie began, but Eloise shook her head.

"Nobody loves me; I'm used to it," Eloise said with a surprising fierceness. "I just wanted one day, one perfect day that was mine. I could pretend, even for a moment, this was all about me for once." Her face softened and the tears flowed again.

"Good way to get back at your mom at the same time," I said. Eloise gave me a weak smile.

"When she said she'd pay for everything, I made sure she did," Eloise said, wiping away her tears with the back of her hand.

"You also had a chance to get the land," Maggie said.

"My father wanted me to have it. But when he made his will, everything changed. She changed," Eloise said. "I'm sure she talked him into all the silly stuff about marrying or owning a business. She tried her hardest to make sure that didn't happen."

"Yeah, your mother has a way with people," I said.

"You're not afraid of her." Eloise stared up at me.

I laughed.

"You've seen my sister, right?" I said. "After Candace, everyone else pales in comparison."

"She's a little bossy and scary sometimes, but nice. At least she loves you," Eloise said, and she was right.

"Did Henry tell you about Jenny?" Maggie asked.

Eloise nodded and looked uncomfortable.

"She comes back into my life wanting to be friends again." Eloise's lower lip quivered.

"She was going to convince you to sell the land away from the nursery," Maggie said.

Eloise's scowled.

"I would never do that. I've known some of those people all my life," she said.

"This is your mother we're talking about. She worked real hard so she could have all of the property and money your father left you," I said.

"Yeah, I know. I don't always like her, but I do love her. I wouldn't have sold the land even to get back at her." Eloise gave me a sly smile. "Maybe charged her rent."

I grinned.

Eloise stared down at herself, gently smoothing the fabric of her dress. "You know Jenny insisted I get this dress. When she told me she saw you wearing it, she said you wouldn't mind and your boyfriend would never marry you."

I took a deep, controlling breath.

"Remind me to kill Jenny later," I told Maggie.

"It's a beautiful dress, Eloise. You'd make someone a wonderful wife one day," Maggie said. By the look on Eloise's face, it was consolation she didn't particular want to hear.

"I think I blew my chance," a dejected Eloise said, as she stared down the hall at Henry. "No one like Henry is going to marry me unless they have too."

"What about Tommy?" I said. "He loves you. Hell, he kidnapped Henry for you."

"I don't love Tommy. It's like dating your brother. Anyway, he'll do anything my mother says," she said.

I nodded in agreement. Tommy wasn't a prize, but was Henry any better? I peered down the hall to see Lee and Henry in a serious discussion about something. Henry shook his head, and a cross Lee pointed at him and was giving him an earful.

"I wonder what that's about," Maggie said.

"Henry has been sweet," Eloise said.

"He tried to steal your inheritance with Jenny," I said in disbelief.

Eloise sat back in her chair and rubbed her face.

"Henry paid attention to me. He was always kind and respectful. He took me out to dinner at fancy restaurants and to my favorite movies. He didn't complain when I wanted to play miniature golf or shopping at the weekend flea markets. He was a little stiff in the beginning, but we really started having fun," she said. She started to cry again. Not only had she lost a husband, she'd lost a friend. Where was the annoying girl who had such demands for her wedding? Where did her fire go?

"Wait a minute," I said and shook Eloise's shoulder. "You need to stop feeling sorry for yourself and do something."

"O, this is not the time," Maggie admonished.

"When will the time be right?" I asked, getting annoyed with them both. "When you're still living in her mother's house still taking her crap? When you're still waiting for your prince to come along? I hate to break the news to you, sweetheart, but the princes are tired of saving us. They don't want to storm the castle, they want split level ranch with a big backyard for their grill. They want to take off their armor and watch Monday Night Football. They want a princess who can save them when they won't read the instruction on the weed whacker and need a trip to the emergency room."

Eloise shook her head.

"I'm not like you," Eloise said. "Every time I tried something, my mother always told me how I couldn't do anything."

"There was a time I thought I couldn't get out of bed. I'd lost my job, a man I thought I loved, and a little bit of my sanity. I had no energy to start over, but I did. I got out of my bed and did," I said.

"I'm not you," Eloise said, her sad eyes searching mine.

"It's not about me or even being strong or anything. It's about belief." I stared down at her hoping she'd understood. "Maggie believes she can be a private investigator when she looks like Tinkerbelle. I believe even when the world is crashing down on me, I can put on my Big Girl Dress and handle anything."

Maggie hugged her again. I wasn't too keen about the hugging stuff, but I wanted to give her something.

"I want to believe that," she said.

"You are you own best religion. Have a little faith, worship the ground you walk on, and don't let anyone tell you otherwise," I demanded.

"If you're lucky and have a great friend, you can have faith in each other." Maggie smiled at me before returning her attention to Eloise. "It's late. We better tell the guests the wedding's off."

Eloise sniffled and nodded.

"It's so embarrassing," she said.

"Don't worry, honey," I said, wrapping an arm around her. "I've embarrassed myself on a daily basis, and I'm still standing."

We all tried to laugh but our hearts weren't in to it.

Maggie laced an arm around Eloise's arm, and we headed toward Lee and Henry. They stopped talking when we approached. A pitiful Henry smiled at Eloise. Maggie had a wistful glint in her eye when she stared at the two. Eloise was devastated, and Henry appeared equally miserable.

"I'm sorry, Eloise," Henry said softly.

"We need to tell the guests," Maggie said. "Then I'm going to take Eloise home."

We all nodded except Lee who kept staring at Eloise. At first, I thought he recognized my dress from the photograph.

"Eloise do you hate Henry?" Lee said.

Eloise blinked and shook her head.

"Lee what are you..." I said but stopped.

"I think you should be together," he said bluntly.

"What?" I said. "I'm all for happy endings but don't you think—" Lee put up a hand to stop me.

"Not as husband and wife but partners," Lee said.

"What is this about?" Maggie asked. Eloise was still to shell-shocked to say anything.

"Henry uses Eloise's land as collateral for a bank loan to keep him afloat," Lee said. "Am I right?"

Henry nodded.

"He doesn't have to marry her to do it?" Maggie said.

"Technically no," Lee said. "Henry will give you twenty-five percent of Bella Vista. Wherein that gives you partial ownership in the development." Lee smiled at her. "Including its net worth, this is more than the amount of the trust."

"That's good, right?" Maggie asked.

"She can float Henry a loan to hold off the banks and right his sinking ship," Lee added.

"What does Eloise get out of it?" I said because I was still not quite sure how this might work in Eloise's favor.

"I get my daddy's gift to me." Eloise beamed.

"Plus a hefty interest rate," Henry said, smiling also as if this was the best idea in the world.

For the first time since Henry told the truth, Eloise smiled and then her smile vanished.

"I want something else," she demanded.

"You're out of your mother's house and have a nice chunk of cash. Eloise, I said empower yourself but what else can you want?" I said.

"I want my own house in Bella Vista," she said. There was a hint of steel back in her eyes.

"Done." Henry didn't hesitate and pulled her into a hug.

"Come by the office tomorrow and I'll write up a contract for you to sign. Once that's done, we'll deal with your mother," Lee said.

The color drained from Eloise face. Since Henry's return, she hadn't spoken to the woman.

"What do I say to her?" Eloise asked meekly, turning to Henry.

"How about goodbye," I said.

"Whatever you want, I'll be by your side," Henry said.

Eloise stared up at him in adoration. Henry returned the look. I caught Maggie smiling so hard, I thought her face would break. We all headed for the door. With the drama that stood on the other side, I still sensed Eloise's dread. Before anyone had had a chance to open the door, I jumped in front of them.

"I believe in revenge," I said as everyone stared back at me.

"She does, it's on the family coat of arms," Lee said dryly.

"The best revenge is living well." I put my hands on my hips and glared at him. "Outside of this room is enough food, music, and enough damn wine to put living well in a whole new stratosphere."

"You want us to have the reception?" a doubtful Eloise said.

"I want us to have a party." I grinned at her. "Your coming out party and your escort for the evening is Henry." I bowed to him.

"I like that idea," Henry said, entwining their arms.

"Also, this will make your mother crazy," I said as I opened the door.

Eloise smiled and said, "I like that idea."

chapter 42

A BRAVE ELOISE stood with Henry in the gazebo as they told their guests there would be no wedding. She hadn't taken off the wedding dress, and in the fading summer afternoon light, she finally looked like a grownup. She didn't whine or cry, just held Henry's hand. The couple apologized profusely about the cancellation. They begged everyone to stay and take part in the food and drinks. All the Verde Nursery employees' eyes shifted to Mrs. Verde, who acted a bit too content with herself. She sat alone at a table dipping a large shrimp into cocktail sauce trying not to grin.

Mrs. Verde's strange behavior left most of the guests confused and unsure of what to do. Some took seats, while others headed straight toward the bar. The bridesmaids went to the buffet. Maggie encouraged the band to play something, and started the evening off with a happy disco song. Eloise stayed away from her mother and close to Henry.

"I've been to happier funerals," I said, staring at the comatose crowd.

"They're all afraid of her," Maggie said. Mrs. Verde sat and surveyed the ruined festivities like a Super Bowl half time show.

"No one is going to have any fun with her around," Maggie said. She was right; it was time for Mrs. Verde to leave the party. One sure way of getting her to go was to tell her the bad news about the arrangement between Henry and Eloise. Lee thought we should keep the deal quiet in case Mrs. Verde tried something desperate. She'd already tried something drastic, stupid and even dangerous. God only knows what would have happened if Zeno had kidnapped Henry. Getting rid of him was a godsend, even though I had a stiff neck from our encounter. I would like to think he was in a small room somewhere, rethinking his lifestyle choices.

"Can I tell her?" I asked Maggie as we walked toward Mrs. Verde.

"And have all the fun?" Maggie said. The corner of her lip inched up into a wicked smile.

This was my influence on her.

Before we'd reached her table, I'd grabbed empty glasses and a bottle of champagne. When we took our seats at Mrs. Verde's table, she smiled up at us. She remained sitting alone; no one dared join her. Obviously pleased with her handiwork, she tipped her empty glass toward Maggie. Maggie poured. We all sat comfortably in our chairs as the rest of the people tried not to stare at us. Lee gave me a scowl from a corner table he shared with Eloise and Henry. The man knew what I was about to do and thankfully stayed in his seat.

The band played an awful cover of an Alicia Keys song to an empty dance floor. The guests remained terrified by a ninety-pound ogre called Mrs. Verde, who drank her champagne and smiled at everyone.

"I think everyone's having a good time," she said. Maggie and I turned to each other, nodded and smiled.

"I think we could have used a few more flowers," Maggie said, looking around the large tent.

"The money I poured into this wedding...." Mrs. Verde lamented but didn't lose her grin. "Well worth it."

"You shouldn't have kidnapped Henry, Mrs. Verde," Maggie scolded and wagged her finger at the elder Verde.

The woman shrugged dismissively.

"Should have left Tommy out of it," I added.

"He wanted to be helpful," she said as she cut her eyes to a contrite Tommy sitting with Frank. "Who is that man?"

"You shouldn't worry about him," I said and pointed to Lee. "You should worry about him."

Mrs. Verde turned to see Lee talking to Henry and Eloise.

"Your boyfriend," she said and turned back to me confused.

"He's a lawyer and right now he's probably working out details of Henry and Eloise's contract," I said.

Mrs. Verde was about to take a sip of her champagne, stopped, and turned back to the table where Henry and Eloise sat.

"What contract?" she asked.

"The one that gives Eloise twenty-five percent of Bella Vista," I said. I couldn't help but smile. "You know the one, Henry's multi-million dollar housing development."

"Amazing, isn't it?" Maggie said, sipping some champagne and smiling at the elder Verde.

"What?" We'd gotten her full attention, and she'd lost her smug grin.

"That would make Eloise a multi-millionaire, wouldn't it, Maggie?" I said cheerfully.

"Amazing," Maggie said, feigning disbelief.

"That's impossible. Why would Henry do something as reckless as that?" she said. Her eyes locked on the table where the couple was deep in conversation with Lee.

"Maybe Henry sees something in her worth that much," I said, as Mrs. Verde's lips tightened with every word.

"Ridiculous," she exclaimed and stood up.

"They're signing the contracts tomorrow. Call it a pre-birthday gift," Maggie said, staring up at the woman. Mrs. Verde slowly turned back to us, probably appraising the silly grins we had on our faces.

"You did this?" Her voice was harsh and unforgiving.

Maggie shrugged.

"Eloise deserved something. Don't you think?" Maggie said.

"I guess Henry thought a simple I'm sorry wouldn't do," I said.

"Over my dead body," she cursed, as she stomped toward Eloise and Henry.

"That could work," I said without remorse.

"Should we stop her?" Maggie said as she poured herself another glass.

"No, Henry will or Lee," I said. Both men stood up as Mrs. Verde approached.

"Fantastic wedding," I said and held my glass for a toast. Maggie held out hers, and we touched glasses.

"Fantastic cake," she said.

"It's a damn fine cake," I said. I put my feet up on another chair as Lee took Mrs. Verde by the elbow and whispered something to her. Even from my vantage point, it was hard to miss Mrs. Verde turning a lovely shade of red. I imagined Lee's conversation had something to do with kidnapping charges. Mrs. Verde twisted away from him, shook her finger at her daughter who was hiding behind Henry. She glowered at them all, turned, and stomped off.

The moment Mrs. Verde left, Henry pulled Eloise on the dance floor and everyone started clapping. They dimmed the lights and put a spot on the couple. The band switched to the Frank Sinatra version of "The Way You Look Tonight", and didn't sound half bad. We all watched. Lee walked over to our table.

"What part about not telling Mrs. Verde didn't you understand?" he asked, taking a seat next to me and draping an arm around my shoulder.

"We couldn't help ourselves," I said. Maggie and I tapped our glasses together again.

"She can try, but it's a done deal. My job might be easier if she didn't interfere," Lee said. When the music changed, more people got up onto the dance floor.

"They make a sweet couple, don't you think?" a wistful Maggie said. She'd already downed two glasses of champagne and I suspect was feeling very little pain.

"Down, Tinker Bell," I warned the woman addicted to happy endings. Maggie pointed to Rocket who was sitting at a table with Bebe, Candace, and Esperanza. An attentive Candace tucked a napkin beneath his chin and set down a plate of food in front of him.

All was right with the world.

A warm summer breeze eased through the tent as the scent of flowers filled the air. The night came slowly as pinpoints of stars hung in a blue-black sky. A perfect evening for a non-wedding, I thought. The music played. The people ate and laughter came up from the vines. Everyone had fun. Even Rocket had a fabulous time. The assistant manager took a shine to him and gave him a tour of the winery. Rocket seemed fascinated by how much effort they took to make grape juice. Tommy started chatting up one of the bridesmaids. Frank found an empty table, sat down, and ate. He had two plates in front of him.

Maggie and I talked to Eloise to make sure she was okay, as the party went into the night. Every now and then, a panic expression came over her, and she needed reassurance. Maggie took every chance to push Henry into Eloise's arm. They were an odd couple, but no one seemed to care. Eloise enjoyed herself. Around Henry, she blushed with his attention. Perhaps with the threat of foreclosure gone, Henry's facade of perfection faded as the night wore on. Don't get me wrong, he still looked like he could walk right out of a men's fashion magazine, and Eloise seemed to be the head of his fan club, but who cared?

After we'd cut the cake, Jenny emerged from whatever rock she'd been hiding under to save her relationship with Eloise or any meal ticket that might come with it. Flanked by her bridesmaids, an angry Eloise stuck out her chin and told her to go away. When Jenny turned to Henry for help, he took Eloise's hand.

"I only wanted to help you get away from your mother," an apologetic Jenny said. "It broke my heart not telling you. I tried to help you."

"You're the worst maid of honor ever," Eloise said.

"You can forgive him but not me?" An indignant Jenny pointed to Henry.

"I guess I can," Eloise said, staring up at him. He stared a Jenny as if realizing for the first time how monumental a mistake she'd been.

"I regret what I did to Eloise, and I will make what I did up to her. Can you?" Henry said.

Jenny's pretty face twisted in fury and she stepped close to him to point in his face.

"If I didn't find out about the money, you wouldn't be here. You owe me. Your precious Bella Vista would be owned by the banks," she said.

"I knew I was wrong, and I did it anyway. I regret that," Henry said. Jenny glared at them both.

"You think she can give you what you want?" Jenny's tone turned cruel. She spread her arms as if to show him what he might be missing. A resolved Henry gazed down at Eloise. Her face flushed with embarrassment.

"She might give me what I need," he said quietly and pulled Eloise away through a small crowd that had gathered. Before she and Henry disappeared into the crowd, Eloise turned back to Jenny and stuck out her tongue. When Jenny tried to follow, the bridesmaids blocked her.

"Henry," Jenny yelled.

Bridesmaid Number One gave Jenny a withering stare. Jenny stepped away as the small group of women dressed in matching pink gowns surrounded her. Unfortunately, she didn't leave fast enough. I found her fifteen minutes later outside the reception tent. I had a piece of cake to give to Lee who'd disappeared on me. I found him cornered by Jenny pleading her case to him. Too polite to push her away, he stood like a deer in headlights. I was beyond being rational about this woman.

"This is not my fault," I heard her say as I approached. Lee's look of relief at the sight of me turned to panic. I guessed I wasn't wearing my happy face.

"It's not what you think," Jenny said as Lee took the opportunity to slip away from her.

"Dessa," Lee warned.

"You don't have a clue as to what I think," I said coolly. Lee stood between us. My gaze remained on Jenny.

"Honey, could you get me a piece of cake?" I said as calmly as I could manage. He stared down at the large slice I held in my hand.

"You already have one, Dessa," he said, sounding a little concerned. "Why don't we go back to the party?"

My smile faded.

"This piece is for Jenny," I said between clenched teeth. Lee turned to her and then to me.

"Odessa," he warned.

"This is the bitter part, honey; the sweet will come later." I turned to him and said, "Go find Maggie, okay?"

Lee took a deep sigh, leaned in to kiss me on the cheek, and promptly walked away from us. He didn't want to be a witness for the defense.

"I don't...." Jenny's protest stopped when I grabbed her by the front of her pink satin dress. I yanked opened the bodice. When I got enough space, I shoved the cake down the front, plate and all. She squealed as I squished the cake further down. I gave her chest a firm slap before licking the butter cream icing from my fingers.

"Are you crazy?" she yelled as she pulled the plate out.

"That's for my dress," I said.

"All of this because of a stupid dress?" she squealed.

I shoved her again in the chest, pushing the cake down further.

"That's for Eloise and for being a lousy friend."

"You bitch," she screamed as she tried to clean herself off.

"I can skip the cake and go straight to dragging your sorry butt through the mud. That would just about make us even for you trying to give my boyfriend a lap dance every time you see him. So do you want some more cake, Jenny?" I glared at her.

She shook her head.

"I didn't think so. Here's some advice. Get a plant and if you haven't killed it within six months, then get a dog. If that survives after a year then get a real job. If you can keep that without sleeping with your boss, then you can get a friend," I said and walked away from her.

When I returned to the party, everyone was laughing and dancing. I found Lee talking to Maggie.

"Is Jenny still alive?" Maggie asked.

I rolled my eyes and I took Lee's hand to pull him onto the dance floor. The band played a brutal rendition of Dean Martin's "You're Nobody til' Somebody Loves You".

"At our wedding, we should have a different band," he said, his lips close to my ear.

"At least one that knows music from this decade," I said.

"No clams."

"No clams," I said. Lee twirled me to the music.

"Any dress you wear will be fine," he said.

"I know what you like." I nodded and smiled.

"Indeed," he said and pulled me closer.

chapter 43

Two weeks after Eloise and Henry's non-wedding, I was back at the Blue Moon filling the dessert case with cakes, pies, and cookies. My hand felt better, so there was no need for Esperanza. She was gone. Without going into too much detail, Lee told me Henry and Eloise's partnership facilitated the necessary loans Bella Vista needed for completion. We were all invited to Eloise's housewarming party. I told her I'd bring the cake.

At the restaurant, Candace stood at her usual spot at the front flirting with Leon. To the untrained eye, they appeared like two business people having a meeting. Candace's freshly applied makeup and a new outfit said otherwise. The whole Swift family sat at the table near the back for a family dinner. Nothing in the kitchen had changed. George still yelled at the kitchen staff, and Bebe worshipped the ground George walked on.

I still designed cakes out of my small house in Queens. I lived with a man who embraced my eccentricities and kept pushing me toward a deeper commitment. Maggie finally convinced Frank to allow her to do more in the detective agency besides filing. Rocket continued to break into his mother's office. Maggie still hadn't figured out how he did it. Mrs. Swift and the Grey Avengers continued to strike terror in the hearts and minds of those in the tri-state area who preyed upon the elderly. The over-seventy set could sleep easy with the Avengers patrolling the neighborhoods. Things were back to normal.

Early in the evening, I finished filling the dessert case, and I super-cleaned my work area under George's watchful eyes. When I finished, I left him to yell at staff and went to the dumpster. The warm night and clear skies made me look up. It was hard to view stars in the city, but I'd remembered the ones at the vineyard, and I smiled. Oddly, I thought of the Bug King who was in the process of finalizing his divorce from his crazy wife. He sent me roses in apology and promised to replace my car. Talking with Horace Fouke was weird, but reassuring. If I had taken everyone's suggestions and gotten the restraining order, Horace would be doing hard time in the Big House. Maybe, in the back of my mind, I knew the Bug King was harmless. I tossed my trash and returned to the restaurant. Inside I found Lee talking to George. Both men stared at me. Bebe leaned up against one of the workstations to stare at me as well.

"What?" I said, checking to see if I threw trash on myself. Before Lee could respond, Candace burst through the double doors with Leon in tow. The Swift family quickly followed them.

"What going on?" I said.

"Honey," Lee said, coming over to me and giving me a hug. Over his shoulder, everyone's eyes were on us. I began to worry.

"Let's get this over with, I have a business to run," an inpatient Candace said.

My mind raced as I thought about all her complaints in the last few weeks and my issues with George. Maybe recognizing my concern, George took pity on me and took me by the arm and out of Lee's embrace.

"Think of this as an intervention," he said as he guided me out of the kitchen. I resisted a little.

"Remember, I love you," Lee added as he followed. He acted as if he were sending me off to war. Something in my stomach shifted. Maggie smiled her silly smile and my stomach fell.

"Is it your birthday, Auntie O?" Rocket asked as I passed him. I shook my head no.

"Will someone tell me what the hell is going on?" I demanded as they paraded me through the dining room with diners watching the procession.

"Close your eyes," Lee said.

"No," I protested.

"Oh, stop being so silly," Candace demanded and grabbed me by the arm and out of Lee and George's hold. We went outside on to the street as everyone followed. I dug in my heels and stopped her.

"Stop being such a baby," Candace said and yanked me along. "Here," she said, pointing to the place that used to be Mrs. Deforest's travel agency. Someone had covered the windows with newspaper.

"Now, Esperanza," George shouted.

Before I had a chance to wonder where Esperanza was, she appeared from inside the small storefront window as the newspaper tore away to reveal a surprising view. George stepped in front of me and opened the door, and Candace nearly pushed me inside.

"This is yours," he said. I glared at him.

"My what?" I said.

Mrs. Deforest had vacated the place almost a week ago. I remembered saying goodbye and wishing her well.

"Leon helped me to buy the agency from Mrs. Deforest. That's what he does, real estate," Candace said, beaming at Leon. "He took care of remodeling and everything."

I narrowed my gaze on Leon.

"Will someone tell me what the hell is going on?" I yelled.

George stepped up.

"Your business is outgrowing your space at home and at the restaurant. You need a place of your own."

I blinked.

"My own what?"

"This is the new location of *O So Sweet Cakes*," Maggie said, almost giddy with excitement.

I glared at them.

"Take a breath, baby," Lee said softly.

I took a breath and another.

"How?" I said.

Everyone turned to Candace.

"I will not turn down another job because you're too busy or don't have enough space or someone to help you." She folded her arms and glared back at everyone. "You have Esperanza to help you now, and it's done."

"Did you think about asking me?" I said, irritated.

She rolled her eyes and placed her hands on her hips. I recognized the universal signs of being pissed and I mirrored it.

"This is your career, act like it," she snapped back. "Ever since you left your job in advertising, you've never taken your cake business seriously. You could double your customer base, but you won't do anything."

"That doesn't give …." I started, but Lee stood between us.

"Everybody, take a breath," he said. "I hate to admit it, but your sister is right. She's worked hard on this."

"Obviously with Leon," I said and pointed at him. "You and I are going to have a long talk about boundaries."

Lee gave him a sympathetic look.

"Oh, please, if I'd told you about this, you would have said I'm running your life. So leave Leon out of this," Candace said.

"So he's not you boyfriend?" I accused, catching her off guard.

She stuck out her chin.

I stuck out mine.

"He's my friend," she said, and Leon smiled at her. If only he had a clue of what he was getting into… well, served him right.

I turned to Lee.

"You knew?" I said. "Everybody knew except me?"

"It's hard to keep a secret from you. You're too stubborn to agree with Candace," Maggie said, stepping forward.

Maggie being Maggie was right, of course. The house in Queens was too small. George made things difficult in the kitchen because he understood I needed more space better than I did. I didn't think I had options. Candace's clear-eyed pragmatism understood the big picture. O So Sweet Cakes was business, pure and simple. She took charge of my life as always with noble intentions. She always wore the Big Girl Dress. It was the advice I'd given Eloise, and I needed to listen when someone gave it to me.

I sighed.

"Thank you, Candy," I said and hugged her. Of course, she pulled away when the embrace lasted too long.

"Everyone's happy." Maggie clapped and popped the cork on a bottle of champagne that appeared from nowhere. Bebe handed everyone a glass as Esperanza helped pour.

"To *O So Sweet Cakes*," George cheered. They all raised their glasses to toast.

"Wait," Lee said, stopping everyone from drinking. "I have something else I want to celebrate."

"Well, hurry up, there are customers who need to eat," Candace said. Lee just smiled at her. It was good to know their relationship was back on track.

"To Dessa, an excellent dessert chef and wonderful woman," he said, raising his glass. "She knows better than anyone else how sometimes you need a new start." His eyes held such hope for me. Suddenly it felt as if no one else were in the room except us. I closed my eyes and took a deep breath. I opened them when he took my hand. Someone had taken his glass of champagne. In its place, he held out a ring. I stared at the glittering emerald cut diamond.

"Breathe, Dessa," he said. I did not realize I'd stopped.

"Oh my God," I heard Maggie squeal.

"What the..." Candace exclaimed. I assume she didn't see this coming.

"Shut up, Candace," George commanded. Surprisingly, Candace did.

"It's about damn time," Bebe added. It was hard to tell, but I think he was smiling.

It took me a moment to focus. My world shifted again and the people I loved were there. I steadied myself, and I gazed into Lee's warm hazel eyes.

"This will change everything if I say yes," I leaned in and whispered to him. He nodded.

"Yeah, as your husband, I can't testify against you." He grinned.

I laughed at the implication as I held out my finger for him to slip the ring on. I admired it, and Lee kissed me soft on the mouth.

I was so ready for this.

Made in the USA
Columbia, SC
10 April 2022